The lion was advancing, and the cruel and selfish audience forgot its momentary anger against injustice in the expected thrill of another bloody encounter. Some, who, a moment before, had been loudly acclaiming Tarzan now cheered the lion, though if the lion were vanquished they would again cheer Tarzan. That, however, they did not anticipate, but believed that they had taken sides with the assured winner, since Tarzan was armed only with a dagger, not having recovered his other weapons after he had thrown them aside.

Naked, but for loincloth and leopard skin, Tarzan presented a magnificent picture of physical perfection, and the people of Castra Sanguinarius gave him their admiration, while they placed their denarii and their talents upon the lion . . .

By Edgar Rice Burroughs
Published by Ballantine Books:

THE TARZAN SERIES
Tarzan of the Apes (#1)
The Return of Tarzan (#2)
The Beasts of Tarzan (#3)
The Son of Tarzan (#4)
Tarzan and the Jewels of Opar (#5)
Jungle Tales of Tarzan (#6)
Tarzan the Untamed (#7)
Tarzan the Terrible (#8)
Tarzan and the Golden Lion (#9)
Tarzan and the Ant Men (#10)
Tarzan, Lord of the Jungle (#11)
Tarzan and the Lost Empire (#12)
Tarzan at the Earth's Core (#13)
Tarzan the Invincible (#14)
Tarzan Triumphant (#15)
Tarzan and the City of Gold (#16)
Tarzan and the Lion Man (#17)
Tarzan and the Leopard Men (#18)
Tarzan's Quest (#19)
Tarzan and the Forbidden City (#20)
Tarzan the Magnificent (#21)
Tarzan and the Foreign Legion (#22)
Tarzan and the Madman (#23)
Tarzan and the Castaways (#24)

COMPLETE AND UNABRIDGED!

And be sure to look for all 11 books of the *Mars* series and all 6 books of the *Pellucidar* series, also published by Ballantine!

By Edgar Rice Burroughs and Joe R. Lansdale:
TARZAN: THE LOST ADVENTURE

TARZAN, LORD OF THE JUNGLE

Edgar Rice Burroughs

TARZAN AND THE LOST EMPIRE

A Del Rey® Book
BALLANTINE BOOKS • NEW YORK

A Del Rey® Book
Published by Ballantine Books

Tarzan, Lord of the Jungle copyright © 1927, 1928 by Consolidated Magazines Corporation
Tarzan and the Lost Empire copyright © 1928, 1929 by Consolidated Magazines Corporation

This Edgar Rice Burroughs, Inc., Authorized Edition published in the United States by Ballantine Books, a division of Random House, Inc., New York, and simultaneously in Canada by Random House of Canada Limited, Toronto.

Trademark TARZAN® Owned by EDGAR RICE BURROUGHS, INC., and Used by Permission

http://www.randomhouse.com

Library of Congress Catalog Card Number: 96-93069

ISBN 0-345-41347-4

This authorized edition published by arrangement with Edgar Rice Burroughs, Inc.

Manufactured in the United States of America

First Edition: July 1997

10   9   8   7   6   5   4   3   2   1

Contents

Tarzan, Lord of the Jungle   1
Tarzan and the Lost Empire   209

TARZAN, LORD OF THE JUNGLE

Contents

CHAPTER   PAGE

Chapter	Title	Page
1.	Tantor the Elephant	5
2.	Comrades of the Wild	14
3.	The Apes of Toyat	23
4.	Bolgani the Gorilla	29
5.	The Tarmangani	38
6.	Ara the Lightning	46
7.	The Cross	55
8.	The Snake Strikes	63
9.	Sir Richard	69
10.	The Return of Ulala	80
11.	Sir James	90
12.	"Tomorrow Thou Diest!"	101
13.	In the Beyt of Zeyd	110
14.	Sword and Buckler	118
15.	The Lonely Grave	130
16.	The Great Tourney	136
17.	"The Saracens!"	146
18.	The Black Knight	152
19.	Lord Tarzan	161
20.	"I Love You!"	172
21.	"For Every Jewel a Drop of Blood!"	182
22.	Bride of the Ape	190
23.	Jad-bal-ja	196
24.	Where Trails Met	202

1

Tantor the Elephant

HIS GREAT BULK swaying to and fro as he threw his weight first upon one side and then upon the other, Tantor the elephant lolled in the shade of the father of forests. Almost omnipotent, he, in the realm of his people. Dango, Sheeta, even Numa the mighty were as naught to the pachyderm. For a hundred years he had come and gone up and down the land that had trembled to the comings and the goings of his forebears for countless ages.

In peace he had lived with Dango the hyena, Sheeta the leopard, and Numa the lion. Man alone had made war upon him. Man, who holds the unique distinction among created things of making war on all living creatures, even to his own kind. Man, the ruthless; man, the pitiless; man, the most hated living organism that Nature has evolved.

Always during the long hundred years of his life, Tantor had known man. There had been black men, always. Big black warriors with spears and arrows, little black warriors, swart Arabs with crude muskets, and white men with powerful express rifles and elephant guns. The white men had been the last to come and were the worst. Yet Tantor did not hate men— not even white men. Hate, vengeance, envy, avarice, lust are a few of the delightful emotions reserved exclusively for Nature's noblest work—the *lower* animals do not know them. Neither do they know fear as man knows it, but rather a certain

5

bold caution that sends the antelope and the zebra, watchful and wary, to the water hole with the lion.

Tantor shared this caution with his fellows and avoided men—especially white men; and so had there been other eyes there that day to see, their possessor might almost have questioned their veracity, or attributed their error to the half-light of the forest as they scanned the figure sprawling prone upon the rough back of the elephant, half dozing in the heat to the swaying of the great body; for, despite the sun-bronzed hide, the figure was quite evidently that of a white man. But there were no other eyes to see and Tantor drowsed in the heat of midday and Tarzan, Lord of the Jungle, dozed upon the back of his mighty friend. A sultry air current moved sluggishly from the north, bringing to the keen nostrils of the ape-man no disquieting perception. Peace lay upon the jungle and the two beasts were content.

In the forest Fahd and Motlog, of the tribe el-Harb, hunted north from the menzil of Sheik Ibn Jad of the Beny Salem fendy el-Guad. With them were black slaves. They advanced warily and in silence upon the fresh spoor of el-fil the elephant, the thoughts of the swart 'Aarab dwelling upon ivory, those of the black slaves upon fresh meat. The 'abd Fejjuan, black Galla slave, sleek, ebon warrior, eater of raw meat, famed hunter, led the others.

Fejjuan, as his comrades, thought of fresh meat, but also he thought of el-Habash, the land from which he had been stolen as a boy. He thought of coming again to the lonely Galla hut of his parents. Perhaps el-Habash was not far off now. For months Ibn Jad had been traveling south and now he had come east for a long distance. El-Habash must be near. When he was sure of that his days of slavery would be over and Ibn Jad would have lost his best Galla slave.

Two marches to the north, in the southern extremity of Abyssinia, stood the round dwelling of the father of Fejjuan, almost on the roughly mapped route that Ibn Jad had planned nearly a year since when he had undertaken this mad adventure upon the advice of a learned Sahar, a magician of repute. But of either the exact location of his father's house or the exact plans of Ibn Jad, Fejjuan was equally ignorant. He but dreamed, and his dreams were flavored with raw meat.

The leaves of the forest drowsed in the heat above the heads of the hunters. Beneath the drowsing leaves of other trees a stone's throw ahead of them Tarzan and Tantor slept, their perceptive faculties momentarily dulled by the soothing influence of fancied security and the somnolence that is a corollary of equatorial midday.

Fejjuan, the Galla slave, halted in his tracks, stopping those behind him by the silent mandate of an upraised hand. Directly before him, seen dimly between the boles and through the foliage, swayed the giant bulk of el-fil. Fejjuan motioned to Fahd, who moved stealthily to the side of the black. The Galla slave pointed through the foliage toward a patch of gray hide. Fahd raised el-Lazzary, his ancient matchlock, to his shoulder. There was a flash of flame, a burst of smoke, a roar, and el-fil, unhit, was bolting through the forest.

As Tantor surged forward at the sound of the report Tarzan started to spring to an upright position, and at the same instant the pachyderm passed beneath a low hanging limb which struck the ape-man's head, sweeping him to the ground, where he lay stunned and unconscious.

Terrified, Tantor thought only of escape as he ran north through the forest, leaving in his wake felled trees, trampled or uptorn bushes. Perhaps he did not know that his friend lay helpless and injured, at the mercy of the common enemy, man. Tantor never thought of Tarzan as one of the Tarmangani, for the white man was synonymous with discomfort, pain, annoyance, whereas Tarzan of the Apes meant to him restful companionship, peace, happiness. Of all the jungle beasts, except his own kind, he fraternized with Tarzan only.

"Billah! Thou missed," exclaimed Fejjuan.

"Gluck!" ejaculated Fahd. "Sheytan guided the bullet. But let us see—perhaps el-fil is hit."

"Nay, thou missed."

The two men pushed forward, followed by their fellows, looking for the hoped-for carmine spoor. Fahd suddenly stopped.

"Wellah! What have we here?" he cried. "I fired at el-fil and killed a Nasrany."

The others crowded about. "It is indeed a Christian dog, and naked, too," said Motlog.

"Or some wild man of the forest," suggested another. "Where didst thy bullet strike him, Fahd?"

They stooped and rolled Tarzan over. "There is no mark of bullet upon him."

"Is he dead? Perhaps he, too, hunted el-fil and was slain by the great beast."

"He is not dead," announced Fejjuan, who had kneeled and placed an ear above the ape-man's heart. "He lives and from the mark upon his head I think but temporarily out of his wits from a blow. See, he lies in the path that el-fil made when he ran away—he was struck down in the brute's flight."

"I will finish him," said Fahd, drawing his khusa.

"By Ullah, no! Put back thy knife, Fahd," said Motlog. "Let the sheykh say if he shall be killed. Thou art always too eager for blood."

"It is but a Nasrany," insisted Fahd. "Think thou to carry him back to the menzil?"

"He moves," said Fejjuan. "Presently he will be able to walk there without help. But perhaps he will not come with us, and look, he hath the size and muscles of a giant. Wellah! What a man!"

"Bind him," commanded Fahd. So with thongs of camel hide they made the ape-man's two wrists secure together across his belly, nor was the work completed any too soon. They had scarce done when Tarzan opened his eyes and looked them slowly over. He shook his head, like some great lion, and presently his senses cleared. He recognized the 'Aarab instantly for what they were.

"Why are my wrists bound?" he asked them in their own tongue. "Remove the thongs!"

Fahd laughed. "Thinkest thou, Nasrany, that thou art some great sheykh that thou canst order about the Beduw as they were dogs?"

"I am Tarzan," replied the ape-man, as one might say, "I am the sheykh of sheykhs."

"Tarzan!" exclaimed Motlog. He drew Fahd aside. "Of all men," he said, lowering his voice, "that it should be our ill fortune to offend this one! In every village that we have entered in the past two weeks we have heard his name. 'Wait,' they have said, 'until Tarzan, Lord of the Jungle, returns. He will slay you when he learns that you have taken slaves in his country.' "

"When I drew my khusa thou shouldst not have stopped my hand, Motlog," complained Fahd; "but it is not too late yet." He placed his hand upon the hilt of his knife.

"Billah, nay!" cried Motlog. "We have taken slaves in this country. They are with us now and some of them will escape. Suppose they carry word to the fendy of this great sheykh that we have slain him? Not one of us will live to return to Beled el-Guad."

"Let us then take him before Ibn Jad that the responsibility may be his," said Fahd.

"Wellah, you speak wisely," replied Motlog. "What the sheykh doeth with this man in the sheykh's business. Come!"

As they returned to where Tarzan stood he eyed them questioningly.

"What have you decided to do with me?" he demanded. "If you are wise you will cut these bonds and lead me to your sheykh. I wish a word with him."

"We are only poor men," said Motlog. "It is not for us to say what shall be done, and so we shall take you to our sheykh who will decide."

The Sheik Ibn Jad of the fendy el-Guad squatted in the open men's compartment of his beyt es-sh'ar, and beside him in the mukaad of his house of hair sat Tollog, his brother, and a young Beduin, Zeyd, who, doubtless, found less attraction in the company of the sheik than in the proximity of the sheik's harem whose quarters were separated from the mukaad only by a breast high curtain suspended between the waist poles of the beyt, affording thus an occasional glimpse of Ateja, the daughter of Ibn Jad. That it also afforded an occasional glimpse of Hirfa, his wife, raised not the temperature of Zeyd an iota.

As the men talked the two women were busy within their apartment at their housewifely duties. In a great brazen jidda Hirfa was placing mutton to be boiled for the next meal while Ateja fashioned sandals from an old bag of camel leather impregnated with the juice of the dates that it had borne upon many a rahla, and meanwhile they missed naught of the conversation that passed in the mukaad.

"We have come a long way without mishap from our own beled," Ibn Jad was remarking, "and the way has been longer because I wished not to pass through el-Habash lest we be set upon or followed by the people of that country. Now may we turn north again and enter el-Habash close to the spot where the magician foretold we should find the treasure city of Nimmr."

"And thinkest thou to find this fabled city easily, once we are within the boundaries of el-Habash?" asked Tollog, his brother.

"Wellah, yes. It is known to the people of his far south Habash. Fejjuan, himself an Habashy, though he has never been there, heard of it as a boy. We shall take prisoners among them and, by the grace of Ullah, we shall find the means to loose their tongues and have the truth from them."

"By Ullah, I hope it does not prove like the treasure that lies upon the great rock el-Howwara in the plain of Medain Salih," said Zeyd. "An afrit guards it where it lay sealed in a stone tower and they say that should it be removed disaster would befall mankind; for men would turn upon their friends, and even upon their brothers, the sons of their fathers and mothers, and the kings of the world would give battle, one against another."

"Yea," testified Tollog, "I had it from one of the fendy Hazim that a wise Moghreby came by there in his travels and consulting the cabalistic signs in his book of magic discovered that indeed the treasure lay there."

"But none dared take it up," said Zeyd.

"Billah!" exclaimed Ibn Jad. "There be no afrit guarding the treasures of Nimmr. Naught but flesh and blood Habush that may be laid low with ball and powder. The treasure is ours for the taking."

"Ullah grant that it may be as easily found as the treasure of Geryeh," said Zeyd, "which lays a journey north of Tebuk in the ancient ruins of a walled city. There, each Friday, the pieces of money roll out of the ground and run about over the desert until sunset."

"Once we are come to Nimmr there will be no difficulty finding the treasure," Ibn Jad assured them. "The difficulty will lie in getting out of el-Habash with the treasure and the woman; and if she is as beautiful as the sahar said, the men of Nimmr may protect her even more savagely than they would the treasure."

"Often do magicians lie," said Tollog.

"Who comes?" exclaimed Ibn Jad, looking toward the jungle that hemmed the menzil upon all sides.

"Billah! It is Fahd and Motlog returning from the hunt," said Tollog. "Ullah grant that they bring ivory and meat."

"They return too soon," said Zeyd.

"But they do not come empty handed," and Ibn Jad pointed toward the naked giant that accompanied the returning hunters.

The group surrounding Tarzan approached the sheik's beyt and halted.

Wrapped in his soiled calico thob, his head kerchief drawn across the lower part of his face, Ibn Jad exposed but two villainous eyes to the intent scrutiny of the ape-man which simultaneously included the pock-marked, shifty-eyed visage of Tollog, the sheik's brother, and the not ill-favored countenance of the youthful Zeyd.

"Who is sheykh here?" demanded Tarzan in tones of authority that belied the camel leather thongs about his wrists.

Ibn Jad permitted his thorrib to fall from before his face. "Wellah, I am sheykh," he said, "and by what name art thou known, Nasrany?"

"They call me Tarzan of the Apes, Moslem."

"Tarzan of the Apes," mused Ibn Jad. "I have heard the name."

"Doubtless. It is not unknown to 'Aarab slave raiders. Why, then, came you to my country, knowing I do not permit my people to be taken into slavery?"

"We do not come for slaves," Ibn Jad assured him. "We do but trade in peace for ivory."

"Thou liest in thy beard, Moslem," returned Tarzan, quietly. "I recognize both Manyuema and Galla slaves in thy menzil, and I know that they are not here of their own choosing. Then, too, was I not present when your henchmen fired a shot at el-fil? Is that peaceful trading for ivory? No! it is poaching, and that Tarzan of the Apes does not permit in his country. You are raiders and poachers."

"By Ullah! we are honest men," cried Ibn Jad. "Fahd and Motlog did but hunt for meat. If they shot el-fil it must be that they mistook him for another beast."

"Enough!" cried Tarzan. "Remove the thongs that bind me and prepare to return north from whence thou came. Thou shalt have an escort and bearers to the Soudan. These will I arrange for."

"We have come a long way and wish only to trade in peace," insisted Ibn Jad. "We shall pay our bearers for their labor and take no slaves, nor shall we again fire upon el-fil. Let us go our way and when we return we will pay you well for permission to pass through your country."

Tarzan shook his head. "No! you shall go at once. Come, cut these bonds!"

Ibn Jad's eyes narrowed. "We have offered thee peace and profits, Nasrany," he said, "but if thou wouldst have war let it be war. Thou art in our power and remember that dead enemies are harmless. Think it over." And to Fahd: "Take him away and bind his feet."

"Be careful, Moslem," warned Tarzan, "the arms of the ape-man are long—they may reach out even in death and their fingers encircle your throat."

"Thou shalt have until dark to decide, Nasrany, and thou mayest know that Ibn Jad will not turn back until he hath that for which he came."

They took Tarzan then and at a distance from the beyt of Ibn

Jad they pushed him into a small hejra; but once within this tent it required three men to throw him to the ground and bind his ankles, even though his wrists were already bound.

In the beyt of the sheik the Beduins sipped their coffee, sickish with clove, cinnamon, and other spice, the while they discussed the ill fortune that had befallen them; for, regardless of his bravado, Ibn Jad knew full well that only speed and most propitious circumstances could not place the seal of success upon his venture.

"But for Motlog," said Fahd, "we would now have no cause for worrying concerning the Nasrany, for I had my knife ready to slit the dog's throat when Motlog interfered."

"And had word of his slaying spread broadcast over his country before another sunset and all his people at our heels," countered Motlog.

"Wellah," said Tollog, the sheik's brother. "I wish Fahd had done the thing he wished. After all how much better off are we if we permit the Nasrany to live? Should we free him we know that he will gather his people and drive us from the country. If we keep him prisoner and an escaped slave carries word of it to his people will they not be upon us even more surely than as though we had slain him?"

"Tollog, thou speakest words of wisdom," said Ibn Jad, nodding appreciatively.

"But wait," said Tollog, "I have within me, unspoken, words of even greater worth." He leaned forward motioning the others closer and lowered his voice. "Should this one whom they call Tarzan escape during the night, or should we set him free, there would be no bad word for an escaped slave to bear to his people."

"Billah!" exclaimed Fahd disgustedly. "There would be no need for an escaped slave to bring word to his people—the Nasrany himself would do that and lead them upon us in person. Bah! the brains of Tollog are as camel's dung."

"Thou hast not heard all that I would say, brother," continued Tollog, ignoring Fahd. "It would only *seem* to the slaves that this man had escaped, for in the morning he would be gone and we would make great lamentation over the matter, or we would say: 'Wellah, it is true that Ibn Jad made peace with the stranger, who departed into the jungle, blessing him.' "

"I do not follow thee, brother," said Ibn Jad.

"The Nasrany lies bound in yonder hejra. The night will be dark. A slim knife between his ribs were enough. There be faithful Habush among us who will do our bidding, nor speak of the matter after. They can prepare a trench from the bottom of which a dead Tarzan may not reach out to harm us."

"By Ullah, it is plain that thou art of skeykhly blood, Tollog," exclaimed Ibn Jad. "The wisdom of thy words proclaims it. Thou shalt attend to the whole matter. Then will it be done secretly and well. The blessings of Ullah be upon thee!" and Ibn Jad arose and entered the quarters of his harem.

2

Comrades of the Wild

DARKNESS FELL UPON the menzil of Ibn Jad the sheik. Beneath the small flitting tent where his captors had left him, Tarzan still struggled with the bonds that secured his wrists, but the tough camel leather withstood even the might of his giant thews. At times he lay listening to the night noises of the jungle, many of them noises that no other human ear could have heard, and always he interpreted each correctly. He knew when Numa passed and Sheeta the leopard; and then from afar and so faintly that it was but the shadow of a whisper, there came down the wind the trumpeting of a bull elephant.

Without the beyt of Ibn Jad Ateja, the sheik's daughter, loitered, and with her was Zeyd. They stood very close to one another and the man held the maiden's hands in his.

"Tell me, Ateja," he said, "that you love no other than Zeyd."

"How many times must I tell you that?" whispered the girl.

"And you do not love Fahd?" insisted the man.

"Billah, no!" she ejaculated.

"Yet your father gives the impression that one day you will be Fahd's."

"My father wishes me to be of the hareem of Fahd, but I mistrust the man, and I could not belong to one whom I neither loved nor trusted."

"I, too, mistrust Fahd," said Feyd. "Listen Ateja! I doubt his loyalty to thy father, and not his alone, but another whose name I durst not even whisper. Upon occasions I have seen them muttering together when they thought that there were no others about."

The girl nodded her head. "I know. It is not necessary even to whisper the name to me—and I hate him even as I hate Fahd."

"But he is of thine own kin," the youth reminded her.

"What of that? Is he not also my father's brother? If that bond does not hold him loyal to Ibn Jad, who hath treated him well, why should I pretend loyalty for him? Nay, I think him a traitor to my father, but Ibn Jad seems blind to the fact. We are a long way from our own country and if aught should befall the sheykh, Tollog, being next of blood, would assume the skeykhly duties and honors. I think he hath won Fahd's support by a promise to further his suit for me with Ibn Jad, for I have noticed that Tollog exerts himself to praise Fahd in the hearing of my father."

"And perhaps a division of the spoils of the ghrazzu upon the treasure city," suggested Zeyd.

"It is not unlikely," replied the girl, "and—Ullah! what was that?"

The Beduins seated about the coffee fire leaped to their feet. The black slaves, startled, peered out into the darkness from their rude shelters. Muskets were seized. Silence fell again upon the tense, listening menzil. The weird, uncanny cry that had unnerved them was not repeated.

"Billah!" ejaculated Ibn Jad. "It came from the midst of the menzil, and it was the voice of a beast, where there are only men and a few domestic animals."

"Could it have been—?" The speaker stopped as though fearful that the thing he would suggest might indeed be true.

"But he is a man and that was the voice of a beast," insisted Ibn Jad. "It could not have been he."

"But he is a Nasrany," reminded Fahd. "Perhaps he has league with Sheytan."

"And the sound came from the direction where he lies bound in a hejra," observed another.

"Come!" said Ibn Jad. "Let us investigate."

With muskets ready the 'Aarab, lighting the way with paper lanterns, approached the hejra where Tarzan lay. Fearfully the foremost looked within.

"He is here," he reported.

Tarzan, who was sitting in the center of the tent, surveyed the 'Aarab somewhat contemptuously. Ibn Jad pressed forward.

"You heard a cry?" he demanded of the ape-man.

"Yes, I heard it. Camest thou, Skeykh Ibn Jad, to disturb my rest upon so trivial an errand, or camest thou to release me?"

"What manner of cry was it? What did it signify?" asked Ibn Jad.

Tarzan of the Apes smiled grimly. "It was but the call of a beast to one of his kind," he replied. "Does the noble Beduwy tremble thus always when he hears the voices of the jungle people?"

"Gluck!" growled Ibn Jad, "the Beduw fear naught. We thought the sound came from this hejra and we hastened hither believing some jungle beast had crept within the menzil and attacked thee. Tomorrow it is the thought of Ibn Jad to release thee."

"Why not tonight?"

"My people fear thee. They would that when you are released you depart hence immediately."

"I shall. I have no desire to remain in thy lice infested menzil."

"We could not send thee alone into the jungle at night where el-adrea is abroad hunting," protested the sheik.

Tarzan of the Apes smiled again, one of his rare smiles. "Tarzan is more secure in his teeming jungle than are the Beduwy in their desert," he replied. "The jungle night has no terrors for Tarzan."

"Tomorrow," snapped the sheik and then, motioning to his followers, he departed.

Tarzan watched their paper lanterns bobbing about the camp to the sheik's beyt and then he stretched himself at full length and pressed an ear to the ground.

When the inhabitants of the 'Aarab menzil heard the cry of the beast shatter the quiet of the new night it aroused within their breasts a certain vague unrest, but otherwise it was meaningless to them. Yet there was one far off in the jungle who caught the call faintly and understood—a huge beast, the great, gray dreadnought of the jungle, Tantor the elephant. Again he raised his trunk aloft and trumpeted loudly. His little eyes gleamed redly wicked as, a moment later, he swung off through the forest at a rapid trot.

Slowly silence fell upon the menzil of Sheik Ibn Jad as the 'Aarab and their slaves sought their sleeping mats. Only the sheik and his brother sat smoking in the sheik's beyt— smoking and whispering in low tones.

"Do not let the slaves see you slay the Nasrany, Tollog," cautioned Ibn Jad. "Attend to that yourself first in secrecy and in silence, then quietly arouse two of the slaves. Fejjuan would be as good as another, as he has been among us since childhood and is loyal. He will do well for one."

"Abbas is loyal, too, and strong," suggested Tollog.

"Yea, let him be the second," agreed Ibn Jad. "But it is well that they do not know how the Nasrany came to die. Tell them that you heard a noise in the direction of his hejra and that when you had come to learn the nature of it you found him thus dead."

"You may trust to my discretion, brother," Tollog assured.

"And warn them to secrecy," continued the sheik. "No man but we four must ever know of the death of the Nasrany, nor of his place of burial. In the morning we shall tell the others that he escaped during the night. Leave his cut bonds within the hejra as proof. You understand?"

"By Ullah, fully."

"Good! Now go. The people sleep." The sheik rose and Tollog, also. The former entered the apartment of his harem and the latter moved silently through the darkness of the night in the direction of the hejra where his victim lay.

Through the jungle came Tantor the elephant and from his path fled gentle beasts and fierce. Even Numa the lion slunk growling to one side as the mighty pachyderm passed.

Into the darkness of the hejra crept Tollog, the sheik's brother; but Tarzan, lying with an ear to the ground, had heard him approaching from the moment that he had left the beyt of Ibn Jad. Tarzan heard other sounds as well and, as he interpreted these others, he interpreted the stealthy approach of Tollog and was convinced when the footsteps turned into the tent where he lay—convinced of the purpose of his visitor. For what purpose but the taking of his life would a Beduin visit Tarzan at this hour of the night?

As Tollog, groping in the dark, entered the tent Tarzan sat erect and again there smote upon the ears of the Beduin the horrid cry that had disturbed the menzil earlier in the evening, but this time it arose in the very hejra in which Tollog stood.

The Beduin halted, aghast. "Ullah!" he cried, stepping back. "What beast is there? Nasrany! Art thou being attacked?"

Others in the camp were awakened, but none ventured forth to investigate. Tarzan smiled and remained silent.

"Nasrany!" reported Tollog, but there was no reply.

Cautiously, his knife ready in his hand, the Beduin backed from the hejra. He listened but heard no sound from within. Running quickly to his own beyt he made a light in a paper lantern and hastened back to the hejra, and this time he carried his musket and it was at full cock. Peering within, the lantern held above his head, Tollog saw the ape-man sitting upon the ground looking at him. There was no wild beast! Then the Beduin understood.

"Billah! It wast thou, Nasrany, who made the fearful cries."

"Beduwy, thou comest to kill the Nasrany, eh?" demanded Tarzan.

From the jungle came the roar of a lion and the trumpeting of a bull elephant, but the boma was high and sharp with thorns and there were guards and beast fire, so Tollog gave no thought to these familiar noises of the night. He did not answer Tarzan's question but laid aside his musket and drew his khusa, which after all was answer enough.

In the dim light of the paper lantern Tarzan watched these preparations. He saw the cruel expression upon the malevolent face. He saw the man approaching slowly, the knife ready in his hand.

The man was almost upon him now, his eyes glittering in the faint light. To the ears of the ape-man came the sound of a commotion at the far edge of the menzil, followed by an Arab oath. Then Tollog launched a blow at Tarzan's breast. The prisoner swung his bound wrists upward and struck the Beduin's knife arm away, and simultaneously he struggled to his knees.

With an oath, Tollog struck again, and again Tarzan fended the blow, and this time he followed swiftly with a mighty sweep of his arms that struck the Beduin upon the side of the head and sent him sprawling across the hejra; but Tollog was instantly up and at him again, this time with the ferocity of a maddened bull, yet at the same time with far greater cunning, for instead of attempting a direct frontal attack Tollog leaped quickly around Tarzan to strike him from behind.

In his effort to turn upon his knees that he might face his antagonist the ape-man lost his balance, his feet being bound together, and fell prone at Tollog's mercy. A vicious smile bared the yellow teeth of the Beduin.

"Die, Nasrany!" he cried, and then: "Billah! What was that?" as, of a sudden, the entire tent was snatched from above his head and hurled off into the night. He turned quickly and a shriek of terror burst from his lips as he saw, red-eyed and angry, the giant form of el-fil towering above him; and in that very instant a supple trunk encircled his body and Tollog, the sheik's brother, was raised high aloft and hurled off into the darkness as the tent had been.

For an instant Tantor stood looking about, angrily, defiantly, then he reached down and lifted Tarzan from the ground, raised him high above his head, wheeled about and trotted rapidly across the menzil toward the jungle. A frightened sentry fired once and fled. The other sentry lay crushed and dead where Tantor had hurled him when he entered the camp. An instant later Tarzan and Tantor were swallowed by the jungle and the darkness.

The menzil of Sheik Ibn Jad was in an uproar. Armed men hastened hither and thither seeking the cause of the disturbance, looking for an attacking enemy. Some came to the spot where had stood the hejra where the Nasrany had been confined, but hejra and Nasrany both had disappeared. Nearby, the beyt of one of Ibn Jad's cronies lay flattened. Beneath it were screaming women and a cursing man. On top of it was Tollog, the sheik's brother, his mouth filled with vile Beduin invective, whereas it should have contained only praises of Allah and thanksgiving, for Tollog was indeed a most fortunate man. Had he alighted elsewhere than upon the top of a sturdily pegged beyt he had doubtless been killed or badly injured when Tantor hurled him thus rudely aside.

Ibn Jad, searching for information, arrived just as Tollog was extricating himself from the folds of the tent.

"Billah!" cried the sheik. "What has come to pass? What, O brother, art thou doing upon the beyt of Abd el-Aziz?"

A slave came running to the sheik. "The Nasrany is gone and he hath taken the hejra with him," he cried.

Ibn Jad turned to Tollog. "Canst thou not explain, brother?" he demanded. "Is the Nasrany truly departed?"

"The Nasrany is indeed gone," replied Tollog. "He is in league with Sheytan, who came in the guise of el-fil and carried the Nasrany into the jungle, after throwing me upon the top of the beyt of Abd el-Aziz whom I still hear squealing and cursing beneath as though it had been he who was attacked rather than I."

Ibn Jad shook his head. Of course he knew that Tollog was a liar—that he always had known—yet he could not understand how his brother had come to be upon the top of the beyt of Abed el-Aziz.

"What did the sentries see?" demanded the sheik. "Where were they?"

"They were at their post," spoke up Motlog. "I was just there. One of them is dead, the other fired upon the intruder as it escaped."

"And what said he of it?" demanded Ibn Jad.

"Wellah, he said that el-fil came and entered the menzil, killing Yemeny and rushing to the hejra where the Nasrany lay bound, ripping it aside, throwing Tollog high into the air. Then he seized the prisoner and bore him off into the jungle, and as he passed him Hasan fired."

"And missed," guessed Ibn Jad.

For several moments the sheik stood in thought, then he turned slowly toward his own beyt. "Tomorrow, early, is the rahla," he said; and the word spread quickly that early upon the morrow they would break camp.

Far into the forest Tantor bore Tarzan until they had come to a small clearing well carpeted with grass, and here the elephant deposited his burden gently upon the ground and stood guard above.

"In the morning," said Tarzan, "when Kudu the Sun hunts again through the heavens and there is light by which to see, we shall discover what may be done about removing these bonds, Tantor; but for now let us sleep."

Numa the lion, Dango the hyena, Sheeta the leopard passed near that night, and the scent of the helpless man-thing was strong in their nostrils, but when they saw who stood guard above Tarzan and heard the mutterings of the big bull, they passed on about their business while Tarzan of the Apes slept.

With the coming of dawn all was quickly astir in the menzil

of Ibn Jad. Scarce was the meagre breakfast eaten ere the beyt
of the sheik was taken down by his women, and at this signal
the other houses of hair came tumbling to the ground, and
within the hour the 'Aarab were winding northward toward
el-Habash.

The Benduins and their women were mounted upon the
desert ponies that had survived the long journey from the
north, while the slaves that they had brought with them from
their own country marched afoot at the front and rear of the
column in the capacity of askari, and these were armed with
muskets. Their bearers were the natives that they had
impressed into their service along the way. These carried the
impedimenta of the camp and herded the goats and sheep along
the trail.

Zeyd rode beside Ateja, the daughter of the sheik, and more
often were his eyes upon her profile than upon the trail ahead.
Fahd, who rode near Ibn Jad, cast an occasional angry glance
in the direction of the two. Tollog, the sheik's brother, saw and
grinned.

"Zeyd is a bolder suitor than thou, Fahd," he whispered to
the young man.

"He has whispered lies into her ears and she will have none
of me," complained Fahd.

"If the sheykh favored thy suit though," suggested Tollog.

"But he does not," snapped Fahd. "A word from you might
aid. You promised it."

"Wellah, yes, but my brother is an over-indulgent sire,"
explained Tollog. "He doth not mislike you, Fahd, but rather
he would have his bint happy, and so leaves the selection of her
mate to her."

"What is there to do, then?" demanded Fahd.

"If I were sheykh, now," suggested Tollog, "but alas I
am not."

"If you were sheykh, what then?"

"My niece would go to the man of my own choosing."

"But you are not sheykh," Fahd reminded him.

Tollog leaned close and whispered in Fahd's ear. "A suitor as bold as Zeyd would find the way to make me sheykh."

Fahd made no reply but only rode on in silence, his head bowed and his brows contracted in thought.

3

The Apes of Toyat

THREE DAYS CRAWLED slowly out of the east and followed one another across the steaming jungle and over the edge of the world beyond. For three days the 'Aarab moved slowly northward toward el-Habash. For three days Tarzan of the Apes lay in the little clearing, bound and helpless, while Tantor the elephant stood guard above him. Once each day the great bull brought the ape-man food and water.

The camel leather thongs held securely and no outside aid appeared to release Tarzan from the ever increasing discomfort and danger of his predicament. He had called to Manu the monkey to come and gnaw the strands apart, but Manu, ever irresponsible, had only promised and forgotten. And so the ape-man lay uncomplaining, as is the way of beasts patiently waiting for release, knowing that it might come in the habiliment of death.

Upon the morning of the fourth day Tantor gave evidences of restlessness. His brief foragings had exhausted the nearby supply of food for himself and his charge. He wanted to move on and take Tarzan with him; but the ape-man was now convinced that to be carried farther into the elephant country would lessen his chances for succor, for he felt that the only one of the jungle people who could release him was Mangani the great ape. Tarzan knew that already he was practically at the outer limits of the Mangani country, yet there was a remote chance that a band of the great anthropoids might pass this way and discover him, while, should Tantor carry him farther north even this meager likelihood of release would be lost forever.

Tantor wanted to be gone. He nudged Tarzan with his trunk and rolled him over. He raised him from the ground.

"Put me down, Tantor," said the ape-man, and the pachyderm obeyed, but he turned and walked away. Tarzan watched him cross the clearing to the trees upon the far side. There Tantor hesitated, stopped, turned. He looked back at Tarzan and trumpeted. He dug up the earth with a great tusk and appeared angry.

"Go and feed," said Tarzan, "and then return. Tomorrow the Mangani may come."

Tantor trumpeted again and, wheeling about, disappeared in the jungle. For a long time the ape-man lay listening to the retreating footfalls of his old friend.

"He is gone," he mused. "I cannot blame him. Perhaps it is as well. What matter whether it be today, tomorrow, or the day after?"

The morning passed. The noonday silence lay upon the jungle. Only the insects were abroad. They annoyed Tarzan as they did the other jungle beasts, but to the poison of their stings he was immune through a lifetime of inoculation.

Suddenly there came a great scampering through the trees. Little Manu and his brothers, his sisters and his cousins came trooping madly through the middle terrace, squealing, chattering and scolding.

"Manu!" called Tarzan. "What comes?"

"The Mangani! The Mangani!" shrieked the monkeys.

"Go and fetch them, Manu!" commanded the ape-man.

"We are afraid."

"Go and call to them from the upper terraces," urged Tarzan.

"They cannot reach you there. Tell them that one of their people lies helpless here. Tell them to come and release me."

"We are afraid."

"They cannot reach you in the upper terraces. Go! They will be your friends then."

"They cannot climb to the upper terraces," said an old monkey. "I will go."

The others, halted in their flight, turned and watched the gray-beard as he scampered quickly off amongst the loftiest branches of the great trees, and Tarzan waited.

Presently he heard the deep gutturals of his own people, the great apes, the Mangani. Perhaps there would be those among them who knew him. Perhaps, again, the band may have come from afar and have no knowledge of him, though that he doubted. In them, however, was his only hope. He lay there, listening, waiting. He heard Manu screaming and chattering as he scampered about high above the Mangani, then, of a sudden, silence fell upon the jungle. There was only the sound of insects, buzzing, humming.

The ape-man lay looking in the direction from which had come the sounds of the approaching anthropoids. He knew what was transpiring behind that dense wall of foliage. He knew that presently a pair of fierce eyes would be examining him, surveying the clearing, searching for an enemy, warily probing for a trick or a trap. He knew that the first sight of him might arouse distrust, fear, rage; for what reason had they to love or trust the cruel and merciless Tarmangani?

There lay great danger in the possibility that, seeing him, they might quietly withdraw without showing themselves. That, then, would be the end, for there were no others than the Mangani to whom he might look for rescue. With this in mind he spoke.

"I am a friend," he called to them. "The Tarmangani caught me and bound my wrists and ankles. I cannot move. I cannot defend myself. I cannot get food nor water. Come and remove my bonds."

From just behind the screen of foliage a voice replied, "You are a Tarmangani."

"I am Tarzan of the Apes," replied the ape-man.

"Yes," screamed Manu, "he is Tarzan of the Apes. The Tarmangani and the Gomangani bound him and Tantor brought him here. Four times has Kudu hunted across the sky while Tarzan of the Apes lay bound."

· "I know Tarzan," said another voice from behind the foliage and presently the leaves parted and a huge, shaggy ape lumbered into the clearing. Swinging along with knuckles to the ground the brute came close to Tarzan.

"M'walat!" exclaimed the ape-man.

"It is Tarzan of the Apes," said the great ape, but the others did not understand.

"What?" they demanded.

"Whose band is this?" asked Tarzan.

"Toyat is king," replied M'walat.

"Then do not tell them it is really I," whispered Tarzan, "until you have cut these bonds. Toyat hates me. He will kill me if I am defenseless."

"Yes," agreed M'walat.

"Here," said Tarzan, raising his bound wrists. "Bite these bonds in two."

"You are Tarzan of the Apes, the friend of M'walat. M'walat will do as you ask," replied the ape.

Of course, in the meager language of the apes, their conversation did not sound at all like a conversation between men, but was rather a mixture of growls and grunts and gestures which, however, served every purpose that could have been served by the most formal and correct of civilized speech since it carried its messages clearly to the minds of both the Mangani and the Tarmangani, the Great Ape and the Great White Ape.

As the other members of the band pressed forward into the clearing, seeing that M'walat was not harmed, the latter stooped and with powerful teeth severed the camel leather thongs that secured the wrists of the ape-man, and similarly he freed his ankles.

As Tarzan came to his feet the balance of the fierce and shaggy band swung into the clearing. In the lead was Toyat, king ape, and at his heels eight more full grown males with perhaps six or seven females and a number of young. The young and the shes hung back, but the bulls pressed forward to where Tarzan stood with M'walat at his side.

The king ape growled menacingly. "Tarmangani!" he cried. Wheeling in a circle he leaped into the air and came down on all fours; he struck the ground savagely with his clenched fists; he growled and foamed, and leaped again and again. Toyat was working himself to a pitch of rage that would nerve him to attack the Tarmangani, and by these maneuvers he hoped also to arouse the savage fighting spirit of his fellows.

"It is Tarzan of the Apes, friend of the Mangani," said M'walat.

"It is a Tarmangani, enemy of the Mangani," cried Toyat. "They come with great thunder sticks and kill us. They make our shes and our balus dead with a loud noise. Kill the Tarmangani."

"It is Tarzan of the Apes," growled Gayat. "When I was a little balu he saved me from Numa. Tarzan of the Apes is the friend of the Mangani."

"Kill the Tarmangani!" shrieked Toyat, leaping high into the air.

Several of the other bulls were now circling and leaping into the air as Gayat placed himself at Tarzan's side. The ape-man knew them well. He knew that sooner or later one of them would have excited himself to such a pitch of maniacal frenzy that he would leap suddenly upon him. M'walat and Gayat would attack in his defense; several more bulls would launch themselves into the battle and there would ensue a free-for-all fight from which not all of them would emerge alive, and none without more or less serious injuries; but Tarzan of the Apes did not wish to battle with his friends.

"Stop!" he commanded raising his opened palm to attract attention. "I am Tarzan of the Apes, mighty hunter, mighty fighter; long did I range with the tribe of Kerchak; when Kerchak died I became king ape; many of you know me; all know that I am first a Mangani; that I am friend to all Mangani. Toyat would have you kill me because Toyat hates Tarzan of the Apes. He hates him not because he is a Tarmangani but because Tarzan once kept Toyat from becoming king. That was many rains ago when some of you were still balus. If Toyat has been a good king Tarzan is glad, but now he is not acting like a good king for he is trying to turn you against your best friend.

"You, Zutho!" he exclaimed, suddenly pointing a finger at a huge bull. "You leap and growl and foam at the mouth. You would sink your fangs into the flesh of Tarzan. Have you forgotten, Zutho, the time that you were sick and the other members of the tribe left you to die? Have you forgotten who brought you food and water? Have you forgotten who it was that kept Sabor the lioness and Sheeta the panther and Dango the hyena from you during those long nights?"

As Tarzan spoke, his tone one of quiet authority, the apes gradually paused to listen to his words. It was a long speech for the jungle folk. The great apes nor the little monkeys long concentrated upon one idea. Already, before he had finished, one of the bulls was overturning a rotted log in search of succulent insects. Zutho was wrinkling his brows in unaccustomed recollection. Presently he spoke.

"Zutho remembers," he said. "He is the friend of Tarzan," and ranged himself beside M'walat. With this the other bulls, except Toyat, appeared to lose interest in the proceedings and either wandered off in search of food or squatted down in the grass.

Toyat still fumed, but as he saw his cause deserted he prosecuted his war dance at a safer distance from Tarzan and his defenders, and it was not long before he, too, was attracted by the more profitable business of bug hunting.

And so Tarzan ranged again with the great apes. And as he loafed lazily through the forest with the shaggy brutes he thought of his foster mother, Kala, the great she-ape, the only mother he had ever known; he recalled with a thrill of pride her savage defense of him against all their natural enemies of the jungle and against the hate and jealousy of old Tublat, her mate, and against the enmity of Kerchak, the terrible old king ape.

As it had been but yesterday since he had seen him, Tarzan's memory projected again upon the screen of recollection the huge bulk and the ferocious features of old Kerchak. What a magnificent beast he had been! To the childish mind of the ape-boy Kerchak had been the personification of savage ferocity and authority, and even today he recalled him with almost a sensation of awe. That he had overthrown and slain this gigantic ruler still seemed to Tarzan almost incredible.

He fought again his battles with Terkoz and with Bolgani the gorilla. He thought of Teeka, whom he had loved, and of Thaka and Tana, and of the little black boy, Tibo, whom he had endeavored to adopt; and so he dreamed through lazy daylight hours while Ibn Jad crept slowly northward toward the leopard city of Nimmr and in another part of the jungle events were transpiring that were to entangle Tarzan in the meshes of a great adventure.

4

Bolgani the Gorilla

A BLACK PORTER caught his foot in an entangling creeper and stumbled, throwing his load to the ground. Of such trivialities are crises born. This one altered the entire life of James Hunter Blake, young, rich, American, hunting big game for the first time in Africa with his friend Wilbur Stimbol who, having spent three weeks in the jungle two years before, was naturally the leader of the expedition and an infallible authority on all matters pertaining to big game, African jungle, safari, food, weather, and Negroes. The further fact that Stimbol was twenty-five years Blade's senior naturally but augmented his claims to omniscience.

These factors did not in themselves constitute the basis for the growing differences between the two men, for Blake was a phlegmatically inclined young man of twenty-five who was rather amused at Stimbol's egotism than otherwise. The first rift had occurred at railhead when, through Stimbol's domineering manner and ill temper, the entire purpose of the expedition had been abandoned by necessity, and what was to have been a quasi-scientific motion picture camera study of wild African life had resolved itself into an ordinary big game hunt.

At railhead, while preparations were going on to secure equipment and a safari, Stimbol had so offended and insulted the cameraman that he had left them flat and returned to the coast. Blake was disappointed, but he made up his mind to go on through and get what pictures he could with a still camera. He was not a man who enjoyed killing for the mere sport of taking life, and as originally planned there was to have been no shooting of game except for food and half a dozen trophies that Stimbol particularly wished to add to his collection.

There had since been one or two altercations relative to Stimbol's treatment of the black porters, but these matters, Blake was hopeful, had been ironed out and Stimbol had promised to leave the handling of the safari to Blake and refrain from any further abuse of the men.

They had come into the interior even farther than they had planned, had had the poorest of luck in the matter of game and were about to turn back toward railhead. It seemed now to Blake that after all they were going to pull through without further difficulty and that he and Stimbol would return to America together, to all intent and purpose still friends; but just then a black porter caught his foot in an entangling creeper and stumbled, throwing his load to the ground.

Directly in front of the porter Stimbol and Blake were walking side by side and, as though guided by a malevolent power, the load crashed into Stimbol, hurling him to the ground. Stimbol and the porter scrambled to their feet amidst the laughter of the Negroes who had witnessed the accident. The porter was grinning. Stimbol was flushed with anger.

"You damned clumsy swine!" he cried, and before Blake could interfere or the porter protect himself the angry white man stepped quickly over the fallen load and struck the black a terrific blow in the face that felled him; and as he lay there, Stimbol kicked him in the side. But only once! Before he could repeat the outrage Blake seized him by the shoulder, wheeled him about and struck him precisely as he had struck the black.

Stimbol fell, rolled over on his side and reached for the automatic that hung at his hip, but quick as he was Blake was quicker. "Cut that!" said Blake, crisply, covering Stimbol with a .45. Stimbol's hand dropped from the grip of his gun. "Get up!" ordered Blake, and when the other had risen: "Now listen to me, Stimbol—this is the end. You and I are through. Tomorrow morning we split the safari and equipment, and whichever way you go with your half I'll go in the opposite direction."

Blake had returned his gun to its holster as he spoke, the black had risen and was nursing a bloody nose, the other blacks were looking sullenly. Blake motioned to the porter to pick up his load and presently the safari was again on the move—a sullen safari without laughter or song.

Blake made camp at the first available ground shortly before noon in order that the division of equipment, food, and men could be made during the afternoon and the two safaris thus be enabled to make an early start the following morning.

Stimbol, sullen, would give no assistance, but, taking a couple of the askari, the armed natives who act as soldiers for the safari, started out from camp to hunt. He had proceeded scarcely a mile along a mould padded game trail which gave forth no sound in answer to their falling footsteps, when one of the natives in the lead held up his hand in warning as he halted in his tracks.

Stimbol advanced cautiously and the black pointed toward the left, through the foliage. Dimly, Stimbol saw a black mass moving slowly away from them.

"What is it?" he whispered.

"Gorilla," replied the black.

Stimbol raised his rifle and fired at the retreating figure. The black was not surprised that he missed.

"Hell!" ejaculated the white. "Come on, get after him! I've got to have him. Gad! what a trophy he'll make."

The jungle was rather more open than usual and again and again they came within sight of the retreating gorilla. Each time Stimbol fired and each time he missed. Secretly the blacks were amused and pleased. They did not like Stimbol.

At a distance Tarzan of the Apes, hunting with the tribe of Toyat, heard the first shot and immediately took to the trees and was racing in the direction of the sound. He felt sure that the weapon had not been discharged by the Beduins, for he well knew and could differentiate between the reports of their muskets and those made by modern weapons.

Perhaps, he thought, there may be among them such a rifle, because such was not impossible, but more likely it meant white men, and in Tarzan's country it was his business to know what strangers were there and why. Seldom they came even now, though once they had never come. It was those days that Tarzan regretted, for when the white man comes peace and happiness depart.

Racing through the trees, swinging from limb to limb, Tarzan of the Apes unerringly followed the direction of the sound of the succeeding shots; and as he approached more closely the scene of the pursuit of Bolgani the gorilla, he heard the crashing of underbrush and the voices of men.

Bolgani, fleeing with greater haste than caution, his mind and attention occupied by thoughts of escape from the hated Tarmangani and the terrifying thunder stick that roared each time the Tarmangani came within sight of him, abandoned his accustomed wariness and hurried through the jungle forgetful of what few other enemies might beset his path; and so it was that he failed to see Histah the snake draped in sinuous loops along an overhanging branch of a nearby patriarch of the forest.

The huge python, naturally short-tempered and irritable, had been disturbed and annoyed by the crashing sounds of pursuit and escape and the roaring voice of the rifle. Ordinarily he would have permitted a full grown bull gorilla to pass unmolested, but in his present state of mind he might have attacked even Tantor himself.

His beady eyes glaring fixedly, he watched the approach of the shaggy Bolgani, and as the gorilla passed beneath the limb to which he clung Histah launched himself upon his prey.

As the great coils, powerful, relentless, silent, encircled Bolgani, he sought to tear the hideous folds from him. Great is the strength of Bolgani, but even greater is that of Histah the snake. A single hideous, almost human scream burst from the lips of Bolgani with the first realization of the disaster that had befallen him, and then he was on the ground tearing futilely at the steadily tightening bands of living steel that would crush the life from him, crush until his bones gave to the tremendous pressure, until only broken pulp remained within a sausagelike thing that would slip between the distended jaws of the serpent.

It was upon this sight that Stimbol and Tarzan came simultaneously—Stimbol stumbling awkwardly through the underbrush, Tarzan of the Apes, demigod of the forest, swinging gracefully through the foliage of the middle terraces.

They arrived simultaneously but Tarzan was the only one of the party whose presence was unsuspected by the others, for, as always, he had moved silently and with the utmost wariness because of the unknown nature of the conditions he might discover.

As he looked down upon the scene below his quick eye and his knowledge of the jungle revealed at a glance the full story of the tragedy that had overtaken Bolgani, and then he saw Stimbol raise his rifle, intent upon bagging two royal specimens with a single shot.

In the heart of Tarzan was no great love for Bolgani the gorilla. Since childhood the shaggy, giant man-beast had been the natural foe of the ape-man. His first mortal combat had been with Bolgani. For years he had feared him, or rather avoided him through caution, for of fear Tarzan was ignorant; and since he had emerged from childhood he had continued to avoid Bolgani for the simple reason that his own people, the great apes, avoided him.

But now when he saw the huge brute beset by two of the natural enemies of both the Mangani and the Bolgani, there flared within his breast a sudden loyalty that burned away the personal prejudices of a lifetime.

He was directly above Stimbol, and with such celerity do the mind and muscles of the ape-man coordinate that even as the American raised his weapon to his shoulder Tarzan had dropped upon his back, felling him to the earth; and before Stimbol could discover what had happened to him, long before he could stumble, cursing, to his feet, Tarzan, who had been unarmed, had snatched the hunter's knife from its scabbard and leaped full upon the writhing, struggling mass of python and gorilla. Stimbol came to his feet ready to kill but what he saw before him temporarily drove the desire for vengeance from his mind.

Naked but for a loincloth, bronzed, black-haired, a giant white man battled with the dread python; and as Stimbol watched he shuddered as he became aware that the low, beast-like growls he had heard came not alone from the savage lips of the gorilla but from the throat of the godlike man-thing that fought for him.

Steel fingers encircled the python just back of its head, while those of the free hand drove Stimbol's hunting knife again and again into the coiling, writhing body of the serpent. With the projection of a new and more menacing enemy into the battle, Histah was forced partially to release his hold upon Bolgani with, at first, the intention of including Tarzan in the same embrace that he might crush them both at once; but soon he discovered that the hairless man-thing constituted a distinct menace to his life that would necessitate his undivided attention, and so he quickly uncoiled from about Bolgani and in a frenzy of rage and pain that whipped his great length into a lashing fury of destruction he sought to encircle the ape-man; but wheresoever his coils approached, the keen knife bit deep into tortured flesh.

Bolgani, the spark of life all but crushed from him, lay gasping upon the ground, unable to come to the aid of his preserver, while Stimbol, goggle-eyed with awe and terror, kept at a safe distance, momentarily forgetful both of his lust for trophies and his bent for revenge.

Thus was Tarzan pitted, single-handed, against one of the mightiest of Nature's creations in a duel to the death, the result of which seemed to the watching American already a foregone conclusion, for what man born of woman could hope, unaided, to escape from the embrace of the deadly coils of a python?

Already Histah had encircled the torso and one leg of the ape-man, but his powers of constriction, lessened by the frightful wounds he had received, had as yet been unable to crush his adversary into helplessness, and Tarzan was now concentrating his attention and the heavy blade of the hunting knife upon a single portion of the weakening body in an attempt to cut Histah in two.

Man and serpent were red with blood; and crimson were the grasses and the brush for yards in all directions as, with a final effort, Histah closed his giant coils spasmodically about his victim at the instant that Tarzan with a mighty upward heavy lunge cut through the vertebrae of the great snake.

Lashing and writhing, the nether portion, headless, flopped aside while the ape-man, still fighting with what remained, exerting his superhuman strength to its ultimate utmost, slowly forced the coils from about his body and cast the dying Histah from him. Then, without a glance at Stimbol, he turned to Bolgani.

"You are hurt to death?" he asked in the language of the great apes.

"No," replied the gorilla. "I am Bolgani! I kill, Tarmangani!"

"I am Tarzan of the Apes," said the ape-man. "I saved you from Histah."

"You did not come to kill Bolgani?" inquired the gorilla.

"No. Let us be friends."

Bolgani frowned in an effort to concentrate upon this remarkable problem. Presently he spoke. "We will be friends," he said. "The Tarmangani behind you will kill us both with his thunder stick. Let us kill him first." Painfully he staggered to his feet.

"No," remonstrated Tarzan. "I will send the Tarmangani away."

"You? He will not go."

"I am Tarzan, Lord of the Jungle," replied the ape-man. "The word of Tarzan is law in the jungle."

Stimbol, who had been watching, was under the impression that the man and the beast were growling at one another and that a new duel impended. Had he guessed the truth and suspicioned that they considered him a common enemy he would have felt far less at ease. Now, his rifle regained, he started toward Tarzan just as the latter turned to address him.

"Stand to one side, young fellow," said Stimbol, "while I finish that gorilla. After the experience you just had with the snake, I doubt if you want that fellow to jump you, too." The American was none too sure of what the attitude of the white giant might be, for all too fresh in his mind was the startling and disconcerting manner of the wild man's introduction; but he felt safe because he held a rifle, while the other was unarmed, and he guessed that the giant might be only too glad to be saved from the attentions of the gorilla, which, from Stimbol's imagined knowledge of such beasts, appeared to him to be quite evidently threatening.

Tarzan halted directly between Bolgani and the hunter and eyed the latter appraisingly for a moment. "Lower your rifle," he said, presently. "You are not going to shoot the gorilla."

"The hell I'm not!" ejaculated Stimbol. "What do you suppose I've been chasing him through the jungle for?"

"Under a misapprehension," replied Tarzan.

"What misapprehension?" demanded Stimbol.

"That you were going to shoot him. You are not."

"Say, young man, do you know who I am?" demanded Stimbol.

"I am not interested," replied Tarzan coldly.

"Well you'd better be. I'm Wilbur Stimbol of Stimbol & Company, brokers, New York!" That was a name to conjure with—in New York. Even in Paris and London it had opened many a door, bent many a knee. Seldom had it failed the purpose of this purse-arrogant man.

"What are you doing in my country?" demanded the ape-man, ignoring Stimbol's egotistical statement of his identity.

"Your country? Who the hell are you?"

Tarzan turned toward the two blacks who had been standing a little in the rear of Stimbol and to one side. "I am Tarzan of the Apes," he said to them in their own dialect. "What is this man doing in my country? How many are there in his party—how many white men?"

'Big Bwana," replied one of the men with sincere deference, "we knew that you were Tarzan of the Apes when we saw you swing from the trees and slay the great snake. There is no other in all the jungle who could do that. This white man is a bad master. There is one other white man with him. The other is kind. They came to hunt Simba the lion and other big game. They have had no luck. Tomorrow they turn back."

"Where is their camp?" demanded Tarzan.

The black who had spoken pointed. "It is not far," he said.

The ape-man turned to Stimbol. "Go back to your camp," he said. "I shall come there later this evening and talk with you and your companion. In the meantime hunt no more except for food in Tarzan's country."

There was something in the voice and manner of the stranger that had finally gone through Stimbol's thick sensibilities and impressed him with a species of awe—a thing he had scarcely ever experienced in the past except in the presence of wealth that was grossly superior to his own. He did not reply. He just stood and watched the bronzed giant turn to the gorilla. He heard them growl at one another for a moment and then, to his vast surprise, he saw them move off through the jungle together, shoulder to shoulder. As the foliage closed about them he removed his helmet and wiped the sweat from his forehead with a silken handkerchief as he stood staring at the green branches that had parted to receive this strangely assorted pair.

Finally he turned to his men with an oath. "A whole day

wasted!" he complained. "Who is this fellow? You seemed to know him."

"He is Tarzan," replied one of the blacks.

"Tarzan? Never heard of him," snapped Stimbol.

"All who know the jungle, know Tarzan."

"Humph!" sneered Stimbol. "No lousy wild man is going to tell Wilbur Stimbol where he can hunt and where he can't."

"Master," said the black who had first spoken, "the word of Tarzan is the law of the jungle. Do not offend him."

"I'm not paying you damn fools for advice," snapped Stimbol. "If I say hunt, we hunt, and don't you forget it." But on their return to camp they saw no game, or at least Stimbol saw none. What the blacks saw was their own affair.

5

The Tarmangani

DURING STIMBOL'S ABSENCE from camp Blake had been occupied in dividing the food and equipment into two equal parts which were arranged for Stimbol's inspection and approval; but the division of the porters and askari he had left until the other's return, and was writing in his diary when the hunting party entered the camp.

He could see at a glance that Stimbol was in bad humor, but as that was the older man's usual state of temper it caused Blake no particular anxiety, but rather gave him cause for added relief that on the morrow he would be rid of his ill-natured companion for good.

Blake was more concerned, however, by the sullen demeanor of the askari who had accompanied Stimbol for it meant to the younger man that his companion had found some new occasion for bullying, abusing, or insulting them, and the difficulty of dividing the safari thus increased. Blake had felt from the moment that he had definitely reached the decision to separate from Stimbol that one of the greatest obstacles they would have to overcome to carry out the plan would be to find sufficient men willing to submit themselves to Stimbol's ideas of discipline, properly to transport his luggage and provisions and guard them and him.

As Stimbol passed and saw the two piles of equipment the frown upon his face deepened. "I see you've got the stuff laid out," he remarked, as he halted before Blake.

"Yes, I wanted you to look it over and see that it is satisfactorily divided before I have it packed."

"I don't want to be bothered with it," replied the other. "I know you wouldn't take any advantage of me on the division."

"Thanks," replied Blake.

"How about the porters?"

"That's not going to be so easy. You know you haven't treated them very well and there will not be many of them anxious to return with you."

"There's where you're dead wrong, Blake. The trouble with you is that you don't know anything about natives. You're too easy with 'em. They haven't any respect for you, and the man they don't respect they don't like. They know that a fellow who beats 'em is their master, and they know that a master is going to look after them. They wouldn't want to trust themselves on a long trek with you. You divided the junk, now let me handle the men—that's more in my line—and I'll see that you get a square deal and a good, safe bunch, and I'll put the fear of God into 'em so they won't dare be anything but loyal to you."

"Just how do you propose selecting the men?" asked Blake.

"Well, in the first place I'd like you to have those men who may wish to accompany you—I'll grant there are a few—so we'll just have 'em all up, explain that we are separating, and I'll tell all those who wish to return with your safari to step forward, then I'll choose some good men from what are left and make up enough that way to complete your quota—see? That's fair enough, isn't it?"

"It's quite fair," agreed Blake. He was hoping that the plan would work out as easily as Stimbol appeared to believe that it would, but he was far from believing and so he thought it best to suggest an alternative that he was confident would have to be resorted to in the end. "In the event that one of us has difficulty in securing the requisite number of volunteers," he said, "I believe that we can enlist the necessary men by offering a bonus to be paid upon safe arrival at railhead. If I am short of men I shall be willing to do so."

"Not a bad idea if you're afraid you can't hold 'em together after I leave you," said Stimbol. "It will be an added factor of safety for you, too; but as for me my men will live up to their original agreement or there'll be some mighty sick porters in these parts. What say we have 'em up and find out just how much of a job we've got on our hands?" He glanced about until his eyes fell on a head man. "Here, you!" he called. "Come here and make it snappy."

The black approached and stopped before the two white men. "You called me, Bwana?" he asked.

"Gather up every one in camp," directed Stimbol. "Have them up here in five minutes for a palaver—every last man jack of them."

"Yes, Bwana."

As the head man withdrew Stimbol turned to Blake. "Any stranger in camp today?" he asked.

"No, why?"

"Ran across a wild man while I was hunting," replied Stimbol. "He ordered me out of the jungle. What do you know about that?" and Stimbol laughed.

"A wild man?"

"Yes. Some crazy nut I suppose. The askari seemed to know about him."

"Who is he?"

"Calls himself Tarzan."

Blake elevated his brows. "Ah!" he exclaimed. "You have met Tarzan of the Apes and he has ordered you out of the jungle?"

"You've heard of him?"

"Certainly, and if he ever orders me out of his jungle, I'll go."

"*You* would, but not Wilbur Stimbol."

"Why did he order you out?" asked Blake.

"He just ordered me out, that's all. Wouldn't let me shoot a gorilla I'd been stalking. The fellow saved the gorilla from a python, killed the python, ordered me out of the jungle, said he'd visit us in camp later and walked away with the gorilla like they were old pals. I never saw anything like it, but it doesn't make any difference to me who or what he thinks he is, I know who and what I am and it's going to take more than a half-wit to scare me out of this country till I'm good and ready to go."

"So you think Tarzan of the Apes is a half-wit?"

"I think anyone's a half-wit who'd run about this jungle naked and unarmed."

"You'll find he's not a half-wit, Stimbol; and unless you want to get in more trouble than you ever imagined existed, you'll do just as Tarzan of the Apes tells you to do."

"What do you know about him? Have you ever seen him?"

"No," replied Blake. "But I have heard a lot about him from our men. He's as much a part of this locality as the jungle, or the lions. Very few, if any, of our men have seen him, but he has the same hold upon their imaginations and superstitions as any of their demons, and they are even more fearful of incurring his displeasure. If they think Tarzan has it in for us we're out of luck."

"Well, all I've got to say is that if this monkey-man knows when he's well off he'll not come butting into the affairs of Wilbur Stimbol."

"And he's coming to visit us, is he?" said Blake. "Well, I certainly want to see him. I've heard of little else since we struck his country."

"It's funny I never heard of him," said Stimbol.

"You never talk with the men," Blake reminded him.

"Gad, it seems as though I'm doing nothing but talk to them," grumbled Stimbol.

"I said, talk *with* them."

"I don't chum with porters," sneered Stimbol.

Blake grinned.

"Here are the men," said Stimbol. He turned toward the waiting porters and askari and cleared his throat. "Mr. Blake and I are going to separate," he announced. "Everything has been divided. I am going to hunt a little farther to the west, make a circle toward the south and return to the coast by a new route. I do not know what Mr. Blake's plans are, but he is going to get half the porters and half the askari, and I want to tell you right now that there isn't going to be any funny business about it. Half of you are going with Mr. Blake whether you like it or not."

He paused, impressively, to let the full weight of his pronouncement sink home. "As usual," he continued. "I wish to keep everyone contented and happy, so I'm going to give you who may want to go with Mr. Blake an opportunity to do so. Now listen! The packs over on that side are Mr. Blake's; those on this side are mine. All those who are willing to accompany Mr. Blake go over on that side!"

There was a moment's hesitation upon the part of the men and then some of them moved quietly over among Blake's packs. Others followed as their understandings slowly grasped the meaning of Stimbol's words until all of the men stood upon Blake's side.

Stimbol turned to Blake with a laugh and a shake of his head. "Gad!" he exclaimed. "Did you ever see such a dumb bunch? No one could have explained the thing more simply than I and yet look at 'em! Not one of them understood me!"

"Are you quite sure of that, Stimbol?" inquired Blake.

Stimbol did not immediately grasp the insinuation. When he did he scowled. "Don't be a fool," he snapped. "Of course they misunderstood me." He turned angrily toward the men. "You thick-skulled, black idiots! Can't you understand anything?" he demanded. "I did not say that you all had to go with Mr. Blake—only those who wished to. Now the rest of you—those who wish to accompany me—get back over here on this side with my packs, and step lively!"

No one moved in the direction of Stimbol's packs. The man flushed.

"This is mutiny!" he stormed. "Whoever is at the bottom of this is going to suffer. Come here, you!" He motioned to a head man. "Who put you fellows up to this? Has Mr. Blake been telling you what to do?"

"Don't be a fool, Stimbol," said Blake. "No one has influenced the men and there is no mutiny. The plan was yours. The men have done just what you told them to. If it had not been for your insufferable egotism you would have known precisely what the outcome would be. These black men are human beings. In some respects they are extremely sensitive human beings, and in many ways they are like children. You strike them, you curse them, you insult them and they will fear you and hate you. You have done all these things to them and they do fear you and hate you. You have sowed and now you are reaping. I hope to God that it will teach you a lesson. There is just one way to get your men and that is to offer them a big bonus. Are you willing to do that?"

Stimbol, his self assurance momentarily shaken at last, wilted in the face of the realization that Blake was right. He looked about helplessly for a moment. The blacks, sullen-faced, stood there like dumb beasts, staring at him. In all those eyes there was no single friendly glance. He turned back to Blake. "See what you can do with them," he said.

Blake faced the men. "It will be necessary for half of you to accompany Mr. Stimbol back to the coast," he said. "He will pay double wages to all those who go with him, provided that you serve him loyally. Talk it over among yourselves and send word to us later by your head man. That is all. You may go."

The balance of the afternoon passed, the two white men keeping to their respective tents; the blacks gathered in groups, whispering. Blake and Stimbol no longer messed together, but after the evening meal each appeared with his pipe to await the report of the head men. After half an hour Blake sent his boy to summon them and presently they came and stood before the young man.

"Well, have the men decided who will accompany Mr. Stimbol?" he asked.

"No one will accompany the old bwana," replied their spokesman. "All will go with the young bwana."

"But Mr. Stimbol will pay them well," Blake reminded, "and half of you must go with him."

The black shook his head. "He could not make the pay big enough," he said. "No boy will go with him."

"You agreed to come out with us and return with us," said Blake. "You must fulfil your agreement."

"We agreed to come out with both of you and return with both of you. There was nothing said about returning separately. We will live up to our agreement and the old bwana may return in safety with the young bwana." There was finality in the tone of the spokesman.

Blake thought for a moment before replying. "You may go," he said. "I will talk with you again in the morning."

The blacks had departed but a moment when the figure of a man appeared suddenly out of the darkness into the light of the campfire.

"Who the—oh, it's you is it?" exclaimed Stimbol. "Here's the wild man, Blake."

The young American turned and surveyed the figure of the bronze giant who was standing just within the circle of the firelight. He noted the clean-cut features, the quiet dignity, the majestic mien and smiled inwardly at recollection of Stimbol's description of this godlike creature—half-wit!

"So you are Tarzan of the Apes!" he said.

Tarzan inclined his head. "And you?" he asked.

"I am Jim Blake of New York," replied the American.

"Hunting of course?"

"With a camera."

"Your companion was using a rifle," Tarzan reminded him.

"I am not responsible for his acts. I cannot control them," replied Blake.

"Nor anyone else," snapped Stimbol.

Tarzan permitted his gaze to move to Stimbol for an instant, but ignored his boast.

"I overheard the conversation between you and the head men," he said, addressing Blake. "Some of your blacks had already told me something about your companion, and twice today I have had an opportunity to form an estimate of my own from personal observation, so I assume that you are separating because you cannot agree. Am I right?"

"Yes," acknowledged Blake.

"And after you separate—what are your plans?"

"I intend to push in a little farther west and then swing—" commenced Stimbol.

"I was speaking to Blake," interrupted Tarzan; "my plans concerning you are already made."

"Well, who the—"

"Silence!" admonished the ape-man. "Go ahead, Blake!"

"We have not had much luck so far," replied Blake, "principally because we never can agree on methods. The result is that I have scarcely a single decent wild animal study. I had planned to go north a way in search of lion pictures. I dislike going back without anything to show for the time and money I have put into the expedition, but now that the men have refused to accompany us separately there is nothing for it but to return to the coast by the shortest route."

"You two don't seem to be taking me into consideration at all," grumbled Stimbol. "I've got as much money and time in this trip as Blake. You forget that I'm here to hunt, and what's more I'm going to hunt and I'm not going straight back to the coast by a damned sight, monkey-man or no monkey-man."

Again Tarzan ignored Stimbol. "Get ready to move out about an hour after sunrise," he said to Blake. "There will be no trouble about dividing the safari. I shall be here to attend to that and give you your final instructions," and as he spoke he turned and disappeared in the darkness.

6

Ara the Lightning

BEFORE DAWN THE camp was astir and by the appointed hour the packs were made and all was in readiness. The porters loitered, awaiting the word that would start the safari upon its eastward journey toward the coast. Blake and Stimbol smoked in silence. The foliage of a nearby tree moved to the swaying of a branch and Tarzan of the Apes dropped lightly into the camp. Exclamations of surprise broke from the lips of the Negroes—surprise clearly tinged with terror. The ape-man turned toward them and addressed them in their own dialect.

"I am Tarzan of the Apes," he said, "Lord of the Jungle. You have brought white men into my country to kill my people. I am displeased. Those of you who wish to live to return to your villages and your families will listen well and do as Tarzan commands.

"You," he pointed at the chief head man, "shall accompany the younger white man whom I will permit to make pictures in my country where and when he will. Select half the men of the safari to accompany the young bwana."

"And you," he addressed another head man, "take those men that remain and escort the other bwana to railhead in the most direct route and without delay. He is not permitted to hunt and there will be no killing except for food or self-defense. Do not fail me. Remember always that Tarzan watches and Tarzan never forgets."

He turned then to the white men. "Blake," he said, "the

arrangements are made. You may leave when you please, with your own safari, and go where you please. The question of hunting is left to your own discretion—you are the guest of Tarzan."

"And you," he addressed Stimbol, "will be taken directly out of the country by the shortest route. You will be permitted to carry firearms for use in self-defense. If you abuse this permission they will be taken away from you. Do not hunt, even for food—your head man will attend to that."

"Now just hold your horses," blustered Stimbol. "If you think I'm going to put up with any such high-handed interference with my rights as an American citizen you're very much mistaken. Why I could buy and sell you and your damned jungle forty times and not know that I'd spent a cent. For God's sake, Blake, tell this poor fool who I am before he gets himself into a lot of trouble."

Tarzan turned to the head man he had selected for Stimbol. "You may up-load and march," he said. "If this white man does not follow you, leave him behind. Take good care of him if he obeys me and deliver him safely at railhead. Obey his orders if they do not conflict with those that I have given you. Go!"

A moment later Stimbol's safari was preparing to depart and, at Tarzan's request, Blake's too was moving out of camp. Stimbol swore and threatened, but his men, sullenly ignoring him, filed off into the jungle toward the east. Tarzan had departed, swinging into the trees and disappearing among the foliage, and at last Stimbol stood alone in the deserted camp.

Thwarted, humiliated, almost frothing with rage he ran after his men, screaming commands and threats that were ignored. Later in the day, sullen and silent, he marched near the head of the long file of porters and askari, convinced at last that the power of the ape-man was greater than his; but in his heart burned resentment and in his mind rioted plans for vengeance—plans that he knew were futile.

Tarzan, wishing to assure himself that his instructions were being carried out, had swung far ahead and was waiting in the crotch of a tree that overhung the trail along which Stimbol must pass. In the distance he could hear the sounds that arose from the marching safari. Along the trail from the opposite direction something was approaching. The ape-man could not see it but he knew what it was. Above the treetops black clouds rolled low, but no air stirred in the jungle.

Along the trail came a great, shaggy, black man-thing. Tarzan of the Apes hailed it as it came in sight of his arboreal perch.

"Bolgani!" he called in low tones.

The gorilla stopped. He stood erect upon his hind feet and looked about.

"I am Tarzan," said the ape-man.

Bolgani grunted. "I am Bolgani," he replied.

"The Tarmangani comes," warned Tarzan.

"I kill!" growled Bolgani.

"Let the Tarmangani pass," said Tarzan. "He and his people have many thunder sticks. I have sent this Tarmangani out of the jungle. Let him pass. Go a little way from the trail—the stupid Gomangani and the Tarmangani, who is stupider, will pass by without knowing that Tarzan and Bolgani are near."

From the darkening sky distant thunder boomed and the two beasts looked upward toward the broad field of Nature's powers, more savage and destructive than their own.

"Pand the thunder hunts in the sky," remarked the ape-man.

"Hunts for Usha the wind," said Bolgani.

"Presently we shall hear Usha fleeing through the trees to escape." Tarzan viewed the lowering, black clouds. "Even Kudu the sun fears Pand, hiding his face when Pand hunts."

Ara the lightning shot through the sky. To the two beasts it was a bolt from Pand's bow and the great drops of rain that commenced to fall shortly after was Meeta, the blood of Usha the wind, pouring from many a wound.

The jungle bent to a great pressure but as yet there was no other noise than the rolling thunder. The trees whipped back and Usha tore through the forest. The darkness increased. The rain fell in great masses. Leaves and branches hurtled through the air, trees crashed amongst their fellows. With deafening roars the elements unleashed their pent anger. The beasts cowered beneath the one awe-inspiring power that they acknowledged as supreme.

Tarzan crouched in the crotch of a great tree with his shoulders arched against the beating rain. Just off the trail Bolgani squatted in drenched and bedraggled misery. They waited. There was nothing else that they could do.

Above them the storm broke again with maniacal fury. The thunder crashed with deafening reverberation. There was a blinding flash of light and the branch upon which Tarzan squatted sagged and hurtled to the trail beneath.

Stunned, the ape-man lay where he had fallen, the great branch partially across his body.

As quickly as it had come, the storm departed. Kudu the sun burst through the clouds. Bolgani, dejected and still terrified, remained where he had squatted, motionless and silent. Bolgani had no desire to attract the attention of Pand the thunder.

Soaked with water, cold, furious, Stimbol slopped along the slippery, muddy trail. He did not know that his safari was some little distance behind him, for he had forged ahead during the storm while they had taken refuge beneath the trees.

At a turn in the trail he came suddenly upon a fallen branch that blocked the way. At first he did not see the body of the man lying beneath it, but when he did he recognized it instantly and a new hope sprang to life within his breast. With Tarzan dead he could be free to do as he pleased; but was the ape-man dead?

Stimbol ran forward and, kneeling, placed an ear to the breast of the prostrate figure. An expression of disappointment crossed his face—Tarzan was not dead. The expression upon Stimbol's face changed—a cunning look came into his eyes as he glanced back down the trail. His men were not in sight! He looked quickly about him. He was alone with the unconscious author of his humiliation!

He thought he was alone. He did not see the shaggy figure that had silently arisen as the sound of Stimbol's approach had come to its sensitive ears and was now peering at him through the foliage—peering at him and at the silent figure of the ape-man.

Stimbol drew his hunting knife from its scabbard. He could

clip its point into the wild man's heart and run back down the trail. His men would find him waiting for them. Later they would come upon the dead Tarzan, but they would not guess how he had met his end.

The ape-man moved—consciousness was returning. Stimbol realized that he must act quickly, and at the same instant a great hairy arm reached out through the foliage and a mighty hand closed upon his shoulder. With a screaming curse he turned to look into the hideous face of Bolgani. He tried to strike at the shaggy breast of his antagonist with his hunting knife, but the puny weapon was torn from his grasp and hurled into the bushes.

The great yellow fangs were bared against Stimbol's throat as Tarzan opened his eyes.

"Kreeg-ah!" cried the ape-man in warning.

Bolgani paused and looked at his fellow beast.

"Let him go," said Tarzan.

"The Tarmangani would have killed Tarzan," explained the gorilla. "Bolgani stopped him. Bolgani kill!" He growled horribly.

"No!" snapped Tarzan. "Free the Tarmangani!"

The gorilla released his grasp upon Stimbol just as the first of the hunter's men came in sight of them, and as Bolgani saw the blacks and how numerous they were his nervousness and irritability increased.

"Take to the jungle, Bolgani," said Tarzan. "Tarzan will take care of this Tarmangani and the Gomangani."

With a parting growl the gorilla merged with the foliage and the shadows of the jungle as Tarzan of the Apes faced Stimbol and his boys.

"You had a close call then, Stimbol," said the ape-man. "It is fortunate for you that you didn't succeed in killing me. I was here for two reasons. One was to see that you obeyed my instructions and the other to protect you from your men. I did not like the way they eyed you in camp this morning. It would not be a difficult thing to lose you in the jungle, you know, and that would put a period to you as surely as poison or a knife. I felt a certain responsibility for you because you are a white man, but you have just now released me from whatever obligation racial ties may have influenced me to acknowledge.

"I shall not kill you, Stimbol, as your deserve; but from now on you may reach the coast on your own, and you will doubtless discover that one cannot make too many friends in the jungle or afford a single unnecessary enemy." He wheeled upon Stimbol's black boys. "Tarzan of the Apes goes his way. You will not see him again, perhaps. Do your duty by this white man as long as he obeys the word of Tarzan, *but see that he does not hunt*!"

With this final admonition the ape-man swung into the lower branches and was gone.

When Stimbol, after repeatedly questioning his men, discovered that Tarzan had practically assured them that they would see no more of him, he regained much of his former assurance and egotistical bluster. Once more he was the leader of men, shouting at the blacks in a loud tone, cursing them, ridiculing them. He thought that it impressed them with his greatness. He believed that they were simple people whom he could deceive into thinking that he was not afraid of Tarzan, and by flaunting Tarzan's commands win their respect. Now that Tarzan had promised not to return Stimbol felt safer in ignoring his wishes, and so it befell that just before they reached a camping ground Stimbol came upon an antelope and without an instant's hesitation fired and killed it.

It was a sullen camp that Stimbol made that night. The men gathered in groups and whispered. "He has shot an antelope and Tarzan will be angry with us," said one.

"He will punish us," said a head man.

"The bwana is a bad man," said another. "I wish he was dead."

"We may not kill him. Tarzan has said that."

"If we leave him in the jungle he will die."

"Tarzan told us to do our duty."

"He said to do it as long as the bad bwana obeyed the commands of Tarzan."

"He has disobeyed them."

"Then we may leave him."

Stimbol, exhausted by the long march, slept like a log. When he awoke the sun was high. He shouted for his boy. There was no response. Again he shouted and louder, adding an oath. No one came. There was no sound in camp.

"The lazy swine," he grumbled. "They'll step a little livelier when I get out there."

He arose and dressed, but as he was dressing the silence of the camp came to impress him as something almost menacing, so that he hastened to be through and out of the tent. As he stepped into the open the truth was revealed at almost the first quick glance about. Not a human being was in sight and all but one of the packs containing provisions were gone. He had been deserted in the heart of Africa!

His first impulse was to seize his rifle and start after the blacks, but second thought impressed him with the danger of such procedure and convinced him that the last thing he should do would be to place himself again in the power of these men who had demonstrated that they felt no compunction in abandoning him to almost certain death. If they wanted to be rid of him they could easily find even a quicker means if he returned and forced himself upon them again.

There was but a single alternative and that was to find Blake and remain with him. He knew that Blake would not abandon him to death in the jungle.

The blacks had not left him without provisions, nor had they taken his rifle or ammunition, but the difficulty that now confronted Stimbol was largely in the matter of transportation for his food. There was plenty of it to last many days, but he knew that he could not carry it through the jungle together with his rifle and ammunition. To remain where the food was would be equally futile. Blake was returning to the coast by another route; the ape-man had said that he would not follow Stimbol's safari farther; it might be years, therefore, before another human being chanced along this little used game trail.

He knew that he and Blake were now separated by about two marches and if he traveled light and Blake did not march too rapidly he might hope to overtake him inside a week. Perhaps Blake would find good camera hunting soon and make a permanent camp. In that case Stimbol would find him even more quickly.

He felt better when he had definitely decided upon a plan of action, and after a good breakfast he made up a small pack of provisions, enough to last him a week, filled his belts and pockets with ammunition, and started off along the back trail.

It was easy going for the trail of the day before was plain and this was the third time that Stimbol had been over it, so he had no difficulty in reaching the camp at which he and Blake had parted company.

As he entered the little clearing early in the afternoon he determined to keep on and cover as much ground on Blake's trail as he could before dark, but for a few minutes he would rest. As he sat down with his back against the bole of a tree he did not notice a movement of the tops of a clump of jungle grasses a few yards distant, and if he had he would, doubtless, have attached no importance to the matter.

Finishing a cigarette Stimbol arose, rearranged his pack, and started off in the direction Blake's men had taken early the preceding morning; but he had covered but a yard or two when he was brought to a sudden halt by an ominous growl that arose from a little clump of jungle grasses close in front of him. Almost simultaneously the fringing grasses parted and there appeared in the opening the head of a great black-maned lion.

With a scream of fear, Stimbol dropped his pack, threw aside his rifle, and started on a run for the tree beneath which he had been sitting. The lion, itself somewhat surprised, stood for an instant watching him and then started in pursuit at an easy lope.

Stimbol, casting an affrighted glance rearward, was horrified—the lion seemed so close and the tree so far away. If distance lends enchantment to the view, proximity may also at times have its advantage. In this instance it served to accelerate the speed of the fleeing man to a most surprising degree, and though he was no longer young he clawed his way to the lower branches of the tree with speed, if not with grace, that would have done justice to a trained athlete.

Nor was he an instant too speedy. Numa's raking talons

touched his boot and sent him swarming up among the higher branches, where he clung weak and panting looking down into the snarling visage of the carnivore.

For a moment Numa growled up at him and then, with a coughing grunt, turned away and strode majestically in the direction of the clump of grasses from which he had emerged. He stopped to sniff at the pack of provisions Stimbol had discarded and, evidently piqued by the man scent clinging to it, cuffed at it angrily. It rolled to one side and Numa stepped back, eyeing it warily, then, with a growl, he leaped upon it and commenced to maul the insensate thing, ripping and tearing until its contents were scattered about upon the ground. He bit into tins and boxes until scarcely an article remained intact, while Stimbol crouched in the tree and watched the destruction of his provisions, utterly helpless to interfere.

A dozen times he cursed himself for having thrown away his rifle and even more frequently he vowed vengeance. He consoled himself, however, with the realization that Blake could not be far away and that with Blake there were ample provisions which could be augmented by trading and hunting. When the lion left he would descend and follow Blake's trail.

Numa, tired of the contents of the pack, resumed his way toward the long grass, but again his attention was distracted—this time by the thunder stick of the Tarmangani. The lion smelled of the discarded rifle, pawed it, and finally picked it up between his jaws. Stimbol looked on, horrified. What if the beast damaged the weapon? He would be left without means of defense or for obtaining food!

"Drop it!" shouted Stimbol. "Drop it!"

Numa, ignoring the ravings of the despised man-thing, strode into his lair, carrying the rifle with him.

That afternoon and night spelled an eternity of terror for Wilbur Stimbol. While daylight lasted the lion remained in the nearby patch of grass effectually deterring the unhappy man from continuing his search for Blake's camp, and after night fell no urge whatever could have induced Stimbol to descend to the paralyzing terrors of the jungle night even had he known that the lion had departed and no sounds had apprised him of the near presence of danger; but sounds did apprise him. From shortly after dark until nearly dawn a perfect bedlam of howls and growls and coughs and grunts and barks arose from directly beneath him as there had been held a convention of all the horrid beasts of the jungle at the foot of the tree that seemed at best an extremely insecure sanctuary.

When morning came the jungle lay silent and peaceful about him and only torn canvas and empty cans bore mute evidence to the feast of the hyenas that had passed into jungle history. Numa had departed leaving the remains of the kill upon which he had lain as the piece de resistance of the hyenian banquet for which Stimbol had furnished the hors d'oeuvres.

Stimbol, trembling, descended. Through the jungle, wild-eyed, startled by every sound, scurried a pitiful figure of broken, terror-stricken old age. Few could have recognized in it Wilbur Stimbol of Stimbol & Company, brokers, New York.

7

The Cross

THE STORM THAT had overtaken Stimbol's safari wrought even greater havoc with the plans of Jim Blake, altering in the instant of a single blinding flash of lightning the course of his entire life.

Accompanied by a single black, who carried his camera and an extra rifle, Blake had struck out from the direct route of his safari in search of lion pictures, there being every indication that the great carnivores might be found in abundance in the district through which they were passing.

It was his intention to parallel the route of his main body and rejoin it in camp in the afternoon. The boy who accompanied him was intelligent and resourceful, the direction and speed of the marching safari were mutually agreed upon and the responsibility for bringing Blake into camp safely was left entirely to the Negro. Having every confidence in the boy, Blake gave no heed to either time or direction, devoting all his energies to the fascinating occupation of searching for photographic studies.

Shortly after leaving the safari Blake and his companion encountered a herd of seven or eight lions which included a magnificent old male, an old lioness and five or six young, ranging from half to full grown.

At sight of Blake and his companion the lions took off leisurely through rather open forest and the men followed, awaiting patiently the happy coincidence of time, light, and grouping that would give the white man such a picture as he desired.

In the mind of the black man was pictured the route of the safari and its relation to the meanderings of the quarry. He knew how far and in what directions he and his companion were being led from their destination. To have returned to the trail of the safari would have been a simple matter to him, but Blake, depending entirely upon the black, gave no heed either to time or direction.

For two hours they clung doggedly to the spoor, encouraged by occasional glimpses of now one, now several members of the regal group, but never was the opportunity afforded for a successful shot. Then the sky became rapidly overcast by black clouds and a few moments later the storm broke in all the terrific fury that only an Equatorial storm can achieve, and an instant later amidst the deafening roar of thunder and a blinding flash of lightning utter disaster engulfed James Hunter Blake.

How long he lay, stunned by the shock of the bolt that had struck but a few feet from him, he did not know. When he opened his eyes the storm had passed and the sun was shining brightly through the leafy canopy of the forest. Still dazed, uncomprehending the cause or extent of the catastrophe, he raised himself slowly upon an elbow and looked about him.

One of the first sights that met his eyes aided materially in the rapid recovery of his senses. Less than a hundred feet from him stood a group of lions, seven of them, solemnly regarding him. The characteristics of individual lions differ as greatly from those of their fellows as do the characteristics of individuals of the human race and, even as a human being, a lion may have his moods as well as his personal idiosyncrasies.

These lions that gravely inspected the man-thing had been spared any considerable experience with the human species; they had seen but few men; they had never been hunted; they were well fed; Blake had done nothing greatly to upset their easily irritated nervous systems. Fortunately for him they were merely curious.

But Blake did not know all this. He knew only that seven lions were standing within a hundred feet of him, that they were not in a cage, and that while he had pursued them to obtain photographs, the thing that he most desired at the moment was not his camera but his rifle.

Stealthily, that he might not annoy them, he looked about him for the weapon. To his consternation it was nowhere in sight, nor was his gun bearer with the extra rifle. Where could the boy be? Doubtless, frightened by the lions, he had decamped. Twenty feet away was a most inviting tree. Blake wondered if the lions would charge the moment that he rose to his feet. He tried to remember all that he had heard about lions and he did recall one fact that applies with almost axiomatic verity to all dangerous animals—if you run from them they will pursue you. To reach the tree it would be necessary to walk almost directly toward the lions.

Blake was in a quandary, and then one of the younger lions moved a few steps nearer! That settled the matter as far as Blake was concerned, for the closer the lions came the shorter his chance of gaining the tree ahead of them in the event that they elected to prevent.

In the midst of a tremendous forest, entirely surrounded by

trees, Nature had chosen to strike him down almost in the center of a natural clearing. There was a good tree a hundred feet away and on the opposite side of the clearing from the lions. Blake stole a longing glance at it and then achieved some rapid mental calculations. If he ran for the farther tree the lions would have to cover two hundred feet while he was covering one hundred, while if he chose the nearer tree, they must come eighty feet while he was going twenty. There seemed, therefore, no doubt as to the greater desirability of the nearer tree which ruled favorite by odds of two to one. Against it, however, loomed the mental hazard that running straight into the face of seven lions involved.

Jim Blake was sincerely, genuinely, and honestly scared; but unless the lions were psychoanalysts they would never have dreamed the truth as he started nonchalantly and slowly toward them—and the tree. The most difficult feat that he had ever accomplished lay in making his legs behave themselves. They wanted to run. So did his feet and his heart and his brain. Only his will held them in leash.

Those were tense moments for Jim Blake—the first half dozen steps he took with seven great lions watching his approach. He saw that they were becoming nervous. The lioness moved uneasily. The old male growled. A younger male, he who had started forward, lashed his sides with his tail, flattened his head, bared his fangs, and stealthily approached.

Blake was almost at the tree when something happened—he never knew what the cause, but inexplicably the lioness turned and bounded away, voicing a low whine, and after her went the other six.

The man leaned against the bole of the tree and fanned himself with his helmet. "Whew!" he breathed, "I hope the next lion I see is in the Central Park Zoo."

But even lions were forgotten in the developments that the next few moments revealed after repeated shouts for the black boy had brought no response and Blake had determined that he must set out in search of him. Nor did he have far to go. On the back track, just inside the clearing, Blake found a few remnants of charred flesh and a blackened and half molten rifle barrel. Of

the camera not a vestige remained. The bolt that had bowled
Blake over must have squarely struck his gun bearer, killing
him instantly, exploding all the ammunition, destroying the
camera, and ruining the rifle that he had carried.

But what had become of the rifle that had been in Blake's
hands? The man searched in all directions, but could not find it
and was finally forced to the conclusion that its disappearance
could be attributed only to one of those freakish tricks which
severe electrical storms so often play upon helpless and futile
humanity.

Frankly aware that he was lost and had not the faintest con-
ception of the direction in which lay the proposed camp of his
safari, Blake started blindly off on what he devoutly hoped
would prove the right route. It was not. His safari was moving
northeast. Blake headed north.

For two days he trudged on through dense forest, sleeping at
night among the branches of trees. Once his fitful slumbers
were disturbed by the swaying of a branch against which he
was braced. As he awoke he felt it sag as to the weight of some
large animal. He looked and saw two fiery eyes gleaming in the
dark. Blake knew it to be a leopard as he drew his automatic
and fired point blank. With a hideous scream the great cat
sprang or fell to the ground. Blake never knew if he hit it. It did
not return and there were no signs of it in the morning.

He found food and water in abundance, and upon the
morning of the third day he emerged from the forest at the foot
of a range of lofty mountains and for the first time in weeks
reveled in an unobstructed view of the blue sky and saw the
horizon again and all that lay between himself and it. He had
not realized that he had been depressed by the darkness and the
crowding pressure of the trees, but now he experienced all the
spiritual buoyancy of a released convict long immured from
freedom and the light of day. Rescue was no longer problem-
atical, merely a matter of time. He wanted to sing and shout;
but he conserved his energies and started toward the mountains. There had been no native villages in the forest and so, he
reasoned, as there must be native villages in a well-watered

country stocked with game, he would find them upon the mountain slopes.

Topping a rise he saw below him the mouth of a canyon in the bed of which ran a small stream. A village would be built on water.

If he followed the water he would come to the village. Quite easy! He descended to the stream where he was deeply gratified to find that a well-worn path paralleled it. Encouraged by the belief that he would soon encounter natives and believing that he would have no difficulty in enlisting their services in aiding him to relocate his safari, Blake followed the path upward into the canyon.

He had covered something like three miles without having discovered any sign of habitation when, at a turn in the path, he found himself at the foot of a great white cross of enormous proportions. Hewn from limestone, it stood directly in the center of the trail and towered above him fully sixty feet. Checked and weatherworn, it gave an impression of great antiquity, which was further borne out by the remains of an almost obliterated inscription upon the face of its massive base.

Blake examined the carved letters, but could not decipher their message. The characters appeared of early English origin, but he dismissed such a possibility as too ridiculous to entertain. He knew that he could not be far from the southern boundary of Abyssinia and that the Abyssinians are Christians. Thus he explained the presence of the cross; but he could not explain the suggestion of sinister menace that this lonely, ancient symbol of the crucifix held for him. Why was it? What was it?

Standing there, tongueless, hoary with age, it seemed to call upon him to stop, to venture not beyond it into the unknown; it warned him back, but not, seemingly, out of a spirit of kindliness and protection, but rather with arrogance and hate.

With a laugh Blake threw off the mood that had seized him and went on; but as he passed the great white monolith he crossed himself, though he was not a Catholic. He wondered what had impelled him to the unfamiliar act, but he could no more explain it than he could the strange and uncanny suggestion of power and personality that seemed to surround the crumbling cross.

Another turn in the path and the trail narrowed where it passed between two huge boulders that might have fallen from the cliff top towering far above. Cliffs closed in closely now in front and upon two sides. Apparently he was close to the canyon's head and yet there was no slightest indication of a village. Yet where did the trail lead? It had an end and a purpose. He would discover the former and, if possible, the latter.

Still under the depressing influence of the cross, Blake passed between the two boulders; and the instant that he had passed them a man stepped out behind him and another in front. They were Negroes, stalwart, fine-featured fellows, and in themselves nothing to arouse wonder or surprise. Blake had expected to meet Negroes in Africa; but not Negroes wearing elaborately decorated leathern jerkins upon the breasts of which red crosses were emblazoned, close-fitting nether garments, and sandals held by doeskin thongs, cross gartered halfway to their knees; not Negroes wearing close-fitting bassinets of leopard skin that fitted their heads closely and reached to below their ears; not Negroes armed with two-handed broadswords and elaborately tipped pikes.

Blake was acutely aware of the pike tips as there was one pressing against his belly and another in the small of his back.

"Who be ye?" demanded the Negro that faced Blake.

Had the man addressed him in Greek Blake would have been no more surprised than he was by the incongruity of this archaic form of speech falling from the lips of a twentieth-century central African black. He was too dumbfounded for an instant to reply.

"Doubtless the fellow be a Saracen, Paul!" said the black behind Blake, "and understands not what thou sayest—a spy, perchance."

"Nay, Peter Wiggs, as my name be Paul Bodkin he be no infidel—that I know of mine own good eyes."

"Whatsoe'er he be it is for ye to fetch him before the captain of the gate who will question him, Paul Bodkin."

"Natheless there be no hurt in questioning him first, an he will answer."

"Stop thy tongue and take him to the captain," said Peter. "I will abide here and guard the way until thou returnest."

Paul stepped aside and motioned for Blake to precede him. Then he fell in behind and the American did not need to glance back to know that the ornate tip of the pike was ever threateningly ready.

The way lay plain before him and Blake followed the trail toward the cliffs where there presently appeared the black mouth of a tunnel leading straight into the rocky escarpment. Leaning against the sides of a niche just within the entrance were several torches made of reeds or twigs bound tightly together and dipped in pitch. One of these Paul Bodkin selected, took some tinder from a metal box he carried in a pouch at his side, struck a spark to it with flint and steel; and having thus ignited the tinder and lighted the torch he pushed Blake on again with the tip of his pike and the two entered the tunnel, which the American found to be narrow and winding, well suited to defense. Its floor was worn smooth until the stones of which it was composed shone polished in the flaring of the torch. The sides and roof were black with the soot of countless thousands, perhaps, of torch-lighted passages along this strange way that led to—what?

8

The Snake Strikes

UNVERSED IN JUNGLE craft, overwhelmed by the enormity of the catastrophe that had engulfed him, his reasoning faculties numbed by terror, Wilbur Stimbol slunk through the jungle, the fleeing quarry of every terror that imagination could conjure. Matted filth caked the tattered remnants of his clothing that scarce covered the filth of his emaciated body. His once graying hair had turned to white, matching the white stubble of a four days' beard.

He followed a broad and well marked trail along which men and horses, sheep and goats had passed within the week, and with the blindness and ignorance of the city dweller he thought that he was on the spoor of Blake's safari. Thus it came that he stumbled, exhausted, into the menzil of the slow moving Ibn Jad.

Fejjuan, the Galla slave, discovered him and took him at once to the sheik's beyt where Ibn Jad, with his brother, Tollog, and several others were squatting in the mukaad sipping coffee.

"By Ullah! What strange creature hast thou captured now, Fejjuan?" demanded the sheik.

"Perhaps a holy man," replied the black, "for he is very poor and without weapons and very dirty—yes, surely he must be a very holy man."

"Who art thou?" demanded Ibn Jad.

"I am lost and starving. Give me food," begged Stimbol.

But neither understood the language of the other.

"Another Nasrany," said Fahd, contemptuously. "A Frenjy, perhaps."

"He looks more like one of el-Engleys," remarked Tollog.

"Perhaps he is from Fransa," suggested Ibn Jad. "Speak to him that vile tongue, Fahd, which thou didst come by among the soldiers in Algeria."

"Who are you, stranger?" demanded Fahd, in French.

"I am an American," replied Stimbol, relieved and delighted to have discovered a medium of communication with the Arabs. "I have been lost in the jungle and I am starving."

"He is from the New World and he has been lost and is starving," translated Fahd.

Ibn Jad directed that food be brought, and as the stranger ate they carried on a conversation through Fahd. Stimbol explained that his men had deserted him and that he would pay well to be taken to the coast. The Beduin had no desire to be further hampered by the presence of a weak old man and was inclined to have Stimbol's throat slit as the easiest solution of the problem, but Fahd, who was impressed by the man's boastings of his great wealth, saw the possibilities of a large reward or ransom and prevailed upon the sheik to permit Stimbol to remain among them for a time at least, promising to take him into his own beyt and be responsible for him.

"Ibn Jad would have slain you, Nasrany," said Fahd to Stimbol later, "but Fahd saved you. Remember that when the time comes for distributing the reward and remember, too, that Ibn Jad will be as ready to kill you tomorrow as he was today and that always your life is in the hands of Fahd. What is it worth?"

"I will make you rich," replied Stimbol.

During the days that followed, Fahd and Stimbol became much better acquainted and with returning strength and a feeling of security Stimbol's old boastfulness returned. He succeeded in impressing the young Beduin with his vast wealth and importance, and so lavish were his promises that Fahd soon commenced to see before him a life of luxury, ease, and power; but with growing cupidity and ambition developed an increasing fear that someone might wrest his good fortune from him. Ibn Jad being the most logical and powerful competitor for the favors of the Nasrany, Fahd lost no opportunity to impress upon Stimbol that the sheik was still thirsting for his blood; though, as a matter of fact, Ibn Jad was so little concerned over the affairs of Wilbur Stimbol that he would have forgotten his presence entirely were he not occasionally reminded of it by seeing the man upon the march or about the camps.

One thing, however, that Fahd accomplished was to acquaint Stimbol with the fact that there was dissension and treachery in the ranks of the Beduins and this he determined to use to his own advantage should necessity demand.

And ever, though slowly, the 'Aarab drew closer to the fabled Leopard City of Nimmr, and as they marched Zeyd found opportunity to forward his suit for the hand of Ateja the daughter of Sheik Ibn Jad, while Tollog sought by insinuation to advance the claims of Fahd in the eyes of the sheik. This he did always and only when Fahd might hear as, in reality, his only wish was to impress upon the young traitor the depth of the latter's obligation to him. When Tollog should become sheik he would not care who won the hand of Ateja.

But Fahd was not satisfied with the progress that was being made. Jealousy rode him to distraction until he could not look upon Zeyd without thoughts of murder seizing his mind; at last they obsessed him. He schemed continually to rid himself and the world of his more successful rival. He spied upon him and upon Ateja, and at last a plan unfolded itself with opportunity treading upon its heels.

Fahd had noticed that nightly Zeyd absented himself from the gatherings of the men in the mukaad of the sheik's tent and that when the simple household duties were performed Ateja slipped out into the night. Fahd followed and confirmed what was really too apparent to be dignified by the name of suspicion—Zeyd and Ateja met.

And then one night, Fahd was not at the meeting in the sheik's beyt. Instead he hid near the tent of Zeyd, and when the latter had left to keep his tryst Fahd crept in and seized the matchlock of his rival. It was already loaded and he had but to prime it with powder. Stealthily he crept by back ways through the camp to where Zeyd awaited his light of love and sneaked up behind him.

At a little distance, sitting in his mukaad with his friends beneath the light of paper lanterns, Ibn Jad the sheik was plainly visible to the two young men standing in the outer darkness. Ateja was still in the women's quarters.

Fahd, standing behind Zeyd, raised the ancient matchlock to his shoulder and aimed—very carefully he aimed, but not at Zeyd. No, for the cunning of Fahd was as the cunning of the fox. Had Zeyd been murdered naught could ever convince Ateja that Fahd was not the murderer. Fahd knew that, and he was equally sure that Ateja would have naught of the slayer of her lover.

Beyond Zeyd was Ibn Jad, but Fahd was not aiming at Ibn Jad either. At whom was he aiming? No one. Not yet was the time ripe to slay the sheik. First must they have their hands upon the treasure, the secret of which he alone was supposed to hold.

Fahd aimed at one of the am'dan of the sheik's tent. He aimed with great care and then he pulled the trigger. The prop splintered and broke a foot above the level of Ibn Jad's head, and simultaneously Fahd threw down the musket and leaped upon the startled Zeyd, at the same time crying loudly for help.

Startled by the shot and the cries, men ran from all directions and with them was the sheik. He found Zeyd being held tightly from behind by Fahd.

"What is the meaning of this?" demanded Ibn Jad.

"By Ullah, Ibn Jad, he would have slain thee!" cried Fahd. "I came upon him just in time, and as he fired I leaped upon his back, else he would have killed you."

"He lies!" cried Zeyd. "The shot came from behind me. If any fired upon Ibn Jad it was Fahd himself."

Ateja, wide-eyed, ran to her lover. "Thou didst not do it, Zeyd; tell me that thou didst not do it."

"As Allah is my God and Mohammed his prophet I did not do it," swore Zeyd.

"I would not have thought it of him," said Ibn Jad.

Cunning, Fahd did not mention the matchlock. Shrewdly he guessed that its evidence would be more potent if discovered by another than he, and that it would be discovered he was sure. Nor was he wrong. Tollog found it.

"Here," he exclaimed, "is the weapon."

"Let us examine it beneath the light," said Ibn Jad. "It should dispel our doubts more surely than any lying tongue."

As the party moved in the direction of the sheik's beyt Zeyd experienced the relief of one reprieved from death, for he knew that the testimony of the matchlock would exonerate him. It could not be his. He pressed the hand of Ateja, walking at his side.

Beneath the light of the paper lanterns in the mukaad Ibn Jad held the weapon beneath his gaze as, with craning necks, the others pressed about him. A single glance sufficed. With stern visage the sheik raised his eyes.

"It is Zeyd's," he said.

Ateja gasped and drew away from her lover.

"I did not do it! It is some trick," cried Zeyd.

"Take him away!" commanded Ibn Jad. "See that he is tightly bound."

Ateja rushed to her father and fell upon her knees. "Do not slay him!" she cried. "It could not have been he. I know it was not he."

"Silence, girl!" commanded the sheik sternly. "Go to thy quarters and remain there!"

They took Zeyd to his own beyt and bound him securely, and in the mukaad of the sheik the elders sat in judgment while from behind the curtains of the women's quarters, Ateja listened.

"At dawn, then, he shall be shot!" This was the sentence that Ateja heard passed upon her lover.

Behind his greasy thorrib Fahd smiled a crooked smile. In his black house of hair Zeyd struggled with the bonds that held him, for though he had not heard the sentence he was aware of what his fate would be. In the quarters of the harem of the Sheik Ibn Jad the sheik's daughter lay sleepless and suffering.

Her long lashes were wet with tears but her grief was silent. Wide-eyed she waited, listening, and presently her patience was rewarded by the sounds of the deep, regular breathing of Ibn Jad and his wife, Hirfa. They slept.

Ateja stirred. Stealthily she raised the lower edge of the tent cloth beside which lay her sleeping mat and rolled quietly beneath it into the mukaad, now deserted. Groping, she found the matchlock of Zeyd where Ibn Jad had left it. She carried also a bundle wrapped in an old thorrib, the contents of which she had gathered earlier in the evening when Hirfa, occupied with her duties, had been temporarily absent from the women's quarters.

Ateja emerged from the tent of her father and crept cautiously along the single, irregular street formed by the pitched tents of the 'Aarab until she came to the beyt of Zeyd. For a moment she paused at the opening, listening, then she entered softly on sandalled feet.

But Zeyd, sleepless, struggling with his bonds, heard her. "Who comes?" he demanded.

"S-s-sh!" cautioned the girl. "It is I, Ateja." She crept to his side.

"Beloved!" he murmured.

Deftly the girl cut the bonds that held his wrists and ankles. "I have brought thee food and thy musket," she told him. "These and freedom I give thee—the rest thou must do thyself. Thy mare stands tethered with the others. Far is the beled el-Guad, beset with dangers is the way, but night and day will Ateja pray to Allah to guide thee safely. Haste, my loved one!"

Zeyd pressed her tightly to his breast, kissed her and was gone into the night.

9

Sir Richard

THE FLOOR OF the tunnel along which Paul Bodkin conducted Blake inclined ever upward, and again and again it was broken by flights of steps which carried them always to higher levels. To Blake the way seemed interminable. Even the haunting mystery of the long tunnel failed to overcome the monotony of its unchanging walls that slipped silently into the torch's dim ken for a brief instant and as silently back into the Cimmerian oblivion behind to make place for more wall unvaryingly identical.

But, as there ever is to all things, there was an end to the tunnel. Blake first glimpsed it in a little patch of distant daylight ahead, and presently he stepped out into the sunlight and looked out across a wide valley that was tree-dotted and beautiful. He found himself standing upon a wide ledge, or shelf, some hundred feet above the base of the mountain through which the tunnel had been cut. There was a sheer drop before him, and to his right the ledge terminated abruptly at a distance of a hundred feet or less. Then he glanced to the left and his eyes went wide in astonishment.

Across the shelf stood a solid wall of masonry flanked at either side by great, round towers pierced by long, narrow embrasures. In the center of the wall was a lofty gateway that was closed by a massive and handsomely wrought portcullis behind which Blake saw two Negroes standing guard. They

69

were clothed precisely as his captors, but held great battle-axes, the butts of which rested upon the ground.

"What ho, the gate!" shouted Paul Bodkin. "Open to the outer guard and a prisoner!"

Slowly the portcullis rose and Blake and his captors passed beneath. Directly inside the gateway and at the left, built into the hillside, was what was evidently a guardhouse. Before it loitered a score or so of soldiers, uniformed like Paul Bodkin, upon the breast of each the red cross. To a heavy wooden rail gaily caparisoned horses were tethered, their handsome trappings recalling to Blake's memory paintings he had seen of mounted knights of medieval England.

There was so much of unreality in the strangely garbed blacks, the massive barbican that guarded the way, the trappings of the horses, that Blake was no longer capable of surprise when one of the two doors in the guardhouse opened and there stepped out a handsome young man clad in a hauberk of chain mail over which was a light surcoat of rough stuff, dyed purple. Upon the youth's head fitted a leopard skin bassinet from the lower edge of which depended a casmail or gorget of chain mail that entirely surrounded and protected his throat and neck. He was armed only with a heavy sword and a dagger, but against the side of the guardhouse, near the doorway where he paused to look at Blake, leaned a long lance, and near it was a shield with a red cross emblazoned upon its boss.

"Od zounds!" exclaimed the young man. "What has thou there, varlet?"

"A prisoner, an' it pleases thee, noble lord," replied Paul Bodkin, deferentially.

"A Saracen, of a surety," stated the young man.

"Nay, an I may make so bold, Sir Richard," replied Paul—"but me thinks he be no Saracen."

"And why?"

"With mine own eyes I didst see him make the sign before the Cross."

"Fetch him hither, lout!"

Bodkin prodded Blake in the rear with his pike, but the American scarce noticed the offense so occupied was his mind by the light of truth that had so suddenly illuminated it. In the instant he had grasped the solution. He laughed inwardly at himself for his denseness. Now he understood everything—and these fellows thought they could put it over on him, did they? Well, they had come near to doing it, all right.

He stepped quickly toward the young man and halted, upon his lips a faintly sarcastic smile. The other eyed him with haughty arrogance.

"Whence comest thou," he asked, "and what doest thou in the Valley of the Sepulcher, varlet?"

Blake's smile faded—too much was too much. "Cut the comedy, young fellow," he drawled in his slow way. "Where's the director?"

"Director? Forsooth, I know not what thou meanest."

"Yes you don't!" snapped Blake, with fine sarcasm. "But let me tell you right off the bat that no seven-fifty a day extra can pull anything like that with me!"

"Ods blud, fellow! I ken not the meaning of all the words, but I mislike thy tone. It savors o'er much of insult to fall sweetly upon the ears of Richard Montmorency."

"Be yourself," advised Blake. "If the director isn't handy send for the assistant director, or the cameraman—even the continuity writer may have more sense than you seem to have."

"Be myself? And who thinkest thee I would be other than Richard Montmorency, a noble knight of Nimmr."

Blake shook his head in despair, then he turned to the soldiers who were standing about listening to the conversation. He thought some of them would be grinning at the joke that was being played on him, but he saw only solemn, serious faces.

"Look here," he said, addressing Paul Bodkin, "don't any of you know where the director is?"

" 'Director'?" repeated Bodkin, shaking his head. "There be none in Nimmr thus y-clept, nay, nor in all the Valley of the Sepulcher that I wot."

"I'm sorry," said Blake, "the mistake is mine; but if there is no director there must be a keeper. May I see him?"

"Ah, keeper!" cried Bodkin, his face lighting with understanding. "Sir Richard is the keeper."

"My gawd!" exclaimed Blake, turning to the young man. "I beg your pardon, I thought that you were one of the inmates."

"Inmates? Indeed thou speakest a strange tongue and yet withall it hath the flavor of England," replied the young man gravely. "But yon varlet be right—I am indeed this day the Keeper of the Gate."

Blake was commencing to doubt his own sanity, or at least his judgment. Neither the young white man nor any of the Negroes had any of the facial characteristics of mad men. He looked up suddenly at the keeper of the gate.

"I am sorry," he said, flashing one of the frank smiles that was famous amongst his acquaintants. "I have acted like a boor, but I've been under a considerable nervous strain for a long time, and on top of that I've been lost in the jungle for days without proper or sufficient food.

"I thought that you were trying to play some sort of a joke on me and, well, I wasn't in any mood for jokes when I expected friendship and hospitality instead.

"Tell me, where am I? What country is this?"

"Thou art close upon the city of Nimmr," replied the young man.

"I suppose this is something of a national holiday or something?" suggested Blake.

"I do not understand thee," replied the young man.

"Why, you're all in a pageant or something, aren't you?"

"Ods bodikins! The fellow speaks an outlandish tongue! Pageant?"

"Yes, those costumes."

"What be amiss with this apparel? True, 'tis not of any wondrous newness, but methinks it be at least more fair than thine. At least it well suffices the daily service of a knight."

"You don't mean that you dress like this every day?" demanded Blake.

"And why not? But enough of this. I have no wish to further bandy words with thee. Fetch him within, two of thee. And thou, Bodkin, return to the outer guard!" The young man turned and reentered the building, while two of the soldiers seized Blake, none too gently, and hustled him within.

He found himself in a high-ceiled room with walls of cut stone and great, hand-hewn beams and rafters blackened with age. Upon the stone floor stood a table behind which, upon a bench, the young man seated himself while Blake was placed facing him with a guard on either hand.

"Thy name," demanded the young man.

"Blake."

"That be all—just Blake?"

"James Hunter Blake."

"What title bearest thou in thine own country?"

"I have no title."

"Ah, thou art not a gentleman, then?"

"I am called one."

"What is thy country?"

"America."

"America! There is no such country, fellow."

"And why not?"

"I never heard of it. What doest thou near the Valley of the Sepulcher? Didst not know 'tis forbidden?"

"I told you I was lost. I didn't know where I was. All I want is to get back to my safari or to the coast."

"That be impossible. We be surrounded by Saracens. For seven hundred and thirty-five years we have been invested by their armies. How come you through the enemies' lines? How passed you through his vast army?"

"There isn't any army."

"Givest thou the lie to Richard Montmorency, varlet? An' thou wert of gentle blood thou shouldst account to me that insult upon the field of honor. Methink'st thou beest some low-born spy sent hither by the Saracen sultan. 'Twould be well an' thou confessed all to me, for if I take thee before the Prince he will wrest the truth from thee in ways that are far from pleasant. What say?"

"I have nothing to confess. Take me before the Prince, or whoever your boss is; perhaps he will at least give me food."

"Thou shalt have food here. Never shall it be said that

Richard Montmorency turned a hungry man from his doorway. Hey! Michel! Michel! Where is the lazy brat? Michel!"

A door opened from an inner apartment to admit a boy, sleepy eyed, digging a grimy fist into one eye. He was clothed in a short tunic, his legs encased in green tights. In his cap was a feather.

"Sleeping again, eh?" demanded Sir Richard. "Thou lazy knave! Fetch bread and meat for this poor wayfarer and be not until the morrow at it!"

Wide-eyed and rather stupidly, the boy stared at Blake. "A Saracen, master?" he asked.

"What boots it?" snapped Sir Richard. "Did not our Lord Jesus feed the multitude, nor ask if there were unbelievers among them? Haste, churl! The stranger be of great hunger."

The youth turned and shuffled from the room, wiping his nose upon his sleeve, and Sir Richard's attention came back to Blake.

"Thou are not ill-favored, fellow," he said. " 'Tis a pity that thou beest not of noble blood, for thy mien appearth not like that of one lowborn."

"I never considered myself lowborn," said Blake, with a grin.

"Thy father, now—was he not at least a sir knight?"

Blake was thinking quickly now. He was far from being able as yet to so much as hazard a guess that might explain his host's archaic costume and language, but he was sure that the man was in earnest, whether sane or not, and were he not sane it seemed doubly wise to humor him.

"Yes, indeed," he replied, "my father is a thirty-second degree Mason and a Knight Templar."

"Sblud! I knew it," cried Sir Richard.

"And so am I," added Blake, when he realized the happy effect his statement had produced.

"Ah, I knew it! I knew it!" cried Sir Richard. "Thy bearing proclaimed thy noble blood; but why didst thou seek to deceive me? And so thou are one of the poor Knights of Christ and of the Temple of Solomon who guard the way of the pilgrims to the Holy Land! This explaineth thy poor raiment and glorifies it."

Blake was mystified by the allusion, as the picture always suggested by a reference to Knights Templar was of waving white plumes, gorgeous aprons, and glittering swords. He did not know that in the days of their origin they were clothed in any old garments that the charity of others might bequeath them.

At this moment Michel returned bearing a wooden trencher containing cold mutton and several pieces of simnel bread and carrying in one hand a flagon of wine. These he set upon the table before Blake and going to a cupboard fetched two metal goblets into which he decanted a portion of the contents of the flagon.

Sir Richard arose and taking one of the goblets raised it before him on a level with his head.

"Hail, Sir James!" he cried, "and welcome to Nimmr and the Valley of the Sepulcher!"

"Here's looking at you!" replied Blake.

"A quaint saying," remarked Sir Richard. "Methinks the ways of England must be changed since the days of Richard the Lion Hearted when my noble ancestor set forth upon the great crusade in the company of his king. Here's looking at you! Ods bodikins! I must not let that from my memory. Here's looking at you! Just wait thou 'til some fair knight doth drink my health—I shall lay him flat with that!

"But, stay! Here, Michel, fetch yon stool for Sir James, and eat, sir knight. Thou must be passing hungry."

"I'll tell the world I am," replied Blake, feelingly, as he sat down on the stool that Michel brought. There were no knives or forks, but there were fingers and these Blake used to advantage while his host sat smiling happily at him from across the rude table.

"Thou art better than a minstrel for pleasure," cried Sir Richard. "I'll tell the world I am! Ho, ho! Thou wilt be a gift from heaven in the castle of the prince. I'll tell the world I am!"

When Blake had satisfied his hunger, Sir Richard ordered Michel to prepare horses. "We ride down to the castle, Sir

James," he explained. "No longer art thou my prisoner, but my friend and guest. That I should have received thee so scurvily shalt ever be to my discredit."

Mounted upon prancing chargers and followed at a respectful distance by Michel, the two rode down the winding mountain road. Sir Richard now carried his shield and lance, a pennon fluttering bravely in the wind from just below the tip of the latter, the sun glancing from the metal of his hauberk, a smile upon his brave face as he chattered with his erstwhile prisoner. To Blake he seemed a gorgeous picture ridden from out the pages of a story book. Yet, belying his martial appearance, there was a childlike simplicity about the man that won Blake's liking from the first, for there was that about him that made it impossible for one to conceive him as the perpetrator of a dishonorable act.

His ready acceptance of Blake's statements about himself bespoke a credulity that seemed incompatible with the high intelligence reflected by his noble countenance, and the American preferred to attribute it to a combination of unsophistication and an innate integrity which could not conceive of perfidy in others.

As the road rounded the shoulder of a hill, Blake saw another barbican barring the way and, beyond, the towers and battlements of an ancient castle. At a command from Sir Richard the warders of the gate opened to them and the three rode through into the ballium. This space between the outer and inner walls appeared unkept and neglected. Several old trees flourished within it and beneath the shade of one of these, close to the outer gateway, lolled several men-at-arms, two of whom were engaged in a game that resembled draughts.

At the foot of the inner wall was a wide moat, the waters of which reflected the gray stones of the wall and the ancient vines that, growing upon its inner side, topped it to form a leaf coping that occasionally hung low upon the outer side.

Directly opposite the barbican was the great gateway in the inner wall and here a drawbridge spanned the moat and a heavy portcullis barred the way into the great court of the castle; but at a word from Sir Richard the gate lifted and, clattering across the drawbridge, they rode within.

Before Blake's astonished eyes loomed a mighty castle of rough hewn stone, while to the right and left, within the great court, spread broad gardens not illy kept, in which were gathered a company of men and women who might have just stepped from Arthur's court.

At sight of Sir Richard and his companion the nearer members of the company regarded Blake with interest and evident surprise. Several called greetings and questions to Sir Richard as the two men dismounted and turned their horses over to Michel.

"Ho, Richard!" cried one. "What bringest thou—a Saracen?"

"Nay," replied Richard. "A fair sir knight who would do his devoir to the prince. Where be he?"

"Yonder," and they pointed toward the far end of the court where a large company was assembled.

"Come, Sir James!" directed Richard, and led him down the courtyard, the knights and ladies following closely, asking questions, commenting with a frankness that brought a flush to Blake's face. The women openly praised his features and his carriage while the men, perhaps prompted by jealousy, made unflattering remarks about his soiled and torn apparel and its, to them, ridiculous cut; and indeed the contrast was great between their gorgeous dalmaticas of villosa or cyclas, their close-fitting tights, their colored caps and Blake's drab shirt, whipcord breeches, and cordovan boots, now soiled, torn, and scratched.

The women were quite as richly dressed as the men, wearing clinging mantles of rich stuff, their hair and shoulders covered with dainty wimples of various colors and often elaborately embroidered.

None of these men, nor any of those in the assemblage they were approaching wore armor, but Blake had seen an armored knight at the outer gateway and another at the inner and he judged that only when engaged in military duties did they wear this heavy and uncomfortable dress.

When they reached the party at the end of the court Sir

Richard elbowed his way among them to the center of the group where stood a tall man of imposing appearance, chatting with those about him. As Sir Richard and Blake halted before him the company fell silent.

"My lord prince," said Richard, bowing, "I bring thee Sir James, a worthy Knight Templar who hath come under the protection of God through the lines of the enemy to the gates of Nimmr."

The tall man eyed Blake searchingly and he had not the appearance of great credulity.

"Thou sayest that thou comest from the Temple of Solomon in the Kingdom of Jerusalem?" he demanded.

"Sir Richard must have misunderstood me," replied Blake.

"Then thou art no Knight Templar?"

"Yes, but I am not from Jerusalem."

"Perchance he is one of those doughty sir knights that guard the pilgrims' way to the Holy Land," suggested a young woman standing near the prince.

Blake glanced quickly at the speaker and as their eyes met, hers fell, but not before he had seen that they were very beautiful eyes set in an equally beautifully, oval face.

"More like it haps he be a Saracen spy sent among us by the sultan," snapped a dark man who stood beside the girl.

The latter raised her eyes to the prince. "He looketh not like a Saracen, my father," she said.

"What knowest thou of the appearance of a Saracen, child?" demanded the prince. "Hast seen so many?" The party laughed and the girl pouted.

"Verily an' I hast seen full as many a Saracen as has Sir Malud or thyself, my lord prince," she snapped, haughtily. "Let Sir Malud describe a Saracen."

The dark young man flushed angrily. "At least," he said, "my lord prince, I knowest an English knight when I seest one, an' if here be an English knight then Sir Malud be a Saracen!"

"Enough," said the prince and then, turning to Blake: "If thou art not from Jerusalem where art thou from?"

"New York," replied the American.

"Ha," whispered Sir Malud to the girl, "didst I not tell you?"

"Tell me what—that he is from New York? Where is that?" she demanded.

"Some stronghold of the infidel," asserted Malud.

"New York?" repeated the prince. "Be that in the Holy Land?"

"It is sometimes called New Jerusalem," explained Blake.

"And thou comest to Nimmr through the lines of the enemy? Tell me, sir knight, had they many men-at-arms? And how were their forces disposed? Be they close upon the Valley of the Sepulcher? Thinkest thou they plan an early attack? Come, tell me all—thou canst be of great service."

"I have come for days through the forest and seen no living man," said Blake. "No enemy surrounds you."

"What?" cried the prince.

"Didst I not tell thee?" demanded Malud. "He is an enemy spy. He wouldst lead us into the belief that we are safe that the forces of the sultan may find us off our guard and take Nimmr and the Valley."

"Ods blud! Methinks thou beest right, Sur Malud," cried the prince. "No enemy indeed! Why else then hast the knights of Nimmr lain here seven and a half centuries if there be no horde of infidels surrounding our stronghold?"

"Search me," said Blake.

"Eh, what?" demanded the prince.

"He hath a quaint manner of speech, my lord prince," explained Richard, "but I do not think him an enemy of England. Myself will vouch for him an' you will take him into your service, my lord prince."

"Wouldst enter my service, sir?" demanded the prince.

Blake glanced at Sir Malud and looked dubious—then his eyes wandered to those of the girl. "I'll tell the world I would!" he said.

10

The Return of Ulala

NUMA WAS HUNGRY. For three days and three nights he had hunted but always the prey had eluded him. Perhaps Numa was growing old. Not so keen were his scent and his vision, not so swift his charges, nor well timed the spring that heretofore had brought down the quarry. So quick the food of Numa that a fraction of a second, a hair's breadth, might mark the difference between a full belly and starvation.

Perhaps Numa was growing old, yet he still was a mighty engine of destruction, and now the pangs of hunger had increased his ferocity manyfold, stimulated his cunning, emboldened him to take great risks that his belly might be filled. It was a nervous, irascible, ferocious Numa that crouched beside the trail. His up-pricked ears, his intent and blazing eyes, his quivering nostrils, the gently moving tail-tip, evidenced his awareness of another presence.

Down the wind to the nostrils of Numa the lion came the man-scent. Four days ago, his belly full, Numa had doubtless slunk away at the first indication of the presence of man, but today is another day and another Numa.

Zeyd, three days upon the back track from the menzil of the sheik Ibn Jad, thought of Ateja, of far Guad, congratulated himself upon the good fortune that had thus far smiled upon his escape and flight. His mare moved slowly along the jungle trail, unurged, for the way was long; and just ahead a beast of prey waited in ambush.

But Numa's were not the only ears to hear, nor his nostrils the only nostrils to scent the coming of the man-thing—another beast crouched near, unknown to Numa.

Overanxious, fearful of being cheated of his meat, Numa made a false move. Down the trail came the mare. She must pass within a yard of Numa, but Numa could not wait. Before she was within the radius of his spring he charged, voicing a horrid roar. Terrified the mare reared and, rearing, tried to turn and bolt. Overbalanced, she toppled backward and fell, and in falling unhorsed Zeyd; but in the instant she was up and flying back along the trail, leaving her master in the path of the charging lion.

Horrified, the man saw the snarling face, the bared fangs almost upon him. Then he saw something else—something equally awe-inspiring—a naked giant who leaped from a swaying branch full upon the back of the great cat. He saw a bronzed arm encircle the neck of the beast of prey as the lion was borne to earth by the weight and impact of the man's body. He saw a heavy knife flashing in the air, striking home again and again as the frenzied lion threw itself about in futile effort to dislodge the thing upon its back. He heard the roars and the growls of el adrea, and mingled with them were growls and snarls that turned his blood cold, for he saw that they came from the lips of the man-beast.

Then Numa went limp and the giant arose and stood above the carcass. He placed one foot upon it and, raising his face toward the heavens, voiced a hideous scream that froze the marrow in the bones of the Beduin—a scream that few men have heard: the victory cry of the bull ape.

It was then that Zeyd recognized his savior and shuddered again as he saw that it was Tarzan of the Apes. The ape-man looked down at him.

"Thou art from the menzil of Ibn Jad," he said.

"I am but a poor man," replied Zeyd. "I but followed where my sheykh led. Hold it not against Zeyd sheykh of the jungle, that he be in thy beled. Spare my poor life I pray thee and may Allah bless thee."

"I have no wish to harm thee, Beduwy," replied Tarzan.

"What wrong hath been done in my country is the fault of Ibn Jad alone. Is he close by?"

"Wellah nay, he be many marches from here."

"Where are thy companions?" demanded the ape-man.

"I have none."

"Thou art alone?"

"Billah, yes."

Tarzan frowned. "Think well Beduwy before lying to Tarzan," he snapped.

"By Ullah, I speak the truth! I am alone."

"And why?"

"Fahd did plot against me to make it appear that I had tried to take the life of Ibn Jad, which, before Allah, is a lie that stinketh to heaven, and I was to be shot; but Ateja, the daughter of the sheykh, cut my bonds in the night and I escaped."

"What is thy name?"

"Zeyd."

"Whither goest thou—to thine own country?"

"Yes, to beled el-Guad, a Beny Salem fendy of el-Harb."

"Thou canst not, alone, survive the perils of the way," Tarzan warned him.

"Of that I be fearful, but death were certain had I not escaped the wrath of Ibn Jad."

For a moment Tarzan was silent in thought. "Great must be the love of Ateja, the daughter of the sheik, and great her belief in you," he said.

"Wellah, yes, great is our love and, too, she knew that I would not slay her father, whom she loves."

Tarzan nodded. "I believe thee and shall help thee. Thou canst not go on alone. I shall take thee to the nearest village and there the chief will furnish you with warriors who will take you to the next village, and thus from village to village you will be escorted to the Soudan."

"May Allah ever watch over and guard thee!" exclaimed Zeyd.

"Tell me," said Tarzan as the two moved along the jungle trail in the direction of the nearest village which lay two marches to the south of them, "tell me what Ibn Jad doth in this country. It is not true that he came for ivory alone. Am I not right?"

"Wellah yes, Sheykh Tarzan," admitted Zeyd. "Ibn Jad came for treasure, but not for ivory."

"What, then?"

"In el-Habash lies the treasure city of Nimmr," explained Zeyd. " This Ibn Jad was told by a learned sahar. So great is the wealth of Nimmr that a thousand camels could carry away not a tenth part of it. It consists of gold and jewels and—a woman."

"A woman?"

"Yes, a woman of such wondrous beauty that in the north she alone would bring a price that would make Ibn Jad rich beyond dreams. Surely thou must have heard of Nimmr."

"Sometimes the Gallas speak of it," said Tarzan, "but always I thought it of no more reality than the other places of their legends. And Ibn Jad undertook this long and dangerous journey on no more than the word of a magician?"

"What could be better than the word of a learned sahar?" demanded Zeyd.

Tarzan of the Apes shrugged.

During the two days that it took them to reach the village Tarzan learned of the white man who had come to the camp of Ibn Jad, but from Zeyd's description of him he was not positive whether it was Blake or Stimbol.

As Tarzan traveled south with Zeyd, Ibn Jad trekked north-ward into el-Habash, and Fahd plotted with Tollog, and Stimbol plotted with Fahd, while Fejjuan, the Galla slave, waited patiently for the moment of his delivery from bondage, and Ateja mourned for Zeyd.

"As a boy thou wert raised in this country, Fejjuan," she said one day to the Galla slave. "Tell me, dost thou think Zeyd could make his way alone to el-Guad?"

"Billah, nay," replied the black. "Doubtless he be dead by now."

The girl stifled a sob.

"Fejjuan mourns with thee, Ateja," said the black, "for Zeyd was a kindly man. Would that Allah had spared your lover and taken him who was guilty."

"What do you mean?" asked Ateja. "Knowest thou, Fejjuan, who fired the shot at Ibn Jad, my father? It was not Zeyd! Tell me it was not Zeyd! But thy words tell me that, which I well knew before. Zeyd could not have sought the life of my father!"

"Nor did he," replied Fejjuan.

"Tell me what you know of this thing."

"And you will not tell another who told you?" he asked. "It would go hard with me if one I am thinking of knew that I had seen what I did see."

"I swear by Allah that I wilt not betray you, Fejjuan," cried the girl. "Tell me, what didst thou see?"

"I did not see who fired the shot at thy father, Ateja," replied the black, "but something else I saw before the shot was fired."

"Yes, what was it?"

"I saw Fahd creep into the beyt of Zeyd and come out again bearing Zeyd's matchlock. That I saw."

"I knew it! I knew it!" cried the girl.

"But Ibn Jad will not believe if you tell him."

"I know; but now that I am convinced perhaps I shall find a way to have Fahd's blood for the blood of Zeyd," cried the girl, bitterly.

For days Ibn Jad skirted the mountains behind which he thought lay the fabled city of Nimmr as he searched for an entrance which he hoped to find without having recourse to the natives whose haunts he had sedulously avoided lest through them opposition to his venture might develop.

The country was sparsely settled, which rendered it easy for the 'Aarab to avoid coming into close contact with the natives, though it was impossible that the Gallas were ignorant of their presence. If however the blacks were willing to leave them alone, Ibn Jad had no intention of molesting them unless he found that it would be impossible to carry his project to a successful issue without their assistance, in which event he was equally ready to approach them with false promises or ruthless cruelty, whichever seemed the more likely to better serve his purpose.

As the days passed Ibn Jad waxed increasingly impatient, for, search as he would, he could locate no pass across the mountains, nor any entrance to the fabled valley wherein lay the treasure city of Nimmr.

"Billah!" he exclaimed one day, "there be a City of Nimmr and there be an entrance to it, and, by Allah, I will find it! Summon the Habush, Tollog! From them or through them we shall have a clue in one way or another."

When Tollog had fetched the Galla slaves to the beyt of Ibn Jad, the old sheik questioned them but there was none who had definite knowledge of the trail leading to Nimmr.

"Then, by Allah," exclaimed Ibn Jad, "we shall have it from the native Habush!"

"They be mighty warriors, O brother," cried Tollog, "and we be far within their country. Should we anger them and they set upon us it might fare ill with us."

"We be Bedauwy," said Ibn Jad proudly, "and we be armed with muskets. What could their simple spears and arrows avail against us?"

"But they be many and we be few," insisted Tollog.

"We shall not fight unless we be driven to it," said Ibn Jad. "First we shall seek, by friendly overtures, to win their confidence and cajole the secret from them.

"Fejjuan!" he exclaimed, turning to the great black. "Thou are a Habushy. I have heard thee say that thou well rememberest the days of thy childhood in the hut of thy father and the story of Nimmr was no new story to you. Go, then, and seek out thy people. Make friends with them. Tell them that the great Sheykh Ibn Jad comes among them in friendliness and that he hath gifts for their chiefs. Tell them also that he would visit the city of Nimmr, and if they will lead him there he will reward them well."

"I but await thy commands," said Fejjuan, elated at this opportunity to do what he had long dreamed of doing. "When shall I set forth?"

"Prepare thyself tonight and when dawn comes depart," replied the sheik.

And so it was that Fejjuan, the Galla slave, set forth early the following morning from the menzil of Ibn Jad, sheik of the fendy el-Guad, to search for a village of his own people.

By noon he had come upon a well-worn trail leading toward the west, and this he followed boldly, guessing that he would best disarm suspicion thus than by attempting to approach a Galla village by stealth. Also he well knew that there was little likelihood that he could accomplish the latter in any event. Fejjuan was no fool. He knew that it might be difficult to convince the Gallas that he was of their blood, for there was against him not alone his 'Aarab garments and weapons but the fact that he would be able to speak the Galla tongue but lamely after all these years.

That he was a brave man was evidenced by the fact that he well knew the suspicious and warlike qualities of his people and their inborn hatred of the 'Aarab and yet gladly embraced this opportunity to go amongst them.

How close he had approached a village Fejjuan did not know. There were neither sounds nor odors to enlighten him when there suddenly appeared in the trail ahead of him three husky Galla warriors and behind him he heard others, though he did not turn.

Instantly Fejjuan raised his hands in sign of peace and at the same time he smiled.

"What are you doing in the Galla country?" demanded one of the warriors.

"I am seeking the house of my father," replied Fejjuan.

"The house of your father is not in the country of the Gallas," growled the warrior. "You are one of these who come to rob us of our sons and daughters."

"No," replied Fejjuan. "I am a Galla."

"If you were a Galla you would speak the language of the Gallas better. We understand you, but you do not speak as a Galla speaks."

"That is because I was stolen away when I was a child and have lived among the Bedauwy since, speaking only their tongue."

"What is your name?"

"The Bedauwy call me Fejjuan, but my Galla name was Ulala."

"Do you think he speaks the truth?" demanded one of the blacks of a companion. "When I was a child I had a brother whose name was Ulala."

"Where is he?" asked the other warrior.

"We do not know. Perhaps Simba the lion devoured him. Perhaps the desert people took him. Who knows?"

"Perhaps he speaks the truth," said the second warrior. "Perhaps he is your brother. Ask him his father's name."

"What was your father's name?" demanded the first warrior.

"Naliny," replied Fejjuan.

At this reply the Galla warriors became excited and whispered among themselves for several seconds. Then the first warrior turned again to Fejjuan.

"Did you have a brother?" he demanded.

"Yes," replied Fejjuan.

"What was his name?"

"Tabo," answered Fejjuan without hesitation.

The warrior who had questioned him leaped into the air with a wild shout.

"It is Ulala!" he cried. "It is my brother. I am Tabo, Ulala. Do you not remember me?"

"Tabo!" cried Fejjuan. "No, I would not know you, for you were a little boy when I was stolen away and now you are a great warrior. Where are our father and mother? Are they alive? Are they well?"

"They are alive and well, Ulala," replied Tabo. "Today they are in the village of the chief, for there is a great council because of the presence of some desert people in our country. Came you with them?"

"Yes, I am a slave to the desert people," replied Fejjuan. "Is it far to the village of the chief? I would see my mother and my father and, too, I would talk with the chief about the desert people who have come to the country of the Gallas."

"Come, brother!" cried Tabo. "We are not far from the village of the chief. Ah, my brother, that I should see you again whom we thought to be dead all these years! Great will be the joy of our father and mother.

"But, tell me, have the desert people turned you against your own people? You have lived with them many years. Perhaps you have taken a wife among them. Are you sure that you do not love them better than you love those whom you have not seen for many years?"

"I do not love the Bedauwy," replied Fejjuan, "nor have I taken a wife among them. Always in my heart has been the hope of returning to the mountains of my own country, to the house of my father. I love my own people, Tabo. Never again shall I leave them."

"The desert people have been unkind to you—they have treated you with cruelty?" demanded Tabo.

"Nay, on the contrary they have treated me well," replied Fejjuan. "I do not hate them, but neither do I love them. They are not of my own blood. I am a slave among them."

As they talked the party moved along the trail toward the village while two of the warriors ran ahead to carry the glad tidings to the father and mother of the long missing Ulala. And so it was that when they came within sight of the village they were met by a great crowd of laughing, shouting Gallas, and in the forerank were the father and mother of Fejjuan, their eyes blinded by the tears of love and joy that welled at sight of this long gone child.

After the greetings were over, and every man, woman, and child in the company must crowd close and touch the returned wanderer, Tabo conducted Fejjuan into the village and the presence of the chief.

Batando was an old man. He had been chief when Ulala was stolen away. He was inclined to be skeptical, fearing a ruse of the desert people, and he asked many questions of Fejjuan concerning matters that he might hold in his memory from the days of his childhood. He asked him about the house of his father and the names of his playmates and other intimate things that an imposter might not know, and when he had done he arose and took Fejjuan in his arms and rubbed his cheek against the cheek of the prodigal.

"You are indeed Ulala," he cried. "Welcome back to the land of your people. Tell me now what the desert people do here. Have they come for slaves?"

"The desert people will always take slaves when they can get them, but Ibn Jad has not come first for slaves, but for treasure."

"Ai! what treasure?" demanded Batando.

"He has heard of the treasure city of Nimmr," replied Fejjuan. "It is a way into the valley where lies Nimmr that he seeks. For this he sent me to find Gallas who would lead him to Nimmr. He will make gifts and he promises rich rewards when he shall have wrested the treasure from Nimmr."

"Are these true words?" asked Batando.

"There is no truth in the beards of the desert dwellers," replied Fejjuan.

"And if he does not find the treasure of Nimmr perhaps he will try to find treasure and slaves in the Galla country to repay the expense of the long journey he has undertaken from the desert country?" asked Batando.

"Batando speaks out of the great wisdom of many years," replied Fejjuan.

"What does he know of Nimmr?" asked the old chief.

"Naught other than what an old medicine man of the 'Aarab told him," replied Fejjuan. "He said to Ibn Jad that great treasure lay hoarded in the City of Nimmr and that there was a beautiful woman who would bring a great price in the far north."

"Nothing more he told him?" demanded Batando. "Did he not tell him of the difficulties of entering the forbidden valley?"

"Nay."

"Then we can guide him to the entrance to the valley," said Batando, smiling slyly.

11

Sir James

As Tarzan and Zeyd journeyed toward the village in which the ape-man purposed to enlist an escort for the Arab upon the first stage of his return journey toward his desert home, the Beduin had time to meditate much upon many matters, and having come to trust and respect his savage guide he at last unbosomed himself to Tarzan.

"Great Skeykh of the Jungle," he said one day, "by thy kindness thou hast won the undying loyalty of Zeyd who begs that thou wilt grant him one more favor."

"And what is that?" asked the ape-man.

"Ateja, whom I love, remains here in the savage country in constant danger so long as Fahd be near her. I dare not now return to the menzil of Ibn Jad even could I find it, but later, when the heat of Ibn Jad's anger will have had time to cool, then I might come again among them and convince him of my innocence, and be near Ateja and protect her from Fahd."

"What, then, would you do?" demanded Tarzan.

"I would remain in the village to which you are taking me until Ibn Jad returns this way toward el-Guad. It is the only chance that I have to see Ateja again in this life, as I could not cross the Soudan alone and on foot should you compel me to leave your country now."

"You are right," replied the ape-man. "You shall remain here six months. If Ibn Jad has not returned in that time I shall leave word that you be sent to my home. From there I can find a way to return you in safety to your own country."

"May the blessings of Allah be upon thee!" cried Zeyd.

And when they came at last to the village Tarzan received the promise of the chief to keep Zeyd until Ibn Jad returned.

After he had left the village again the ape-man headed north, for he was concerned over the report that Zeyd had given him of the presence of a European prisoner among the 'Aarab. That Stimbol, whom he had sent eastward toward the coast, should be so far north and west as Zeyd had reported appeared inconceivable, and so it seemed more probable that the prisoner was young Blake, for whom Tarzan had conceived a liking. Of course the prisoner might not be either Stimbol or Blake, but whoever he was Tarzan could not readily brook the idea of a white man being permitted to remain a prisoner of the Beduins.

But Tarzan was in no hurry, for Zeyd had told him that the prisoner was to be held for ransom. He would have a look about for Blake's camp first and then follow up the spoor of the Arabs. His progress, therefore, was leisurely. On the second day he met the apes of Toyat and for two days he hunted with them, renewing his acquaintance with Gayat and Zutho, listening to the gossip of the tribe, often playing with the balus.

Leaving them, he loafed on through the jungle, stopping once for half a day to bait Numa where he lay upon a fresh kill, until the earth trembled to the thunderous roars of the maddened king of beasts as the ape-man taunted and annoyed him.

Sloughed was the thin veneer of civilization that was Lord Greystoke; back to the primitive, back to the savage beast the ape-man reverted as naturally, as simply, as one changes from one suit to another. It was only in his beloved jungle, surrounded by its savage denizens, that Tarzan of the Apes was truly Tarzan, for always in the presence of civilized men there was a certain restraint that was the outcome of that inherent suspicion that creatures of the wild ever feel for man.

Tired of throwing ripe fruit at Numa, Tarzan swung away through the middle terraces of the forest, lay up for the night far away and in the morning, scenting Bara the deer, made a kill and fed. Lazy, he slept again, until the breaking of twigs and the rustle of down-tramped grasses awoke him.

He sniffed the air with sensitive nostrils and listened with ears that could hear an ant walk, and then he smiled, Tantor was coming.

For half a day he lolled on the huge back, listening to Manu the Monkey chattering and scolding among the trees. Then he moved on again.

A day or two later he came upon a large band of monkeys. They seemed much excited and at sight of him they all commenced to jabber and chatter.

"Greetings, Manu!" cried the ape-man. "I am Tarzan, Tarzan of the Apes. What happens in the jungle?"

"Gomangani! Gomangani!" cried one.

"Strange Gomangani!" cried another.

"Gomangani with thunder sticks!" chattered a third.

"Where?" asked the ape-man.

"There! There!" they shouted in chorus, pointing toward the northeast.

"Many sleeps away?" asked Tarzan.

"Close! Close!" the monkeys answered.

"There is one Tarmangani with them?"

"No, only Gomangani. With their thunder sticks they kill little Manu and eat him. Bad Gomangani!"

"Tarzan will talk with them," said the ape-man.

"They will kill Tarzan with their thunder sticks and eat him," prophesied a graybeard.

The ape-man laughed and swung off through the trees in the direction Manu had indicated. He had not gone far when the scent spoor of blacks came faintly to his nostrils and this spoor he followed until presently he could hear their voices in the distance.

Silently, warily Tarzan came through the trees, noiseless as the shadows that kept him company, until he stood upon a swaying limb directly above a camp of Negroes.

Instantly Tarzan recognized the safari of the Young American, Blake, and a second later he dropped to the ground before the astonished eyes of the blacks. Some of them would have run, but others recognized him.

"It is Big Bwana!" they cried. "It is Tarzan of the Apes!"

"Where is your head man?" demanded Tarzan.

A stalwart Negro approached him. "I am head man," he said.

"Where is your master?"

"He is gone, many days," replied the black.

"Where?"

"We do not know. He hunted with a single askar. There was a great storm. Neither of them ever returned. We searched the jungle for them, but could not find them. We waited in camp where they were to have joined us. They did not come. We did not know what to do. We would not desert the young Bwana, who was kind to us; but we feared that he was dead. We have not provisions to last more than another moon. We decided to return home and tell our story to the friends of the young Bwana."

"You have done well," said Tarzan. "Have you seen a company of the desert people in the jungle?"

"We have not seen them," replied the head man, "but while we were searching for the young Bwana we saw where desert people had camped. It was a fresh camp."

"Where?"

The black pointed. "It was on the trail to the north Galla country in Abyssinia and when they broke camp they went north."

"You may return to your village," said Tarzan, "but first take those things which are the young Bwana's to his friends to keep for him and send a runner to the home of Tarzan with this message: Send one hundred Waziri to Tarzan in the north Galla country. From the water hole of the smooth, round rocks follow the trail of the desert people."

"Yes, Big Bwana, it will be done," said the head man.

"Repeat my message."

The black boy did as he was bidden.

"Good!" said Tarzan. "I go. Kill not Manu the monkey if

you can find other food, for Manu is the cousin of Tarzan and of you."

"We understand, Big Bwana."

In the castle of Prince Gobred in the City of Nimmr James Hunter Blake was being schooled in the duties of a Knight of Nimmr. Sir Richard had taken him under his protection and made himself responsible for his training and his conduct.

Prince Gobred, quick to realize Blake's utter ignorance of even the simplest observances of knighthood, was frankly skeptical, and Sir Malud was almost openly antagonistic, but the loyal Sir Richard was a well-beloved knight and so he had his way. Perhaps, too, the influence of the Princess Guinalda was not without its effect upon her sire, for first among the treasurers of the Prince of Nimmr ranked his daughter Guinalda; and Guinalda's curiosity and interest had been excited by the romance of the coming of this fair stranger knight to the buried and forgotten city of Nimmr.

Sir Richard had clothed Blake from his own wardrobe until a weaver, a cutter of cloth, a seamstress, and an armorer could fashion one for him. Nor did it take long. A week found Sir James clothed, armored, and horsed as befitted a Knight of Nimmr, and when he spoke to Sir Richard of payment for all this he found that money was almost unknown among them. There were, Sir Richard told him, a few pieces of coin that their ancestors had brought here seven hundred and thirty-five years before, but payment was made by service.

The knights served the prince and he kept them. They protected the laborers and the artisans and in return received what they required from them. The slaves received their food and clothing from the prince or from whichever knight they served. Jewels and precious metals often changed hands in return for goods or service, but each transaction was a matter of barter as there were no standards of value.

They cared little for wealth. The knights valued most highly their honor and their courage upon which there could be no price. The artisan found his reward in the high perfection of his handicraft and in the honors that it brought him.

The valley provided food in plenty for all; the slaves tilled the ground; the freedmen were the artisans, the men-at-arms, the herders of cattle; the knights defended Nimmr against its enemies, competed in tourneys, and hunted wild game in the valley and its surrounding mountains.

As the days passed Blake found himself rapidly acquiring a certain proficiency in knightly arts under the wise tutorage of Sir Richard. The use of sword and buckler he found most difficult, notwithstanding the fact that he had been proficient with the foils in his college days, for the knights of Nimmr knew naught of the defensive use of their two edged weapons and seldom used the point for other purpose than the *coup-de-grace*. For them the sword was almost wholly a cutting weapon, the buckler their sole defense; but as Blake practiced with this weapon it dawned upon him that his knowledge of fencing might be put to advantage should the necessity arise, to the end that his awkwardness with the buckler should be outweighed by his nicer defensive handling of his sword and his offensive improved by the judicious use of the point, against which they had developed little or no defense.

The lance he found less difficult, its value being so largely dependent upon the horsemanship of him who wielded it, and that Blake was a splendid horseman was evidenced by his polo rating as an eight goal man.

The ballium, or outer court, which lay between the inner and outer walls of the castle and entirely surrounded it, was, upon the north or valley side, given over entirely to knightly practice and training. Here the ballium was very wide, and against the inner wall was built a wooden grandstand that could be quickly removed in the event of an attack upon the castle.

Jousts and tilts were held here weekly, while the great tourneys that occurred less often were given upon a field outside the castle wall upon the floor of the valley.

Daily many knights and ladies came to watch the practice and training that filled the ballium with life and action and color during the morning hours. Good-natured banter flew back and forth, wagers were laid, and woe betide the contender who was unhorsed during these practice bouts, for the thing that a knight dreaded even more than he dreaded death was ridicule.

In the formal jousts that were held weekly greater decorum was observed by the audience, but during the daily practice their raillery verged upon brutality.

It was before such an audience as this that Blake received his training, and because he was a novelty the audiences were larger than usual, and because the friends of Sir Malud and the friends of Sir Richard had tacitly acknowledged him as an issue both the applause and the ridicule were loud and boisterous.

Even the Prince came often and Guinalda always was there. It was soon apparent that Prince Gobred leaned slightly to the side of Sir Malud, with the natural result that Malud's party immediately acquired numerous recruits.

The training of the lads who were squires to the knights and who would one day be admitted to the charmed circle of knighthood occupied the earlier hours of the morning. This was followed by practice tilts between knights, during which Sir Richard or one of his friends undertook the training of Blake at the far side of the ballium, and it was during this practice that the American's outstanding horsemanship became apparent, even Gobred being led to applause.

"Ods bodikins," he exclaimed, "the man be a part of his charger!"

" 'Twas but chance that saved him from a fall," said Malud.

"Mayhap," agreed Gobred, "but at that me likes the looks of him within a saddle."

"He doeth not too ill with his lance," admitted Malud. "But, ods blud! didst ever see a more awkward lout with a buckler? Methinks he hath had more use for a trencher." This sally elicited roars of laughter in which the Princess Guinalda did not join, a fact which Malud, whose eyes were often upon her, was quick to note. "Thou still believest this churl to be a knight, Princess Guinalda?" he demanded.

"Have I said aught?" she asked.

"Thou didst not laugh," he reminded her.

"He is a stranger knight, far from his own country and it

seemeth not a knightly nor a gentle thing to ridicule him," she replied. "Therefore I did not laugh, for I was not amused."

Later that day as Blake joined the others in the great court, he ran directly into Malud's party, nor was it at all an accident, as he never made any effort to avoid Malud or his friends and was, seemingly, oblivious to their thinly veiled taunts and insinuations. Malud himself attributed this to the density and ignorance of a yokel, which he insisted Blake to be, but there were others who rather admired Blake for his attitude, seeing in it a studied affront that Malud was too dense to perceive.

Most of the inmates of the grim castle of Nimmr were inclined pleasantly toward the newcomer. He had brought with him an air of freshness and newness that was rather a relief from the hoary atmosphere that had surrounded Nimmr for nearly seven and a half centuries. He had brought them new words and new expressions and new views, which many of them were joyously adopting, and had it not been for the unreasoning antagonism of the influential Sir Malud, Blake had been accepted with open arms.

Sir Richard was far more popular than Malud, but lacked the latter's wealth in horses, arms, and retainers, and consequently had less influence with Prince Gobred. However, there were many independent souls who either followed Sir Richard because they were fond of him or arrived at their own decisions without reference to the dictates of policy, and many of these were staunch friends to Blake.

Not all of those who surrounded Malud this afternoon were antagonistic to the American, but the majority of them laughed when Malud laughed and frowned when he frowned, for in the courts of kings and princes flourished the first order of "yes men."

Blake was greeted by many a smile and nod as he advanced and bowed low before the Princess Guinalda who was one of the company and, being of princely blood, entitled to his first devoirs.

"Thou didst well this morning, Sir James," said the princess, kindly. "It pleases me greatly to see thee ride."

"Methinketh 'twould be a rarer treat to see him serve a side of venison," sneered Malud.

This provoked so much laughter that Malud was encouraged to seek further applause.

"Odzooks!" he cried, "arm him with a trencher and carving knife and he would be at home."

"Speaking of serving," said Blake, "and Sir Malud's mind seems to be more occupied with that than with more knightly things, does any of you know what is necessary quickly to serve fresh pig?"

"Nay, fair sir knight," said Guinalda, "we know not. Prithee tell us."

"Yes, tell us," roared Malud, "thou, indeed, shouldst know."

"You said a mouthful, old scout, I do know!"

"And what be necessary that you may quickly serve fresh pig?" demanded Malud, looking about him and winking.

"A trencher, a carving knife, and you, Sir Malud," replied Blake.

It was several seconds before the thrust penetrated their simple minds and it was the Princess Guinalda who first broke into merry laughter and soon all were roaring, while some explained the quip to others.

No, not all were laughing—not Sir Malud. When he grasped the significance of Blake's witticism he first turned very red and then went white, for the great Sir Malud liked not to be the butt of ridicule, which is ever the way of those most prone to turn ridicule upon others.

"Sirrah," he cried, "darest thou affront Malud? Ods blud, fellow! Lowborn varlet! Only thy blood canst atone this affront!"

"Hop to it, old think!" replied Blake. "Name your poison!"

"I knowest not the meaning of thy silly words," cried Malud, "but I know that an' thou doest not meet me in fair tilt upon the morrow I shalt whip thee across the Valley of the Holy Sepulcher with a barrel stave."

"You're on!" snapped back Blake. "Tomorrow morning in the south ballium with——"

"Thou mayst choose the weapons, sirrah," said Malud.

"Don't call me sirrah, I don't like it," said Blake very quietly, and now he was not smiling. "I want to tell you something, Malud, that may be good for your soul. You are really the only man in Nimmr who didn't want to treat me well and give me a chance, a fair chance, to prove that I am all right.

"You think you are a great knight, but you are not. You have no intelligence, no heart, no chivalry. You are not what we would call in my country a good sport. You have a few horses and a few men-at-arms. That is all you have, for without them you would not have the favor of the Prince, and without his favor you would have no friends.

"You are not so good or great a man in any way as is Sir Richard, who combines all the qualities of chivalry that for centuries have glorified the order of knighthood; nor are you so good a man as I, who, with your own weapons, will best you on the morrow when, in the north ballium, I meet you on horseback with sword and buckler!"

The members of the party, upon seeing Malud's wrath, had gradually fallen away from Blake until, as he concluded his speech, he stood alone a few paces apart from Malud and those who surrounded him. Then it was that one stepped from among those at Malud's side and walked to Blake. It was Guinalda.

"Sir James," she said with a sweet smile, "thou spokest with thy mouth full!" She broke into a merry laugh. "Walk with me in the garden, sir knight," and taking his arm she guided him toward the south end of the eastern court.

"You're wonderful!" was all that Blake could find to say.

"Dost really think I be wonderful?" she demanded " 'Tis hard to know if men speak the truth to such as I. The truth, as people see it, is spoke more oft to slaves than princes."

"I hope to prove it by my conduct," he said.

They had drawn a short distance away from the others now and the girl suddenly laid her hand impulsively upon his.

"I brought thee away, Sir James, that I might speak with thee alone," she said.

"I do not care what the reason was so long as you did it," he replied, smiling.

"Thou art a stranger among us, unaccustomed to our ways, unversed in knightly practice—so much so that there are many who doubt thy claims to knighthood. Yet thou art a brave man, or else a very simple one, or thou wouldst never have chosen to meet Sir Malud with sword and buckler, for he be skilled with these while thou art clumsy with them.

"Because I thinkest that thou goest to thy death tomorrow I have brought thee aside to speak with thee."

"What can be done about it now?" asked Blake.

"Thou art passing fair with thy lance," she said, "and it is still not too late to change thy selection of weapons. I beg thee to do so."

"You care?" he asked. There can be a world of meaning in two words.

The girl's eyes dropped for an instant and then flashed up to his and there was a touch of hauteur in them. "I am the daughter of the Prince of Nimmr," she said. "I care for the humblest of my father's subjects."

"I guess that will hold you for a while, Sir James," thought Blake, but to the girl he said nothing, only smiled.

Presently she stamped her foot. "Thou hast an impudent smile, sirrah!" she exclaimed angrily. "Meliketh it not. Then thou art too forward with the daughter of a prince."

"I merely asked you if you cared whether I was killed. Even a cat could ask that."

"And I replied. Why then didst thou smile?"

"Because your eyes had answered me before your lips had spoken and I knew that your eyes had told the truth."

Again she stamped her foot angrily. "Thou art indeed a forward boor," she exclaimed. 'I shall not remain to be insulted further."

Her head held high she turned and walked haughtily away to rejoin the other party.

Blake stepped quickly after her. "Tomorrow," he whispered, "I meet Sir Malud with sword and buckler. With your favor upon my helm I could overthrow the best sword in Nimmr."

The Princes Guinalda did not deign to acknowledge that she had heard his words as she walked to join the others clustered about Sir Malud.

12

"Tomorrow Thou Diest!"

THERE WAS A great celebration in the village of Batondo the chief the night that Ulala returned. A goat was killed and many chickens, and there were fruit and cassava bread and native beer in plenty for all. There was music, too, and dancing. With all of which it was morning before they sought their sleeping mats, with the result that it was after noon the following day before Fejjuan had an opportunity to speak of serious matters with Batando.

When finally he sought him out he found the old chief squatting in the shade before his hut, slightly the worse for the orgy of the preceding night.

"I have come to talk with you, Batando," he said, "of the desert people."

Batando grunted. His head ached.

"Yesterday you said that you would lead them to the entrance to the forbidden valley," said Fejjuan. "You mean, then, that you will not fight them?"

"We shall not have to fight them if we lead them to the entrance to the forbidden valley," replied Batando.

"You speak in riddles," said Fejjuan.

"Listen, Ulala," replied the old chief. "In childhood you were stolen from your people and taken from your country. Being young, there were many things you did not know and there are others that you have forgotten.

"It is not difficult to enter the forbidden valley, especially from the north. Every Galla knows how to find the northern pass through the mountains or the tunnel beyond the great cross that marks the southern entrance. There are only these two ways in—every Galla knows them; but every Galla also knows that there is no way out of the forbidden valley."

"What do you mean, Batando?" demanded Fejjuan. "If there are two ways in, there must be two ways out."

"No—there is no way out," insisted the chief. "As far back as goes the memory of man or the tales of our fathers and our fathers' fathers it is known that many men have entered the forbidden valley, and it is also known that no man has ever come out of it."

"And why have they not come out?"

Batando shook his head. "Who knows?" he asked. "We cannot even guess their fate."

"What sort of people inhabit the valley?" asked Fejjuan.

"Not even that is known. No man has seen them and returned to tell. Some say they are the spirits of the dead, others that the valley is peopled by leopards; but no one knows.

"Go therefore, Ulala, and tell the chief of the desert people that we will lead him to the entrance to the valley. If we do this we shall not have to fight him and his people, nor shall we ever again be bothered by them," and Batando laughed at his little joke.

"Will you send guides back with me to lead the Bedauwy to the valley?" asked Fejjuan.

"No," replied the chief. "Tell them we shall come in three days. In the meantime I shall gather together many warriors from other villages, for I do not trust the desert people. Thus we shall conduct them through our country. Explain this to their chief and also that in payment he must release to us all the Galla slaves he has with him—before he enters the valley."

"That Ibn Jad will not do," said Fejjuan.

"Perhaps, when he sees himself surrounded by Galla warriors, he will be glad to do even more," replied Batando.

And so Fejjuan, the Galla slave, returned to his masters and reported all that Batando had told him to report.

Ibn Jad at first refused to give up his slaves, but when Fejjuan had convinced him that under no other terms would Batando lead him to the entrance to the valley, and that his refusal to liberate the slaves would invite the hostile attentions of the Gallas, he finally consented; but in the back of his mind was the thought that before his promise was consummated he might find an opportunity to evade it.

Only one regret had Fejjuan in betraying the Beduins, and that was caused by his liking for Ateja, but being a fatalist he was consoled by the conviction that whatever was to be, would be, regardless of what he might do.

And as Ibn Jad waited and Batando gathered his black warriors from far and near, Tarzan of the Apes came to the water hole of the smooth, round rocks and took up the trail of the Beduins.

Since he had learned from Blake's blacks that the young American was missing and also that they had seen nothing of Stimbol since the latter had separated from Blake and started for the coast, the ape-man was more convinced than ever that the white prisoner among the Arabs was Blake.

Still he felt no great concern for the man's safety, for if the Beduins had sufficient hopes of reward to spare his life at all he was in no great danger from them. Reasoning thus Tarzan made no pretense of speed as he followed the spoor of Ibn Jad and his people.

Two men sat upon rough benches at opposite sides of a rude table. Between them a cresset of oil with a cotton wick laying in it burned feebly, slightly illuminating the stone flagging of the floor and casting weird shadows of themselves upon the rough stone walls.

Through a narrow window, innocent of glass, the night air blew, driving the flame of the cresset now this way, now that. Upon the table, between the men, lay a square board blocked off into squares, and within some of these were several wooden pieces.

"It is your move, Richard," said one of the men. "You don't appear to be very keen about the game tonight. What's the matter?"

"I be thinking of the morrow, James, and my heart be heavy within me," replied the other.

"And why?" demanded Blake.

"Malud is not the best swordsman in Nimmr," replied Sir Richard, "but—" he hesitated.

"I am the worst," Blake finished the sentence for him laughingly.

Sir Richard looked up and smiled. "Thou wilt always joke, even in the face of death," he said. "Art all the men of this strange country thou tell'st of alike?"

"It is your move, Richard," said Blake.

"Hide not his sword from thine eyes with thy buckler, James," cautioned Richard. "Ever keep thine eyes upon his eyes until thou knowest whereat he striketh, then, with thy buckler ready, thou mayst intercept the blow, for he be over slow and always his eyes proclaim where his blade will fall. Full well I knoweth that for often have I exercised against him."

"And he hasn't killed you," Blake reminded him.

"Ah, we did but practice, but on the morrow it will be different, for Malud engages thee to the death, in mortal combat my friend, to wash away in blood the affront thou didst put upon him."

"He wants to kill me, just for that?" asked Blake. "I'll tell the world he's a touchy little rascal!"

"Were it only that, he might be satisfied merely to draw blood, but there is more that he hath against thee."

"More? What? I've scarcely spoken to him a dozen times," said Blake.

"He be jealous."

"Jealous? Of whom?"

"He would wed the Princess and he hath seen in what manner thou lookest at her," explained Richard.

"Poppycock!" cried Blake, but he flushed.

"Nay, he be not the only one who hath marked it," insisted Richard.

"You're crazy," snapped Blake.

"Often men look thus at the princess, for she be beautiful beyond compare, but—"

"Has he killed them all?" demanded the American.

"No, for the princess didst not look back at *them* in the same manner."

Blake leaned back upon his bench and laughed. "Now I know you're crazy," he cried, "all of you. I'll admit that I think the princess is a mighty sweet kid, but say young fellow, she can't see me a little bit."

"Enough of thy outlandish speech I grasp to gather thy meaning, James, but thou canst not confuse me upon the one subject nor deceive me upon the other. The eyes of the princess seldom leave thee whilst thou art at practice upon the lists and the look in thine when they rest upon her—hast ever seen a hound adoring his master?"

"Run along and sell your papers," admonished Blake.

"For this, Malud wouldst put thee out of the way and it is because I know this that I grieve, for I have learned to like thee over well, my friend."

Blake arose and came around the end of the table. "You're a good old scout, Richard," he said, placing a hand affectionately upon the other's shoulder, "but do not worry—I am not dead yet. I know I seem awkward with the sword, but I have learned much about its possibilities within the past few days and I think that Sir Malud has a surprise awaiting him."

"Thy courage and thy vast assurance should carry thee far, James, but they may not overcome a lifetime of practice with the sword, and that is the advantage Malud hath over thee."

"Does Prince Gobred favor Malud's suit?" demanded Blake.

"Why not? Malud is a powerful knight, with a great castle of his own and many horses and retainers. Besides a dozen knights he hath fully an hundred men-at-arms."

"There are several knights who have their own castles and following are there not?" asked Blake.

"Twenty, perchance," replied Richard.

"And they live close to Gobred's castle?"

"At the edge of the hills, within three leagues upon either hand of Gobred's castle," explained Richard.

"And no others live in all this great valley?" demanded Blake.

"You have heard mention made of Bohun?" asked Richard.

"Yes, often—why?"

"He calls himself king, but never will we refer to him as king. He and his followers dwell upon the opposite side of the valley. They number, perchance, as many as we and we be always at war against them."

"But I've been hearing quite a bit about a great tournament for which the knights are practicing now. I thought that Bohun and his knights were to take part in it."

"They be. Once each year, commencing upon the first Sunday of Lent and extending over a period of three days, there hath been from time immemorial a truce declared between the Fronters and the Backers, during which is held the Great Tourney, one year in the plain before the city of Nimmr and the next year in the plain before the City of the Sepulcher, as they call it."

"Fronters and Backers! What in heck do those mean?" demanded Blake.

"Thou art a knight of Nimmr and know not that?" exclaimed Richard.

"What I know about knighting would rattle around in a peanut shell," admitted Blake.

"Thou shouldst know and I shalt tell thee. Hark thee well, then," said Richard, "for I must need go back to the very beginning." He poured two goblets of wine from a flagon standing on the floor beside him, took a long drink and proceeded with his tale. "Richard I sailed from Sicily in the spring of 1191 with all his great following bound for Acre, where he was to meet the French king, Philip Augustus, and wrest the Holy Land from the power of the Saracen. But Richard tarried upon the way to conquer Cyprus and punish the vile despot who had placed an insult upon Berengaria, whom Richard was to wed.

"When the great company again set their sails for Acre there were many Cyprian maidens hidden away upon the ships by knights who had taken a fancy to their lovely faces, and it so befell that two of these ships, encountering a storm, were blown from their course and wrecked upon the Afric shore.

"One of these companies was commanded by a knight y-clept Bohun and the other by one Gobred and though they marched together they kept separate other than when attacked.

"Thus, searching for Jerusalem, they came upon this valley which the followers of Bohun declared was the Valley of the Holy Sepulcher and that the crusade was over. Their crosses, that they had worn upon their breasts as do all crusaders who have not reached their goal, they removed and placed upon their backs to signify that the crusade was over and that they were returning home.

"Gobred insisted that this was not the Valley of the Holy Sepulcher and that the crusade was not accomplished. He, therefore, and all his followers, retained their crosses upon their breasts and built a city and a strong castle to defend the entrance of the valley that Bohun and his followers might be prevented from returning to England until they had accomplished their mission.

"Bohun crossed the valley and built a city and a castle to prevent Gobred from pushing on in the direction in which the latter knew that the true Sepulcher lay, and for nearly seven and a half centuries the descendants of Bohun have prevented the descendants of Gobred from pushing on and rescuing the Holy Land from the Saracen, while the descendants of Gobred have prevented the descendants of Bohun from returning to England, to the dishonor of knighthood.

"Gobred took the title of prince and Bohun that of king and these titles have been handed down from father to son during the centuries, while the followers of Gobred still wear the cross upon their breasts and are called therefrom, the Fronters, and the followers of Bohun wear theirs upon their backs and are called Backers."

"And you would still push on and liberate the Holy Land?" asked Blake.

"Yes," replied Richard, "and the Backers would return to England; but long since have we realized the futility of either hope since we be surrounded by a vast army of Saracens and our numbers be too few to pit against them.

"Thinkest thou not that we are wise to remain here under such stress?" he demanded.

"Well, you'd certainly surprise 'em if you rode into Jerusalem, or London, either," admitted Blake. "On the whole Richard, I'd remain right here, if I were you. You see, after seven hundred and thirty-five years most of the home folks may have forgotten you and even the Saracens might not know what it was all about if you came charging into Jerusalem."

"Mayhap you speak wisely, James," said Richard, "and then, too, we be content here, knowing no other country."

For a while both men were silent, in thought. Blake was the first to speak. "This big tourney interests me," he said. "You say it starts the first Sunday in Lent. That's not far away."

"No, not far. Why?"

"I was wondering if you thought I'd be in shape to have a part in it. I'm getting better and better with the lance every day."

Sir Richard looked sadly at him and shook his head. "Tomorrow thou wilt be dead," he said.

"Say! You're a cheerful party," exclaimed Blake.

"I am only truthful, good friend," replied Richard. "It grieveth my heart sorely that it should be true, but true it be—thou canst prevail over Sir Malud on the morrow. Wouldst that I might take thy place in the lists against him, but that may not be. But I console myself with the thought that thou will comport thyself courageously and die as a good sir knight should, with no stain upon thy escutcheon. Greatly will it solace the Princess Guinalda to know that thou didst die thus."

"You think so?" ventured Blake.

"Verily."

"And if I don't die—will she be put out?"

"Put out! Put out of what?" demanded Richard.

"Will she be sore vexed, then," corrected Blake.

"I should not go so far as to say that," admitted Richard, "but natheless it appears certain that no lady would rejoice to see her promised husband overthrown and killed, and if thou art not slain it may only be because thou hast slain Malud."

"She is his affianced wife?" demanded Blake.

" 'Tis understood, that be all. As yet no formal marriage bans have been proclaimed."

"I'm going to turn in," snapped Blake. "If I've got to be killed tomorrow I ought to get a little sleep tonight."

As he stretched himself upon a rough wool blanket that was spread over a bed of rushes upon the stone floor in one corner of the room and drew another similar blanket over him, he felt less like sleep than he had ever felt before. The knowledge that on the morrow he was to meet a medieval knight in mortal combat naturally gave him considerable concern, but Blake was too self-reliant and too young to seriously harbor the belief that he would be the one to be killed. He knew it was possible but he did not intend to permit the thought to upset him. There was, however, another that did. It upset him very much and, too, it made him angry when he realized that he was concerned about it—about the proposed marriage of Sir Malud of West Castle and Guinalda, Princess of Nimmr.

Could it be that he had been ass enough, he soliloquized, to have fallen in love with this little medieval princess who probably looked upon him as dirt beneath her feet? And what was he going to do about Malud? Suppose he should get the better of the fellow on the morrow? Well, what about it? If he killed him that would make Guinalda unhappy. If he didn't kill him—what? Sir James did not know.

13

In the Beyt of Zeyd

IBN JAD WAITED three days in his menzil but no Galla guides arrived to lead him into the valley as Batando had promised, and so he sent Fejjuan once more to the chief to urge him to hasten, for always in the mind of Ibn Jad was the fear of Tarzan of the Apes and the thought that he might return to thwart and punish him.

He knew he was out of Tarzan's country now, but he also knew that where boundaries were so vague he could not definitely count upon this fact as an assurance of safety from reprisal. His one hope was that Tarzan was awaiting his return through Tarzan's country, and this Ibn Jad had definitely decided not to attempt. Instead he was planning upon moving directly west, passing north of the ape-man's stamping grounds, until he picked up the trail to the north down which he had traveled from the desert country.

In the mukaad of the sheik with Ibn Jad sat Tollog, his brother, and Fahd and Stimbol, besides some other 'Aarab. They were speaking of Batando's delay in sending guides and they were fearful of treachery, for it had long been apparent to them that the old chief was gathering a great army of warriors, and though Fejjuan assured them that they would not be used against the 'Aarab if Ibn Jad resorted to no treachery, yet they were all apprehensive of danger.

Ateja, employed with the duties of the harem, did not sing nor smile as had been her wont, for her heart was heavy with mourning for her lover. She heard the talk in the mukaad but it did not interest her. Seldom did her eyes glance above the curtain that separated the women's quarters from the mukaad, and when they did the fires of hatred blazed within them as they crossed the countenance of Fahd.

She chanced to be thus glancing when she saw Fahd's eyes, which were directed outward across the menzil, go suddenly wide with astonishment.

"Billah, Ibn Jad!" cried the man. "Look!"

With the others Ateja glanced in the direction Fahd was staring and with the others she voiced a little gasp of astonishment, though those of the men were rounded into oaths.

Walking straight across the menzil toward the sheik's beyt strode a bronzed giant armed with a spear, arrows, and a knife. Upon his back was suspended an oval shield and across one shoulder and his breast was coiled a rope, hand plaited from long fibers.

"Tarzan of the Apes!" ejaculated Ibn Jad. "The curse of Ullah be upon him!"

"He must have brought his black warriors with him and left them hidden in the forest," whispered Tollog. "Not else would he dare enter the menzil of the Beduw."

Ibn Jad was heartsick and he was thinking fast when the ape-man halted directly in the outer opening of the mukaad. Tarzan let his eyes run quickly over the assemblage. They stopped upon Stimbol, finally.

"Where is Blake?" he demanded of the American.

"You ought to know," growled Stimbol.

"Have you seen him since you and he separated?"

"No."

"You are sure of that?" insisted the ape-man.

"Of course I am."

Tarzan turned to Ibn Jad. "You have lied to me. You are not here to trade but to find and sack a city; to take its treasure and steal its women."

"That is a lie!" cried Ibn Jad. "Whoever told thee that, lied."

"I do not think he lied," replied Tarzan. "He seemed an honest youth."

"Who was he?" demanded Ibn Jad.

"His name is Zeyd." Ateja heard and was suddenly galvanized to new interest. "He says all this and more, and I believe him."

"What else did he tell thee, Nasrany?"

"That another stole his musket and sought to slay thee, Ibn Jad, and then put the blame upon him."

"That is a lie, like all he hath told thee!" cried Fahd.

Ibn Jad sat in thought, his brows contracted in a dark scowl, but presently he looked up at Tarzan with a crooked smile. "Doubtless the poor youth thought that he spoke the truth," he said. "Just as he thought that he should slay his sheykh and for the same reason. Always hath his brain been sick, but never before did I think him dangerous.

"He hath deceived thee, Tarzan of the Apes, and that I can prove by all my people as well as by this Nasrany I have befriended, for all will tell thee that I am seeking to obey thee and leave thy country. Why else then should I have travelled north back in the direction of my own beled?"

"If thou wished to obey me why didst thou hold me prisoner and send thy brother to slay me in the night?" asked Tarzan.

"Again thou wrongst Ibn Jad," said the sheik sadly. "My brother came to cut thy bonds and set thee free, but thou set upon him and then came el-fil and carried thee away."

"And what meant thy brother when he raised his knife and cried: 'Die, Nasrany!' " demanded the ape-man. "Sayeth a man thus who cometh to do a kindness?"

"I did but joke," mumbled Tollog.

"I am here again," said Tarzan, "but not to joke. My Waziri are coming. Together we shall see you well on your way toward the desert."

"It is what we wish," said the sheik quickly. "Ask this other Nasrany if it be not true that we are lost and would be but too glad to have thee lead us upon the right way. Here we be beset by Galla warriors. Their chief hath been gathering them for days and momentarily we fear that we shall be attacked. Is that not true, Nasrany?" he turned to Stimbol as he spoke.

"Yes, it is true," said Stimbol.

"It is true that you are going to leave the country," said Tarzan, "and I shall remain to see that you do so. Tomorrow you will start. In the meantime set aside a beyt for me—and let there be no more treachery."

"Thou needst fear nothing," Ibn Jad assured him, then he turned his face toward the women's quarters. "Hirfa! Ateja!" he called. "Make ready the beyt of Zeyd for the sheykh of the jungle."

To one side but at no great distance from the beyt of Ibn Jad the two women raised the black tent for Tarzan, and when the am'dan had been placed and straightened and the tunb el-beyt made fast to the pegs that Ateja drove into the earth Hirfa returned to her household duties, leaving her daughter to stretch the side curtains.

The instant that Hirfa was out of earshot Ateja ran to Tarzan.

"Oh, Nasrany," she cried, "thou hast seen my Zeyd? He is safe?"

"I left him in a village where the chief will care for him until such time as thy people come upon thy return to the desert country. He is quite safe and well."

"Tell me of him, oh, Nasrany, for my heart hungers for word of him," implored the girl. "How came you upon him? Where was he?"

"His mare had been dragged down by el-adrea who was about to devour your lover. I chanced to be there and slew el-adrea. Then I took Zeyd to the village of a chief who is my friend, for I knew that he could not survive the perils of the jungle should I leave him afoot and alone. It was my thought to send him from the country in safety, but he begged to remain until you returned that way. This I have permitted. In a few weeks you will see your lover."

Tears were falling from Ateja's long, black lashes—tears of joy—as she seized Tarzan's hand and kissed it. "My life is thine, Nasrany," she cried, "for that thou hast given me back my lover."

That night as the Galla slave, Fejjuan, walked through the menzil of his masters he saw Ibn Jad and Tollog sitting in the sheik's mukaad whispering together and Fejjuan, well aware of the inherent turpitude of this precious pair, wondered what might be the nature of their plotting.

Behind the curtain of the harem Ateja lay huddled upon her sleeping mat, but she did not sleep. Instead she was listening to the whispered conversation of her father and her uncle.

"He must be put out of the way," Ibn Jad insisted.

"But his Waziri are coming," objected Tollog. "If they do not find him here what can we say? They will not believe us, whatever we say. They will set upon us. I have heard that they are terrible men."

"By Ullah!" cried Ibn Jad. "If he stays we are undone. Better risk something than to return empty-handed to our own country after all that we have passed through."

"If thou thinkest that I shall again take this business upon myself thou art mistaken, brother," said Tollog. "Once was enough."

"No, not thee; but we must find a way. Is there none among us who might wish more than another to be rid of the Nasrany?" asked Ibn Jad, but to himself as though he were thinking aloud.

"The other Nasrany!" exclaimed Tollog. "He hateth him."

Ibn Jad clapped his hands together. "Thou hast it, brother!"

"But still shall we be held responsible," reminded Tollog.

"What matter if he be out of the way. We can be no worse off than we now are. Suppose Batando came tomorrow with the guides? Then indeed would the jungle sheykh know that we have lied to him, and it might go hard with us. No, we must be rid of him this very night."

"Yes, but how?" asked Tollog.

"Hold! I have a plan. Listen well, O brother!" and Ibn Jad rubbed his palms together and smiled, but he would not have smiled, perhaps had he known that Ateja listened, or had he seen the silent figure crouching in the dark just beyond the outer curtain of his beyt.

"Speak, Ibn Jad," urged Tollog, "tell me thy plan."

"Wellah, it is known by all that the Nasrany Stimbol hates the sheykh of the jungle. With loud tongue he hath proclaimed it many times before all when many were gathered in my mukaad."

"You would send Stimbol to slay Tarzan of the Apes?"

"Thou guessed aright," admitted Ibn Jad.

"But how wilt that relieve us of responsibility? He wilt have been slain by thy order in thine own menzil," objected Tollog.

"Wait! I shall not command the one Nasrany to slay the other; I shall but suggest it, and when it is done I shall be filled with rage and horror that this murder hath been done in my menzil. And to prove my good faith I shall order that the murderer be put to death in punishment for his crime. Thus we shall be rid of two unbelieving dogs and at the same time be able to convince the Waziri that we were indeed the friends of their sheykh, for we shall mourn him with loud lamentations— when the Waziri shall have arrived."

"Allah be praised for such a brother!" exclaimed Tollog, enraptured.

"Go thou now, at once, and summon the Nasrany Stimbol," directed Ibn Jad. "Send him to me alone, and after I have spoken with him and he hath departed upon his errand come thee back to my beyt."

Ateja trembled upon her sleeping mat, while the silent figure crouching outside the sheik's tent arose after Tollog had departed and disappeared in the darkness of the night.

Hastily summoned from the beyt of Fahd, Stimbol, cautioned to stealth by Tollog, moved silently through the darkness to the mukaad of the sheik where he found Ibn Jad awaiting him.

"Sit, Nasrany," invited the Beduin.

"What in hell do you want of me this time of night?" demanded Stimbol.

"I have been talking with Tarzan of the Apes," said Ibn Jad, "and because you are my friend and he is not I have sent for you to tell you what he plans for you. He has interfered in all my designs and is driving me from the country, but that is as nothing compared with what he intends for you."

"What in hell is he up to now?" demanded Stimbol. "He's always butting into someone else's business."

"Thou dost not like him?" asked Ibn Jad.

"Why should I?" and Stimbol applied a vile epithet to Tarzan.

"Thou wilt like him less when I tell thee," said Ibn Jad.

"Well, tell me."

"He says that thou hast slain thy companion, Blake," explained the sheik, "and for that Tarzan is going to kill thee on the morrow."

"Eh? What? Kill me?" demanded Stimbol. "Why he can't do it! What does he think he is—a Roman emperor?"

"Nevertheless he will do as he says," insisted Ibn Jad. "He is all powerful here. No one questions the acts of this great jungle sheykh. Tomorrow he will kill thee."

"But—you won't let him, Ibn Jad! Surely, you won't let him?" Stimbol was already trembling with terror.

Ibn Jad elevated his palms. "What can I do?" he asked.

"You can—you can—why there must be something that you can do," wailed the frightened man.

"There is naught that any can do—save yourself," whispered the sheik.

"What do you mean?"

"He lies asleep in yon beyt and—thou hast a sharp khusa."

"I have never killed a man," whispered Stimbol.

"Nor hast thou ever been killed," reminded the sheik; "but tonight thou must kill or tomorrow thou wilt be killed."

"God!" gasped Stimbol.

"It is late," said Ibn Jad, "and I go to my sleeping mat. I have warned thee—do what thou wilt in the matter," and he arose as though to enter the women's quarters.

Trembling, Stimbol staggered out into the night. For a moment he hesitated, then he crouched and crept silently through the darkness toward the beyt that had been erected for the ape-man.

But ahead of him ran Ateja to warn the man who had saved her lover from the fangs of el-adrea. She was almost at the beyt she had helped to erect for the ape-man when a figure stepped from another tent and clapping a palm across her mouth and an arm about her waist held her firmly.

"Where goest thou?" whispered a voice in her ear, a voice that she recognized at once as belonging to her uncle; but Tollog did not wait for a reply, he answered for her. "Thou goest to warn the Nasrany because he befriended thy lover! Get thee back to thy father's beyt. If he knew this he would slay thee. Go!" And he gave her a great shove in the direction from which she had come.

There was a nasty smile upon Tollog's lips as he thought how neatly he had foiled the girl, and he thanked Allah that chance had placed him in a position to intercept her before she had been able to ruin them all; and even as Tollog, the brother of the sheik, smiled in his beard a hand reached out of the darkness behind him and seized him by the throat—fingers grasped him and dragged him away.

Trembling, bathed in cold sweat, grasping in tightly clenched fingers the hilt of a keen knife, Wilbur Stimbol crept through the darkness toward the tent of his victim.

Stimbol had been an irritable man, a bully and a coward; but he was no criminal. Every fiber of his being revolted at the thing he contemplated. He did not want to kill, but he was a cornered human rat and he thought that death stared him in the face, leaving open only this one way of escape.

As he entered the beyt of the ape-man he steeled himself to accomplish that for which he had come, and he was indeed a very dangerous, a very formidable man, as he crept to the side of the figure lying in the darkness, wrapped in an old burnous.

14

Sword and Buckler

As THE SUN touched the turrets of the castle of the Prince of Nimmr a youth rolled from between his blankets, rubbed his eyes, and stretched. Then he reached over and shook another youth of about his own age who slept beside him.

"Awaken, Edward! Awaken, thou sluggard!" he cried.

Edward rolled over on his back and essayed to say "Eh?" and to yawn at the same time.

"Up, lad!" urged Michel. "Forgottest thou that thy master fares forth to be slain this day?"

Edward sat up, now fully awake. His eyes flashed. " 'Tis a lie!" he cried, loyally. "He will cleave Sir Malud from poll to breast plate with a single blow. Livest no sir knight with such mighty thews as hast Sir James. Thou art disloyal, Michel, to Sir Richard's friend who hath been a good and kindly friend to us as well."

Michel patted the other lad upon the shoulder. "Nay, I did but jest, Edward," he said. "My hopes be all for Sir James, and yet—" he paused, "I fear—"

"Fear what?" demanded Edward.

"That Sir James be not well enough versed in the use of sword and buckler to overcome Sir Malud, for even were his strength the strength of ten men it shall avail him naught without the skill to use it."

"Thou shalt see!" maintained Edward, stoutly.

"I see that Sir James hath a loyal squire," said a voice behind them, and turning they saw Sir Richard standing in the doorway, "and may all his friends wish him well this day thus loyally!"

"I fell asleep last night praying to our Lord Jesus to guide his blade through Sir Malud's helm," said Edward.

"Good! Get thee up now and look to thy master's mail and to the trappings of his steed, that he may enter the lists bedight as befits a noble sir knight of Nimmr," instructed Richard, and left them.

It was eleven o'clock of this February morning. The sun shone down into the great north ballium of the castle of Nimmr, glinting from the polished mail of noble knights and from pike and battle-ax of men-at-arms, picking out the gay colors of the robes of the women gathered in the grandstand below the inner wall.

Upon a raised dais at the front and center of the grandstand sat Prince Gobred and his party, and upon either side of them and extending to the far ends of the stand were ranged the noble knights and ladies of Nimmr, while behind them sat men-at-arms who were off duty, then the freedmen, and last of all, the serfs, for under the beneficent rule of the house of Gobred these were accorded many privileges.

At either end of the lists was a tent, gay with pennons and the colors and devices of its owner; one with the green and gold of Sir Malud and the other with the blue and silver of Sir James.

Before each of these tilts stood two men-at-arms, resplendent in new apparel, the metal of their battle-axes gleaming brightly, and here a groom held a restive, richly caparisoned charger, while the squire of each of the contestants busied himself with last-minute preparations for the encounter.

A trumpeter, statuesque, the bell of his trumpet resting upon his hip, waited for the signal to sound the fanfare that would announce the entrance of his master into the lists.

A few yards to the rear a second charger champed upon his bit as he nuzzled the groom that held him in waiting for the knight who would accompany each of the contestants upon the field.

In the blue and silver tilt sat Blake and Sir Richard, the latter issuing instructions and advice, and of the two he was the more nervous. Blake's hauberk, gorget, and bassinet were of heavy chain mail, the latter lined inside and covered outside, down to the gorget, with leopard skin, offering fair protection for his head from an ordinary, glancing blow; upon his breast was sewn a large, red cross and from one shoulder depended the streamers of a blue and silver rosette. Hanging from the pole of the tilt, upon a wooden peg, were Blake's sword and buckler.

The grandstand was filled. Prince Gobred glanced up at the sun and spoke to a knight at his side. The latter gave a brief command to a trumpeter stationed at the princely loge and presently, loud and clear, the notes of a trumpet rang in the ballium. Instantly the tilts at either end of the lists were galvanized to activity, while the grandstand seemed to spring to new life as necks were craned first toward the tent of Sir Malud and then toward that of Sir James.

Edward, flushed with excitement, ran into the tilt and seizing Blake's sword passed the girdle about his hips and buckled it in place at his left side, then, with the buckler, he followed his master out of the tilt.

As Blake prepared to mount, Edward held his stirrup while the groom sought to quiet the nervous horse. The lad pressed Blake's leg after he had swung into the saddle (no light accomplishment, weighed down as he was by heavy chain mail) and looked up into his face.

"I have prayed for thee, Sir James," he said. "I know that thou wilt prevail."

Blake saw tears in the youth's eyes as he looked down at him and he caught a choking note in his voice. "You're a good boy, Eddie," he said. "I'll promise that you won't have to be ashamed of me."

"Ah, Sir James, how could I? Even in death thou wilt be a noble figure of a knight. A fairer one it hath never been given one to see, methinks," Edward assured him as he handed him his round buckler.

Sir Richard had by now mounted, and at a signal from him that they were ready there was a fanfare from the trumpet at Sir

Malud's tilt and that noble sir knight rode forward, followed by a single knight.

Blake's trumpeter now announced his master's entry and the American rode out close along the front of the grandstand, followed by Sir Richard. There was a murmur of applause for each contestant, which increased as they advanced and met before Prince Gobred's loge.

Here the four knights reined in and faced the Prince and each raised the hilt of his sword to his lips and kissed it in salute. As Gobred cautioned them to fight honorably, as true knights, and reminded them of the rules governing the encounter Blake's eyes wandered to the face of Guinalda.

The little princess sat stiffly erect, looking straight before her. She seemed very white, Blake thought, and he wondered if she were ill.

How beautiful, thought Blake, and though she did not once appear to look at him he was not cast down, for neither did she look at Malud.

Again the trumpet sounded and the four knights rode slowly back to opposite ends of the lists and the principals waited for the final signal to engage. Blake disengaged his arm from the leather loop of his buckler and tossed the shield upon the ground.

Edward looked at him aghast. "My Lord knight!" he cried. "Art ill? Art fainting? Didst drop thy buckler?" and he snatched it up and held it aloft to Blake, though he knew full well that his eyes had not deceived him and that his master had cast aside his only protection.

To the horrified Edward there seemed but one explanation and that his loyalty would not permit him to entertain for an instant—that Blake was preparing to dismount and refuse to meet Sir Malud, giving the latter the victory by default and assuring himself of the contempt and ridicule of all Nimmr.

He ran to Richard who had not seen Blake's act. "Sir Richard! Sir Richard!" he cried in a hoarse whisper. "Some terrible affliction hath befallen Sir James!"

"Hey, what?" exclaimed Richard. "What meaneth thou lad?"

"He has cast aside his buckler," cried the youth. "He must be stricken sore ill, for it cannot be that otherwise he would refuse combat."

Richard spurred to Blake's side. "Hast gone mad, man?" he demanded. "Thou canst not refuse the encounter now unless thou wouldst bring dishonor upon thy friends!"

"Where did you get that line?" demanded Blake. "Who said I was going to quit?"

"But thy buckler?" cried Sir Richard.

The trumpet at the Prince's loge rang out peremptorily. Sir Malud spurred forward to a fanfare from his own trumpeter.

"Let her go!" cried Blake to his.

"Thy buckler!" screamed Sir Richard.

"The damned thing was in my way," shouted Blake as he spurred forward to meet the doughty Malud, Richard trailing behind him, as did Malud's second behind that knight.

There was a confident smile upon the lips of Sir Malud and he glanced often at the knights and ladies in the grandstand, but Blake rode with his eyes always upon his antagonist.

Both horses had broken immediately into a gallop, and as they neared one another Malud spurred forward at a run and Blake saw that the man's aim was doubtless to overthrow him at the first impact, or at least to so throw him out of balance as to make it easy for Malud to strike a good blow before he could recover himself.

Malud rode with his sword half raised at his right side, while Blake's was at guard, a position unknown to the knights of Nimmr, who guarded solely with their bucklers.

The horsemen approached to engage upon each other's left, and as they were about to meet Sir Malud rose in his stirrups and swung his sword hand down, to gain momentum, described a circle with his blade and launched a terrific cut at Blake's head.

It was at that instant that some few in the grandstand realized that Blake bore no buckler.

"His buckler!" "Sir James hath no buckler!" "He hath lost his buckler!" rose now from all parts of the stand; and from right beside him, where the two knights met before the loge of

Gobred, Blake heard a woman scream, but he could not look to see if it were Guinalda.

As they met Blake reined his horse suddenly toward Malud's, so that the two chargers' shoulders struck, and at the same time he cast all his weight in the same direction, whereas Malud, who was standing in his stirrups to deliver his blow, was almost in a state of equilibrium and having his buckler ready for defense was quite helpless insofar as maneuvering his mount was concerned.

Malud, overbalanced, lost the force and changed the direction of his blow, which fell, much to the knight's surprise, upon Blake's blade along which it spent its force and was deflected from its target.

Instantly, his horse well in hand by reason that his left arm was unencumbered by a buckler, Blake reined in and simultaneously cut to the left and rear, his point opening the mail on Malud's left shoulder and biting into the flesh before the latter's horse had carried him out of reach.

A loud shout of approbation arose from the stands for the thing had been neatly done and then Malud's second spurred to the Prince's loge and entered a protest.

"Sir James hath no buckler!" he cried. " 'Tis no fair combat!"

" 'Tis fairer for thy knight than for Sir James," said Gobred.

"We would not take that advantage of him," parried Malud's second, Sir Jarred.

"What sayest thou?" demanded Gobred of Sir Richard who had quickly ridden to Jarred's side. "Is Sir James without a buckler through some accident that befell before he entered the lists?"

"Nay, he cast it aside," replied Richard, "and averred that the 'damned thing' did annoy him; but if Sir Jarred feeleth that, because of this, they be not fairly matched we are willing that Sir Malud, also, should cast aside his buckler."

Gobred smiled. "That be fair," he said.

The two men, concerned with their encounter and not with the argument of their seconds, had engaged once more. Blood was showing upon Malud's shoulder and trickling down his back, staining his skirts and the housing of his charger.

The stand was in an uproar, for many were still shouting aloud about the buckler and others were screaming with delight over the neat manner in which Sir James had drawn his first blood. Wagers were being freely made, and though Sir Malud still ruled favorite in the betting, the odds against Blake were not so great, and while men had no money to wager they had jewels and arms and horses. One enthusiastic adherent of Sir Malud bet three chargers against one that his champion would be victorious and the words were scarce out of his mouth ere he had a dozen takers, whereas before the opening passage at arms offers as high as ten to one had found no takers.

Now the smile was gone from Malud's lips and he glanced no more at the grandstand. There was rage in his eyes as he spurred again toward Blake, who he thought had profited by a lucky accident.

Unhampered by a buckler Blake took full advantage of the nimbleness of the wiry horse he rode and which he had ridden daily since his arrival in Nimmr, so that man and beast were well accustomed to one another.

Again Sir Malud saw his blade glance harmlessly from the sword of his antagonist and then, to his vast surprise, the point of Sir James' blade leaped quickly beneath his buckler and entered his side. It was not a deep wound, but it was painful and again it brought blood.

Angrily Malud struck again, but Blake had reined his charger quickly to the rear and before Malud could gather his reins Blake had struck him again, this time a heavy blow upon the helm.

Half stunned and wholly infuriated Malud wheeled and charged at full tilt, once again determined to ride his adversary down. They met with a crash directly in front of Gobred's loge, there was a quick play of swords that baffled the eyesight of the onlookers and then, to the astonishment of all, most particularly Malud, that noble sir knight's sword flew from his grasp and hurtled to the field, leaving him entirely to the mercy of his foe.

Malud reined in and sat erect, waiting. He knew and Blake knew that under the rules that governed their encounter Blake was warranted in running him through unless Malud sued for mercy, and no one, Blake least of all, expected this of so proud and haughty a knight.

Sir Malud sat proudly on his charger waiting for Blake to advance and kill him. Utter silence had fallen upon the stands, so that the champing of Malud's horse upon its bit was plainly audible. Blake turned to Sir Jarred.

"Summon a squire, sir knight," he said, "to return Sir Malud's sword to him."

Again the stands rocked to the applause, but Blake turned his back upon them and rode to Richard's side to wait until his adversary was again armed.

"Well, old top," he inquired of Sir Richard, "just how much a dozen am I offered for bucklers now?"

Richard laughed. "Thou hast been passing fortunate, James," he replied; "but methinks a good swordsman would long since have cut thee through."

"I know Malud would have if I had packed that chopping bowl along on the party," Blake assured him, though it is doubtful if Sir Richard understood what he was talking about, as was so often the case when Blake discoursed that Richard had long since ceased to even speculate as to the meaning of much that his friend said.

But now Sir Malud was rearmed and riding toward Blake. He stopped his horse before the American and bowed low. "I do my devoirs to a noble and generous knight," he said, graciously.

Blake bowed. "Are you ready sir?" he asked.

Malud nodded.

"On guard, then!" snapped the American.

For the moment the two jockeyed for position. Blake feinted and Malud raised his buckler before his face to catch the blow, but as it did not fall he lowered his shield, just as Blake had known that he would, and as he did so the edge of the

American's weapon fell heavily upon the crown of his bassinet.

Malud's arm dropped at his side, he slumped in his saddle and then toppled forward and rolled to the ground. Agile, even in his heavy armor, Blake dismounted and walked to where his foe lay stretched upon his back almost in front of Gobred's loge. He placed a foot upon Malud's breast and pressed the point of his sword against his throat.

The crowd leaned forward to see the coup-de-grace administered, but Blake did not drive his point home. He looked up at Prince Gobred and addressed him.

"Here is a brave knight," he said, "with whom I have no real quarrel. I spare him to your service, Prince, and to those who love him," and his eyes went straight to the eyes of the Princess Guinalda. Then he turned and walked back along the front of the grandstand to his own tilt, while Richard rode behind him, and the knights and the ladies, the men-at-arms, the freedmen and the serfs stood upon their seats and shouted their applause.

Edward was beside himself with joy, as was Michel. The former knelt and embraced Blake's legs, he kissed his hand, and wept, so great were his happiness and his excitement.

"I knew it! I knew it!" he cried. "Didst I not tell thee, Michel, that my own sir knight would overthrow Sir Malud?"

The men-at-arms, the trumpeter, and the grooms at Blake's tilt wore grins that stretched from ear to ear. Whereas a few minutes before they had felt ashamed to have been detailed to the losing side, now they were most proud and looked upon Blake as the greatest hero of Nimmr. Great would be their boasting among their fellows as they gathered with their flagons of ale about the rough deal table in their dining hall.

Edward removed Blake's armor and Michel got Richard out of his amidst much babbling upon the part of the youths who could not contain themselves, so doubly great was their joy because so unexpected.

Blake went directly to his quarters and Richard accompanied him, and when the two men were alone Richard placed a hand upon Blake's shoulder.

"Thou hast done a noble and chivalrous thing, my friend," he said, "but I know not that it be a wise one."

"And why?" demanded Blake. "You didn't think I could stick the poor mutt when he was lying there defenseless?"

Richard shook his head. " 'Tis but what he would have done for thee had thy positions been reversed," said he.

"Well, I couldn't do it. We're not taught to believe that it is exactly ethical to hit a fellow when he's down, where I come from," explained Blake.

"Had your quarrel been no deeper than appeared upon the surface thou might well have been thus magnanimous; but Malud be jealous of thee and that jealousy will be by no means lessened by what hath transpired this day. Thou might have been rid of a powerful and dangerous enemy had thou given him the coup-de-grace, as was thy right; but now thou hast raised up a greater enemy since to his jealousy is added hatred and envy against thee for thy prowess over him. Thou didst make him appear like a monkey, James, and that Sir Malud wilt never forgive, and I know the man."

The knights and ladies attached to the castle of Gobred ate together at a great table in the huge hall of the castle. Three hundred people could be accommodated at the single board and it took quite a company of serving men to fill their needs. Whole pigs, roasted, were carried in upon great trenchers and there were legs of mutton and sides of venison and bowls of vegetables, with wine and ale, and at the end immense puddings.

There was much laughter and loud talking, and it all presented a wild and fascinating picture to Sir James Blake as he sat at the lower end of the table far below the salt that night, in his accustomed place as one of the latest neophytes in the noble ranks of the knighthood of Nimmr.

The encounter between himself and Malud was the subject of the moment and many were the compliments bestowed upon him and many the questions as to where and how he had acquired his strange technique of swordsmanship. Although they had seen him accomplish it, yet they still appeared to believe it inconceivable that a man might prevail without a buckler over one who carried this essential article of defense.

Prince Gobred and his family sat, with the higher nobles of Nimmr, at a table slightly raised above the rest of the board and running across its upper end, the whole forming a huge T. When he wished to speak to anyone farther down the table he resorted to the simple expedient of raising his voice, so that if several were so inclined at the same time the room became a bedlam of uproar and confusion.

And as Blake sat at the farthest end of the table it was necessary for one at Gobred's end to scream to attract attention, though when it was discovered that it was the prince who was speaking the rest of the company usually lapsed into silence out of respect for him, unless they were too far gone in drink.

Shortly after the feasters were seated Gobred had arisen and lifted his goblet high in air, and silence had fallen upon the whole company as knights and ladies rose and faced their prince.

"Hail to our King!" cried Gobred. "Hail to our liege lord, Richard of England!"

And in a great chorus rose the answering "Hail!" as the company drank the health of Richard Coeur de Lion seven hundred and twenty-eight years after his death!

Then they drank the health of Gobred and of the Princess Brynilda, his wife, and of the Princess Guinalda, and each time a voice boomed from just below the dais of the prince: "Here I be looking at thee!" as Sir Richard with a proud smile displayed his newly acquired knowledge.

Again Prince Gobred arose. "Hail!" he cried, "to that worthy sir knight who hath most nobly and chivalrously acquitted himself in the lists this day! Hail to Sir James, Knight Templar, and, now, Knight of Nimmr!"

Not even the name of Richard I of England had aroused the enthusiasm that followed the drinking to Sir James. The length of the long hall Blake's eyes travelled straight to where Guinalda stood. He saw her drink to him and he saw that her eyes were regarding him, but the distance was too great and the light of the pitch torches and the oil cressets too dim for him to see whether her glance carried a message of friendship or dislike.

When the noise had partially subsided and the drinkers had retaken their seats Blake arose.

"Prince Gobred," he called the length of the room, "knights and ladies of Nimmr, I give you another toast! To Sir Malud!"

For a moment there was silence, the silence of surprise, and then the company arose and drank the health of the absent Sir Malud.

"Thou art a strange sir knight, with strange words upon thy lips and strange ways, Sir James," shouted Gobred, "but though thou callest a hail 'a toast' and thy friends be 'old top' and 'kid,' yet withal it seemeth that we understand thee and we would know more about thy country and the ways of the noble knights that do abide there.

"Tell us, are they all thus chivalrous and magnanimous to their fallen foes?"

"If they're not they get the raspberry," explained Blake.

" 'Get the raspberry'!" repeated Gobred. " 'Tis some form of punishment, methinks."

"You said it, Prince!"

"Of a surety I said it, Sir James!" snapped Gobred with asperity.

"I mean, Prince, that you hit the nail on the head—you guessed it the first time. You see the raspberry is about the only form of punishment that the Knights of the Squared Circle, or the Knights of the Diamond can understand."

" 'Knights of the Squared Circle'! 'Knights of the Diamond'! Those be knightly orders of which I wot not. Be they doughty knights?"

"Some of them are dotty, but a lot of them are regulars. Take Sir Dempsey, for instance, a knight of the Squared Circle. He showed 'em all he was a regular knight in defeat, which is much more difficult than being a regular knight in victory."

"Be there other orders of knighthood these days?" demanded Gobred.

"We're lousy with them!"

"What?" cried Gobred.

"We're all knights these days," explained Blake.

"All knights! Be there no serfs nor yeomen? 'Tis incredible!"

"Well, there are some yeomen in the navy, I think; but all the rest of us, pretty much, are knights. You see things have changed a lot since the days of Richard. The people have sort of overthrown the old order of things. They poked a lot of ridicule at knights and wanted to get rid of knighthood, and as soon as they had they all wanted to be knights themselves; so we have Knights Templar now and Knights of Pythias and Knights of Columbus and Knights of Labor and a lot more I can't recall."

"Methinks it must be a fine and noble world," cried Gobred, "for what with so many noble sir knights it would seemeth that they must often contend, one against another—is that not true?"

"Well, they do scrap some," Blake admitted.

15

The Lonely Grave

WITHIN THE DARK interior of the beyt Stimbol could see nothing. Just before him he heard a man breathing heavily as might one in a troubled sleep. The would-be murderer paused to steady his nerves. Then, on hands and knees, he crept forward inch by inch.

Presently one of his hands touched the prostrate figure of the sleeper. Lightly, cautiously, Stimbol groped until he had definitely discovered the position in which his victim lay. In one hand, ready, he grasped the keen knife. He scarce dared breathe for fear he might awaken the ape-man. He prayed that Tarzan was a sound sleeper, and he prayed that the first blow of his weapon would reach that savage heart.

Now he was ready! He had located the exact spot where he must strike! He raised his knife and struck. His victim shuddered spasmodically. Again and again with savage maniacal force and speed the knife was plunged into the soft flesh. Stimbol felt the warm blood spurt out upon his hand and wrist.

At length, satisfied that his mission had been accomplished, he scurried from the beyt. Now he was trembling so that he could scarcely stand—terrified, revolted by the horrid crime he had committed.

Wild-eyed, haggard, he stumbled to the mukaad of Ibn Jad's beyt and there he collapsed. The sheik stepped from the women's quarters and looked down upon the trembling figure that the dim light of a paper lantern revealed.

"What doest thou here, Nasrany?" he demanded.

"I have done it, Ibn Jad!" muttered Stimbol.

"Done what?" cried the sheik.

"Slain Tarzan of the Apes."

"Ai! Ai!" screamed Ibn Jad. "Tollog! Where art thou? Hirfa! Ateja! Come! Didst hear what the Nasrany sayeth?"

Hirfa and Ateja rushed into the mukaad.

"Didst hear him?" repeated Ibn Jad. "He hath slain my good friend the great sheykh of the jungle. Motlog! Fahd! Haste!" His voice had been rising until now he was screaming at the top of his lungs and 'Aarab were streaming toward his beyt from all directions.

Stimbol, stunned by what he had done, dumb from surprise and terror at the unexpected attitude of Ibn Jad, crouched speechless in the center of the mukaad.

"Seize him!" cried the sheik to the first man that arrived. "He hath slain Tarzan of the Apes, our great friend, who was to preserve us and lead us from this land of dangers. Now all will be our enemies. The friends of Tarzan will fall upon us and slay us. Allah, bear witness that I be free from guilt in this matter and let Thy wrath and the wrath of the friends of Tarzan fall upon this guilty man!"

By this time the entire population of the menzil was gathered in front of the sheik's beyt, and if they were surprised by his protestations of sudden affection for Tarzan they gave no evidence of it.

"Take him away!" commanded Ibn Jad. "In the morning we shall gather and decided what we must do."

They dragged the terrified Stimbol to Fahd's beyt, where they bound him hand and foot and left him for Fahd to guard. When they had gone the Beduin leaned low over Stimbol, and whispered in his ear.

"Didst really slay the jungle sheykh?" he demanded.

"Ibn Jad forced me to do so and now he turns against me," whispered Stimbol.

"And tomorrow he will have you killed so that he may tell the friends of Tarzan that he hath punished the slayer of Tarzan," said Fahd.

"Save me, Fahd!" begged Stimbol. "Save me and I will give you twenty million francs—I swear it! Once I am safe in the nearest European colony I will get the money for you. Think of it, Fahd—twenty million francs!"

"I am thinking of it, Nasrany," replied the Beduin, "and I think that thou liest. There be not that much money in the world!"

"I swear that I have ten times that amount. If I have lied to you, you may kill me. Save me! Save me!"

"Twenty million francs!" murmured Fahd. "Perchance he does not lie! Listen, Nasrany. I do not know that I can save thee, but I shall try, and if I succeed and thou forgettest the twenty million francs I shall kill thee if I have to follow thee across the world—dost understand?"

Ibn Jad called two ignorant slaves to him and commanded them to go to the beyt that had been Zeyd's and carry Tarzan's body to the edge of the menzil where they were to dig a grave and bury it.

With paper lanterns they went to the beyt of death and wrapping the dead man in the old burnous that already covered him they carried him across the menzil and laid him down while they dug a shallow grave; and so, beneath a forest giant in the land that he loved the grave of Tarzan of the Apes was made.

Roughly the slaves rolled the corpse into the hole they had made, shoveled the dirt upon it and left it in its lonely, unmarked tomb.

Early the next morning Ibn Jad called about him the elders of the tribe, and when they were gathered it was noted that Tollog was missing, and though a search was made he could not be found. Fahd suggested that he had gone forth early to hunt.

Ibn Jad explained to them that if they were to escape the wrath of the friends of Tarzan they must take immediate steps to disprove their responsibility for the slaying of the ape-man and that they might only do this and express their good faith by punishing the murderer.

It was not difficult to persuade them to take the life of a Christian and there was only one that demurred. This was Fahd.

"There are two reasons, Ibn Jad, why we should not take the life of this Nasrany," he said.

"By Ullah, there never be any reason why a true believer should not take the life of a Nasrany!" cried one of the old men.

"Listen," admonished Fahd, "to what I have in mind and then I am sure that you will agree that I am right."

"Speak, Fahd," said Ibn Jad.

"This Nasrany is a rich and powerful man in his own beled. If it be possible to spare his life he will command a great ransom—dead he is worth nothing to us. If by chance, the friends of Tarzan do not learn of his death before we are safely out of this accursed land it will have profited us naught to have killed Stimbol and, billah, if we kill him now they may not believe us when we say that he slew Tarzan and we took his life in punishment.

"But if we keep him alive until we are met with the friends of Tarzan, should it so befall that they overtake us, then we may say that we did hold him prisoner that Tarzan's own people might mete out their vengeance for him, which would suit them better."

"Thy words are not without wisdom," admitted Ibn Jad, "but suppose the Nasrany spoke lies concerning us and said that it was we who slew Tarzan? Wouldst they not believe him above us?"

"That be easily prevented," said the old man who had spoken before. "Let us cut his tongue out forthwith that he may not bear false witness against us."

"Wellah, thou hast it!" exclaimed Ibn Jad.

"Billah, nay!" cried Fahd. "The better we treat him the larger will be the reward that he will pay us."

"We can wait until the last moment," said Ibn Jad, "and we see that we are to lose him and our reward, then may we cut out his tongue."

Thus the fate of Wilbur Stimbol was left to the gods, and Ibn Jad, temporarily freed from the menace of Tarzan, turned his attention once more to his plans for entering the valley. With a strong party he went in person and sought a palaver with the Galla chief.

As he approached the village of Batando he passed through the camps of thousands of Galla warriors and realized fully what he had previously sensed but vaguely—that his position was most precarious and that with the best grace possible he must agree to whatever terms the old chief might propose.

Batando received him graciously enough, though with all the majesty of a powerful monarch, and assured him that on the following day he would escort him to the entrance to the valley, but that first he must deliver to Batando all the Galla slaves that were with his party.

"But that will leave us without carriers or servants and will greatly weaken the strength of my party," cried Ibn Jad.

Batando but shrugged his black shoulders.

"Let them remain with us until we have returned from the valley," implored the sheik.

"No Galla man may accompany you," said Batando with finality.

Early the next morning the tent of Ibn Jad was struck in signal that all were to prepare for the rahla, and entirely surrounded by Galla warriors they started toward the rugged mountains where lay the entrance to the valley of Ibn Jad's dreams.

Fejjuan and the other Galla slaves that the 'Aarab had brought with them from beled el-Guad marched with their own people, happy in their new-found freedom. Stimbol, friendless, fearful, utterly cowed, trudged wearily along under guard of two young Beduins, his mind constantly reverting to the horror of the murdered man lying in his lonely grave behind them.

Winding steadily upward along what at times appeared to be an ancient trail and again no trail at all, the 'Aarab and their escort climbed higher and higher into the rugged mountains that rim the Valley of the Sepulcher upon the north. At the close of the second day, after they had made camp beside a rocky mountain brook, Batando came to Ibn Jad and pointed to the entrance to a rocky side ravine that branched from the main canyon directly opposite the camp.

"There," he said, "lies the trail into the valley. Here we leave you and return to our villages. Upon the morrow we go."

When the sun rose the following morning Ibn Jad discovered that the Gallas had departed during the night, but he did not know it was because of the terror they felt for the inhabitants of the mysterious valley from which no Galla ever had returned.

That day Ibn Jad spent in making a secure camp in which to leave the women and children until the warriors had returned from their adventure in the valley or had discovered that they might safely fetch their women, and the next morning, leaving a few old men and boys to protect the camp, he set forth with those who were accounted the fighting men among them, and presently the watchers of the camp saw the last of them disappear in the rocky ravine that lay opposite the menzil.

16

The Great Tourney

KING BOHUN WITH many knights and squires and serving
men had ridden down from his castle above the City of the
Sepulcher two days ago to take his way across the valley to
the field before the city of Nimmr for the Great Tourney that
is held once each year, commencing upon the first Sunday
in Lent.

Gay pennons fluttered from a thousand lance tips and gay
with color were the housings of the richly caparisoned chargers
that proudly bore the Knights of the Sepulcher upon whose
backs red crosses were emblazoned to denote that they had
completed the pilgrimage to the Holy Land and were returning
to home and England.

Their bassinets, unlike those of the Knights of Nimmr, were
covered with bullock hide, and the devices upon their bucklers
differed, and their colors. But for these and the crosses upon
their backs they might have been Gobred's own good knights
and true.

Sturdy sumpter beasts, almost as richly trapped as the
knight's steeds, bore the marquees and tilts that were to house
the knights during the tourney, as well as their personal
belongings, their extra arms and their provisions for the three
days of the tourney; for custom, over seven centuries old, for-
bade the Knights of Nimmr and the Knights of the Sepulcher
breaking bread together.

The Great Tourney was merely a truce during which they

carried on their ancient warfare under special rules which transformed it into a gorgeous pageant and an exhibition of martial prowess which noncombatants might witness in comfort and with impunity. It did not permit friendly intercourse between the two factions as this was not compatible with the seriousness of the event, in which knights of both sides often were killed, or the spirit in which the grand prize was awarded.

This prize as much as any other factor had kept open the breach of seven and a half centuries' duration that separated the Fronters from the Backers, for it consisted of five maidens whom the winners took back with them to their own city and who were never again seen by their friends or relatives.

Though the sorrow was mitigated by the honorable treatment that custom and the laws of knighthood decreed should be accorded these unfortunate maidens, it was still bitter because attached to it was the sting of defeat.

Following the tournament the maidens became the especial charges of Gobred or Bohun, dependent of course upon whether the honors of the tourney had fallen to the Fronters or the Backers, and in due course were given in honorable marriage to knights of the victorious party.

The genesis of the custom, which was now fully seven centuries old, doubtless lay in the wise desire of some ancient Gobred or Bohun to maintain the stock of both factions strong and virile by the regular infusion of new blood, as well, perhaps, as to prevent the inhabitants of the two cities from drifting too far apart in manners, customs, and speech.

Many a happy wife of Nimmr had been born in the City of the Sepulcher and seldom was it that the girls themselves repined for long. It was considered an honor to be chosen and there were always many more who volunteered than the requisite number of five that annually made the sacrifice.

The five who constituted the prize offered by the City of the Sepulcher this year rode on white palfreys and were attended by a guard of honor in silver mail. The girls, selected for their beauty to thus honor the city of their birth, were gorgeously attired and weighed down with ornaments of gold and silver and precious stones.

Upon the plain before the city of Nimmr preparations for the tourney had been in progress for many days. The lists were being dragged and rolled with heavy wooden rollers, the ancient stands of stone from which the spectators viewed the spectacle were undergoing their annual repairs and cleansing, a frame superstructure was being raised to support the canopies that would shade the choice seats reserved for the nobility, and staffs for a thousand pennons had been set around the outer margin of the lists—these and a hundred other things were occupying a company of workmen; and in the walled city and in the castle that stood above it the hammers of armorers and smiths rang far into the night forging iron shoes and mail and lance tips.

Blake had been assured that he was to have a part in the Great Tourney and was as keen for it as he had been for the big game of the season during his football days at college. He had been entered in two sword contests—one in which five Knights of Nimmr met five Knights of the Sepulcher and another in which he was pitted against a single antagonist—but his only contest with the lance was to be in the grand finale when a hundred Fronters faced a hundred Backers, since, whereas, before his encounter with Malud he had been considered hopeless with sword and buckler, now Prince Gobred looked to him to win many points with these, his lance work being held but mediocre.

King Bohun and his followers were camped in a grove of oaks about a mile north of the lists, nor did the laws governing the Great Tourney permit them to come nearer until the hour appointed for their entrance upon the first day of the spectacle.

Blake, in preparing for the tourney, had followed the custom adopted by many of the knights of wearing distinctive armor and trapping his charger similarly. His chain mail was all of solid black, relieved only by the leopard skin of his bassinet and the blue and silver pennon upon his lance. The housings of his mount were of black, edged with silver and blue, and there were, of course, the prescribed red crosses upon his breast and upon his horse housings.

As he came from his quarters upon the opening morning of

the tourney, followed by Edward bearing his lance and buckler, he appeared a somber figure among the resplendently caparisoned knights and the gorgeously dressed women that were gathered in the great court awaiting the word to mount their horses which were being held in the north ballium by the grooms.

That his black mail was distinctive was evidenced by the attention he immediately attracted, and that he had quickly become popular among the knights and ladies of Nimmr was equally apparent by the manner in which they clustered about him, but opinion was divided in the matter of his costume, some holding that it was too dismal and depressing.

Guinalda was there but she remained seated upon a bench where she was conversing with one of the maidens that had been chosen as Nimmr's prize. Blake quickly disengaged himself from those who had crowded about him and crossed the court to where Guinalda sat. At his approach the princess looked up and inclined her head slightly in recognition of his bow and then she resumed her conversation with the maiden.

The rebuff was too obvious to permit of misunderstanding, but Blake was not satisfied to accept it and go his way without an explanation. He could scarce believe, however, that the princess was still vexed merely because he had intimated that he had believed that she took a greater interest in him than she had admitted. There must be some other reason.

He did not turn and walk away, then, although she continued to ignore him, but stood quietly before her waiting patiently until she should again notice him.

Presently he noted that she was becoming nervous as was also the maiden with whom she spoke. There were lapses in their conversation; one of Guinalda's feet was tapping the flagging irritably; a slow flush was creeping upward into her cheeks. The maiden fidgeted, she plucked at the ends of the wimple that lay about her shoulders, she smoothed the rich cyclas of her mantle and finally she arose and bowing before the princess asked if she might go and bid farewell to her mother.

Guinalda bade her begone and then, alone with Blake and no

longer able to ignore him, nor caring to, she turned angrily upon him.

"I was right!" she snapped. "Thou art a forward boor. Why standeth thou thus staring at me when I have made it plain that I wouldst not be annoyed by thee? Go!"

"Because—" Blake hesitated, "because I love you."

"Sirrah!" cried Guinalda, springing to her feet. "How darest thou!"

"I would dare anything for you, my princess," replied Blake, "because I love you."

Guinalda looked straight at him for a moment in silence, then her short upper lip curved in a contemptuous sneer.

"Thou liest!" she said. "I have heard what thou hast said concerning me!" and without waiting for a reply she brushed past him and walked away.

Blake hurried after her. "What have I said about you?" he demanded. "I have said nothing that I would not repeat before all Nimmr. Not even have I presumed to tell my best friend, Sir Richard, that I love you. No other ears than yours have heard that."

"I have heard differently," said Guinalda, haughtily, "and I care not to discuss the matter further."

"But—" commenced Blake, but at that instant a trumpet sounded from the north gate leading into the ballium. It was the signal for the knights to mount. Guinalda's page came running to her to summon her to her father's side. Sir Richard appeared and seized Blake by the arm.

"Come, James!" he cried. "We should have been mounted before now for we ride in the forerank of the knights today." And so Blake was dragged away from the princess before he could obtain an explanation of her, to him, inexplicable attitude.

The north ballium presented a scene of color and activity, crowded as it was with knights and ladies, pages, squires, grooms, men-at-arms, and horses, nor would it accommodate them all, so that the overflow stretched into the east and south balliums and even through the great east gate out upon the road that leads down into the valley.

For half an hour something very like chaos reigned about the castle of the Prince of Nimmr, but eventually perspiring marshals and shouting heralds whipped the cortege into shape as it took its slow and imposing way down the winding mountain road toward the lists.

First rode the marshals and heralds and behind them a score of trumpeters; then came Prince Gobred, riding alone, and following was a great company of knights, their colored pennons streaming in the wind. They rode just before the ladies and behind the ladies was another company of knights, while in the rear marched company after company of men-at-arms, some armed with crossbows, others with pikes, and still others again with battle-axes of huge proportions.

Perhaps a hundred knights and men-at-arms all told were left behind to guard the castle and the entrance to the Valley of the Sepulcher, but these would be relieved to witness the second and third days' exercises.

As the Knights of Nimmr wound down to the lists, the Knights of the Sepulcher moved out from their camp among the oaks, and the marshals of the two parties timed their approach so that both entered the lists at the same time.

The ladies of Nimmr dropped out of the procession and took their places in the stand; the five maidens of Nimmr and the five from the City of Sepulcher were escorted to a dais at one end of the lists, after which the knights lined up in solid ranks, the Knights of Nimmr upon the south side of the lists, the Knights of Sepulcher upon the north.

Gobred and Bohun rode forward and met in the center of the field, where, in measured and imposing tones, Bohun delivered the ancient challenge prescribed by custom and the laws of the Great Tourney and handed Gobred the gage, the acceptance of which constituted an acceptance of the challenge and marked the official opening of the tourney.

As Gobred and Bohun reined about and faced their own knights these rode out of the lists, those who were not to take part in the encounters of the day seeking places in the stands after turning their chargers over to grooms, while those who were to participate formed again to ride once around the lists, for the double purpose of indicating to their opponents and the spectators the entrants for that day and of viewing the prizes offered by their opponents.

In addition to the maidens there were many minor prizes consisting of jeweled ornaments, suits of mail, lances, swords, bucklers, splendid steeds, and the many articles that were valued by knights or that might find favor in the eyes of their ladies.

The Knights of the Sepulcher paraded first, with Bohun at their head, and it was noticeable that the eyes of the king were often upon the women in the stands as he rode past. Bohun was a young man, having but just ascended the throne following the recent death of his father. He was arrogant and tyrannical and it had been common knowledge in Nimmr that for years he had been at the head of a faction that was strong for war with Nimmr, that the city might be reduced and the entire Valley of the Sepulcher brought under the rule of the Bohuns.

His charger prancing, his colors flying, his great company of knights at his back, King Bohun rode along the stands reserved for the people of Nimmr, and when he came to the central loge in which sat Prince Gobred with the Princess Brynilda and Princess Guinalda, his eyes fell upon the face of the daughter of Gobred.

Bohun reined in his charger and stared straight into the face of Guinalda. Gobred flushed angrily, for Bohun's act was a breach of courtesy, and half rose from his seat, but at that moment Bohun, bowing low across his mount's withers, moved on, followed by his knights.

That day the honors went to the Knights of the Sepulcher, for they scored two hundred and twenty-seven points against one hundred and six that the Knights of Nimmr were able to procure.

Upon the second day the tourney opened with the riding past of the entrants who, ordinarily, were conducted by a herald, but to the surprise of all, Bohun again led his knights past the stands and again he paused and looked full at the Princess Guinalda.

This day the Knights of Nimmr fared a little better, being for the day but seven points behind their opponents, though the score for the two days stood two hundred and sixty-nine to three hundred and ninety-seven in favor of the Knights of the Sepulcher.

So the third day opened with the knights from the north boasting what seemed an insuperable lead of one hundred and twenty eight points and the Knights of Nimmr spurred to greater action by the knowledge that to win the tourney they must score two hundred and thirty-two of the remaining three hundred and thirty-four points.

Once again, contrary to age-old custom, Bohun led his entrants about the lists as they paraded before the opening encounter, and once again he drew rein before the loge of Gobred and his eye rested upon the beautiful face of Guinalda for an instant before he addressed her sire.

"Prince Gobred of Nimmr," he said in his haughty and arrogant voice, "as ye well know my valiant sir knights have bested thine by more than six score points and the Great Tourney be as good as ours already. Yet we would make thee a proposition."

"Speak Bohun! The Great Tourney is yet far from won, but an' ye have any proposition that an honorable prince may consider thou hast my assurance that 'twill be given consideration."

"Thy five maidens are as good as ours," said Bohun, "but give me thy daughter to be queen of the Valley of the Sepulcher and I will grant thee thy tourney."

Gobred went white with anger, but when he replied his voice was low and even for he was master of his own emotions, as befitted a princely man.

"Sir Bohun," he said, refusing to accord to his enemy the title of king, "thy words are an offense in the ears of honorable men, implying as they do that the daughter of a Gobred be for sale and that the honor of the knighthood of Nimmr may be bartered for.

"Get thee hence to thine own side of the lists before I set serfs upon ye to drive ye there with staves."

"So that be thine answer, eh?" shouted Bohun. "Then know ye that I shall take the five maidens by the rules of the Great

Tourney and thy daughter by force of arms!" With this threat delivered he wheeled his steed and spurred away.

Word of Bohun's proposition and his rebuff spread like wildfire throughout the ranks of the Knight of Nimmr so that those who were to contend this last day of the tourney were keyed to the highest pitch of derring-do in the defence of the honor of Nimmr and the protection of the Princess Guinalda.

The great lead attained by the Knights of the Sepulcher during the first two days was but an added incentive to greater effort, provoking them, as a spur, to the utmost limits of daring and exertion. There was no need that their marshals should exhort them. The youth and chivalry of Nimmr had heard the challenge and would answer it in the lists!

Blake's sword and buckler encounter with the Knight of the Sepulcher was scheduled for the first event of the day. When the lists were cleared he rode in to a fanfare of trumpets, moving parallel with the south stands while his adversary rode along the front of the north stands, the latter halting before the loge of Bohun as Blake drew rein in front of that of Gobred, where he raised the hilt of his sword to his lips to the Prince, though his eyes were upon Guinalda.

"Conduct thyself as a true knight this day to the glory and honor of Nimmr," charged Gobred, "and may the blessings of Our Lord Jesus be upon thee and thy sword, our well-beloved Sir James!"

"To the glory and honor of Nimmr I pledge my sword and my life!" should have been Blake's reply according to the usages of the Great Tourney.

"To the glory and honor of Nimmr and to the protection of my Princess I pledge my sword and my life!" is what he said, and it was evident from the expression on Gobred's face that he was not displeased, while the look of haughty disdain which had been upon Guinalda's face softened.

Slow she arose and tearing a ribbon from her gown stepped to the front of the loge. "Receive this favor from thy lady, sir knight," she said, "bearing it with honor and to victory in thy encounter."

Blake reined close to the rail of the loge and bent low while

Guinalda pinned the ribbon upon his shoulder. His face was close to hers; he sensed the intoxicating perfume of her hair; he felt her warm breath upon his cheek.

"I love you," he whispered, so low that no other ears than hers could hear.

"Thou art a boor," she replied in a voice as low as his. "It be for the sake of the five maidens that I encourage ye with this favor."

Blake looked straight into her eyes. "I love you, Guinalda," he said, "and—you love me!"

Before she could reply he had wheeled away, the trumpets had sounded, and he was cantering slowly toward the end of the field where the tilts of the Knights of Nimmr stood.

Edward, very much excited, was there and Sir Richard and Michel, with a marshal, heralds, trumpeters, men-at-arms—a martial company to urge him on with encouragement and advice.

Blake cast aside his buckler, nor was there any to reprove him now. Instead they smiled proudly and knowingly, for had they not seen him best Sir Malud without other defense than his horsemanship and his sword?

The trumpets blared again. Blake turned and put spurs to his charger. Straight down the center of the lists he rode. From the opposite end came a Knight of the Sepulcher to meet him!

"Sir James! Sir James!" cried the spectators in the stands upon the south side, while the north stands answered with the name of their champion.

"Who is the black knight?" asked many a man in the north stands of his neighbor.

"He hath no buckler!" cried some. "He be mad!" "Sir Guy wilt cleave him open at the first pass!" "Sir Guy! Sir Guy!"

17

"The Saracens!"

JUST AS THE second day of the Great Tourney had opened in the Valley of the Sepulcher upon the plains below the city of Nimmr, a band of swart men in soiled thobs and carrying long matchlocks topped the summit of the pass upon the north side of the valley and looked down upon the City of the Sepulcher and the castle of King Bohun.

They had followed upward along what may once have been a trail, but for so long a time had it been unused, or so infrequently had it been used that it was scarce distinguishable from the surrounding brush; but below them now Ibn Jad saw at a short distance a better marked road and, beyond, what appeared to him a fortress. Beyond that again he glimpsed the battlements of Bohun's castle.

What he saw in the foreground was the barbican guarding the approach to the castle and the city, both of which were situated in much the same relative position as were the barbican and castle upon the south side of the valley where Prince Gobred guarded the city of Nimmr and the valley beyond it against the daily expected assault of the Saracens.

Seeking cover, Ibn Jad and his Beduins crept down toward the barbican where an old knight and a few men-at-arms kept perfunctory ward. Hiding in the mountain brush the 'Aarab saw two strangely apparelled blacks hunting just outside the great gateway. They were armed with crossbows and arrows and their prey was rabbits. For years they had seen no stranger

146

come down this ancient road, and for years they had hunted between the gate and the summit of the mountains, though farther than this they were not permitted to wander. Nor had they any great desire to do so, for, though they were descendants of Gallas who lived just beyond this mountaintop, they thought that they were Englishmen and that a horde of Saracens awaited to annihilate them should they venture too far afield.

Today they hunted as they had often hunted when they chanced to be placed in the guard at the outer barbican. They moved silently forward, warily awaiting the break of a rabbit. They did not see the dark-faced men in the brush.

Ibn Jad saw that the great gateway was open and that the gate that closed it raised and lowered vertically. It was raised now. Great was the laxity of the old knight and the men-at-arms, but King Bohun was away and there was none to reprove them.

Ibn Jad motioned those nearest him to follow and crept slowly closer to the gateway.

What of the old knight and the other watchers? The former was partaking of a late breakfast just within one of the great towers of the barbican and the latter were taking advantage of the laxity of his discipline to catch a few more winks of sleep as they stretched beneath the shade of some trees within the ballium.

Ibn Jad won to within a few yards of the gateway and waited for the others to reach his side. When they were all there he whispered to them and then trotted on silent sandals toward the gate, his matchlock ready in his hands. Behind him came his fellows. They were all within the ballium before the men-at-arms were aware that there was an enemy this side of Palestine.

With crossbow and battle-ax the men-at-arms sprang to defend the gate. Their cries of "The Saracens! The Saracens!" brought the old sir knight and the hunters running toward the ballium.

Below, at the castle of King Bohun, the men at the gates and the other retainers who had been left while Bohun sallied forth to the Great Tourney heard strange noises from the direction of the outer barbican. The shouts of men floated down to them and strange, sharp sounds that were like thunder and yet unlike it. Such sounds they had never heard before, nor any of their forbears. They rallied at the outer castle gate and the knights with them consulted as to what was best to be done.

Being brave knights there seemed but one thing open for them. If those at the far outer barbican had been attacked they must hasten to their defense. Summoning all but four of the knights and men-at-arms at his disposal the marshal of the castle mounted and rode forth toward the outer gate.

Halfway there they were espied by Ibn Jad and his men who, having overcome the poorly armed soldiers at the gate, were advancing down the road toward the castle. At sight of these reinforcements Ibn Jad hastened to secrete his followers and himself in the bushes that lined the roadway. So it fell that the marshal rode by them and did not see them and, when they had passed, Ibn Jad and his followers came out of the bushes and continued down the winding mountain road toward the castle of King Bohun.

The men at the castle gate, now fully upon the alert, stood ready with the portcullis raised as the marshal instructed them, so that in the event that those who had ridden out should be hard pressed upon their return by an enemy at their rear they could still find sanctuary within the ballium. The plan was, in such event, to lower the portcullis behind the men of the Sepulcher and in the faces of the pursuing Saracens, for that an enemy must be such was a forgone conclusion—had not they and their ancestors waited for near seven and a half centuries now for this momentarily expected assault? They wondered if it really had come at last.

While they discussed the question Ibn Jad watched them from a concealing clump of bushes a few yards away.

The wily Beduin knew the purpose of the portcullis and he was trying to plan best how he might enter the enclosure beyond before it could be dropped before his face. At last he found a plan and smiled. He beckoned three men to come close and into their ears he whispered that which he had in mind.

There were four men-at-arms ready to drop the portcullis at the psychological moment and all four of them stood in plain sight of Ibn Jad and the three that were beside him. Carefully, cautiously, noiselessly the four 'Aarab raised their ancient matchlocks and took careful aim.

"Now!" whispered Ibn Jad and four matchlocks belched forth flame and black powder and slugs of lead.

The four men-at-arms dropped to the stone flagging and Ibn Jad and all his followers raced forward and stood within the ballium of the castle of King Bohun. Before them, across the ballium, was another gate and a broad moat, but the drawbridge was lowered, the portcullis raised, and the gateway unguarded.

The marshal and his followers had ridden unhindered into the ballium of the outer barbican and there they had found all its defenders lying in their own blood, even to the little squire of the old knight who should have watched the gate and did not.

One of the men-at-arms still lived and in his dying breath he gasped the terrible truth. The Saracens had come at last!

"Where are they?" demanded the marshal.

"Didst thou not see them, sir?" asked the dying man. "They marched down the road toward the castle."

"Impossible!" cried the marshal. "We didst but ride along that very road and saw no one."

"They marched down toward the castle," gasped the man.

The marshal knit his brows. "Were there many?" he demanded.

"There are few," replied the man-at-arms. "It was but the advance guard of the armies of the sultan."

Just then the volley that laid low the four warders at the castle gate crashed upon the ears of the marshal and his men.

"Ods blud!" he cried.

"They must have hid themselves in the bush as we passed," exclaimed a knight at the marshal's side, "for of a surety they be there and we be here and there be one road between."

"There be but four men at the castle gate," said the marshal, "and I did bid them keep the 'cullis up till we returned. God pity me! I have given over the Sepulcher to the Saracens. Slay me, Sir Morley!"

"Nay, man! We need every lance and sword and crossbow that we may command. This be no time to think of taking thy life when thou canst give it to Our Lord Jesus in defense of His Sepulcher against the infidels!"

"Thou art right, Morley," cried the marshal. "Remain you here, then, with six men and hold this gate. I shall return with the others and give battle at the castle!"

But when the marshal came again to the castle gate he found the portcullis down and a dark-faced, bearded Saracen glaring at him through the iron bars. The marshal at once ordered the crossbowmen to shoot the fellow down, but as they raised their weapons to their shoulder there was a loud explosion that almost deafened them and flame leaped from a strange thing that the Saracen held against his shoulder and pointed at them. One of the crossbowmen screamed and lunged forward upon his face and the others turned and fled.

They were brave men in the face of dangers that were natural and to be expected, but in the presence of the supernatural, the weird, the uncanny, they reacted as most men do, and what could have been more weird than death leaping in flame and with a great noise through space to strike their fellow down?

But Sir Bulland, the marshal, was a knight of the Sepulcher. He might wish to run away fully as much as the simple and lowly men-at-arms, but there was something that held him there that was more potent than fear of death. It is called Honor.

Sir Bulland could not run away and so he sat there on his great horse and challenged the Saracens to mortal combat; challenged them to send their doughtiest sir knight to meet him and thus decide who should hold the gate.

But the 'Aarab already held it. Furthermore they did not understand him. In addition to all this they were without honor as Sir Bulland knew it, and perhaps as anyone other than a Beduin knows it, and would but have laughed at his silly suggestion.

One thing they did know—two things they knew—that he was a Nasrany and that he was unarmed. They did not count his great lance and his sword as weapons, for he could not reach them with either. So one of them took careful aim and shot Sir Bulland through his chain mail where it covered his noble and chivalrous heart.

Ibn Jad had the run of the castle of King Bohun and he was sure that he discovered the fabled City of Nimmr that the sahar had told him of. He herded together the women and children and the few men that remained and held them under guard. For a while he was minded to slay them, since they were but Nasrany, but he was so pleased at having found and taken the treasure city that he let them live—for the time at least.

At his command his followers ransacked the castle in search of the treasure. Nor were they disappointed, for the riches of Bohun were great. There was gold in the hills of the Valley of the Sepulcher and there were precious stones to be found there, also. For seven and a half centuries the slaves of the Sepulcher and of Nimmr had been washing gold from the creekbeds and salvaging precious stones from the same source. The real value of such was not to the men of the Sepulcher and Nimmr what it would be to men of the outer world. They but esteemed these things as trinkets, yet they liked them and saved them and even bartered for them on occasion, but they did not place them in vaults under lock and key. Why should they in a land where such things were not stolen? Their women and their horses they guarded, but not their gold or their jewels.

And so Ibn Jad gathered a great sack full of treasure, enough to satisfy the wildest imaginings of his cupidity. He gathered all that he could find in the castle of King Bohun, more than he had hoped to find in this fabled city; and then a strange thing happened. Having more wealth than he possibly could use he wanted more. No, not so strange after all, for Ibn Jad was human.

He spent the night with his followers in the castle of King Bohun and during the night he planned, for he had seen a wide valley stretching far away to other mountains and at the base of those mountains he had seen that which appeared to be a city. "Perhaps," thought Ibn Jad, "it is a richer city than this. I shall start on the morrow to see."

18

The Black Knight

DOWN THE FIELD thundered the two chargers. Silence fell upon the stands. They were almost met when Sir Guy realized that his adversary bore no shield. But what of that? He had been sent to the lists by his own people—the responsibility was theirs, the advantage Sir Guy's. Had they sent him in without a sword Sir Guy might still have slain him without besmirching his knightly honor, for such were the laws of the Great Tourney.

Yet his discovery had its effect upon the Knight of the Sepulcher as just for an instant it had distracted his attention from the thought that should have been uppermost in his mind—gaining the primary advantage by the skill of his opening attack.

He saw his antagonist's horse swing out just before they met. He stood in his stirrups, as had Sir Malud, to deliver a terrific cut; then Blake threw his horse straight into the shoulder of Sir Guy's. The latter's sword fell and with a loud, clanging noise slipped harmlessly from the blade of the Knight of Nimmr. Guy had raised his buckler to protect his own head and neck and could not see Sir James. Guy's horse stumbled and nearly fell. As it recovered itself Blake's blade slipped beneath the buckler of the Knight of the Sepulcher and its point pierced the gorget of his adversary and passed through his throat.

With a cry that ended in a blood choked gurgle Sir Guy of the Sepulcher toppled backward upon his horse's rump and rolled upon the ground while the south stands went mad with joy.

The laws of the Great Tourney account the knight who is unhorsed as slain, so the coup-de-grace is never given and no knight is killed unnecessarily. The victor rides to the tilt of the vanquished, wheels about and gallops to his own tilt, the full length of the lists, where he waits until a herald of the opposing side fetches the prize to him.

And so it was that as Blake swung from his saddle, sword in hand, and approached the fallen Sir Guy, a gasp arose from the south stands and a roar of angry protest from the north.

Marshals and heralds galloped madly from the tilt of the fallen Backer and, seeing this, Sir Richard, fearing that Blake would be set upon and slain, led a similar party from his end of the field.

Blake approached the fallen knight, who lay upon his back, feebly struggling to arise, and when the spectators looked to see him run Sir Guy through with his sword they saw him instead toss the weapon to the ground and kneel beside the wounded man.

With an arm beneath Sir Guy's shoulders he raised him and held him against his knee while he tore off his helm and gorget, and when the marshals and the heralds and the others drew rein beside him Blake was trying to staunch the flow of blood.

"Quick!" he cried to them, "a chirurgeon! His jugular is not touched, but this flow of blood must be stopped."

Several of the knights dismounted and gathered about, and among them was Sir Richard. A herald of Sir Guy's faction kneeled and took the youth from Blake's arms.

"Come!" said Richard. "Leave the sir knight to his own friends."

Blake arose. He saw how peculiar were the expressions upon the faces of the knights about him, but as he drew away one of them spoke. An older man, who was one of Bohun's marshals.

"Thou art a generous and chivalrous knight," he said to Blake, "and a courageous one too who would thus set at naught the laws of the Great Tourney and the customs of centuries."

Blake faced him squarely. "I do not give a damn for your laws or your customs," he said. "Where I come from a decent man wouldn't let a yellow dog bleed to death without trying to save him, much less a brave and gallant boy like this, and because he fell by my hand, by the customs of my country I should be compelled to aid him."

"Yes," explained Sir Richard, "as otherwise he would be punished with a raspberry."

The winning of the first event of the day was but a fore-runner of a series of successes on the part of the Knights of Nimmr until, at the opening of the last event, the score showed four hundred fifty-two points for them against four hundred forty-eight points for their opponents. A margin of four points, how-ever, was as nothing at this stage of the tourney, as the final event held one hundred points which Fate might allot almost entirely to one side.

This was the most spectacular event of the whole tourney and one which the spectators always looked forward to with the greatest anticipation. Two hundred knights were engaged in it, one hundred Knights of Nimmr against one hundred Knights of the Sepulcher. They formed at opposite ends of the lists and as the trumpets sounded the signal they charged with lances, and thus they fought until all of one side had been unhorsed or had retired from the field because of wounds. Broken lances could be replaced as a polo player may ride out and obtain a fresh mallet when he breaks his. Otherwise there were few rules to govern this concluding number of the Great Tourney, which more nearly approximated a battle scene than any other event of the three days of conflict.

Blake had won his fifteen points for the Knights of Nimmr in the opening event of the day and again with four other com-rades, pitted against five mounted swordsmen from the north, he had helped to add still further points to the growing score of the Fronters.

He was entered in the last event largely because the mar-shals appreciated the value of his horsemanship and felt that it would more than compensate for his inexperience with the lance.

The two hundred mailed knights had paraded for the final event and were forming lines at opposite ends of the lists, one hundred Knights of the Sepulcher at one end and one hundred Knights of Nimmr at the other. Their chargers, especially selected for this encounter, were powerful and fleet, chosen for their courage as were the youths who bestrode them.

The knights, with few exceptions, were youths in their twenties, for to youth went the laurels of this great sport of the Middle Ages as they still do in the sports of today. Here and there was a man of middle age, a hardened veteran whose heart and hand had withstood the march of years and whose presence exerted a steadying influence upon the young knights the while it spurred them to their utmost efforts, for these were champions whose deeds were sung by minstrels in the great halls of the castles of Nimmr.

In proud array, with upright lances and fluttering pennons, the sunlight glinting from burnished mail and bit and boss and shining brightly upon the gorgeous housings of their mounts, the two hundred presented a proud and noble spectacle as they awaited the final summons of the trumpet.

Rearing and plunging, eager to be off, many a warhorse broke the line as will a thoroughbred at the barrier, while at one side and opposite the center of the lists a herald waited for the moment that both lines should be formed before he gave the signal that would send these iron men hurtling into combat.

Blake found himself well toward the center of the line of Nimmr's knights, beneath him a great black that fretted to be off, before him the flower of the knighthood of the Sepulcher. In his right hand he grasped a heavy, iron-shod lance, the butt of which rested in a boot at his stirrup, and upon his left arm he bore a great shield, nor had he any wish to discard it in the face of all those sturdy, iron-tipped lances.

As he looked down the long length of the lists upon the hundred knights that would presently be racing toward him in solid array with lance points projecting far ahead of their horses, Blake felt that his shield was entirely inadequate and he experienced a certain nervousness that reminded him of similar moments of tense waiting for the referee's whistle during his football days—those seemingly long-gone days of another life that he sensed now as a remote and different incarnation.

At last came the signal! He saw the herald raise his sword on high. With the two hundred he gathered his restive charger and couched his lance. The sword fell! From the four corners of the lists trumpets blared; from two hundred throats rose the cri de guerre; four hundred spurs transmitted the awaited signal from man to horse.

The thundering lines bore down the field while a score of heralds raced along the flanks and rear to catch any infraction of the sole regulation that bore upon the final tumultuous collision. Each knight must engage the foe upon his bridle hand, for to couch his lance upon the one to his right was an unknightly act, since thus a single knight might have two lances set upon him at once, against which there could be no defence.

From above the rim of his shield Blake saw the solid front of lances, iron-shod chargers, and great shields almost upon him. The speed, the weight, the momentum seemed irresistible and, metaphorically, with deep respect Blake took his hat off to the knights of old.

Now the two lines were about to meet! The spectators sat in spellbound silence; the riders, grim-jawed, with tight-set lips, were voiceless now.

Blake, his lance across his horse's withers, picked the knight racing toward him upon his left hand; for an instant he caught the other's eyes and then each crouched behind his shield as the two lines came together with a deafening crash.

Blake's shield smashed back against his face and body with such terrific force that he was almost carried from his saddle. He felt his own lance strike and splinter and then, half stunned, he was through the iron line, his charger, frantic and uncontrolled, running wildly toward the tilts of Bohun's knights.

With an effort Blake pulled himself together, gathered his reins, and finally managed to get his horse under control, and it was not until he had reined him about that he got his first glimpse of the result of the opening encounter. A half dozen chargers were scrambling to their feet and nearly a score more were galloping, riderless, about the lists. A full twenty-five knights lay upon the field and twice that many squires and serving men were running in on foot to succor their masters.

Already several of the knights had again set their lances against an enemy and Blake saw one of the Knights of the Sepulcher bearing down upon him, but he raised his broken spear shaft above his head to indicate that he was momentarily hors de combat and galloped swiftly back to his own end of the lists where Edward was awaiting him with a fresh weapon.

"Thou didst nobly well, beloved master," cried Edward.

"Did I get my man?" asked Blake.

"That thou didst, sir," Edward assured him, beaming with pride and pleasure, "and all be thou breakest thy lance upon his shield thou didst e'en so unhorse him."

Armed anew Blake turned back toward the center of the lists where many individual encounters were taking place. Already several more knights were down and the victors looking for new conquests in which the stands were assisting with hoarse cries and advice, and as Blake rode back into the lists he was espied by many in the north stands occupied by the knights and followers of the Sepulcher.

"The black knight!" they cried. "Here! Here! Sir Wildred! Here is the black knight that overthrew Sir Guy. Have at him, Sir Wildred!"

Sir Wildred, a hundred yards away, couched his lance. "Have at thee, Sir Black Knight!" he shouted.

"You're on!" Blake shouted back, putting spurs to the great black.

Sir Wildred was a large man and he bestrode a raw-boned roan with the speed of a deer and the heart of a lion. The pair would have been a match for the best of Nimmr's knighthood.

Perhaps it was as well for Blake's peace of mind that Wildred appeared to him like any other knight and that he did not know that he was the most sung of all the heroes of the Sepulcher.

As a matter of fact, any knight looked formidable to Blake, who was still at a loss to understand how he had unhorsed his man in the first encounter of this event.

"The bird must have lost both stirrups," is what he had mentally assured himself when Edward had announced his victory.

But he couched his lance like a good sir knight and true and bore down upon the redoubtable Sir Wildred. The Knight of the Sepulcher was charging diagonally across the field from the south stands. Beyond him Blake caught a glimpse of a slim, girlish figure standing in the central loge. He could not see her eyes, but he knew that they were upon him.

"For my Princess!" he whispered as Sir Wildred loomed large before him.

Lance smote on shield as the two knights crashed together with terrific force and Blake felt himself lifted clear of his saddle and hurled heavily to the ground. He was neither stunned nor badly hurt and as he sat up a sudden grin wreathed his face, for there, scarce a lance length from him, sat Sir Wildred. But Sir Wildred did not smile.

" 'Sdeath!" he cried. "Thou laughest at me, sirrah?"

"If I look as funny as you do," Blake assured him, "you've got a laugh coming too."

Sir Wildred knit his brows. "Ods blud!" he exclaimed. "An' thou beest a knight of Nimmr I be a Saracen! Who beest thou? Thy speech savoreth not of the Valley."

Blake had arisen. "Hurt much?" he asked stepping forward. "Here, I'll give you a hand up."

"Thou art, of a certainty, a strange sir knight," said Wildred. "I recall now that thou didst offer succor to Sir Guy when thou hadst fairly vanquished him."

"Well, what's wrong with that?" asked Blake. "I haven't anything against you. We've had a bully good scrap and are out of it. Why should we sit here and make faces at one another?"

Sir Wildred shook his head. "Thou art beyond my comprehension," he admitted.

By this time their squires and a couple of serving men had arrived, but neither of the fallen knights was so badly injured that he could not walk without assistance. As they started for their respective tilts Blake turned and smiled at Wildred.

"So long, old man," he cried cheerily. "Hope we meet again some day."

Still shaking his head Sir Wildred limped away, followed by the two who had come to assist him.

At his tilt Blake learned that the outcome of the Great Tourney still hung in the balance and it was another half hour before the last of the Knights of Nimmr went down in defeat, leaving two Knights of the Sepulcher victorious upon the field. But this was not enough to overcome the lead of four points that the Fronters had held at the opening of the last event and a moment later the heralds announced that the Knights of Nimmr had won the Great Tourney by the close margin of two points.

Amidst the shouting of the occupants of the stands at the south the Knights of Nimmr who had taken part in the tourney and had won points for the Fronters formed to ride upon the lists and claim the grand prize. Not all were there, as some had been killed or wounded in encounters that had followed their victories, though the toll on both sides had been much smaller than Blake had imagined that it would be. Five men were dead and perhaps twenty too badly injured to ride, the casualties being about equally divided.

As the Knight of Nimmr rode down the field to claim the five maidens from the City of the Sepulcher, Bohun gathered all his knights at his side of the lists as though preparing to ride back to his camp. At the same time a Knight of the Sepulcher, wearing the leopard skin bassinet of Nimmr, entered the stands upon the south side of the field and made his way toward the loge of Prince Gobred.

Bohun watched. The Knights of Nimmr were at the far end of the field engrossed in the ritualistic rites that the laws of the Great Tourney prescribed for the reception of the five maidens.

Close beside Bohun two young knights sat their chargers, their eyes upon their king, and one of them held the bridle of a riderless horse.

Suddenly Bohun raised his hand and spurred across the field followed by his knights. They moved a little toward the end of the field where the Knights of Nimmr were congregated so that the bulk of them were between this end of the field and Gobred's loge.

The young knight who had sat close beside Bohun, and his companion leading the riderless horse, spurred at a run straight for the stands of Nimmr and the loge of the Prince. As they drew in abreast of it a knight leaped into the loge from the rear, swept Guinalda into his arms, tossed her quickly to the young knight waiting to receive her, sprang to the edge of the rail and leaped into the saddle of the spare horse being held in readiness for him; then they both wheeled and spurred away before the surprised Gobred or those about him could raise a hand to stay them. Behind them swept Bohun and the Knights of the Sepulcher, out toward the camp among the oaks.

Instantly all was pandemonium. A trumpeter in Gobred's loge sounded the alarm; the prince ran from the stands to the spot where his horse was being held by a groom; the Knights of Nimmr, ignorant of what had occurred, not knowing where to rally or against whom, milled about the lists for a few moments.

Then Gobred came, spurring swiftly before them. "Bohun has stolen the Princess Guinalda!" he cried. "Knights of Nimmr—" but before he could say more, or issue orders to his followers, a black knight on a black charger spurred roughly through the ranks of surrounding men and was away after the retreating Knights of the Sepulcher.

19

Lord Tarzan

THERE WAS A nasty smile upon Tollog's lips as he thought how neatly he had foiled Ateja, who would have warned the Nasrany of the plot to slay him, and he thanked Allah that chance had placed him in a position to intercept her before she had been able to ruin them all. Even as Tollog, the brother of the sheik, smiled in his beard a hand reached out of the darkness behind him and seized him by the throat—fingers grasped him and he was dragged away.

Into the beyt that had been Zeyd's and which had been set up for the Nasrany, Tollog was dragged. He struggled and tried to scream for help, but he was powerless in the grip of steel that held him and choked him.

Inside the beyt a voice whispered in his ear. "Cry out, Tollog," it said, "and I shall have to kill you." Then the grasp upon his throat relaxed, but Tollog did not call for help, for he had recognized the voice that spoke and he knew that it had made no idle threat.

He lay still while the bonds were drawn tight about his wrists and ankles and a gag fastened securely in his mouth. He felt the folds of his burnous drawn across his face and then— silence.

He heard Stimbol creep into the beyt, but he thought that it was still he who had bound him. And thus died Tollog, the brother of Ibn Jad, died as he had planned that Tarzan of the Apes should die.

And, knowing that he would die thus, there was a smile upon the lips of the ape-man as he swung through the forest toward the southeast.

Tarzan's quest was not for Beduins but for Blake. Having assured himself that the white man in the menzil of Ibn Jad was Stimbol and that none knew the whereabouts of the other American, he was hastening back to the locality where Blake's boys had told him their bwana had disappeared, in the hope of picking up his trail and, if unable to assist him, at least to learn what fate had overtaken him.

Tarzan moved swiftly and his uncanny senses of sight and smell aided him greatly in wresting its secrets from the jungle, yet it was three days before he found the spot where Ara the lightning had struck down Blake's gun bearer.

Here he discovered Blake's faint spoor leading toward the north. Tarzan shook his head, for he knew that there was a stretch of uninhabited forest laying between this place and the first Galla villages. Also he knew that if Blake survived hunger and the menace of wild beasts he might only live to fall victim to a Galla spear.

For two days Tarzan followed a spoor that no other human eye might have discerned. On the afternoon of the second day he came upon a great stone cross built directly in the center of an ancient trail. Tarzan saw the cross from the concealment of bushes for he moved as beasts of prey moved, taking advantage of every cover, suspicious of every strange object, always ready for flight or battle as occasion might demand.

So it was that he did not walk blindly into the clutches of the two men-at-arms that guarded the outer way to the City of Nimmr. To his keen ears was borne the sound of their voices long before he saw them.

Even as Sheeta or Numa approach their prey, so Tarzan of the Apes crept through the brush until he lay within a few yards of the men-at-arms. To his vast astonishment he heard them conversing in a quaint form of English that, while understandable to him, seemed yet a foreign tongue. He marvelled at their antiquated costumes and obsolete weapons, and in them he saw an explanation of Blake's disappearance and a suggestion of his fate.

For a time Tarzan lay watching the two with steady, unblinking eyes—it might have been Numa himself, weighing the chances of a sudden charge. He saw that each was armed with a sturdy pike and a sword. They could speak English, after a fashion, therefore, he argued, they might be able to give him word of Blake. But would they receive him in a friendly spirit or would they attempt to set upon and slay him?

He determined that he could never ascertain what their attitude would be by lying hidden among the brush, and so he gathered himself, as Numa does when he is about to spring.

The two blacks were idly gossiping, their minds as far from thoughts of danger as it were possible they could be, when suddenly without warning Tarzan launched himself full upon the back of the nearer, hurling him to the ground. Before the other could gather his wits the ape-man had dragged his victim into the concealment of the bush from which he had sprung, while the fellow's companion turned and fled in the direction of the tunnel.

The man in Tarzan's grasp fought and struggled to be free but the ape-man held him as easily as he might have held a child.

"Lie still," he advised, "I shall not harm you."

"Ods blud!" cried the black. "What matter of creature be thou?"

"One who will not harm you if you will tell him the truth," replied Tarzan.

"What wouldst thou know?" demanded the black.

"A white man came this way many weeks ago. Where is he?"

"Thou speakest of Sir James?" asked the soldier.

"Sir James!" mused Tarzan and then he recollected that Blake's first name was James. "His name was James," he replied, "James Blake."

"Verily, 'tis the same," said the soldier.

"You have seen him? Where is he now?"

"He be defending the honor of Our Lord Jesus and the

Knights of Nimmr in the Great Tourney in the lists upon the plain below the city, and have ye come to wreak dispite upon our good Sir James thou wilt find many doughty knights and men-at-arms who will take up the gage in his behalf."

"I am his friend," said Tarzan.

"Then why didst thou leap upon me thus, if thou art a friend to Sir James?" demanded the man.

"I did not know how you had received him or how you would receive me."

"A friend of Sir James will be received well in Nimmr," said the man.

Tarzan took the man's sword from him and permitted him to rise—his pike he had dropped before being dragged among the bushes.

"Go before me and lead me to your master," commanded the ape-man, "and remember that your life will be the forfeit that you must pay for treachery."

"Do not make me leave the road unguarded against the Saracens," begged the man. "Soon my companion will return with others and then I shall beg them to take thee where thou wilt."

"Very well," agreed the ape-man. They had not waited long before he heard the sound of hastening footsteps and a strange jingling and clanking that might have been caused by the shaking of many chains and the striking against them of objects of metal.

Shortly afterward he was surprised to see a white man clothed in chain mail and carrying a sword and buckler descending the trail at a trot, a dozen pikemen at his back.

"Tell them to halt!" commanded Tarzan, placing the point of the man's sword in the small of his back. "Tell them I would talk with them before they approach too closely."

"Stop, I pray thee!" cried the fellow. "This be a friend of Sir James, but he wilt run me through with my own sword an' ye press him too close. Parley with him, most noble sir knight, for I wouldst live at least to know the result of the Great Tourney."

The knight halted a few paces from Tarzan and looked him up and down from feet to head. "Thou art truly a friend to Sir James?" he demanded.

Tarzan nodded. "I have been seeking him for days."

"And some mishap befell thee and thou lost thy apparel."

The ape-man smiled. "I go thus, in the jungle," he said.

"Art thou a sir knight and from the same country as Sir James?"

"I am an Englishman," replied Tarzan of the Apes.

"An Englishman! Thrice welcome then to Nimmr! I be Sir Bertram and a good friend to Sir James."

"And I am called Tarzan," said the ape-man.

"And thy rank?" inquired Sir Bertram.

Tarzan was mystified by the strange manners and garb of his seemingly friendly inquisitor, but he sensed that whatever the man might be he took himself quite seriously and would be more impressed if he knew that Tarzan was a man of position, and so he answered him truthfully, in his quiet way.

"A Viscount," he said.

"A peer of the realm!" exclaimed Sir Bertram. "Prince Gobred will be o'er pleased to greet thee, Lord Tarzan. Come thou with me and I wilt furnish thee with apparel that befits thee."

At the outer barbican Bertram took Tarzan into the quarters reserved for the knight commanding the warders and kept him there while he sent his squire to the castle to fetch raiment and a horse, and while they waited Bertram told Tarzan all that had befallen Blake since his arrival in Nimmr and, too, much of the strange history of this unknown British colony.

When the squire returned with the clothing it was found that it fitted the ape-man well, for Bertram was a large man, and presently Tarzan of the Apes was garbed as a Knight of Nimmr and was riding down toward the castle with Sir Bertram. Here the knight announced him at the gate as the Lord Viscount Tarzan. Once within he introduced him to another knight whom he persuaded to relieve him at the gate while he conducted Tarzan to the lists that he might be presented to Gobred and witness the final scenes of the tourney, were it not concluded before they arrived.

And so it was that Tarzan of the Apes, clad in chain mail, and armed with lance and sword, rode down into the Valley of the Sepulcher just as Bohun put his foul scheme into execution and carried off the Princess Guinalda.

Long before they reached the lists Bertram was aware that something was amiss, for they could see the dust clouds racing rapidly north away from the lists as though one body of knights pursued another. He put spurs to his mount and Tarzan followed suit, and so they came at a stiff run to the lists and there they found all pandemonium.

The women were mounting preparatory to riding back to Nimmr under escort of a few knights that Gobred had sent back to guard them. The men-at-arms were forming themselves into companies, but all was being done in a confused manner since every now and then a great part of the company would rush to the highest part of the stands and peer off toward the north after the clouds of dust that revealed nothing to them.

Sir Bertram accosted one of his fellows. "What hath befallen?" he demanded

"Bohun hath seized the Princess Guinalda and carried her away," came the astounding reply.

"Zounds!" cried Bertram, reining about. "Wilt ride with me in the service of our princess, Lord Tarzan?"

For answer Tarzan spurred his horse alongside of Bertram's and stirrup to stirrup the two set out across the plain, while far ahead of them Blake drew gradually closer and closer to the fleeing Knights of the Sepulcher. So thick was the cloud of dust they threw up that they were hid from their pursuer even as he was hid from them and so were unaware that Blake was near them.

The American carried no lance nor shield, but his sword clattered and clashed at his side and at his right hip swung his forty-five. Whenever he had been armed, since he entered Nimmr, he had carried this weapon of another world and another age. To their queries he had answered that it was but a lucky talisman that he carried, but in his heart was the thought that some day it might stand him in better stead than these simple knights and ladies could dream.

He knew that he would never use it except in battle, or as a last resort against overwhelming odds or unfair tactics, but he was glad that he carried it today as it might mean the difference between liberty and captivity for the woman he loved.

Slowly he drew closer to the rearmost Knights of the Sepulcher. Their mounts bred and trained to the utmost endurance and to carry the great weight of man and mail kept to a brisk canter even after the first long spurt of speed that had carried them away from the lists of Nimmr.

The dust rolled up in clouds from iron-shod feet. Through it Blake groped, catching vague glimpses of mounted men just ahead. The black, powerful, fleet, courageous, showed no sign of fatigue. The rider carried his sword in his hand, ready. He was no longer a black knight, but a gray. Bassinet, hauberk, all the rich caparisons of his horse, the horse itself, were gray with dust.

Blake glimpsed a knight toward whom he was slowly drawing closer. This knight was gray! Like a flash Blake realized the value of the camouflage that chance had laid upon him. He might ride among them and they would not suspect that he was not of them!

Instantly he sheathed his sword and pressed forward, but he edged off a little from the knight before he passed him. Urging the black ever a little faster Blake crept up through the ranks of Bohun's knights. Somewhere a knight was carrying double and this knight he sought.

The nearer the head of the column he forged the greater became the danger of discovery, for now the dust was less thick and men could see farther, but yet his own armor, his face, the leopard skin of his bassinet were coated thick with gray and though knights peered intently at him as he passed none recognized him.

Once one hailed him. "Is't thou, Percival?" he demanded.

"Nay," replied Blake and spurred on a trifle faster.

Now, dimly, just ahead, he saw several knights bunched close and once he thought he glimpsed the fluttering garments of a woman in their midst. Pressing on, he drew close behind these and there, surrounded by knights, he saw a woman held before one of the riders.

Drawing his sword he spurred straight between two knights

who rode close behind he who carried Guinalda, and as Blake passed he cut to the right and left and the two knights rolled from their saddles.

At a touch of the spurs the black leaped abreast the young knight that was bearing off the princess. So quickly was the thing accomplished that the knights who rode scarce an arm's length from him had not the time to realize what was occurring and prevent it.

Blake slipped his left arm about the girl and at the same time thrust to the left above his left forearm, driving his blade far into the body of the youthful knight. Then he spurred forward carrying Guinalda from the dead arms as the knight pitched headlong from his saddle.

Blake's sword was wrenched from his grasp, so far had he driven it into the body of the man who dared commit this wrong against the woman Blake loved.

Cries of rage arose about him as knights spurred in pursuit and the black ran free with no guiding hand upon the reins. A huge fellow loomed just at Blake's rear and another was closing in from the other side. The first man swung his sword as he stood in his stirrups and the second was already reaching for Blake with his point.

Strange oaths were on their lips and their countenances were contorted with rage as they strove to have the life of the rash man who had almost thwarted them in their design, but that he could succeed they had not the remotest belief, for he was one against a thousand.

Then something happened the like of which had never been known to them or their progenitors. A blue barreled forty-five flashed from the holster at Blake's hip, there was a loud report and the knight upon Blake's right rear lunged head foremost to the ground. Blake turned in his saddle and shot the knight upon his other side between the eyes.

Terrified, the horses of the other knights close by, who might have menaced him, bolted, as did the great black that Blake bestrode; but while the American was trying to replace his weapon in its holster and gather the reins in his right hand he leaned to the left and thus forced the horse slowly around toward the direction he wished him to go, Blake's plan being to cut across the front of the Knights of the Sepulcher and then turn southward toward Nimmr.

He was sure that Gobred and his followers must be close in pursuit, and that it would be but a matter of minutes before he would have Guinalda safe behind a thousand or more knights, any one of whom would lay down his life for her.

But the Knights of the Sepulcher had spread out over a greater front than Blake had anticipated, and now he saw them coming rapidly upon his left and was forced to swerve in a more northerly direction.

Closer and closer they came and once more the American found it necessary to drop his reins and draw his forty-five. One shot sent the horses of the menacing knights rearing and plunging away from the terrifying sound, and it sent the black into a new paroxysm of terror that almost resulted in Blake and the girl being unhorsed.

When the man finally brought the animal again under control the dust cloud that marked the position of the Knights of the Sepulcher was far behind, and close upon Blake's left was a great forest, whose dark depths offered concealment for the moment at least.

Reining quickly within Sir James drew up and gently lowered Guinalda to the ground. Then he dismounted and tied the black to a tree, for Blake was spent after what he had been through this day since his first entry upon the lists, and the black was spent as well.

He slipped the housing and the heavy saddle from the horse's back and took the great bit from his mouth, replacing a portion of the housing to serve as a cooler until the horse should be less heated, nor once did he glance at the princess until he had finished caring for his horse.

Then he turned and faced her. She was standing leaning against a tree, looking at him.

"Thou art brave, sir knight," she said softly, and then added, arrogantly, "but still a boor."

Blake smiled, wanly. He was very tired and had no wish to argue.

"I'm sorry to ask you to do it," he said, ignoring what she had said to him, "but Sir Galahad here will have to be kept moving about a bit until he cools off and I'm too fagged to do it."

The Princess Guinalda looked at him in wide-eyed amazement. "Ye—ye," she stammered, "ye mean that I should lead the beast? I, a princess!"

"I can't do it, Guinalda," replied Blake. "I tell you I'm just about all in, lugging all these skid chains about since sunrise. I guess you'll have to do it."

"Have to! Durst thou command, knave?"

"Snap out of it girl!" advised Blake curtly. "I'm responsible for your safety and it may all depend on this horse. Get busy, and do as I tell you! Lead him back and forth slowly."

There were tears of rage in the eyes of the Princess Guinalda as she prepared to make an angry retort, but there was something in Blake's eyes that silenced her. She looked at him for a long moment and then turned and walked to the black. Untying the rope that tethered him to the tree she led him slowly to and fro, while Blake sat with his back against a great tree and watched out across the plain for the first sign of pursuit.

But there was no pursuit, for the knights of Nimmr had taken the Knights of the Sepulcher and the two forces were engaging in a running fight that was leading them farther and farther away toward the City of the Sepulcher upon the north side of the valley.

Guinalda led the black for half an hour. She led him in silence and in silence Blake sat gazing out across the valley. Presently he turned toward the girl and rose to his feet.

"That'll be good," he said, approaching her. "Thank you. I'll rub him a bit now. I was too exhausted to do it before."

Without a word she turned the black over to him and with dry leaves he rubbed the animal from muzzle to dock. When he had finished he threw the housing over him again and came and sat down beside the girl.

He let his eyes wander to her profile—to her straight nose, her short upper lip, her haughty chin. "She is beautiful," thought Blake, "but selfish, arrogant, and cruel." But when she turned her eyes toward him, even though they passed over him as though he had not been there, they seemed to belie all the other evidence against her.

He noticed that her eyes were never quiet. Her glances roved from place to place, but more often into the depths of the wood and upward among the branches of the trees. Once she started and turned suddenly to gaze intently into the forest.

"What is it?" asked Blake.

"Methought something moved within the wood," she said. "Let us be gone."

"It is almost dusk," he replied. "When it is dark we can ride to Nimmr in safety. Some of Bohun's knights may still be searching for you."

"What!" she exclaimed. "Remain here until dark? Knowest thou not where we be?"

"Why, what's wrong with this place?" demanded the man.

She leaned toward him, her eyes wide with terror. "It be the Wood of the Leopards!" she whispered.

"Yes?" he queried casually.

"Here lair the great leopards of Nimmr," she continued, "and after night falls only a camp with many guards and beast fires be safe from them. And even so not always then, for they have been known to leap upon a warder and, dragging him into the wood, devour him within hearing of the camp.

"But," suddenly her eyes responded to a new thought, "I hadst forgot the strange, roaring weapon with which thou slew the knights of Bohun! Of a surety with that thou couldst slay all the leopards of the wood!"

Blake hesitated to undeceive her and add to her alarm. "Perhaps," he said, "it will be as well to start now, for we have a long ride and it will soon be dark."

As he spoke he started toward Sir Galahad. He had almost reached the horse when the animal suddenly raised its head and with up-pricked ears and dilated nostrils looked into the gathering shadows of the wood. For an instant Sir Galahad trembled like a leaf and then, with a wild snort, he lay back with all his weight upon the tether, and as it parted with a snap he wheeled and raced out upon the plain.

Blake drew his gun and peered into the wood, but he saw nothing nor could his atrophied sense of smell catch the scent that had come so clearly to the nostrils of Sir Galahad.

Eyes that he could not see were watching him, but they were not the eyes of Sheeta the leopard.

20

"I Love You!"

LORD TARZAN RODE with Sir Bertram in the wake of the Knights of Nimmr, nor did they overtake them until after Blake had borne Guinalda out of the battle which had followed immediately the hosts of Gobred had overhauled the Knights of the Sepulcher.

As the two approached, Tarzan saw opposing knights paired off in mortal combat. He saw a Knight of Nimmr go down before an adversary's lance and then the victor espied Tarzan.

"Have at you, sir knight!" cried he of the Sepulcher, and couched his lance and put spurs to his charger.

This was a new experience for the ape-man, a new adventure, a new thrill. He knew as much about jousting as he did about ping-pong, but from childhood he had wielded a spear, and so he smiled as the knight charged upon him.

Lord Tarzan waited, and the Knight of the Sepulcher was disconcerted to see his adversary awaiting him, motionless, his spear not even couched to receive him.

Lord Bertram had reined in his horse to watch the combat

and observe how this English peer accounted for himself in battle and he too was perplexed. Was the man mad, or was he fearful of the issue?

As his antagonist approached him, Tarzan rose in his stirrups and carried his lance hand above and behind his head, and when the tip of the other's lance was yet five paces from him the ape-man launched the heavy weapon as he had so often launched his hunting spear and his war spear in the chase and in battle.

It was not Viscount Greystoke who faced the Knight of the Sepulcher; it was not the king of the great apes. It was the chief of the Waziri, and no other arm in the world could cast a war spear as could his.

Forward his spear hand shot, straight as an arrow sped the great lance. It struck the shield of the Knight of the Sepulcher just above the boss and, splitting the heavy wood, drove into the heart of Tarzan's foe, and at the same instant the ape-man reined his horse aside as that of his fallen antagonist thundered past.

Sir Bertram shook his head and spurred to meet an antagonist that had just challenged him. He was not sure that the act of Lord Tarzan had been entirely ethical, but he had to admit that it had been magnificent.

The fortunes of the battle carried Tarzan toward the west. His lance gone, he fought with his sword. Luck and his great strength and wondrous agility carried him through two encounters. By this time the battle had drawn off toward the northeast.

Tarzan had accounted for his second man since he had lost his lance and a Knight of the Sepulcher had slain a Knight of Nimmr. Now these two remained alone upon the field, nor did the other lose a moment in shouting his challenge to the ape-man.

Never in his life had Tarzan seen such fierce, bold men, such gluttons for battle. That they gloried in conflict and in death with a fierce lust that surpassed the maddest fanaticism he had ever witnessed filled Tarzan's breast with admiration. What men! What warriors!

Now the last knight was upon him. Their swords clashed on ready buckler. They wheeled and turned and struck again. They passed and spurred once more to close quarters. Each rose in his stirrups to deliver a terrified cut, each sought to cleave the other's skull.

The blade of the Knight of the Sepulcher glanced from Tarzan's buckler and bit into the skull of the ape-man's charger, but Tarzan's edge smote true.

As his horse went down Tarzan leaped free, his antagonist falling dead at his feet, while the riderless horse of the slain knight galloped swiftly off in the direction in which lay the City of the Sepulcher.

Tarzan looked about him. He was alone upon the field. Far to the north and east he saw the dust of battle. The City of Nimmr lay across the plain toward the south. When the battle was over it was there that Blake would ride and it was Blake whom Tarzan wanted to find. The sun was sinking behind the western hills as Tarzan turned toward Nimmr.

The chain mail that he wore was heavy, hot, and uncomfortable, and Tarzan had not gone far before he discarded it. He had his knife and his rope. These he always kept with him, but he left the sword with the armor and with a sigh of relief continued on his way.

Ibn Jad, as he had come across the valley from the City of the Sepulcher toward the city that he had seen upon the opposite side, had been perturbed by the great clouds of dust that had been raised by the Knights of the Sepulcher and the pursuing Nimmrians.

Seeing a forest close upon his right hand he had thought it wiser to seek its concealing shadows until he could learn more concerning that which caused so great a dust cloud, which he saw was rapidly approaching.

Within the forest it was cool and here Ibn Jad and his followers rested.

"Let us remain here," suggested Abd el-Aziz, "until evening, when we may approach the city under cover of darkness."

Ibn Jad approved the plan and so they camped just within

the forest and waited. They watched the dust cloud pass and continue on toward the City of the Sepulcher.

"Billah, it is well we did escape that village before yon host returned," said Ibn Jad.

They saw a horseman enter the forest, or pass to the south of it—they could not know which—but they were not interested in single horsemen, or in any horsemen, so they did not investigate. He seemed to be either carrying another person upon his horse with him, or some great bundle. At a distance they could not see which.

"Perhaps," said Abd el-Aziz, "we shall find greater treasure in the city to the south."

"And perhaps the beautiful woman of whom the sahar spoke," added Ibn Jad, "for she was not within the city we left this morning."

"There were some there that were beautiful," said Fahd.

"The one I seek is more beautiful than an houri," said Ibn Jad.

When they took up their march again, just before dark they moved cautiously just within the edge of the forest. They had covered a mile, perhaps, when those in the lead heard voices ahead. Ibn Jad sent one to investigate.

The man was soon back. His eyes were bright with excitement. "Ibn Jad," he whispered, "thou needest seek no farther—the houri is just ahead!"

Following the suggestion of the scout Ibn Jad, followed by his companions, went deeper into the woods and approached Blake and Guinalda from the west. When Sir Galahad broke loose and Blake drew his forty-five Ibn Jad knew that they could remain in concealment no longer. He called Fahd to him.

"Many of the Nasranys speak the language thou didst learn among the soldiers of the North," he said. "Speak thou therefore to this one in the same tongue, telling him we are friends and that we are lost."

When Fahd saw the Princess Guinalda his eyes narrowed and he trembled almost as might a man with ague. Never in his life had Fahd seen so beautiful a woman, never had he dreamed that an houri might be so lovely.

"Do not fire upon us," he called to Blake from the conceal-ment of some bushes. "We are friends. We are lost."

"Who are you?" demanded Blake, surprised to hear French spoken in the Valley of the Sepulcher.

"We be poor men from the desert country," replied Fahd. "We are lost. Help us to find our way and the blessings of Allah shall be upon thee."

"Come out and let me see you," said Blake. "If you are friendly you need not fear me. I've had all the trouble I'm looking for."

Fahd and Ibn Jad stepped out into view and at sight of them Guinalda voiced a little scream and seized Blake's arm. "The Saracens!" she gasped.

"I guess they're Saracens all right," said Blake, "but you needn't worry—they won't hurt you."

"Not harm a crusader?" she demanded incredulously.

"These fellows never heard of a crusader."

"Melikes not the way they look at me," whispered Guinalda.

"Well, neither do I, but perhaps they mean no harm."

With many smiles the Arabs gathered around the two and through Fahd Ibn Jad repeated his protestations of friendship and his delight at meeting one who could direct him from the valley. He asked many questions about the City of Nimmr; and all the while his followers pressed closer to Blake.

Of a sudden the smiles vanished from their faces as, at a signal from their sheik, four stalwart Beduins leaped upon the American and bore him to the ground, snatching his gun from him, while simultaneously two others seized the Princess Guinalda.

In a moment Blake was securely bound and the 'Aarab were debating what disposition to make of him. Several wanted to slit his throat, but Ibn Jad counseled against it since they were in a valley filled with the man's friends and should the fortunes of war decide to throw some of the Beduins into the hands of the enemy such would fare better if they spared this one's life.

Blake threatened, promised, begged that they give Guinalda her liberty, but Fahd only laughed at him and spit upon him. For a time it seemed almost certain that they were going to kill

Blake, as one of the Beduins stood over him with a keen khusa in his hand, awaiting the word from Ibn Jad.

It was then that Guinalda tore free from those who held her and threw herself upon Blake to shield his body from the blade with her own.

"Thou shalt not slay him!" she cried. "Take my life an' thou must have Christian blood, but spare him."

"They cannot understand you, Guinalda," said Blake. "Perhaps they will not kill me, but that does not matter. You must escape them."

"Oh, they must not kill thee—they shall not! Canst ever forgive me the cruel words I spoke? I did not mean them. My pride was hurt that thou shouldst say of me what Malud told me thou didst say and so I spoke to hurt thee and not from my heart. Canst forgive me?"

"Forgive you? God love you, I could forgive you murder! But what did Malud tell you I had said?"

"Oh, mind not now. I care not what thou said. I tell thee I forgive it! Say to me again thy words that thou didst speak when I pinned my favor upon thy hauberk and I can forgive thee anything."

"What did Malud say?" insisted Blake.

"That thou hadst bragged that thou wouldst win me and then cast my love aside," she whispered.

"The cur! You must know that he lied, Guinalda."

"Say what I have asked and I shall know he lied," she insisted.

"I love you! I love you, Guinalda!" cried Blake.

The Arabs laid heavy hands upon the girl and dragged her to her feet. Ibn Jad and the others still argued about the disposition to be made of Blake.

"By Ullah!" exclaimed the sheik, at last, "we shall leave the Nasrany where he lies and if he dies none can say that the Beduw did slay him.

"Abd el-Aziz," he continued, "let thou take men and continue across the valley to that other city. Come, I shall accompany you a way and we will talk out of hearing of this Nasrany who, perchance, understandeth more of our tongue than he would have us guess."

As they moved away toward the south Guinalda tried to free herself again from the grasp of her captors, but they dragged her with them. Until the last Blake saw her struggling and saw her dear face turned toward him, and as they passed out of sight among the trees she called back through the falling night three words that meant more to him than all the languages of all the world combined: "I love you!"

At a distance from Blake the 'Aarab halted. "I leave thee here, Abd el-Aziz," said Ibn Jad. "Go thou and see if the city appears to be a rich place, and if it be too strongly guarded make no attempt to loot it, but return to the menzil that will be just beyond the northern summit where it now is, or, if we move it, we shall make our trail plain that you may follow us.

"I shall hasten from the valley with this rich treasure that we now have, not the least of which is the woman. Billah! in the north she will fetch the ransom of a dozen sheykh.

"Go, Abd el-Aziz, and may Allah be with thee!"

Ibn Jad turned directly north. His belief that the great body of horsemen he had glimpsed amid the distant dust were returning to the city he had sacked argued against his attempting to leave the valley by the same route that he had entered it, and so he had determined to attempt to scale the steep mountains at a point west of the City of the Sepulcher, avoiding the castle and its defenders entirely.

Blake heard the retreating footsteps of the Beduins die away in the distance. He struggled with his bonds, but the camel leather held securely. Then he lay quiet. How silent, how lonely the great, black wood—the Wood of the Leopards! Blake listened. Momentarily he expected to hear the fall of padded feet, the sound of a great, furred body approaching through the underbrush. The slow minutes dragged. An hour had passed.

The moon rose—a great, swollen, red moon that floated silently up from behind distant mountains. This moon was looking down upon Guinalda as it was on him. He whispered a message to it—a message for his princess. It was the first time that Blake ever had been in love and he almost forgot his bonds and the leopards in recalling those three words that Guinalda had called back at the instant of their separation.

What was that? Blake strained his eyes into the darkness of the shadowy wood. Something was moving! Yes, it was the sound of stealthy, padded feet—the scraping of a furred body against leaves and twigs. The leopard of the wood was coming!

Hark! There must be another in a nearby tree, for he was sure that he could see a shadowy form almost above him.

The moonlight, shining from the low moon near the eastern horizon, crept beneath the trees and lighted the ground upon which Blake lay and beyond him for a dozen yards and more.

Presently into this moonlit space stepped a great leopard.

Blake saw the blazing eyes, felt them burning into him like fire. He could not tear his own from the great snarling figure, where they were held in awful fascination.

The carnivore crouched and crept closer. Inch by inch it crept upon him as though with the studied cruelty of premeditated torture. He saw the sinuous tail lashing from side to side. He saw the great fangs bared. He saw the beast flatten against the ground, its muscles tensed. It was about to spring! Helpless, horrified, Blake could not take his eyes from the hideous, snarling face.

He saw it leap suddenly with the lightness and agility of a house cat, and at the same instant he saw something flash through the air. The leopard stopped in mid-leap and was hauled upward into a tree that overhung the spot.

He saw the shadowy form that he had seen before, but now he saw that it was a man and that he was hauling the leopard upward by a rope that had been cast about its neck at the instant that it had risen to leap upon him.

Screaming, pawing with raking talons, Sheeta the leopard was dragged upward. A mighty hand reached out and grasped the great cat by the scruff of the neck and another hand drove a knife blade into the savage heart.

When Sheeta ceased to struggle, and hung quiet, the hand

released its grasp and the dead body of the carnivore thudded to the ground beside Blake. Then the godlike figure of an almost naked white man dropped lightly to the leafy mold.

Blake voiced an exclamation of surprised delight. "Tarzan of the Apes!" he cried.

"Blake?" demanded the ape-man, and then: "At last! And I didn't find you much too soon, either."

"I'll tell the world you didn't!" exclaimed Blake.

Tarzan cut the bonds that held the American.

"You've been looking for me?" asked Blake.

"Ever since I learned that you had become separated from your safari."

"By George, that was white of you!"

"Who left you trussed up here?"

"A bunch of Arabs."

Something like a growl escaped the lips of the ape-man. "That villainous old Ibn Jad here?" he demanded incredulously.

"They took a girl who was with me," said Blake. "I do not need to ask you to help me rescue her, I know."

"Which way did they go?" asked Tarzan.

"There." Blake pointed toward the south.

"When?"

"About an hour ago."

"You'd better shed that armor," advised Tarzan, "it makes walking a punishment—I just tried it."

With the ape-man's help Blake got out of his coat of mail and then the two set out upon the plain trail of the Arabs. At the point where Ibn Jad had turned back toward the north they were at a loss to know which of the two spoors to follow, for here the footprints of Guinalda, that the ape-man had been able to pick up from time to time since they left the spot where the girl had been seized, disappeared entirely.

They wondered what had become of them. They could not know that here, when she found that Ibn Jad was going to turn back with her away from Nimmr, she had refused to walk farther. It had been all right as long as they were approaching

Nimmr, but she refused absolutely to be a party to her own abduction when it led away from home.

What breeze there was was blowing from the east, nullifying the value of Tarzan's sense of smell so that even the great ape-man could not know in what direction or with which party Guinalda had been carried off.

"The most reasonable assumption," said Tarzan, "is that your princess is with the party that has gone north, for I know that Ibn Jad's menzil must lay in that direction. He did not enter the valley from the south. That I know because I just came in that way myself and Sir Bertram assured me that there are only two entrances—the one through which I came and a pass above the City of the Sepulcher.

"Ibn Jad would want to get the girl out of the valley and into his camp as soon as possible whether he is going to hold her for ransom or take her north to sell her. The party that went south toward Nimmr may have been sent to treat with her people for a ransom; but the chances are that she is not with that party.

"However, it is at best but a matter of conjecture. We must ascertain definitely, and I suggest that you follow the northern spoor, which is, I am certain, the one that will lead to the girl, while I overtake the party to the south.

"I can travel faster than you and if I am right and the girl is with the northern party I'll turn back and overtake you without much loss of time. If you catch up with the other band and find the girl is not with them, you can turn back and join me; but if she is with them you'd better not risk trying to recover her until you have help, for you are unarmed and those Beduins would think no more of cutting your throat than they would of drinking a cup of coffee.

"Now, good-bye and good luck!" And Tarzan of the Apes was off at a trot upon the trail of the party that had gone in the direction of Nimmr, while Blake turned northward to face a dismal journey through the black depths of the Wood of the Leopards.

21

"For Every Jewel
a Drop of Blood!"

ALL NIGHT IBN Jad and his party marched northward. Though they were hampered by the refusal of Guinalda to walk, yet they made rapid progress for they were spurred on by their great desire to escape from the valley with their booty before they should be discovered and set upon by the great host of fighting men they were now convinced were quartered in the castle and city they had been fortunate enough to find almost deserted.

Avarice gave them strength and endurance far beyond that which they normally displayed, with the result that dawn found them at the foot of the ragged mountains that Ibn Jad had determined to scale rather than attempt an assault upon the castle which guarded the easy way from the valley.

It was a jaded party that won eventually to the pass just above the outer barbican that guarded the road to the City of the Sepulcher, nor were they discovered by the warders there until the last man of them was safely on the trail leading to the low saddle at the summit of the mountains, beyond which lay the menzil of the Beduins.

The defenders of the barbican made a sortie against them and approached their rear so closely that the knight who commanded saw Guinalda and recognized her, but a volley from the matchlocks of the desert people sent the crudely armed soldiers of Bohun back in retreat, though the brave knight couched his lance and charged again until his horse was brought down by a bullet and he lay pinned beneath it.

It was afternoon before Ibn Jad with his fagged company staggered into the menzil. Though they dropped in their tracks from sheer exhaustion, he allowed them but an hour of sleep before he gave the signal for the rahla, for the sheik of the fendy el-Guad was filled with an ever increasing fear that the treasure and the woman would be taken away from him before he could reach the sandy wastes of his own barren beled.

The heavy weight of the treasure had been divided into several bundles and these were distributed among his least mistrusted followers, while the custody of the girl captive was placed in the hands of Fahd, whose evil eyes filled the princess with fear and loathing.

Stimbol, who had secretly scoffed at the stories of treasure and the mad tales of a beautiful woman that the 'Aarab expected to find in some fabulous, hidden city, was dumbfounded when he viewed the spoils of the Beduin, and at first was inclined to attribute them to the hallucinations of his fever-wracked brain.

Weak, Stimbol staggered feebly along the trail, keeping as close to Fahd as he could, for he knew that of all the company this unscrupulous scoundrel would be most likely to assist him, for to Fahd a live Stimbol meant great wealth; nor was Fahd unmindful of the fact. And now there was another purpose in the evil mind of the Beduin who had conceived for the white girl an infatuation that was driving him to the verge of madness.

With the wealth that Stimbol had promised him Fadh realized that he could afford to possess this lovely houri whom otherwise a poor Beduwy must sell for the great price that she would bring, and so there revolved in the mind of Fahd many schemes whereby he might hope to gain sole possession of both Guinalda and Stimbol; but always there loomed in the path of every plan that he considered the dour figure of his greedy sheik.

At the foot of the Mountains of the Sepulcher Ibn Jad turned toward the east, thus to avoid passing again through the country of Batando. Beyond the eastern end of the range he would turn south again and later strike west just above the northern limits of the territory that was nominally Tarzan's, for though he knew that the Lord of the Jungle was dead he yet feared the vengeance of his people.

It was late before Ibn Jad made camp. The preparations for the evening meal were hurried. The light from the cooking fire and the paper lanterns in the beyt of the sheik was dim and flickering, yet not so dim but that Ateja saw Fahd drop something into the bowl of food that she had prepared for Ibn Jad and which stood upon the ground between him and his would-be assassin.

As the sheik reached for the receptacle Ateja stepped from the women's quarters and struck it from his hand, but before she could explain her act or charge Fahd with his villainy the culprit, realizing that his perfidy had been discovered, leaped to his feet and seizing his matchlock sprang into the women's quarters where Guinalda had been left under the watchful care of Hirfa and Ateja.

Seizing the girl by the wrist and dragging her after him Fahd broke through the curtains at the rear of the beyt and ran in the direction of his own tent. By this time the mukaad of Ibn Jad was in an uproar. The sheik was demanding an explanation from Ateja, still unaware that Fahd had escaped through the rear of the beyt; no one had followed him into the women's quarters.

"He placed *simm* in thy food!" cried Ateja. "I saw him and the proof of it be that he fled when he knew that I had seen."

"Billah," exclaimed Ibn Jad. "The son of a jackal would poison me? Seize him and fetch him to me!"

"He hath fled through the beyt!" cried Hirfa, "and taken the Nasrawia with him."

The Beduins sprang to their feet and took after Fahd, but at his own beyt he stopped them with a bullet and they retreated. In his tent he seized Stimbol who was lying upon a filthy sleeping mat and dragged him to his feet.

"Hasten!" he hissed in the American's ear. "Ibn Jad has

ordered that thou be slain! Quick! follow me and I will save thee."

Again Fahd had recourse to the rear curtains of a beyt and as his fellows approached the front in anger but with caution, Fahd, dragging Guinalda and followed by Stimbol, sneaked through the darkness of the menzil and turned toward the west.

It was dusk when James Blake, following the plain trail of Ibn Jad, finally clambered over the last escarpment and stood upon the trail that led through the pass toward the outer world beyond the valley of the Sepulcher.

A hundred yards to his right loomed the gray towers of the barbican, to his left was the trail that led in the direction of his heart's desire, and all about him, concealed in the bushes, were the men-at-arms of King Bohun of the Sepulcher; but this he did not guess, for how could he know that for hours the eyes of the warders had been watching his slow ascent toward the pass trail?

Spent by the long climb following hours of gruelling exertion without food or rest, unarmed, Blake was helpless to resist or to attempt escape when a dozen armed men stepped from the surrounding bushes and encircled him in a band of steel. And so Sir James of Nimmr was seized and hauled before King Bohun, and when he was questioned and Bohun found that he was the same black knight that had thwarted his plan to abduct the Princess Guinalda he could scarce contain himself.

Assuring Blake only of the fact that he would be put to death as soon as Bohun could determine upon a fate commensurate with the heinousness of the crime, the king ordered him to be placed in chains, and the American was led away by guards to a black hole beneath the castle, where by the light of flares a smith forged a heavy iron band about one ankle and he was chained to a damp stone wall.

In the light of the flare Blake saw two emaciated, naked creatures similarly chained, and in a far corner glimpsed a skeleton among the bones of which rusted a length of chain and a great anklet. Then silently the guards and the smith departed, taking the flares with them, and James Blake was left in darkness and despair.

Upon the plain, below the City of Nimmr, Tarzan had overtaken the party of Beduins led by Abd el-Aziz, and after assuring himself that the girl was not with them he had turned without revealing himself to them and hurried northward to take up the trail of the other party.

Requiring food and rest he lay up in the Wood of the Leopards during the heat of the day after stalking Horta the boar and making a quick kill. His belly filled, the ape-man found a high flung tree crotch where there was little likelihood of the heavy leopards of Nimmr disturbing his slumbers, and here he slept until the sun was sinking behind the western menzil where Ibn Jad's people had camped during his incursion of the Valley of the Sepulcher.

Some time since, he had lost the spoor of Blake, but that of the girl frequently recurred, and as her rescue now took precedence over other considerations he followed doggedly along the trail of Ibn Jad. For a time he was mystified by the fact that Guinalda's spoor, well marked by the imprints of the tiny sandals of medieval design, did not appear among the footprints of those who left the Beduin menzil.

He lost some time searching about in an effort to discover a clue to the riddle and presently he hit upon the truth, which lay in the fact that Guinalda's light sandals having been badly worn by her journey and far too tight for comfortable walking she had been given a pair belonging to Ateja, and thus it became difficult to differentiate between the spoor of the two girls, who were of equal weight and of a similarity of carriage that rendered their footprints practically identical.

Tarzan therefore contented himself with following the spoor of the party, and so it was that he passed their first night's camp, where Fahd had stolen Guinalda from the Sheik, without discovering that three of its members had there turned to the west, while the main body of the 'Aarab marched toward the east.

And as Tarzan followed the spoor of Ibn Jad a hundred stalwart Waziri moved northward from the water hole of the smooth, round rocks upon the old trail of the Beduins. With them was Zeyd, who had begged so hard to accompany them when they passed the village where he had been waiting that at last the sub-chief had consented.

When Tarzan overtook the 'Aarab they had already turned south around the eastern end of the Mountains of the Sepulcher. He saw the bags they carried and the evident concern with which Ibn Jad watched and guarded them, and he shrewdly guessed that the wily old thief had indeed found the treasure he had sought; but he saw no evidence of the presence of the Princess, and Stimbol, too, was missing.

Tarzan was furious. He was furious at the thieving Beduins for daring to invade his country and he was furious at himself because he felt that in some way he had been tricked.

Tarzan had his own methods of inflicting punishment upon his enemies and he had, as well, his own grim and grisly sense of humor. When men were doing wrong it pleased him to take advantage of whatever might cause them the greatest suffering and in this he was utterly ruthless with his enemies.

He was confident that the 'Aarab thought him dead and it did not suit his whim to reveal their error to them at this time, but it did accord with his fancy to let them commence to feel the weight of his displeasure and taste the first fruits of their villainy.

Moving silently through the trees Tarzan paralleled the course of the 'Aarab. They were often plainly visible to him; but none saw Tarzan, nor dreamed that savage eyes were watching their every move.

Five men carried the treasure, though its weight was not so great but that one powerful man might have borne it for a short distance. Tarzan watched these men most often, these and the Sheik Ibn Jad.

The trail was wide and the sheik walked beside one of those who bore the treasure. It was very quiet in the jungle. Even the 'Aarab, garrulous among themselves, were quiet, for they were very tired and the day was hot and they were unused to the burdens they were forced to carry since Batando had robbed them of their slaves.

Of a sudden, without warning and with only the swish of its flight through the air to announce it, an arrow passed through the neck of the Beduin who walked beside Ibn Jad.

With a scream the man lunged forward upon his face and the 'Aarab, warned by their sheik, cocked their muskets and prepared to receive an attack, but look where they would they saw no sign of an enemy. They waited, listening, but there was no sound other than the droning of insects and the occasional raucous cry of a bird; but when they moved on again, leaving their fellow dead upon the trail, a hollow voice called to them from a distance.

"For every jewel a drop of blood!" it wailed dismally, for its author knew well the intensely superstitious nature of the desert dwellers and how best to affright them.

It was a shaken column that continued on its way, nor was there any mention of making camp until almost sunset, so anxious were they all to leave behind this gloomy wood and the horrid afrit that inhabited it; but the forest persisted and at length it became necessary to make camp.

Here the campfires and food relieved the tension upon their overwrought nerves, and their spirits had revived to such an extent that there were again singing and laughter in the menzil of Ibn Jad.

The old sheik himself sat in his mukaad surrounded by the five bags of treasure, one of which he had opened and beneath the light of a lantern was fondling the contents. About him were his cronies, sipping their coffee.

Suddenly something fell heavily upon the ground before the beyt and rolled into the mukaad among them. It was the severed head of a man! Glaring up at them were the dead eyes of their fellow, whose corpse they had left lying in the trail earlier in the day.

Horror-struck, spellbound, they sat staring at the gruesome thing when, from out of the dark forest, came the hollow voice again: *"For every jewel a drop of blood!"*

Ibn Jad shook as a man with ague. The men of the camp gathered close together in front of the beyt of the sheik. Each grasped a musket in one hand and searched for his hijab with the other, for each carried several of these amulets, and that in demand this night was the one written against the jin, for certainly none but a jin could have done this thing.

Hirfa stood half within the mukaad staring at the dead face of her fellow while Ateja crouched upon a sleeping mat in the quarters of the women. She did not see the back curtain rise, nor the figure that crept within. It was dark in the quarters of the harem since little light filtered in from the lanterns in the mukaad.

Ateja felt a hand clapped across her mouth at the same instant that another grasped her by the shoulder. A voice whispered in her ear. "Make no sound! I shall not hurt thee. I am a friend to Zeyd. Tell me the truth and no harm will befall you or him. Where is the woman Ibn Jad brought from the valley?"

He who held her placed his ear close to her lips and removed his hand from them. Ateja trembled like a leaf. She had never seen a jin. She could not see the creature that leaned close to her, but she knew that it was one of those fearsome creatures of the night.

"Answer!" whispered the voice in her ear. "If thou wouldst save Zeyd, speak and speak the truth!"

"Fahd took the woman from our menzil last night," she gasped. "I do not know where they went."

As it came, in silence the presence left the side of the terrified girl. When Hirfa sought her a moment later she found her in a swoon.

22

Bride of the Ape

BLAKE SQUATTED UPON the stone floor in the utter darkness of his dungeon. After his jailers had left he had spoken to his fellow prisoners, but only one had replied and his jibbering tones assured the American that the poor wretch had been reduced to stark insanity by the horrors of imprisonment in this foul hole.

The young man, accustomed to freedom, light, activity, already felt the hideousness of his position and wondered how long it would be before he, too, jibbered incoherently at the end of a rusting chain, how long before he, too, was but mildewed bones upon a clammy floor.

In utter darkness and in utter silence there is no time, for there is no means by which one may compute the passage of time. How long Blake crouched in the stifling air of his dank dungeon he could not know. He slept once, but whether he had dozed for an instant or slept the clock around he could not even hazard a guess. And of what moment was it? A second, a day, a year meant nothing here. There were only two things that could mean anything to Jim Blake now—freedom or death. He knew that it would not be long before he would welcome the latter.

A sound disturbed the silence of the buried vault. Footsteps were approaching. Blake listened as they came nearer. Presently he discerned a flickering light that grew in intensity until a pine torch illuminated the interior of his prison. At first it blinded his eyes so that he could not see who came, bearing the light, but whoever it was crossed and stopped before him.

Blake looked up, his eyes more accustomed to the unwonted brilliance, and saw two knights standing before him.

"It be he," said one.

"Dost thou not know us, Sir Black Knight?" demanded the other.

Blake looked at them closely. A slow smile lighted his face, as he saw a great bandage wrapped about the neck of the younger man.

"I suppose," he said, "here is where I get mine."

"Get thine! What meanest thou?" demanded the older man.

"Well, you two certainly haven't come to pin any medals on me, Sir Wildred," said Blake, with a wry smile.

"Thou speakest in riddles," said Wildred. "We have come to free thee that the young king may not bring disgrace upon the Knights of the Sepulcher by carrying out his wicked will with thee. Sir Guy and I heard that he would burn thee at the stake, and we said to one another that while blood flowed in our bodies we would not let so valorous a knight be thus shamelessly wronged by any tyrant."

As he spoke Wildred stooped and with a great rasp commenced filing upon the iron rivets that held the hinged anklet in place.

"You are going to help me to escape!" exclaimed Blake. "But suppose you are discovered—will not the king punish you?"

"We shall not be discovered," said Wildred, "though I would take that chance for so noble a knight as thee. Sir Guy be upon the outer barbican this night and 'twill be no trick to get thee that far. He can pass thee through and thou canst make thy way down the mountainside and cross to Nimmr. We cannot get thee through the city gates for these be held by two of Bohun's basest creatures, but perchance upon the morrow Sir Guy or I may find the way to ride out upon the plain with a led horse, and that we shall if so it hap that it be possible."

"Tell us a thing that hath filled us with questioning," said Sir Guy.

"I don't follow you," said Blake.

"Thou didst, and mighty prettily too, take the Princess Guinalda from under the very nose of Bohun," continued Guy, "and yet later she was seen in the clutches of the Saracens. How came this to pass?"

"She was seen?" demanded Blake. "Where?"

"Beyond the outer barbican she was and the Saracens carried her away through the pass that leadeth no man knoweth where," said Wildred.

Blake told them of all that had transpired since he had taken Guinalda from Bohun, and by the time he had finished the rivets had been cut and he stood again a free man.

Wildred smuggled him through secret passages to his own quarters and there gave him food and new clothing and a suit of armor, for now that they knew he was riding out over the pass into the strange country they had decided that he could only be permitted to do so properly armored, armed, and mounted.

It was midnight when Wildred smuggled Blake through the castle gate and rode with him toward the outer barbican. Here Sir Guy met them and a few minutes later Blake bid these chivalrous enemies good-bye and, mounted on a powerful charger, his own colors flying from his lance tip, rode beneath the portcullis and out upon the starlit road that led to the summit of the Mountains of the Sepulcher.

Toyat, the king ape, picked a succulent beetle from the decaying bark of a fallen tree. About him were the great, savage people of his tribe. It was afternoon and the apes loafed in the shade of great trees beside a little natural clearing in the jungle. They were content and at peace with all the world.

Coming toward them were three people, but the wind blew from the apes toward the people and so neither Toyat nor any of his fellows caught the scent spoor of the Tarmangani. The jungle trail was soft with damp mold, for it had rained the night before, and the feet of the three gave forth no sound that the apes heard. Then, too, the three were moving cautiously for they had not eaten for two days and they were hunting for food.

There was a gray old man, emaciated by fever, tottering along with the aid of a broken tree branch; there was a wicked-eyed Beduin carrying a long musket; and the third was a girl whose strange garments of splendid stuffs were torn and soiled. Her face was streaked with dirt and was drawn and thin, yet still it was a face of almost heavenly beauty. She walked with an effort, and though she sometimes stumbled from weariness never did she lose a certain regalness of carriage, nor lower the haughty elevation of her well moulded chin.

The Beduin was in the lead. It was he who first sighted a young ape playing at the edge of the clearing, farthest from the great bulls of the tribe of Toyat. Here was food! The Beduin raised his ancient weapon and took aim. He pressed the trigger and the ensuing roar mingled with the scream of pain and terror that burst from the wounded balu.

Instantly the great bulls leaped to action. Would they flee the feared and hated thunder stick of the Tarmangani, or would they avenge the hurting of the balu? Who might know? Today they might do the one, tomorrow, under identical circumstances, the other. Today they chose vengeance.

Led by Toyat, growling hideously, the bulls lumbered forward to investigate. It was this sight that met the horrified gaze of the three as they followed up Fahd's shot to learn if at last they were to eat or if they must plod on hopelessly, weakened by the hunger gnawing at their vitals.

Fahd and Stimbol turned and bolted back down the trail, the Arab, in his cowardly haste, pushing Guinalda to one side and hurling her to the ground. The leading bull, seeing the girl, leaped upon her and was about to sink his teeth into her neck when Toyat seized him and dragged him from her, for Toyat had recognized her for what she was. The king ape had once seen another Tarmangani she and had decided that he would like to have one as a wife.

The other ape, a huge bull, seeing that Toyat wanted the prey and angered by the bullying manner of the king, immediately decided to contest Toyat's right to what he had first claimed. Baring his fangs he advanced menacingly toward Toyat who had dragged the girl back into the clearing.

Toyat snarled back at him. "Go away," said Toyat. "This is Toyat's she."

"It is Go-yad's," replied the other, advancing.

Toyat turned back. "I kill!" he screamed.

Go-yad came on and suddenly Toyat seized Guinalda in his hairy arms and fled into the jungle. Behind him, bellowing and screaming, pursued Go-yad.

The Princess Guinalda, wide-eyed with horror, fought to free herself from the hideous, hairy creature that was bearing her off. She had never seen nor even heard of such a thing as a great ape, and she thought them now some hideous, low inhabitant of that outer world that she had always been taught consisted of encircling armies of Saracens and beyond and at a great distance a wonderful country known as England. What else was there she had not even tried to guess, but evidently it was a horrid place peopled by hideous creatures, including dragons.

Toyat had run no great distance when he realized that he could not escape while burdened with the she, and as he had no mind to give her up he turned suddenly and faced the roaring Go-yad. Go-yad did not stop. He came on frothing at the mouth, bristling, snarling—a picture of bestial savagery, power, and frenzied rage.

Toyat, relinquishing his hold upon the girl, advanced to meet the charge of his rebellious subject, while Guinalda, weakened by unaccustomed exertion and lack of nourishment, appalled by the hideous circumstances of her plight, sank panting to the ground.

Toyat and Go-yad, immersed in the prospect of battle, were oblivious to all else. Could Guinalda have taken advantage of this temporary forgetfulness of her she might have escaped; but she was too stunned, too exhausted to take advantage of her opportunity. Spellbound, fascinated by the horror of it, she watched these terrifying, primordial man-beasts preparing to battle for possession of her.

Nor was Guinalda the sole witness of these savage preliminaries. From the concealment of a low bush behind which he lay another watched the scene with steady, interested eyes.

Absorbed by their own passion neither Toyat nor Go-yad noted the occasional movement of the outer leaves of the bush behind which this other watcher lay, a movement imparted by the body of the watcher with each breath and with each slightest change of position.

Perhaps the watcher discovered no sporting interest in the impending duel, for just as the two apes were about to engage he arose and stepped into the open—a great black-maned lion, whose yellow coat gleamed golden in the sunlight.

Toyat saw him first and with a growl of rage turned and fled, leaving his adversary and their prize to whatever fate Providence might hold in store for them.

Go-yad, thinking his rival had abandoned the field through fear of him, beat loudly upon his breast and roared forth the victory cry of the bull ape, then, swaggering as became a victor and a champion, he turned to claim the prize.

Between himself and the girl he saw the lion standing, gazing with serious mien straight into his eyes. Go-yad halted. Who would not have? The lion was within springing distance but he was not crouched. Go-yad backed away, snarling, and when the lion made no move to follow, the great ape suddenly turned and lumbered off into the jungle, casting many a backward glance in the direction of the great cat until intervening foliage shut him from his view.

Then the lion turned toward the girl. Poor little Princess! Hopeless, resigned, she lay upon the ground staring, wide-eyed, at this new engine of torture and destruction. The king of beasts surveyed her for a moment and then walked toward her. Guinalda clasped her hands and prayed—not for life, for hope of that she had long since resigned, but for death, speedy and painless.

The tawny beast came close. Guinalda closed her eyes to shut out the fearsome sight. She felt hot breath upon her cheek, its fetid odor assailed her nostrils. The lion sniffed about her. God! why did he not end it? Tortured nerves could endure no more and Guinalda swooned. Merciful surcease of her suffering.

23

Jad-bal-ja

NERVE SHAKEN, THE remnants of Ibn Jad's company turned toward the west and hastened by forced marches to escape the hideous forest of the jin. Abd el-Aziz and those who had accompanied him from the Wood of the Leopards toward Nimmr had not rejoined them. Nor ever would they, for upon the plain below the treasure city of the Beduins' dreaming the knights of Gobred had discovered them and, despite the thundering havoc of the ancient matchlocks, the iron Knights of Nimmr had couched their spears against the Saracens and once again the victorious cri de guerre of the Crusaders had rung out after seven centuries of silence to announce a new engagement in the hoary war for the possession of the Holy Land—the war that is without end.

From the north a mailed knight rode down through the forest of Galla land. A blue and silver pennon fluttered from his lance. The housings of his great charger were rich with gold and silver from the treasure vaults of Wildred of the Sepulcher, Wide-eyed Galla warriors viewed this solitary anachronism from afar, and fled.

Tarzan of the Apes, ranging westward, came upon the spoor of Fahd and Stimbol and Guinalda and followed it toward the south.

Northward marched a hundred ebon giants, veterans of a hundred battles—the famed Waziri—and with them came Zeyd, the lover of Ateja. One day they came upon a fresh spoor crossing their line of march diagonally toward the southwest. It was the spoor of Arab sandals, those of two men and a woman, and when the Waziri pointed them out to Zeyd the young Beduin swore that he recognized those of the woman as belonging to Ateja, for who knew better the shape and size of her little foot, or the style of the sandals she fabricated? He begged the Waziri to turn aside for a time and aid him in finding his sweetheart, and while the subchief was debating the question in his mind the sound of something hurrying through the jungle attracted the attention of every ear.

While they listened a man staggered into view. It was Fahd. Zeyd recognized him instantly and as immediately became doubly positive that the footprints of the woman had been made by Ateja.

Zeyd approached Fahd menacingly. "Where is Ateja?" he demanded.

"How should I know? I have not seen her for days," replied Fahd, truthfully enough.

"Thou liest!" cried Zeyd, and pointed at the ground. "Here are her own footprints beside thine!"

A cunning expression came into the eyes of Fahd. Here he saw an opportunity to cause suffering to the man he hated. He shrugged his shoulders.

"Wellah, if you know, you know," he said.

"Where is she?" demanded Zeyd.

"She is dead. I would have spared you," answered Fahd.

"Dead?" The suffering in that single word should have melted a heart of stone—but not Fahd's.

"I stole her from her father's beyt," continued Fahd, wishing to inflict as much torture as possible upon his rival. "For days and nights she was mine; then a huge ape stole her from me. By now she must be dead."

But Fahd had gone too far. He had encompassed his own undoing. With a scream of rage Zeyd leaped upon him with drawn khusa, and before the Waziri could interfere or Fahd defend himself the keen blade had drunk thrice in the heart of the lying Beduin.

With bent head and dull eyes Zeyd marched on northward

with the Waziri, as, a mile behind them, a wasted old man, burning with fever, stumbled in the trail and fell. Twice he tried to regain his feet, only to sink weakly back to earth. A filthy, ragged bundle of old bones, he lay—sometimes raving in delirium, sometimes so still that he seemed dead.

Down from the north came Tarzan of the Apes upon the spoor of Guinalda and the two who had accompanied her. Knowing well the windings of the trail he took short cuts, swinging through the branches of the trees, and so it happened that he missed the Waziri at the point where their trail had encountered that of Fahd, where Zeyd had slain his rival, and presently his nostrils picked up the scent of the Mangani in the distance.

Toward the great apes he made his way swiftly for he feared that harm might befall the girl should she, by any mischance, fall into the hands of the anthropoids. He arrived in the clearing where they lazed, a short time after the return of Toyat and Go-yad, who, by now, had abandoned their quarrel, since the prize had been taken by one stronger than either of them.

The preliminaries of meeting over and the apes having recognized and acknowledged Tarzan, he demanded if any had seen the Tarmangani she who had recently passed through the jungle.

M'walat pointed at Toyat and Tarzan turned toward the king.

"You have seen the she?" demanded Tarzan, fearful, for he did not like the manner of the king ape.

Toyat jerked a thumb toward the south. "Numa," he said and went on hunting for food, but Tarzan knew what the ape meant as surely as though he had spoken a hundred words of explanation.

"Where?" asked Tarzan.

Toyat pointed straight to where he had abandoned Guinalda to the lion, and the ape-man, moving straight through the jungle along the line indicated by the king ape, went sadly to investigate, although he already guessed what he would find. At least he could drive Numa from his kill and give decent burial to the unfortunate girl.

*   *   *

Slowly consciousness returned to Guinalda. She did not open her eyes, but lay very quiet wondering if this was death. She felt no pain.

Presently a sickly sweet and pungent odor assailed her nostrils and something moved very close to her, so close that she felt it against her body, pressing gently, and where it pressed she felt heat as from another body.

Fearfully she opened her eyes and the horror of her predicament again swept over her for she saw that the lion had lain down almost against her. His back was toward her, his noble head was lifted, his black mane almost brushed her face. He was looking off, intently, toward the north.

Guinalda lay very quiet. Presently she felt, rather than heard, a low rumbling growl that seemed to have its origin deep in the cavernous chest of the carnivore.

Something was coming! Even Guinalda sensed that, but it could not be succor, for what could succor her from this hideous beast?

There was a rustling among the branches of the trees a hundred feet away and suddenly the giant figure of a demigod dropped to the ground. The lion rose and faced the man. The two stood thus, eyeing one another for a brief moment. Then the man spoke.

"Jad-bal-ja!" he exclaimed, and then: "Come to heel!"

The great, golden lion whined and strode across the open space, stopping before the man. Guinalda saw the beast look up into the face of the demigod and saw the latter stroke the tawny head affectionately, but meanwhile the eyes of the man, or god, or whatever he was, were upon Guinalda and she saw the sudden relief that came to them as Tarzan realized that the girl was unharmed.

Leaving the lion the ape-man crossed to where the princess lay and knelt beside her.

"You are the Princess Guinalda?" he asked.

The girl nodded, wondering how he knew her. As yet she was too stunned to command her own voice.

"Are you hurt?" he asked.

She shook her head.

"Do not be afraid," he assured her in a gentle voice. "I am your friend. You are safe now."

There was something in the way he said it that filled Guinalda with such a sense of safety as all the mailed knights of her father's realm had scarce imparted.

"I am not afraid—any more," she said simply.

"Where are your companions?" he asked.

She told him all that had happened.

"You are well rid of them," said the ape-man, "and we shall not attempt to find them. The jungle will account for them in its own way and in its own good time."

"Who art thou?" asked the girl.

"I am Tarzan."

"How didst thou know my name?" she queried.

"I am a friend of one whom you know as Sir James," he explained. "He and I were searching for you."

"Thou art his friend?" she cried. "Oh, sweet sir, then thou art mine as well!"

The ape-man smiled. "Always!" he said.

"Why did the lion not kill thee, Sir Tarzan?" she demanded, thinking him a simple knight, for in her land there were only these beside the members of her princely house and the pseudo king of the City of the Sepulcher. For in the original company that had been wrecked upon the coast of Africa at the time of the Third Crusade there were only knights, except one bastard son of Henry II, who had been the original Prince Gobred. Never having been in contact with an English king since they parted from Richard at Cyprus no Gobred had assumed the right to issue patents of nobility to his followers, solely the prerogative of the king.

"Why did the lion not kill me?" repeated Tarzan. "Because he is Jad-bal-ja, the Golden Lion, which I raised from cubhood. All his life he has known me only as friend and master. He would not harm me and it was because of his lifelong association with human beings that he did not harm you; though I was fearful when I saw him beside you that he had, for a lion is always a lion!"

"Thou dwellest nearby?" asked the girl.

"Far away," said Tarzan, "But there must be some of my people nearby, else Jad-bal-ja would not be here. I sent for my warriors and doubtless he has accompanied them."

Finding that the girl was hungry Tarzan bade the Golden Lion remain and guard her while he went in search of food.

"Do not fear him," he told her, "and remember that you could not have a protector more competent than he to discourage the approach of enemies."

"And well mayst I believe it," admitted Guinalda.

Tarzan returned with food and then, as the day was not done, he started back toward Nimmr with the rescued girl, carrying her, as she was now too weak to walk; and beside them strode the great, black-maned lion of gold.

During that journey Tarzan learned much of Nimmr and also discovered that Blake's love for his princess was apparently fully reciprocated by the girl, for she seemed never so content as when talking about her Sir James and asking questions concerning his far country and his past life, of which, unfortunately, Tarzan could tell her nothing.

Upon the second day the three came to the great cross and here Tarzan hailed the warders and bade them come and take their princess.

She urged the ape-man to accompany her to the castle and receive the thanks of her father and mother, but he told her that he must leave at once to search for Blake, and at that she ceased her urging.

"An' thou findst him," she said, "tell him that the gates of Nimmr be always open to him and that the Princess Guinalda awaits his return."

Down from the Cross went Tarzan and Jad-bal-ja and before she turned back to enter the tunnel that led to her father's castle the Princess Guinalda stood watching them until a turn in the trail hid them from her view.

"May Our Lord Jesus bless thee, sweet sir knight," she murmured, "and watch o'er thee and fetch thee back once more with my beloved!"

24

Where Trails Met

DOWN THROUGH THE forest rode Blake searching for some clue to the whereabouts of the Arabs, ranging this way and that, following trails and abandoning them.

Late one day he came suddenly in to a large clearing where once a native village had stood. The jungle had not yet reclaimed it and as he entered it he saw a leopard crouching upon the far side, and before the leopard lay the body of a human being. At first Blake thought the poor creature dead, but presently he saw it attempt to rise and crawl away.

The great cat growled and advanced toward it. Blake shouted and spurred forward, but Sheeta paid no attention to him, evidently having no mind to give up his prey; but as Blake came nearer the cat turned to face him with an angry growl.

The American wondered if his horse would dare the close proximity of the beast of prey, but he need not have feared. Nor would he had he been more fully acquainted with the customs of the Valley of the Sepulcher, where one of the greatest sports of the knights of the two enemy cities is hunting the giant cats with lance alone when they venture from the sanctuary of the Wood of the Leopards.

The charger that Blake bestrode had faced many a savage cat, and larger, too, by far than this one, and so he fell into his charging stride with no show of fear or nervousness and the two thundered down upon Sheeta while the creature that was to have been its prey looked on with wide, astounded eyes.

Within the length of its spring Sheeta rose swiftly to meet the horse and man. He leaped and as he leaped he struck full on the metal tip of the great lance, and the wooden shaft passed through him so far that it was with difficulty that the man forced the carcass from it. When he had done so he turned and rode to the side of the creature lying helpless on the ground.

"My God!" he cried as his eyes rested on the face below him. "Stimbol!"

"Blake!"

The younger man dismounted.

"I'm dying, Blake," whispered Stimbol. "Before I go I want to tell you that I'm sorry. I acted like a cad. I guess I've got what was coming to me."

"Never mind that, Stimbol," said Blake. "You're not dead yet. The first thing is to get you where there are food and water." He stooped and lifted the emaciated form and placed the man in his saddle. "I passed a small native village a few miles back. They all ran when they saw me, but we'll try there for food."

"What are you doing here?" asked Stimbol. "And in the name of King Arthur, where did you get the outfit?"

"I'll tell you about it when we get to the village," said Blake. "It's a long story. I'm looking for a girl that was stolen by the Arabs a few days ago."

"God!" ejaculated Stimbol.

"You know something about her?" demanded Blake.

"I was with the man that stole her," said Stimbol, "or at least who stole her from the other Arabs."

"Where is she?"

"She's dead, Blake!"

"Dead?"

"A bunch of those big anthropoid apes got her. The poor child must have been killed immediately."

Blake was silent for a long time, walking with bowed head as, weighted down by heavy armor, he led the horse along the trail.

"Did the Arabs harm her?" he asked presently.

"No," said Stimbol. "The sheik stole her either for ransom or to sell her in the north, but Fahd stole her for himself. He took me along because I had promised him a lot of money if he'd save me, and I kept him from harming the girl by telling him that he'd never get a cent from me if he did. I felt sorry for the poor child and I made up my mind that I was going to save her if I could."

When Blake and Stimbol approached the village the blacks fled, leaving the white men in full possession of the place. It did not take Blake long to find food for them both.

Making Stimbol as comfortable as possible, Blake found fodder for his horse and presently returned to the old man. He was engaged in narrating his experiences when he was suddenly aware of the approach of many people. He could hear voices and the pad of naked feet. Evidently the villagers were returning.

Blake prepared to meet them with friendly overtures, but the first glimpse he had of the approaching party gave him a distinct shock, for these were not the frightened villagers he had seen scurrying into the jungle a short time before.

With white plumes waving about their heads a company of stalwart warriors came swinging down the trail. Great oval shields were upon their backs, long war spears in their hands.

"Well," said Blake, "I guess we're in for it. The villagers have sent for their big brothers."

The warriors entered the village and when they saw Blake they halted in evident wonder. One of their number approached him and to Blake's surprise addressed him in fairly good English.

"We are the Waziri of Tarzan," he said. "We search for our chief and master. Have you seen him, Bwana?"

The Waziri! Blake could have hugged them. He had been at his wits end to know what he was to do with Stimbol. Alone he never could have brought the man to civilization, but now he knew that his worries were over.

Had it not been for the grief of Blake and Zeyd, it had been a merry party that made free with the cassava and beer of the villagers that night, for the Waziri were not worrying about their chief.

"Tarzan cannot die," said the subchief to Blake, when the latter asked if the other felt any fear as to the safety of his master, and the simple conviction of the quiet words almost succeeded in convincing Blake of their truth.

Along the trail plodded the weary 'Aarab of the Beny Salem fendy, el-Guad. Tired men staggered beneath the weight of half-loads. The women carried even more. Ibn Jad watched the treasure with greedy eyes. An arrow came from nowhere and pierced the heart of a treasure bearer close before Ibn Jad. A hollow voice sounded from the jungle: *"For every jewel a drop of blood!"*

Terrified, the Beduins hastened on. Who would be next? They wanted to cast aside the treasure, but Ibn Jad, greedy, would not let them. Behind them they caught a glimpse of a great lion. He terrified them because he did not come nearer or go away—he just stalked silently along behind. There were no stragglers.

An hour passed. The lion paced just within sight of the tail end of the column. Never had the head of one of Ibn Jad's columns been so much in demand. Everyone wished to go in the lead.

A scream burst from another treasure carrier. An arrow had passed through his lungs. *"For every jewel a drop of blood!"*

The men threw down the treasure. "We will not carry the accursed thing more!" they cried, and again the voice spoke.

"Take up the treasure, Ibn Jad!" it said. *"Take up the treasure! It is thou who murdered to acquire it. Pick it up, thief and murderer, and carry it thyself!"*

Together the 'Aarab made the treasure into one load and lifted it to Ibn Jad's back. The old sheik staggered beneath the weight.

"I cannot carry it!" he cried aloud. "I am old and I am not strong."

"Thou canst carry it, or—die!" boomed the hollow voice, while the lion stood in the trail behind them, his eyes glaring fixedly at them.

Ibn Jad staggered on beneath the great load. He could not now travel as fast as the others and so he was left behind with only the lion as company; but only for a short time. Ateja saw his predicament and came back to his side, bearing a musket in her hands.

"Fear not," she said, "I am not the son thou didst crave, but yet I shall protect thee even as a son!"

It was almost dusk when the leaders of the Beduin company stumbled upon a village. They were in it and surrounded by a hundred warriors before they realized that they were in the midst of the one tribe of all others they most feared and dreaded—the Waziri of Tarzan.

The subchief disarmed them at once.

"Where is Ibn Jad?" demanded Zeyd.

"He cometh!" said one.

They looked back along the trail and presently Zeyd saw two figures approaching. One was a man bent beneath a great load and the other was that of a young girl. What he did not see was the figure of a great lion in the shadows behind them.

Zeyd held his breath because, for an instant, his heart had stopped beating.

"Ateja!" he cried and ran forward to meet her and clasp her in his arms.

Ibn Jad staggered into the village. He took one look at the stern visages of the dread Waziri and sank weakly to the ground, the treasure almost burying him as it fell upon his head and shoulders.

Hirfa voiced a sudden scream as she pointed back along the trail, and as every eye turned in that direction, a great golden lion stepped into the circle of the firelight in the village, and at its side strode Tarzan, Lord of the Jungle.

As Tarzan entered the village Blake came forward and grasped his hand.

"We were too late!" said the American sadly.

"What do you mean?" asked the ape-man.

"The Princess Guinalda is dead!"

"Nonsense!" exclaimed Tarzan. "I left her this morning at the entrance to the City of Nimmr."

A dozen times Tarzan was forced to assure Blake that he was not playing a cruel joke upon him. A dozen times Tarzan had to repeat Guinalda's message: "An' thou findst him tell him that the gates of Nimmr be always open to him and that the Princess Guinalda awaits his return!"

Later in the evening Stimbol, through Blake, begged Tarzan to come to the hut in which he lay.

"Thank God!" exclaimed the old man fervently. "I thought that I had killed you. It has preyed on my mind and now I know that it was not you I believe that I can recover."

"You will be taken care of properly, Stimbol," said the ape-man, "and as soon as you are well enough you will be taken to the coast," then he walked away. He would do his duty by the man who had disobeyed him and tried to kill him, but he would not feign a friendship he did not feel.

The following morning they prepared to leave the village. Ibn Jad and his Arabs, with the exception of Zeyd and Ateja, who had asked to come and serve Tarzan in his home, were being sent to the nearest Galla village under escort of a dozen Waziri. Here they would be turned over to the Galla and doubtless sold into slavery in Abyssinia.

Stimbol was borne in a litter by four stout Waziri as the party prepared to take up its march toward the south and the country of Tarzan. Four others carried the treasure of the City of the Sepulcher.

Blake, dressed again in his iron mail, bestrode his great charger as the column started out of the village and down the trail into the south. Tarzan and the Golden Lion stood beside him. Blake reached down and extended his hand to the ape-man.

"Good-bye, sir!" he said.

"Good-bye?" demanded Tarzan. "Aren't you coming home with us?"

Blake shook his head.

"No," he said, "I'm going back into the middle ages with the woman I love!"

Tarzan and Jad-bal-ja stood in the trail watching as Sir James rode out toward the City of Nimmr, the blue and silver of his pennon fluttering bravely from the iron tip of his great lance.

TARZAN
AND THE
LOST EMPIRE

To Jean Hulbert

1

NKIMA DANCED EXCITEDLY upon the naked, brown shoulder of his master. He chattered and scolded, now looking up inquiringly into Tarzan's face and then off into the jungle.

"Something is coming, Bwana," said Muviro, subchief of the Waziri. "Nkima has heard it."

"And Tarzan," said the ape-man.

"The big Bwana's ears are as keen as the ears of Bara the antelope," said Muviro.

"Had they not been, Tarzan would not be here today," replied the ape-man, with a smile. "He would not have grown to manhood had not Kala, his mother, taught him to use all of the senses that Mulungu gave him."

"What comes?" asked Muviro.

"A party of men," replied Tarzan.

"Perhaps they are not friendly," suggested the African. "Shall I warn the warriors?"

Tarzan glanced about the little camp where a score of his fighting men were busy preparing their evening meal and saw that, as was the custom of the Waziri, their weapons were in order and at hand.

"No," he said. "It will, I believe, be unnecessary, as these people who are approaching do not come stealthily as enemies would, nor are their numbers so great as to cause us any apprehension."

But Nkima, a born pessimist, expected only the worst, and

as the approaching party came nearer his excitement increased. He leaped from Tarzan's shoulder to the ground, jumped up and down several times and then, springing back to Tarzan's side, seized his arm and attempted to drag him to his feet.

"Run, run!" he cried, in the language of the apes. "Strange Gomangani are coming. They will kill little Nkima."

"Do not be afraid, Nkima," said the ape-man. "Tarzan and Muviro will not let the strangers hurt you."

"I smell a strange Tarmangani," chattered Nkima. "There is a Tarmangani with them. The Tarmangani are worse than the Gomangani. They come with thundersticks and kill little Nkima and all his brothers and sisters. They kill the Mangani. They kill the Gomangani. They kill everything with their thundersticks. Nkima does not like the Tarmangani. Nkima is afraid."

To Nkima, as to the other denizens of the jungle, Tarzan was no Tarmangani, no white man. He was of the jungle. He was one of them, and if they thought of him as being anything other than just Tarzan it was as a Mangani, a great ape, that they classified him.

The advance of the strangers was now plainly audible to everyone in the camp. The Waziri warriors glanced into the jungle in the direction from which the sounds were coming and then back to Tarzan and Muviro, but when they saw that their leaders were not concerned they went quietly on with their cooking.

A tall Negro warrior was the first of the party to come within sight of the camp. When he saw the Waziri he halted and an instant later a bearded white man stopped beside him.

For an instant the white man surveyed the camp and then he came forward, making the sign of peace. Out of the jungle a dozen or more warriors followed him. Most of them were porters, there being but three or four rifles in evidence.

Tarzan and the Waziri realized at once that it was a small and harmless party, and even Nkima, who had retreated to the safety of a nearby tree, showed his contempt by scampering fearlessly back to climb to the shoulder of his master.

"Doctor von Harben!" exclaimed Tarzan, as the bearded stranger approached. "I scarcely recognized you at first."

"God has been kind to me, Tarzan of the Apes," said von Harben, extending his hand. "I was on my way to see you and I have found you a full two days' march sooner than I expected."

"We are after a cattle-killer," explained Tarzan. "He has come into our kraal several nights of late and killed some of our best cattle, but he is very cunning. I think he must be an old lion to outwit Tarzan for so long.

"But what brings you into Tarzan's country, Doctor? I hope it is only a neighborly visit and that no trouble has come to my good friend, though your appearance belies my hope."

"I, too, wish that it were nothing more than a friendly call," said von Harben, "but as a matter of fact I am here to seek your help because I am in trouble—very serious trouble, I fear."

"Do not tell me that the Arabs have come down again to take slaves or to steal ivory, or is it that the leopard men are way-laying your people upon the jungle trails at night?"

"No, it is neither the one nor the other. I have come to see you upon a more personal matter. It is about my son, Erich. You have never met him."

"No," said Tarzan; "but you are very tired and hungry. Let your men make camp here. My evening meal is ready; while you and I eat you shall tell me how Tarzan may serve you."

As the Waziri, at Tarzan's command, assisted von Harben's men in making their camp, the doctor and the ape-man sat cross-legged upon the ground and ate the rough fare that Tarzan's Waziri cook had prepared.

Tarzan saw that his guest's mind was filled with the trouble that had brought him in search of the ape-man, and so he did not wait until they had finished the meal to reopen the subject, but urged von Harben to continue his story at once.

"I wish to preface the real object of my visit with a few words of explanation," commenced von Harben. "Erich is my only son. Four years ago, at the age of nineteen, he completed his university course with honors and received his first degree. Since then he has spent the greater part of his time in pursuing his studies in various European universities, where he has specialized in archaeology and the study of dead languages. His one hobby, outside of his chosen field, has been mountain climbing and during succeeding summer vacations he scaled every important Alpine peak.

"A few months ago he came here to visit me at the mission and immediately became interested in the study of the various Bantu dialects that are in use by the several tribes in our district and those adjacent thereto.

"While pursuing his investigation among the natives he ran across that old legend of The Lost Tribe of the Wiramwazi Mountains, with which we are all so familiar. Immediately his mind became imbued, as have the minds of so many others, with the belief that this fable might have originated in fact and that if he could trace it down he might possibly find descendants of one of the lost tribes of Biblical history."

"I know the legend well," said Tarzan, "and because it is so persistent and the details of its narration by the natives so circumstantial, I have thought that I should like to investigate it myself, but in the past no necessity has arisen to take me close to the Wiramwazi Mountains."

"I must confess," continued the doctor, "that I also have had the same urge many times. I have upon two occasions talked with men of the Bagego tribe that live upon the slopes of the Wiramwazi Mountains and in both instances I have been assured that a tribe of white men dwells somewhere in the depths of that great mountain range. Both of these men told me that their tribe has carried on trade with these people from time immemorial and each assured me that he had often seen members of The Lost Tribe both upon occasions of peaceful trading and during the warlike raids that the mountaineers occasionally launched upon the Bagego.

"The result was that when Erich suggested an expedition to the Wiramwazi I rather encouraged him, since he was well fitted to undertake the adventure. His knowledge of Bantu and his intensive, even though brief, experience among the natives gave him an advantage that few scholars otherwise equipped by education to profit by such an expedition would have, while his considerable experience as a mountain climber would, I felt, stand him in good stead during such an adventure.

"On the whole I felt that he was an ideal man to lead such an expedition, and my only regret was that I could not accompany him, but this was impossible at the time. I assisted him in every way possible in the organization of his safari and in equipping and provisioning it.

"He has not been gone a sufficient length of time to accomplish any considerable investigation and return to the mission, but recently a few of the members of his safari were reported to me as having returned to their villages. When I sought to interview them they avoided me, but rumors reached me that convinced me that all was not well with my son. I therefore determined to organize a relief expedition, but in all my district I could find only these few men who dared accompany me to the Wiramwazi Mountains, which, their legends assure them, are inhabited by malign spirits—for, as you know, they consider The Lost Tribe of the Wiramwazi to be a band of bloodthirsty ghosts. It became evident to me that the deserters of Erich's safari had spread terror through the district.

"Under the circumstances I was compelled to look elsewhere for help and naturally I turned, in my perplexity, to Tarzan, Lord of the Jungle.... Now you know why I am here."

"I will help you, Doctor," said Tarzan, after the other had concluded.

"Good!" exclaimed von Harben; "but I knew that you would. You have about twenty men here, I should judge, and I have about fourteen. My men can act as carriers, while yours, who are acknowledged to be the finest fighting men in Africa, can serve as askaris. With you to guide us we can soon pick up the trail and with such a force, small though it be, there is no country that we cannot penetrate."

Tarzan shook his head. "No, Doctor," he said, "I shall go alone. That is always my way. Alone I may travel much more rapidly and when I am alone the jungle holds no secrets from me—I shall be able to obtain more information along the way than would be possible were I accompanied by others. You know the jungle people consider me as one of themselves. They do not run away from me as they would from you and other men."

"You know best," said von Harben. "I should like to accompany you. I should like to feel that I am doing my share, but if you say no I can only abide by your decision."

"Return to your mission, Doctor, and wait there until you hear from me."

"And in the morning you leave for the Wiramwazi Mountains?" asked von Harben.

"I leave at once," said the ape-man.

"But it is already dark," objected von Harben.

"There is a full moon and I wish to take advantage of it," explained the other. "I can lie up in the heat of the day for what rest I need." He turned and called Muviro to him. "Return home with my warriors, Muviro," he instructed, "and hold every fighting man of the Waziri in readiness in the event that I find it necessary to send for you."

"Yes, Bwana," replied Muviro; "and how long shall we wait for a message before we set out for the Wiramwazi Mountains in search of you?"

"I shall take Nkima with me and if I need you I shall send him back to fetch and to guide you."

"Yes, Bwana," replied Muviro. "They will be in readiness—all the fighting men of the Waziri. Their weapons will be at hand by day and by night and fresh war paint will be ready in every pot."

Tarzan swung his bow and his quiver of arrows across his back. Over his left shoulder and under his right arm lay the coils of his grass rope and at his hip dangled the hunting knife of his long-dead sire. He picked up his short spear and stood for a moment with head up, sniffing the breeze. The firelight played upon his bronzed skin.

For a moment he stood thus, every sense alert. Then he called to Nkima in the tongue of the ape folk and as the little monkey scampered toward him, Tarzan of the Apes turned without a word of farewell and moved silently off into the jungle, his lithe carriage, his noiseless tread, his majestic mien suggesting to the mind of von Harben a personification of another mighty jungle animal, Numa the lion, king of beasts.

2

Erich von Harben stepped from his tent upon the slopes of the Wiramwazi Mountains to look upon a deserted camp.

When he had first awakened, the unusual quiet of his surroundings had aroused within him a presentiment of ill, which was augmented when repeated calls for his body-servant, Gabula, elicited no response.

For weeks, as the safari had been approaching the precincts of the feared Wiramwazi, his men had been deserting by twos and threes until the preceding evening when they had made this camp well upon the mountain slopes only a terrified remnant of the original safari had remained with him. Now even these, overcome during the night by the terrors of ignorance and superstition, had permitted fear to supplant loyalty and had fled from the impending and invisible terrors of this frowning range, leaving their master alone with the bloodthirsty spirits of the dead.

A hasty survey of the campsite revealed that the men had stripped von Harben of everything. All of his supplies were gone and his gun carriers had decamped with his rifles and all of his ammunition, with the exception of a single Luger pistol and its belt of ammunition that had been in the tent with him.

Erich von Harben had had sufficient experience with these natives to understand fairly well the mental processes based upon their deep-rooted superstition that had led them to this seemingly inhuman and disloyal act and so he did not place so much blame upon them as might another less familiar with them.

While they had known their destination when they embarked upon the undertaking, their courage had been high in direct proportion to the great distance that they had been from the Wiramwazi, but in proportion as the distance lessened with each day's march their courage had lessened until now upon the very threshold of horrors beyond the ken of human minds the last vestige of self-control had deserted them and they had fled precipitately.

That they had taken his provisions, his rifles, and his ammunition might have seemed the depth of baseness had von Harben not realized the sincerity of their belief that there could be no possible hope for him and that his immediate death was a foregone conclusion.

He knew that they had reasoned that under the circumstances it would be a waste of food to leave it behind for a man who was already as good as dead when they would need it for their return journey to their villages, and likewise, as the weapons of mortal man could avail nothing against the ghosts of Wiramwazi, it would have been a needless extravagance to have surrendered fine rifles and quantities of ammunition that von Harben could not use against his enemies of the spirit world.

Von Harben stood for some time looking down the mountain slope toward the forest, somewhere in the depths of which his men were hastening toward their own country. That he might overtake them was a possibility, but by no means a certainty, and if he did not he would be no better off alone in the jungle than he would be on the slopes of the Wiramwazi.

He faced about and looked up toward the rugged heights above him. He had come a long way to reach his goal, which now lay somewhere just beyond that serrated skyline, and he was of no mind to turn back now in defeat. A day or a week in these rugged mountains might reveal the secret of The Lost Tribe of legend, and surely a month would be sufficient to determine beyond a reasonable doubt that the story had no basis in fact, for von Harben believed that in a month he could fairly well explore such portions of the range as might naturally lend themselves to human habitation, where he hoped at best to find relics of the fabled tribe in the form of ruins or burial mounds. For to a man of von Harben's training and intelligence there could be no thought that The Lost Tribe of legend, if it had ever existed, could be anything more than a vague memory surrounding a few moldy artifacts and some crumbling bones.

It did not take the young man long to reach a decision and presently he turned back to his tent and, entering it, packed a few necessities that had been left to him in a light haversack, strapped his ammunition belt about him, and stepped forth once more to turn his face upward toward the mystery of the Wiramwazi.

In addition to his Luger, von Harben carried a hunting knife and with this he presently cut a stout staff from one of the small trees that grew sparsely upon the mountainside against the time when he might find an alpenstock indispensable.

A mountain rill furnished him pure, cold water to quench his thirst, and he carried his pistol cocked, hoping that he might bag some small game to satisfy his hunger. Nor had he gone far before a hare broke cover, and as it rolled over to the crack of the Luger, von Harben gave thanks that he had devoted much time to perfecting himself in the use of small arms.

On the spot he built a fire and grilled the hare, after which he lit his pipe and lay at ease while he smoked and planned. His was not a temperament to be depressed or discouraged by seeming reverses, and he was determined not to be hurried by excitement, but to conserve his strength at all times during the strenuous days that he felt must lie ahead of him.

All day he climbed, choosing the long way when it seemed safer, exercising all the lore of mountain climbing that he had accumulated, and resting often. Night overtook him well up toward the summit of the highest ridge that had been visible from the base of the range. What lay behind, he could not even guess, but experience suggested that he would find other ridges and frowning peaks before him.

He had brought a blanket with him from the last camp and in this he rolled up on the ground. From below there came the noises of the jungle subdued by distance—the yapping of jackals and faintly from afar the roaring of a lion.

Toward morning he was awakened by the scream of a leopard, not from the jungle far below, but somewhere upon the mountain slopes nearby. He knew that this savage night prowler constituted a real menace, perhaps the greatest he would have to face, and he regretted the loss of his heavy rifle.

He was not afraid, for he knew that after all there was little likelihood that the leopard was hunting him or that it would attack him, but there was always that chance and so to guard against it he started a fire of dry wood that he had gathered for the purpose the night before. He found the warmth of the blaze welcome, for the night had grown cold, and he sat for some time warming himself.

Once he thought he heard an animal moving in the darkness beyond the range of the firelight, but he saw no shining eyes and the sound was not repeated. And then he must have slept, for the next thing that he knew it was daylight and only embers remained to mark where the beast fire had blazed.

Cold and without breakfast, von Harben continued the ascent from his cheerless camp, his eyes, under the constant urging of his stomach, always alert for food. The terrain offered few obstacles to an experienced mountain climber, and he even forgot his hunger in the thrill of expectancy with which he anticipated the possibilities hidden by the ridge whose summit now lay but a short distance ahead of him.

It is the summit of the next ridge that ever lures the explorer onward. What new sights lie just beyond? What mysteries will its achievement unveil to the eager eyes of the adventurer? Judgment and experience joined forces to assure him that when his eyes surmounted the ridge ahead they would be rewarded with nothing more startling than another similar ridge to be negotiated; yet there was always that other hope hanging like a shining beacon just below the next horizon, above which the rays of its hidden light served to illuminate the figments of his desire, and his imagination transformed the figments into realities.

Von Harben, sane and phlegmatic as he was, was now keyed to the highest pitch of excitement as he at last scaled the final barrier and stood upon the crest of the ridge. Before him stretched a rolling plateau, dotted with stunted wind-swept trees, and in the distance lay the next ridge that he had anticipated, but indistinct and impurpled by the haze of distance. What lay between him and those far hills? His pulse quickened at the thought of the possibilities for exploration and discovery that lay before him, for the terrain that he looked upon was entirely different from what he had anticipated. No lofty peaks were visible except in the far distance, and between him and them there must lie intriguing ravines and valleys—virgin fields at the feet of the explorer.

Eagerly, entirely forgetful of his hunger or his solitude, von Harben moved northward across the plateau. The land was gently rolling, rock-strewn, sterile, and uninteresting, and when he had covered a mile of it he commenced to have misgivings, for if it continued on without change to the dim hills in the distance, as it now seemed was quite likely the case, it could offer him neither interest nor sustenance.

As these thoughts were commencing to oppress him, he became suddenly conscious of a vague change in the appearance of the terrain ahead. It was only an impression of unreality. The hills far away before him seemed to rise out of a great void, and it was as though between him and them there existed nothing. He might have been looking across an inland sea to distant, hazy shores—a waterless sea, for nowhere was there any suggestion of water—and then suddenly he came to a halt, startled, amazed. The rolling plateau ceased abruptly at his feet, and below him, stretching far to the distant hills, lay a great abyss—a mighty canyon similar to that which has made the gorge of the Colorado world-famous.

But here there was a marked difference. There were indications of erosion. The grim walls were scarred and water-worn. Towers and turrets and minarets, carved from the native granite, pointed upward from below, but they clung close to the canyon's wall, and just beyond them he could see the broad expanse of the floor of the canyon, which from his great height above it appeared as level as a billiard table. The scene held him in a hypnosis of wonderment and admiration as, at first swiftly and then slowly, his eyes encompassed the whole astounding scene.

Perhaps a mile below him lay the floor of the sunken canyon, the further wall of which he could but vaguely estimate to be somewhere between fifteen and twenty miles to the north, and this he realized was the lesser dimension of the canyon. Upon his right, to the east, and upon his left, to the west, he could see that the canyon extended to considerable distances—just how far he could not guess. He thought that to the east he could trace the wall that hemmed it upon that side, but from where he stood the entire extent of the canyon to the west was not visible, yet he knew that the floor that was visible to him must stretch fully twenty-five or thirty miles from east to west. Almost below him was a large lake or marsh that seemed to occupy the greater part of the east end of the canyon. He could see lanes of water winding through what appeared to be great growths of reeds and, nearer the northern shore, a large island. Three streams, winding ribbons far below, emptied into the lake, and in the far distance was another ribbon that might be a road. To the west the canyon was heavily wooded, and between the forest and the lake he saw moving figures of what he thought to be grazing game.

The sight below him aroused the enthusiasm of the explorer to its highest pitch. Here, doubtless, lay the secret of The Lost Tribe of the Wiramwazi and how well Nature had guarded this secret with stupendous barrier cliffs, aided by the superstitions of the ignorant inhabitants of the outer slopes, was now easily understandable.

As far as he could see, the cliffs seemed sheer and impossible of descent, and yet he knew that he must find a way—that he would find a way down into that valley of enchantment.

Moving slowly along the rim he sought some foothold, however slight, where Nature had lowered her guard, but it was almost night and he had covered but a short distance before he found even a suggestion of hope that the canyon was hemmed at any point by other than unbroken cliffs, whose perpendicular faces rose at their lowest point fully a thousand feet above any possible foothold for a human being.

The sun had already set when he discovered a narrow fissure in the granite wall. Crumbled fragments of the mother rock had fallen into and partially filled it so that near the surface, at least, it offered a means of descent below the level of the cliff top, but in the gathering darkness he could not determine how far downward this rough and precarious pathway led.

He could see that below him the cliffs rose in terraced battlements to within a thousand feet of where he stood, and if the narrow fissure extended to the next terrace below him, he felt that the obstacles thereafter would present fewer difficulties than those that had baffled him up to the present time—for while he would still have some four thousand feet to descend, the formation of the cliffs was much more broken at the foot of the first sheer drop and consequently might be expected to offer some avenues of descent of which an experienced mountain climber could take advantage.

Hungry and cold, he sat beneath the descending night, gazing down into the blackening void below. Presently, as the darkness deepened, he saw a light twinkling far below and then another and another and with each his excitement rose, for he knew that they marked the presence of man. In many places upon the marshlike lake he saw the fires twinkling, and at a point which he took to mark the site of the island there were many lights.

What sort of men were they who tended these fires? Would he find them friendly or hostile? Were they but another tribe of Africans, or could it be that the old legend was based upon truth and that far below him white men of The Lost Tribe cooked their evening meals above those tantalizing fires of mystery?

What was that? Von Harben strained his ears to catch the faint suggestion of a sound that arose out of the shadowy abyss below—a faint, thin sound that barely reached his ears, but he was sure that he could not be mistaken—the sound was the voices of men.

And now from out of the valley came the scream of a beast and again a roar that rumbled upward like distant thunder. To the music of these sounds, von Harben finally succumbed to exhaustion, sleep for the moment offering him relief from cold and hunger.

When morning came he gathered wood from the stunted trees nearby and built a fire to warm himself. He had no food, nor all the previous day since he had reached the summit had he seen any sign of a living creature other than the game a mile beneath him on the verdant meadows of the canyon bottom.

He knew that he must have food and have it soon and food lay but a mile away in one direction. If he sought to circle the canyon in search of an easier avenue of descent, he knew that he might not find one in the hundred miles or more that he must travel. Of course he might turn back. He was sure that he could reach the base of the outer slopes of the Wiramwazi, where he knew that game might be found before exhaustion overcame him, but he had no mind to turn back and the thought of failure was only a vague suggestion that scarcely ever rose above the threshold of his conscious mind.

Having warmed himself before the fire, he turned to examine the fissure by the full light of day. As he stood upon its brink he could see that it extended downward for several hundred feet, but there it disappeared. However, he was by no means sure that it ended, since it was not a vertical cleft, but tilted slightly from the perpendicular.

From where he stood he could see that there were places in the fissure where descent would be just possible, though it might be very difficult to reascend. He knew, therefore, that should he reach the bottom of the fissure and find that further descent was impossible he would be caught in a trap from which there might be no escape.

Although he felt as fit and strong as ever, he realized perfectly that the contrary was the fact and that his strength must be ebbing and that it would continue to ebb still more rapidly the longer that he was forced to expend it in arduous efforts to descend the cliff and without any possibility of rebuilding it with food.

Even to Erich von Harben, young, self-confident, and enthusiastic, his next step seemed little better than suicidal. To another the mere idea of attempting the descent of these towering cliffs would have seemed madness, but in other mountains von Harben had always found a way, and with this thin thread upon which to hang his hopes he faced the descent into the unknown. Now he was just about to lower himself over the edge of the fissure when he heard the sounds of footsteps behind him. Wheeling quickly, he drew his Luger.

3

LITTLE NKIMA CAME racing through the treetops, jabbering excitedly, and dropped to the knee of Tarzan of the Apes where the latter lay stretched upon the great branch of a jungle giant, his back against the rough bole, where he was lying up after making a kill and feeding.

"Gomangani! Gomangani!" shrilled Nkima. "They come! They come!"

"Peace," said Tarzan. "You you are a greater nuisance than all the Gomangani in the jungle."

"They will kill little Nkima," cried the monkey. "They are strange Gomangani, and there are no Tarmangani among them."

"Nkima thinks everything wants to kill him," said Tarzan, "and yet he has lived many years and is not dead yet."

"Sabor and Sheeta and Numa, the Gomangani, and Histah the snake like to eat poor little Nkima," wailed the monkey. "That is why he is afraid."

"Do not fear, Nkima," said the ape-man. "Tarzan will let no one hurt you."

"Go and see the Gomangani," urged Nkima. "Go and kill them. Nkima does not like the Gomangani."

Tarzan rose leisurely. "I go," he said. "Nkima may come or he may hide in the upper terraces."

"Nkima is not afraid," blustered the little monkey. "He will go and fight the Gomangani with Tarzan of the Apes," and he leaped to the back of the ape-man and clung there with his arms about the bronzed throat, from which point of vantage he peered fearfully ahead, first over the top of one broad shoulder and then over the top of the other.

Tarzan swung swiftly and quietly through the trees toward a point where Nkima had discovered the Gomangani, and presently he saw below him some score of natives straggling along the jungle trail. A few of them were armed with rifles and all carried packs of various sizes—such packs as Tarzan knew must belong to the equipment of a white man.

The Lord of the Jungle hailed them and, startled, the men halted, looking up fearfully.

"I am Tarzan of the Apes. Do not be afraid," Tarzan reassured them, and simultaneously he dropped lightly to the trail among them, but as he did so Nkima leaped frantically from his shoulders and scampered swiftly to a high branch far above, where he sat chattering and scolding, entirely forgetful of his vain boasting of a few moments before.

"Where is your master?" demanded Tarzan.

The Africans looked sullenly at the ground, but did not reply.

"Where is the Bwana, von Harben?" Tarzan insisted.

A tall man standing near fidgeted uneasily. "He is dead," he mumbled.

"How did he die?" asked Tarzan.

Again the man hesitated before replying. "A bull elephant that he had wounded killed him," he said at last.

"Where is his body?"

"We could not find it."

"Then how do you know that he was killed by a bull elephant?" demanded the ape-man.

"We do not know," another spoke up. "He went away from camp and did not return."

"There was an elephant about and we thought that it had killed him," said the tall man.

"You are not speaking true words," said Tarzan.

"I shall tell you the truth," said the third. "Our Bwana ascended the slopes of the Wiramwazi and the spirits of the dead being angry seized him and carried him away."

"I shall tell you the truth," said Tarzan. "You have deserted your master and run away, leaving him alone in the forest."

"We were afraid," the man replied. "We warned him not to ascend the slopes of the Wiramwazi. We begged him to turn back. He would not listen to us, and the spirits of the dead carried him away."

"How long ago was that?" asked the ape-man.

"Six, seven, perhaps ten marchings. I do not remember."

"Where was he when you last saw him?"

As accurately as they could the men described the location of their last camp upon the slopes of the Wiramwazi.

"Go your way back to your own villages in the Urambi country. I shall know where to find you if I want you. If your Bwana is dead, you shall be punished," and swinging into the branches of the lower terrace, Tarzan disappeared from the sight of the unhappy natives in the direction of the Wiramwazi, while Nkima, screaming shrilly, raced through the trees to overtake him.

From his conversation with the deserting members of von Harben's safari, Tarzan was convinced that the young man had been traitorously abandoned and that in all likelihood he was making his way alone back upon the trail of the deserters.

Not knowing Erich von Harben, Tarzan could not have guessed that the young man would push on alone into the unknown and forbidding depths of the Wiramwazi, but assumed on the contrary that he would adopt the more prudent alternative and seek to overtake his men as rapidly as possible. Believing this, the ape-man followed back along the trail of the safari, expecting momentarily to meet von Harben.

This plan greatly reduced his speed, but even so he traveled with so much greater rapidity than the natives that he came to the slopes of the Wiramwazi upon the third day after he had interviewed the remnants of von Harben's safari.

It was with great difficulty that he finally located the point at which von Harben had been abandoned by his men, as a heavy rain and windstorm had obliterated the trail, but at last he stumbled upon the tent, which had blown down, but nowhere could he see any signs of von Harben's trail.

Not having come upon any signs of the white man in the jungle or any indication that he had followed his fleeing safari, Tarzan was forced to the conclusion that if von Harben was not indeed dead he must have faced the dangers of the unknown alone and now be either dead or alive somewhere within the mysterious fastnesses of the Wiramwazi.

"Nkima," said the ape-man, "the Tarmangani have a saying that when it is futile to search for a thing, it is like hunting for a needle in a haystack. Do you believe, Nkima, that in this great mountain range we shall find our needle?"

"Let us go home," said Nkima, "where it is warm. Here the wind blows and up there it is colder. It is no place for little Manu, the monkey."

"Nevertheless, Nkima, there is where we are going."

The monkey looked up toward the frowning heights above.

"Little Nkima is afraid," he said. "It is in such places that Sheeta, the panther, lairs."

Ascending diagonally and in a westerly direction in the hope of crossing von Harben's trail, Tarzan moved constantly in the opposite direction from that taken by the man he sought. It was his intention, however, when he reached the summit, if he had in the meantime found no trace of von Harben, to turn directly eastward and search at a higher altitude in the opposite direction. As he proceeded, the slope became steeper and more rugged until at one point near the western end of the mountain mass he encountered an almost perpendicular barrier high up on the mountainside along the base of which he picked his precarious way among loose boulders that had fallen from above. Underbrush and stunted trees extended at different points from the forest below quite up to the base of the vertical escarpment.

So engrossed was the ape-man in the dangerous business of picking his way along the mountainside that he gave little heed to anything beyond the necessities of the trail and his constant search for the spoor of von Harben, and so he did not see the little group of warriors that were gazing up at him from the shelter of a clump of trees far down the slope, nor did Nkima, usually as alert as his maser, have eyes or ears for anything beyond the immediate exigencies of the trail. Nkima was unhappy. The wind blew and Nkima did not like the wind. All about him he smelled the spoor of Sheeta, the panther, while he considered the paucity and stunted nature of the few trees along the way that his master had chosen. From time to time he noted, with sinking heart, ledges just above them from which Sheeta might spring down upon them; and the way was a way of terror for little Nkima.

Now they had come to a particularly precarious point upon the mountainside. A sheer cliff rose above them on their right and at their left the mountainside fell away so steeply that as Tarzan advanced his body was pressed closely against the granite face of the cliff as he sought a foothold upon the ledge of loose rubble. Just ahead of them the cliff shouldered out boldly against the distant skies. Perhaps beyond that clear-cut corner the going might be better. If it should develop that it was worse, Tarzan realized that he must turn back.

At the turn where the footing was narrowest a stone gave beneath Tarzan's foot, throwing him off his balance for an instant and at that same instant Nkima, thinking that Tarzan was falling, shrieked and leaped from his shoulder, giving the ape-man's body just the impetus that was required to over-balance it entirely.

The mountainside below was steep, though not perpendicular, and if Nkima had not pushed the ape-man outward he doubtless would have slid but a short distance before being able to stay his fall, but as it was he lunged headforemost down the embankment, rolling and tumbling for a short distance over the loose rock until his body was brought to a stop by one of the many stunted trees that clung tenaciously to the wind-swept slope.

Terrified, Nkima scampered to his master's side. He screamed and chattered in his ear and pulled and tugged upon him in an effort to raise him, but the ape-man lay motionless, a tiny stream of blood trickling from a cut on his temple into his shock of black hair.

As Nkima mourned, the warriors, who had been watching them from below, clambered quickly up the mountainside toward him and his helpless master.

4

As Erich von Harben turned to face the thing that he had heard approaching behind him, he saw a Negro armed with a rifle coming toward him.

"Gabula!" exclaimed the white man, lowering his weapon. "What are you doing here?"

"Bwana," said the warrior, "I could not desert you. I could not leave you to die alone at the hands of the spirits that dwell upon these mountains."

Von Harben eyed him incredulously. "But if you believe that, Gabula, are you not afraid that they will kill you, too?"

"I expect to die, Bwana," replied Gabula. "I cannot understand why you were not killed the first night or the second night. We shall both surely be killed tonight."

"And yet you followed me! Why?"

"You have been kind to me, Bwana," replied the man. "Your father has been kind to me. When the others talked they filled me with fear and when they ran away I went with them, but I have come back. There was nothing else that I could do, was there?"

"No, Gabula. For you or for me there would have been nothing else to do, as we see such things, but as the others saw them they found another thing to do and they did it."

"Gabula is not as the others," said the man, proudly. "Gabula is a Batoro."

"Gabula is a brave warrior," said von Harben. "I do not

believe in spirits and so there was no reason why I should be afraid, but you and all your people do believe in them and so it was a very brave thing for you to come back, but I shall not hold you. You may return, Gabula, with the others."

"Yes?" Gabula exclaimed eagerly. "The Bwana is going back? That will be good. Gabula will go back with him."

"No, I am going down into that canyon," said von Harben, pointing over the rim.

Gabula looked down, surprise and wonder reflected by his wide eyes and parted lips.

"But, Bwana, even if a human being could find a way down these steep cliffs, where there is no place for either hand or foot, he would surely be killed the moment he reached the bottom, for this indeed must be the Land of the Lost Tribe where the spirits of the dead live in the heart of the Wiramwazi."

"You do not need to come with me, Gabula," said von Harben. "Go back to your people."

"How are you going to get down there?" demanded the Negro.

"I do not know just how, or where, or when. Now I am going to descend as far along this fissure as I can go. Perhaps I shall find my way down here, perhaps not."

"But suppose there is no foothold beyond the fissure?" asked Gabula.

"I shall have to find footing."

Gabula shook his head. "And if you reach the bottom, Bwana, and you are right about the spirits and there are none or they do not kill you, how will you get out again?"

Von Harben shrugged his shoulders and smiled. Then he extended his hand. "Good-bye, Gabula," he said. "You are a brave man."

Gabula did not take the offered hand of his master. "I am going with you," he said, simply.

"Even though you realize that should we reach the bottom alive we may never be able to return?"

"Yes."

"I cannot understand you, Gabula. You are afraid and I

know that you wish to return to the village of your people. Then why do you insist on coming with me when I give you leave to return home?"

"I have sworn to serve you, Bwana, and I am a Batoro," replied Gabula.

"And I can only thank the Lord that you are a Batoro," said von Harben, "for the Lord knows that I shall need help before I reach the bottom of this canyon, and we must reach it, Gabula, unless we are content to die by starvation."

"I have brought food," said Gabula. "I knew that you might be hungry and I brought some of the food that you like," and, unrolling the small pack that he carried, he displayed several bars of chocolate and a few packages of concentrated food that von Harben had included among his supplies in the event of an emergency.

To the famished von Harben, the food was like manna to the Israelites, and he lost no time in taking advantage of Gabula's thoughtfulness. The sharp edge of his hunger removed, von Harben experienced a feeling of renewed strength and hopefulness, and it was with a light heart and a buoyant optimism that he commenced the descent into the canyon.

Gabula's ancestry, stretching back through countless generations of jungle-dwelling people, left him appalled as he contemplated the frightful abyss into which his master was leading him, but so deeply had he involved himself by his protestations of loyalty and tribal pride that he followed von Harben with no outward show of the real terror that was consuming him.

The descent through the fissure was less difficult than it had appeared from above. The tumbled rocks that had partially filled it gave more than sufficient footing and in only a few places was assistance required, and it was at these times that von Harben realized how fortunate for him had been Gabula's return.

When at last they reached the bottom of the cleft they found themselves, at its outer opening, flush with the face of the cliff and several hundred feet below the rim. This was the point beyond which von Harben had been unable to see and which he had been approaching with deep anxiety, since there was every likelihood that the conditions here might put a period to their further descent along this route.

Creeping over the loose rubble in the bottom of the fissure to its outer edge, von Harben discovered a sheer drop of a hundred feet to the level of the next terrace and his heart sank. To return the way they had come was, he feared, a feat beyond their strength and ingenuity, for there had been places down which one had lowered the other only with the greatest difficulty, which would be practically unscalable on the return journey.

It being impossible to ascend and as starvation surely faced them where they were, there was but one alternative. Von Harben lay upon his belly, his eyes at the outer edge of the fissure, and, instructing Gabula to hold tightly to his ankles, he wormed himself forward until he could scan the entire face of the cliff below him to the level of the next terrace.

A few feet from the level on which he lay he saw that the fissure lay open again to the base of the cliff, its stoppage at the point where they were having been caused by a large fragment of rock that had wedged securely between the sides of the fissure, entirely choking it at this point.

The fissure, which had narrowed considerably since they had entered it at the summit, was not more than two or three feet wide directly beneath the rock on which he lay and extended with little variation at this width the remaining hundred feet to the comparatively level ground below.

If he and Gabula could but get into this crevice he knew that they could easily brace themselves against its sides in such a way as to descend safely the remaining distance, but how with the means at hand were they to climb over the edge of the rock that blocked the fissure and crawl back into the fissure again several feet farther down?

Von Harben lowered his crude alpenstock over the edge of the rock fragment. When he extended his arms at full length the tip of the rod fell considerably below the bottom of the rock on which he lay. A man hanging at the end of the alpenstock might conceivably swing into the fissure, but it would necessitate a feat of acrobatics far beyond the powers of either himself or Gabula.

A rope would have solved their problem, but they had no rope. With a sigh, von Harben drew back when his examination of the fissure convinced him that he must find another way, but he was totally at a loss to imagine in what direction to look for a solution.

Gabula crouched back in the fissure, terrified by the anticipation of what von Harben's attempted exploration had suggested. The very thought of even looking out over the edge of that rock beyond the face of the cliff left Gabula cold and half paralyzed, while the thought that he might have to follow von Harben bodily over the edge threw the Negro into a fit of trembling; yet had von Harben gone over the edge Gabula would have followed him.

The white man sat for a long time buried in thought. Time and again his eyes examined every detail of the formation of the fissure within the range of his vision. Again and again they returned to the huge fragment upon which they sat, which was securely wedged between the fissure's sides. With this out of the way he felt that they could make unimpeded progress to the next terrace, but he knew that nothing short of a charge of dynamite could budge the heavy granite slab. Directly behind it were loose fragments of various sizes, and as his eyes returned to them once again he was struck with the possibility that they suggested.

"Come, Gabula," he said. "Help me throw out some of these rocks. This seems to be our only possible hope of escaping from the trap that I have got us into."

"Yes, Bwana," replied Gabula, and fell to work beside von Harben, though he could not understand why they should be picking up these stones, some of which were very heavy, and pushing them out over the edge of the flat fragment that clogged the fissure.

He heard them crash heavily where they struck the rocks below and this interested and fascinated him to such an extent that he worked feverishly to loosen the larger blocks of stone for the added pleasure he derived from hearing the loud noise that they made when they struck.

"It begins to look," said von Harben, after a few minutes, "as though we may be going to succeed, unless by removing these rocks here we cause some of those above to slide down and thus loosen the whole mass above us—in which event, Gabula, the mystery of The Lost Tribe will cease to interest us longer."

"Yes, Bwana," said Gabula, and lifting an unusually large rock he started to roll it toward the edge of the fissure. "Look! Look, Bwana!" he exclaimed, pointing at the place where the rock had lain.

Von Harben looked and saw an opening about the size of a man's head extending into the fissure beneath them.

"Thank Nsenene, the grasshopper, Gabula," cried the white man, "if that is the totem of your clan—for here indeed is a way to salvation."

Hurriedly the two men set to work to enlarge the hole by throwing out other fragments that had long been wedged in together to close the fissure at this point, and as the fragments clattered down upon the rocks below, a tall, straight warrior standing in the bow of a dugout upon the marshy lake far below looked up and called the attention of his comrades.

They could plainly hear the reverberations of the falling fragments as they struck the rocks at the foot of the fissure and, keen-eyed, they could see many of the larger pieces that von Harben and Gabula tossed downward.

"The great wall is falling," said the warrior.

"A few pebbles," said another. "It is nothing."

"Such things do not happen except after rains," said the first speaker. "It is thus that it is prophesied that the great wall will fall."

"Perhaps it is a demon who lives in the great rift in the wall," said another. "Let us hasten and tell the masters."

"Let us wait and watch," said the first speaker, "until we have something to tell them. If we went and told them that a few rocks had fallen from the great wall they would only laugh at us."

Von Harben and Gabula had increased the size of the

opening until it was large enough to permit the passage of a man's body. Through it the white man could see the rough sides of the fissure extending to the level of the next terrace and knew that the next stage of the descent was already as good as an accomplished fact.

"We shall descend one at a time, Gabula," said von Harben. "I shall go first, for I am accustomed to this sort of climbing. Watch carefully so that you may descend exactly as I do. It is easy and there is no danger. Be sure that you keep your back braced against one wall and your feet against the other. We shall lose some hide in the descent, for the walls are rough, but we shall get down safely enough if we take it slowly."

"Yes, Bwana. You go first," said Gabula. "If I see you do it then, perhaps, I can do it."

Von Harben lowered himself through the aperture, braced himself securely against the opposite walls of the fissure, and started slowly downward. A few minutes later Gabula saw his master standing safely at the bottom, and though his heart was in his mouth the Negro followed without hesitation, but when he stood at last beside von Harben he breathed such a loud sigh of relief that von Harben was forced to laugh aloud.

"It is the demon himself," said the warrior in the dugout, as von Harben had stepped from the fissure.

From where the dugout of the watchers floated, half concealed by lofty papyrus, the terrace at the base of the fissure was just visible. They saw von Harben emerge and a few moments later the figure of Gabula.

"Now, indeed," said one of the men, "we should hasten and tell the masters."

"No," said the first speaker. "Those two may be demons, but they look like men and we shall wait until we know what they are and why they are here before we go away."

For a thousand feet the descent from the base of the fissure was far from difficult, a rough slope leading in an easterly direction down toward the canyon bottom. During the descent their view of the lake and of the canyon was often completely shut off by masses of weather-worn granite around which they sometimes had difficulty in finding a way. As a rule the easiest descent lay between these towering fragments of the main body of the cliff, and at such times as the valley was hidden from them so were they hidden from the watchers on the lake.

A third of the way down the escarpment von Harben came to the verge of a narrow gorge, the bottom of which was densely banked with green, the foliage of trees growing luxuriantly, pointing unquestionably to the presence of water in abundance. Leading the way, von Harben descended into the gorge, at the bottom of which he found a spring from which a little stream trickled downward. Here they quenched their thirst and rested. Then, following the stream downward, they discovered no obstacles that might not be easily surmounted.

For a long time, hemmed in by the walls of the narrow gorge and their view further circumscribed by the forestlike growth along the banks of the stream, they had no sight of the lake or the canyon bottom, but, finally, when the gorge debouched upon the lower slopes von Harben halted in admiration of the landscape spread out before him. Directly below, another stream entered that along which they had descended, forming a little river that dropped steeply to what appeared to be vivid green meadowland through which it wound tortuously to the great swamp that extended out across the valley for perhaps ten miles.

So choked was the lake with some feathery-tipped aquatic plant that von Harben could only guess as to its extent, since the green of the water plant and the green of the surrounding meadows blended into one another, but here and there he saw signs of open water that appeared like winding lanes or passages leading in all directions throughout the marsh.

As von Harben and Gabula stood looking out across this (to them) new and mysterious world, the warriors in the dugout watched them attentively. The strangers were still so far away that the men were unable to identify them, but their leader assured them that these two were no demons.

"How do you know that they are not demons?" demanded one of these fellows.

"I can see that they are men," replied the other.

"Demons are very wise and very powerful," insisted the

doubter. "They may take any form they choose. They might come as birds or animals or men."

"They are not fools," snapped the leader. "If a demon wished to descend the great wall he would not choose the hardest way. He would take the form of a bird and fly down."

The other scratched his head in perplexity, for he realized that here was an argument that would be difficult to controvert. For want of anything better to say, he suggested that they go at once and report the matter to their masters.

"No," said the leader. "We shall remain here until they come closer. It will be better for us if we can take them with us and show them to our masters."

The first few steps that von Harben took onto the grassy meadowland revealed the fact that it was a dangerous swamp from which only with the greatest difficulty were they able to extricate themselves.

Floundering back to solid ground, von Harben reconnoitered in search of some other avenue to more solid ground on the floor of the canyon, but he found that upon both sides of the river the swamp extended to the foot of the lowest terrace of the cliff, and low as these were in comparison to their lofty fellows towering far above them, they were still impassable barriers.

Possibly by reascending the gorge he might find an avenue to more solid ground toward the west, but as he had no actual assurance of this and as both he and Gabula were well-nigh exhausted from the physical strain of the descent, he preferred to find an easier way to the lake shore if it were possible.

He saw that while the river at this point was not swift, the current was rapid enough to suggest that the bottom might be sufficiently free from mud to make it possible for them to utilize it as an avenue to the lake, if it were not too deep.

To test the feasibility of the idea, he lowered himself into the water, holding to one end of his alpenstock, while Gabula seized the other. He found that the water came to his waistline and that the bottom was firm and solid.

"Come on, Gabula. This is our way to the lake, I guess," he said.

As Gabula slipped into the water behind his master, the dugout containing the warriors pushed silently along the watery lane among the papyrus and with silent paddles was urged swiftly toward the mouth of the stream where it emptied into the lake.

As von Harben and Gabula descended the stream they found that the depth of the water did not greatly increase. Once or twice they stumbled into deeper holes and were forced to swim, but in other places the water shallowed until it was only to their knees, and thus they made their way down to the lake at the verge of which their view was shut off by clumps of papyrus rising twelve or fifteen feet above the surface of the water.

"It begins to look," said von Harben, "as though there is no solid ground along the shoreline, but the roots of the papyrus will hold us and if we can make our way to the west end of the lake I am sure that we shall find solid ground, for I am positive that I saw higher land there as we were descending the cliff."

Feeling their way cautiously along, they came at last to the first clump of papyrus and just as von Harben was about to clamber to the solid footing of the roots, a canoe shot from behind the mass of floating plants and the two men found themselves covered by the weapons of a boatload of warriors.

5

LUKEDI, THE BAGEGO, carried a gourd of milk to a hut in the village of his people on the lower slopes at the west end of the Wiramwazi range.

Two stalwart spearmen stood guard at the doorway of the hut. "Nyuto has sent me with milk for the prisoner," said Lukedi. "Has his spirit returned to him?"

"Go in and see," directed one of the sentries.

Lukedi entered the hut and in the dim light saw the figure of a giant white man sitting upon the dirt floor gazing at him. The man's wrists were bound together behind his back and his ankles were secured with tough fiber strands.

"Here is food," said Lukedi, setting the gourd upon the ground near the prisoner.

"How can I eat with my hands tied behind my back?" demanded Tarzan. Lukedi scratched his head. "I do not know," he said. "Nyuto sent me with the food. He did not tell me to free your hands."

"Cut the bond," said Tarzan, "otherwise I cannot eat."

One of the spearmen entered the hut. "What is he saying?" he demanded.

"He says that he cannot eat unless his hands are freed," said Lukedi.

"Did Nyuto tell you to free his hands?" asked the spearman.

"No," said Lukedi.

The spearman shrugged his shoulders. "Leave the food then; that is all you were asked to do."

Lukedi turned to leave the hut. "Wait," said Tarzan. "Who is Nyuto?"

"He is chief of the Bagegos," said Lukedi.

"Go to him and tell him that I wish to see him. Tell him also that I cannot eat with my hands tied behind my back."

Lukedi was gone for half an hour. When he returned he brought an old, rusted slave chain and an ancient padlock.

"Nyuto says that we may chain him to the center pole and then cut the bonds that secure his hands," he said to the guard.

The three men entered the hut where Lukedi passed one end of the chain around the center pole, pulling it through a ring on the other end; the free end he then passed around Tarzan's neck, securing it there with the old slave padlock.

"Cut the bonds that hold his wrists," said Lukedi to one of the spearmen.

"Do it yourself," retorted the warrior. "Nyuto sent you to do it. He did not tell me to cut the bonds."

Lukedi hesitated. It was apparent that he was afraid.

"We will stand ready with our spears," said the guardsmen; "then he cannot harm you."

"I shall not harm him," said Tarzan. "Who are you anyway and who do you think I am?"

One of the guardsmen laughed. "He asked who we are as though he did not know!"

"We know who you are, all right," said the other warrior.

"I am Tarzan of the Apes," said the prisoner, "and I have no quarrel with the Bagegos."

The guardsman who had last spoken laughed again derisively. "That may be your name," he said. "You men of The Lost Tribe have strange names. Perhaps you have no quarrel with the Bagegos, but the Bagegos have a quarrel with you," and still laughing he left the hut followed by his companion, but the youth Lukedi remained, apparently fascinated by the prisoner at whom he stood staring as he might have stared at a deity.

Tarzan reached for the gourd and drank the milk it contained, and never once did Lukedi take his eyes from him.

"What is your name?" asked Tarzan.

"Lukedi," replied the youth.

"And you have never heard of Tarzan of the Apes?"

"No," replied the youth.

"Who do you think I am?" demanded the ape-man.

"We know that you belong to The Lost Tribe."

"But I thought the members of The Lost Tribe were supposed to be the spirits of the dead," said Tarzan.

"That we do not know," replied Lukedi. "Some think one way, some another; but you know, for you are one of them."

"I am not one of them," said Tarzan. "I come from a country farther south, but I have heard of the Bagegos and I have heard of The Lost Tribe."

"I do not believe you," said Lukedi.

"I speak the truth," said Tarzan.

Lukedi scratched his head. "Perhaps you do," he said. "You do not wear clothes like the members of The Lost Tribe, and the weapons that we found with you are different."

"You have seen members of The Lost Tribe?" asked Tarzan.

"Many times," replied Lukedi. "Once a year they come out of the bowels of the Wiramwazi and trade with us. They bring dried fish, snails, and iron and take in exchange salt, goats, and cows."

"If they come and trade with you peacefully, why do you make me a prisoner if you think I am one of them?" demanded Tarzan.

"Since the beginning we have been at war with the members of The Lost Tribe," replied Lukedi. "It is true that once a year we trade with them, but they are always our enemies."

"Why is that?" demanded the ape-man.

"Because at other times we cannot tell when they will come with many warriors and capture men, women, and children whom they take away with them into the Wiramwazi. None ever returns. We do not know what becomes of them. Perhaps they are eaten."

"What will your chief, Nyuto, do with me?" asked Tarzan.

"I do not know," said Lukedi. "They are discussing the question now. They all wish to put you to death, but there are some who believe that this would arouse the anger of the ghosts of all the dead Bagegos."

"Why should the ghosts of your dead wish to protect me?" demanded Tarzan.

"There are many who think that you members of The Lost Tribe are the ghosts of our dead," replied Lukedi.

"What do you think, Lukedi?" asked the ape-man.

"When I look at you I think that you are a man of flesh and blood the same as I, and so I think that perhaps you are telling me the truth when you say that you are not a member of The Lost Tribe, because I am sure that they are all ghosts."

"But when they come to trade with you and when they come to fight with you, can you not tell whether they are flesh and blood or not?"

"They are very powerful," said Lukedi. "They might come in the form of men in the flesh or they might come as snakes or lions. That is why we are not sure."

"And what do you think the council will decide to do with me?" asked Tarzan.

"I think that there is no doubt but that they will burn you alive, for thus both you and your spirit will be destroyed so that it cannot come back to haunt and annoy us."

"Have you seen or heard of another white man recently?" asked Tarzan.

"No," replied the youth. "Many years ago, before I can remember, two white men came who said that they were not members of The Lost Tribe, but we did not believe them and they were killed. I must go now. I shall bring you more milk tomorrow."

After Lukedi had left, Tarzan commenced examining the chain, padlock, and the center pole of the hut in an effort to discover some means of escape. The hut was cylindrical and surmounted by a conical roof of grass. The side walls were of stakes set upright a few inches in the ground and fastened together at their tops and bottoms by creepers. The center pole was much heavier and was secured in position by rafters radiating from it to the top of the wall. The interior of the hut was plastered with mud, which had been thrown on with force and then smoothed with the palm of the hand. It was a common type with which Tarzan was familiar. He knew that there was a possibility that he might be able to raise the center pole and withdraw the chain from beneath it.

It would, of course, be difficult to accomplish this without attracting the attention of the guards, and there was a possibility that the center pole might be set sufficiently far in the ground to render it impossible for him to raise it. If he were given time he could excavate around the base of it, but inasmuch as one or the other of the sentries was continually poking his head into the hut to see that all was well, Tarzan saw little likelihood of his being able to free himself without being discovered.

As darkness settled upon the village Tarzan stretched himself upon the hard dirt floor of the hut and sought to sleep. For some time the noises of the village kept him awake, but at last he slept. How long thereafter it was that he was awakened he did not know. From childhood he had shared with the beasts, among whom he had been raised, the ability to awaken quickly and in full command of all his faculties. He did so now, immediately conscious that the noise that had aroused him came from an animal upon the roof of the hut. Whatever it was, it was working quietly, but to what end the ape-man could not imagine.

The acrid fumes of the village cook fires so filled the air that Tarzan was unable to catch the scent of the creature upon the roof. He carefully reviewed all the possible purposes for which an animal might be upon the thatched, dry-grass roof of the Bagego hut and through a process of elimination he could reach but one conclusion. That was that the thing upon the outside wished to come in and either it did not have brains enough to know that there was a doorway, or else it was too cunning to risk detection by attempting to pass the sentries.

But why should any animal wish to enter the hut? Tarzan lay upon his back, gazing up through the darkness in the direction of the roof above him as he tried to find an answer to his question. Presently, directly above his head, he saw a little ray of moonlight. Whatever it was upon the roof had made an opening that grew larger and larger as the creature quietly tore away the thatching. The aperture was being made close to the wall where the radiating rafters were farthest apart, but whether this was through intent or accident Tarzan could not guess. As the hole grew larger and he caught occasional glimpses of the thing silhouetted against the moonlit sky, a broad smile illuminated the face of the ape-man. Now he saw strong little fingers working at the twigs that were fastened laterally across the rafters to support the thatch and presently, after several of these had been removed, the opening was entirely closed by a furry little body that wriggled through and dropped to the floor close beside the prisoner.

"How did you find me, Nkima?" whispered Tarzan.

"Nkima followed," replied the little monkey. "All day he has been sitting in a high tree above the village watching this place and waiting for darkness. Why do you stay here, Tarzan of the Apes? Why do you not come away with little Nkima?"

"I am fastened here with a chain," said Tarzan. "I cannot come away."

"Nkima will go and bring Muviro and his warriors," said Nkima.

Of course he did not use these words at all, but what he said in the language of the apes conveyed the same meaning to Tarzan. Black apes carrying sharp, long sticks was the expression that he used to describe the Waziri warriors, and the name for Muviro was one of his own coining, but he and Tarzan understood one another.

"No," said Tarzan. "If I am going to need Muviro, he could not get here in time now to be of any help to me. Go back into the forest, Nkima, and wait for me. Perhaps I shall join you very soon."

Nkima scolded, for he did not want to go away. He was afraid alone in this strange forest; in fact, Nkima's life had been one long complex of terror, relieved only by those occasions when he could snuggle in the lap of his master, safe within the solid walls of Tarzan's bungalow. One of the sentries heard the voices within the hut and crawled partway in.

"There," said Tarzan to Nkima, "you see what you have done. Now you had better do as Tarzan tells you and get out of here and into the forest before they catch you and eat you."

"Who are you talking to?" demanded the sentry. He heard a scampering in the darkness and at the same instant he caught sight of the hole in the roof and almost simultaneously he saw something dark go through it and disappear. "What was that?" he demanded, nervously.

"That," said Tarzan, "was the ghost of your grandfather. He came to tell me that you and your wives and all your children would take sick and die if anything happens to me. He also brought the same message for Nyuto."

The sentry trembled. "Call him back," he begged, "and tell him that I had nothing to do with it. It is not I, but Nyuto, the chief, who is going to kill you."

"I cannot call him back," said Tarzan, "and so you had better tell Nyuto not to kill me."

"I cannot see Nyuto until morning," wailed the sentry. "Perhaps then it will be too late."

"No," said Tarzan. "The ghost of your grandfather will not do anything until tomorrow."

Terrified, the sentry returned to his post where Tarzan heard him fearfully and excitedly discussing the matter with his companions until the ape-man finally dropped off to sleep again.

It was late the following morning before anyone entered the hut in which Tarzan was confined. Then came Lukedi with another gourd of milk. He was very much excited.

"Is what Ogonyo says true?" he demanded.

"Who is Ogonyo?" asked Tarzan.

"He was one of the warriors who stood guard here last night, and he has told Nyuto and all the village that he heard the ghost of his grandfather talking with you and that the ghost said that he would kill everyone in the village if you were harmed, and now everyone is afraid."

"And Nyuto?" asked Tarzan.

"Nyuto is not afraid of anything," said Lukedi.

"Not even of ghosts of grandfathers?" asked Tarzan.

"No. He alone of all the Bagegos is not afraid of the men of The Lost Tribe, and now he is very angry at you because you have frightened his people and this evening you are to be burned. Look!" And Lukedi pointed to the low doorway of the hut. "From here you can see them placing the stake to which you are to be bound, and the boys are in the forest gathering fagots."

Tarzan pointed toward the hole in the roof. "There," he said, "is the hole made by the ghost of Ogonyo's grandfather. Fetch Nyuto and let him see. Then, perhaps, he will believe."

"It will make no difference," said Lukedi. "If he saw a thousand ghosts with his own eyes, he would not be afraid. He is very brave, but he is also very stubborn and a fool. Now we shall all die."

"Unquestionably," said Tarzan.

"Can you not save me?" asked Lukedi.

"If you will help me to escape, I promise you that the ghosts shall not harm you."

"Oh, if I could but do it," said Lukedi, as he passed the gourd of milk to the ape-man.

"You bring me nothing but milk," said Tarzan. "Why is that?"

"In this village we belong to the Buliso clan and, therefore, we may not drink the milk nor eat the flesh of Timba, the black cow, so when we have guests or prisoners we save this food for them."

Tarzan was glad that the totem of the Buliso clan was a cow instead of a grasshopper, or rainwater from the roofs of houses or one of the hundreds of other objects that are venerated by different clans, for while Tarzan's early training had not placed grasshoppers beyond the pale as food for men, he much preferred the milk of Timba.

"I wish that Nyuto would see me and talk with me," said Tarzan of the Apes. "Then he would know that it would be better to have me for a friend than for an enemy. Many men have tried to kill me, many chiefs greater than Nyuto. This is not the first hut in which I have lain a prisoner, nor is it the first time that men have prepared fires to receive me, yet I still live, Lukedi, and many of them are dead. Go, therefore, to Nyuto and advise him to treat me as a friend, for I am not from The Lost Tribe of the Wiramwazi."

"I believe you," said Lukedi, "and I shall go and beg Nyuto to hear me, but I am afraid that he will not."

As the youth reached the doorway of the hut, there suddenly arose a great commotion in the village. Tarzan heard men issuing orders. He heard children crying and the pounding of many naked feet upon the hard ground. Then the war-drums boomed and he heard clashing of weapons upon shields and loud shouting. He saw the guards before the doorway spring to their feet and run to join the other warriors and then Lukedi, at the doorway, shrank back with a cry of terror.

"They come! They come!" he cried, and ran to the far side of the hut where he crouched in terror.

6

ERICH VON HARBEN looked into the faces of the tall, almost naked, warriors whose weapons menaced him across the gunwale of their low dugout, and the first thing to attract his attention was the nature of those weapons.

Their spears were unlike any that he had ever seen in the hands of modern savages. Corresponding with the ordinary spear of the African savage, they carried a heavy and formidable javelin that suggested to the mind of the young archaeologist nothing other than the ancient Roman pike, and this similarity was further confirmed by the appearance of the short, broad, two-edged swords that dangled in scabbards supported by straps passing over the left shoulders of the warriors. If this weapon was not the *gladius Hispanus* of the Imperial Legionary, von Harben felt that his studies and researches had been for naught.

"Ask them what they want, Gabula," he directed. "Perhaps they will understand you."

"Who are you and what do you want of us?" demanded Gabula in the Bantu dialect of his tribe.

"We wish to be friends," added von Harben in the same dialect. "We have come to visit your country. Take us to your chief."

A tall Negro in the stern of the dugout shook his head. "I do not understand you," he said. "You are our prisoners. We are going to take you with us to our masters. Come, get into the boat. If you resist or make trouble we shall kill you."

"They speak a strange language," said Gabula. "I do not understand them."

Surprise and incredulity were reflected in the expression on von Harben's face, and he experienced such a sensation as one might who looked upon a man suddenly resurrected after having been dead for nearly two thousand years.

Von Harben had been a close student of ancient Rome and its long dead language, but how different was the living tongue, which he heard and which he recognized for what it was, from the dead and musty pages of ancient manuscripts.

He understood enough of what the man had said to get his meaning, but he recognized the tongue as a hybrid of Latin and Bantu root words, though the inflections appeared to be uniformly those of the Latin language.

In his student days von Harben had often imagined himself a citizen of Rome. He had delivered orations in the Forum and had addressed his troops in the field in Africa and in Gaul, but how different it all seemed now when he was faced with the actuality rather than the figment of imagination. His voice sounded strange in his own ears and his words came haltingly as he spoke to the tall man in the language of the Cæsars.

"We are not enemies," he said. "We have come as friends to visit your country," and then he waited, scarce believing that the man could understand him.

"Are you a citizen of Rome?" demanded the warrior.

"No, but my country is at peace with Rome," replied von Harben.

The man looked puzzled as though he did not understand the reply. "You are from Castra Sanguinarius." His words carried the suggestion of a challenge.

"I am from Germania," replied von Harben.

"I never heard of such a country. You are a citizen of Rome from Castra Sanguinarius."

"Take me to your chief," said von Harben.

"That is what I intend to do. Get in here. Our masters will know what to do with you."

Von Harben and Gabula climbed into the dugout, so awkwardly that they almost overturned it, much to the disgust of the warriors, who seized hold of them none too gently and forced them to squat in the bottom of the frail craft. This was now turned about and paddled along a winding canal, bordered on either side of tufted papyrus rising ten to fifteen feet above the surface of the water.

"To what tribe do you belong?" asked von Harben, addressing the leader of the warriors.

"We are barbarians of the Mare Orientis, subjects of Validus Augustus, Emperor of the East; but why do you ask such questions? You know these things as well as I."

A half hour of steady paddling along winding water-lanes brought them to a collection of beehive huts built upon the floating roots of the papyrus, from which the tall plants had been cleared just sufficiently to make room for the half dozen huts that constituted the village. Here von Harben and Gabula became the center of a curious and excited company of men, women, and children, and von Harben heard himself and Gabula described by their captors as spies from Castra Sanguinarius and learned that on the morrow they were to be taken to Castrum Mare, which he decided must be the village of the mysterious "masters" to whom his captors were continually alluding. The Negroes did not treat them unkindly, though they evidently considered them as enemies.

When they were interviewed by the head man of the village, von Harben, his curiosity aroused, asked him why they had not been molested if all of his people believed, as they seemed to, that they were enemies.

"You are a citizen of Rome," replied the head man, "and this other is your slave. Our masters do not permit us barbarians to injure a citizen of Rome even though he may be from Castra Sanguinarius, except in self-defense or upon the battlefield of war."

"Who are your masters?" demanded von Harben.

"Why, the citizens of Rome who live in Castrum Mare, of course, as one from Castra Sanguinarius well knows."

"But I am not from Castra Sanguinarius," insisted von Harben.

"You may tell that to the officers of Validus Augustus," replied the head man. "Perhaps they will believe you, but it is certain that I do not."

"Are these people who dwell in Castrum Mare Negroes?" asked von Harben.

"Take them away," ordered the head man, "and confine them safely in a hut. There they may ask one another foolish questions. I do not care to listen to them further."

Von Harben and Gabula were led away by a group of warriors and conducted into one of the small huts of the village. Here they were brought a supper of fish and snails and a dish concocted of the cooked pith of papyrus.

When morning dawned the prisoners were again served with food similar to that which had been given them the previous evening and shortly thereafter they were ordered from the hut.

Upon the water-lane before the village floated half a dozen dugouts filled with warriors. Their faces and bodies were painted as for war and they appeared to have donned all the finery of barbaric necklaces, anklets, bracelets, armbands, and feathers that each could command; even the prows of the canoes bore odd designs in fresh colors.

There were many more warriors than could have been accommodated in the few huts within the small clearing, but, as von Harben learned later, these came from other clearings, several of which comprised the village. Von Harben and Gabula were ordered into the chief's canoe and a moment later the little fleet pushed off into the water-lane. Strong paddlers propelled the dugouts along the winding waterway in a northeasterly direction.

During the first half hour they passed several small clearings in each of which stood a few huts from which the women and children came to the water's edge to watch them as they passed, but for the most part the water-lane ran between monotonous walls of lofty papyrus, broken only occasionally by short stretches of more open water.

Von Harben tried to draw the chief into conversation, especially relative to their destination and the nature of the "masters" into whose hands they were to be delivered, but the taciturn warrior ignored his every advance and finally von Harben lapsed into the silence of resignation.

They had been paddling for hours, and the heat and monotony had become almost unbearable, when a turn in the water-lane revealed a small body of open water, across the opposite side of which stretched what appeared to be lowland surmounted by an earthen rampart, along the top of which was a strong stockade. The course of the canoe was directed toward two lofty towers that apparently marked the gateway through the rampart.

Figures of men could be seen loitering about this gateway, and as they caught sight of the canoes a trumpet sounded and a score of men sallied from the gateway and came down to the water's edge.

As the boat drew nearer, von Harben saw that these men were soldiers, and at the command of one of them the canoes drew up a hundred yards offshore and waited there while the chief shouted to the soldiers on shore telling them who he was and the nature of his business. Permission was then given for the chief's canoe to approach, but the others were ordered to remain where they were.

"Stay where you are," commanded one of the soldiers, evidently an under-officer, as the dugout touched the shore. "I have sent for the centurion."

Von Harben looked with amazement upon the soldiers drawn up at the landing. They wore the tunics and cloaks of Cæsar's legionaries. Upon their feet were the sandallike caligae. A helmet, a leather cuirass, an ancient shield with pike and Spanish sword completed the picture of antiquity; only their skin belied the suggestion of their origin. They were not white men; neither were they Negroes, but for the most part of a light-brown color with regular features.

They seemed only mildly curious concerning von Harben,

and on the whole appeared rather bored than otherwise. The under-officer questioned the chief concerning conditions in the village. They were casual questions on subjects of no particular moment, but they indicated to von Harben a seemingly interested and friendly relationship between the Negroes of the outlying villages in the papyrus swamp and the evidently civilized brown people of the mainland; yet the fact that only one canoe had been permitted to approach the land suggested that other and less pleasant relations had also existed between them at times. Beyond the rampart von Harben could see the roofs of buildings and far away, beyond these, the towering cliffs that formed the opposite side of the canyon.

Presently two more soldiers emerged from the gateway opposite the landing. One of them was evidently the officer for whom they were waiting, his cloak and cuirass being of finer materials and more elaborately decorated; while the other, who walked a few paces behind him, was a common soldier, probably the messenger who had been dispatched to fetch him.

And now another surprise was added to those which von Harben had already experienced since he had dropped over the edge of the barrier cliffs into this little valley of anachronisms—the officer was unquestionably white.

"Who are these, Rufinus?" he demanded of the under-officer.

"A barbarian chief and warriors from the villages of the western shore," replied Rufinus. "They bring two prisoners that they captured in the Rupes Flumen. As a reward they wish permission to enter the city and see the Emperor."

"How many are they?" asked the officer.

"Sixty," replied Rufinus.

"They may enter the city," said the officer. "I will give them a pass, but they must leave their weapons in their canoes and be out of the city before dark. Send two men with them. As to their seeing Validus Augustus, that I cannot arrange. They might go to the palace and ask the præfect there. Have the prisoners come ashore."

As von Harben and Gabula stepped from the dugout, the expression upon the officer's face was one of perplexity.

"Who are you?" he demanded.

"My name is Erich von Harben," replied the prisoner.

The officer jerked his head impatiently. "There is no such family in Castra Sanguinarius," he retorted.

"I am not from Castra Sanguinarius."

"Not from Castra Sanguinarius!" The officer laughed.

"That is the story he told me," said the chief, who had been listening to the conversation.

"I suppose that he will be saying next that he is not a citizen of Rome," said the officer.

"That is just what he does say," said the chief.

"But wait," exclaimed the officer, excitedly. "Perhaps you are indeed from Rome herself!"

"No, I am not from Rome," von Harben assured him.

"Can it be that there are white barbarians in Africa!" exclaimed the officer. "Surely your garments are not Roman. Yes, you must be a barbarian unless, as I suspect, you are not telling me the truth and you are indeed from Castra Sanguinarius."

"A spy, perhaps," suggested Rufinus.

"No," said von Harben. "I am no spy nor am I an enemy," and with a smile, "I am a barbarian, but a friendly barbarian."

"And who is this man?" asked the officer, indicating Gabula. "Your slave?"

"He is my servant, but not a slave."

"Come with me," directed the officer. "I should like to talk with you. I find you interesting, though I do not believe you."

Von Harben smiled. "I do not blame you," he said, "for even though I see you before me I can scarcely believe that you exist."

"I do not understand what you mean," said the officer, "but come with me to my quarters."

He gave orders that Gabula was to be confined to the guardhouse temporarily, and then he led von Harben back to one of the towers that guarded the entrance to the rampart.

The gate lay in a vertical plane at right angles to the rampart with a high tower at either side, the rampart curving inward at this point to connect with the tower at the inner end of the gate. This made a curved entrance that forced an enemy attempting to enter to disclose its right or unprotected side to the defenders upon the rampart, a form of camp fortification that von Harben knew had been peculiar to the ancient Romans.

The officer's quarters consisted of a single, small, bare room directly off a larger room occupied by the members of the guard. It contained a desk, a bench, and a couple of roughly made chairs.

"Sit down," said the officer, after they had entered, "and tell me something about yourself. If you are not from Castra Sanguinarius, from whence do you come? How did you get into our country and what are you doing here?"

"I am from Germania," replied von Harben.

"Bah!" exclaimed the officer. "They are wild and savage barbarians. They do not speak the language of Rome at all; not even as poorly as you."

"How recently have you come in contact with German barbarians?" von Harben asked.

"Oh, I? Never, of course, but our historians knew them well."

"And how lately have they written of them?"

"Why, Sanguinarius himself mentions them in the story of his life."

"Sanguinarius?" questioned von Harben. "I do not recall ever having heard of him."

"Sanguinarius fought against the barbarians of Germania in the 839th year of Rome."

"That was about eighteen hundred and thirty-seven years ago," von Harben reminded the officer, "and I think you will have to admit that there may have been much progress in that time."

"And why?" demanded the other. "There have been no changes in this country since the days of Sanguinarius and he has been dead over eighteen hundred years. It is not likely then that barbarians would change greatly if Roman citizens have not. You say you are from Germania. Perhaps you were taken to Rome as a captive and got your civilization there, but your apparel is strange. It is not of Rome. It is not of any place which I have ever heard. Go on with your story."

"My father is a medical missionary in Africa," explained von Harben. "Often when I have visited him I heard the story of a lost tribe that was supposed to live in these mountains. The natives told strange stories of a white race living in the depths of the Wiramwazi. They said that the mountains were inhabited by the ghosts of their dead. Briefly, I came to investigate the story. All but one of my men, terrified after we reached the outer slopes of the mountains, deserted me. That one and I managed to descend to the floor of the canyon. Immediately we were captured and brought here."

For a while the other sat in silence, thinking.

"Perhaps you are telling me the truth," he said, at last. "Your apparel is not that of Castra Sanguinarius and you speak our language with such a peculiar accent and with so great effort that it is evidently not your mother tongue. I shall have to report your capture to the Emperor, but in the meantime I shall take you to the home of my uncle, Septimus Favonius. If he believes your story he can help you, as he has great influence with the Emperor, Validus Augustus."

"You are kind," said von Harben, "and I shall need a friend here if the customs of Imperial Rome still prevail in your country, as you suggest. Now that you know so much about me, perhaps you will tell me something about yourself."

"There is little to tell," said the officer. "My name is Mallius Lepus. I am a centurion in the army of Validus Augustus. Perhaps, if you are familiar with Roman customs, you will wonder that a patrician should be a centurion, but in this matter as in some others we have not followed the customs of Rome. Sanguinarius admitted all his centurions to the patrician class, and since then for over eighteen hundred years only patricians have been appointed centurions.

"But here is Aspar," exclaimed Mallius Lepus, as another officer entered the room. "He has come to relieve me and when he has taken over the gate you and I shall go at once to the home of my uncle, Septimus Favonius."

7

Tarzan of the apes looked at Lukedi in surprise and then out through the low doorway of the hut in an effort to see what it was that had so filled the breast of the youth with terror.

The little section of the village street, framed by the doorway, showed a milling mass of brown bodies, waving spears, terrified women and children. What could it mean?

At first he thought that Lukedi meant that the Bagegos were coming for Tarzan, but now he guessed that the Bagegos were being beset by troubles of their own, and at last he came to the conclusion that some other savage tribe had attacked the village.

But, whatever the cause of the uproar, it was soon over. He saw the Bagegos turn and flee in all directions. Strange figures passed before his eyes in pursuit, and for a time there was comparative silence, only a hurrying of feet, an occasional command, and now and then a scream of terror.

Presently three figures burst into the hut—enemy warriors searching the village for fugitives. Lukedi, trembling, inarticulate, paralyzed by fright, crouched against the far wall. Tarzan sat leaning against the center pole to which he was chained. At sight of him, the leading warrior halted, surprise written upon his face. His fellows joined him and they stood for a moment in excited conversation, evidently discussing their find. Then one of them addressed Tarzan, but in a tongue that the ape-man could not understand, although he realized that there was something vaguely and tantalizingly familiar about it.

Then one of them discovered Lukedi and, crossing the hut, dragged him to the center of the floor. They spoke again to Tarzan, motioning him toward the door so that he understood that they were ordering him from the hut, but in reply he pointed to the chain about his neck.

One of the warriors examined the lock that secured the chain, spoke to his fellows, and then left the hut. He returned very shortly with two rocks and, making Tarzan lie upon the ground, placed the padlock upon one of the rocks and pounded upon it with the other until it broke.

As soon as he was released, Tarzan and Lukedi were ordered from the hut, and when they had come out into the open the ape-man had an opportunity to examine his captors more closely. In the center of the village there were about one hundred light-brown warriors surrounding their Bagego prisoners, of whom there were some fifty men, women, and children.

The tunics, cuirasses, helmets, and sandals of the raiders Tarzan knew that he had never seen before, and yet they were as vaguely familiar as was the language spoken by their wearers.

The heavy spears and the swords hanging at their right sides were not precisely like any spears or swords that he had ever seen, and yet he had a feeling that they were not entirely unfamiliar objects. The effect of the appearance of these strangers was tantalizing in the extreme. It is not uncommon for us to have experiences that are immediately followed by such a sensation of familiarity that we could swear we had lived through them before in their minutest detail, and yet we are unable to recall the time or place or any coincident occurrences.

It was such a sensation that Tarzan experienced now. He

thought that he had seen these men before, that he had heard them talk; he almost felt that at some time he had understood their language, and yet at the same time he knew that he had never seen them. Then a figure approached from the opposite side of the village—a white man, garbed similarly to the warriors, but in more resplendent trappings, and of a sudden Tarzan of the Apes found the key and the solution of the mystery, for the man who came toward him might have stepped from the pedestal of the statue of Julius Cæsar in the Palazzo dei Conservatori in Rome.

These were Romans! A thousand years after the fall of Rome he had been captured by a band of Cæsar's legionaries, and now he knew why the language was so vaguely familiar, for Tarzan, in his effort to fit himself for a place in the civilized world into which necessity sometimes commanded him, had studied many things and among them Latin, but the reading of Cæsar's Commentaries and scanning Vergil do not give one a command of the language and so Tarzan could neither speak nor understand the spoken words, though the smattering that he had of the language was sufficient to make it sound familiar when he heard others speaking it.

Tarzan looked intently at the Cæsar-like white man approaching him and at the dusky, stalwart legionaries about him. He shook himself. This indeed must be a dream, and then he saw Lukedi with the other Bagego prisoners. He saw the stake that had been set up for his burning and he knew that as these were realities so were the strange warriors about him.

Each soldier carried a short length of chain, at one end of which was a metal collar and a padlock, and with these they were rapidly chaining the prisoners neck to neck.

While they were thus occupied the white man, who was evidently an officer, was joined by two other whites similarly garbed. The three caught sight of Tarzan and immediately approached and questioned him, but the ape-man shook his head to indicate that he could not understand their language. Then they questioned the soldiers who had discovered him in the hut and finally the commander of the company issued some instructions relative to the ape-man and turned away.

The result was that Tarzan was not chained to the file of prisoners, but though he again wore the iron collar, the end of the chain was held by one of the legionaries in whose keeping he had evidently been placed.

Tarzan could only believe that this preferential treatment was accorded him because of his color and the reluctance of the white officers to chain another white with Negroes.

As the raiders marched away from the village one of the officers and a dozen legionaries marched in advance. These were followed by the long line of prisoners accompanied by another officer and a small guard. Behind the prisoners, many of whom were compelled to carry the live chickens that were a part of the spoils of the raid, came another contingent of soldiers herding the cows and goats and sheep of the villagers, and behind all a large rear guard compromising the greater part of the legionaries under the command of the third officer.

The march led along the base of the mountains in a northerly direction and presently upward diagonally across the rising slopes at the west end of the Wiramwazi range.

It chanced that Tarzan's position was at the rear of the line of prisoners, at the end of which marched Lukedi.

"Who are these people, Lukedi?" asked Tarzan, after the party had settled down to steady progress.

"These are the ghost people of the Wiramwazi," replied the young Bagego.

"They have come to prevent the killing of their fellow," said another, looking at Tarzan. "I knew Nyuto should not have made him prisoner. I knew that harm would come from it. It is well for us that the ghost people came before we had slain him."

"What difference will it make?" said another. "I would rather have been killed in my own village than to be taken into the country of the ghost people and killed there."

"Perhaps they will not kill us," suggested Tarzan.

"They will not kill you because you are one of them, but they will kill the Bagegos because they did dare to take you prisoner."

"But they have taken him prisoner, too," said Lukedi. "Can you not see that he is not one of them? He does not even understand their language."

The other men shook their heads, but they were not convinced. They had made up their minds that Tarzan was one of the ghost people and they were determined that nothing should alter this conviction.

After two hours of marching the trail turned sharply to the right and entered a narrow and rocky gorge, the entrance to which was so choked with trees and undergrowth that it could not have been visible from any point upon the slopes below.

The gorge soon narrowed until its rocky walls could be spanned by a man's outstretched arms. The floor, strewn with jagged bits of granite from the lofty cliffs above, afforded poor and dangerous footing, so that the speed of the column was greatly reduced.

As they proceeded Tarzan realized that, although they were entering more deeply into the mountains, the trend of the gorge was downward rather than upward. The cliffs on either side rose higher and higher above them until in places the gloom of night surrounded them and, far above, the stars twinkled in the morning sky.

For a long hour they followed the windings of the dismal gorge. The column halted for a minute or two and immediately after the march was resumed Tarzan saw those directly ahead of him filing through an arched gateway in the manmade wall of solid masonry that entirely blocked the gorge to a height of at least a hundred feet. Also, when it was the ape-man's turn to pass the portal, he saw that it was guarded by other soldiers similar to those into whose hands he had fallen and that it was further re-enforced by a great gate of huge, hand-hewn timbers that had been swung open to permit the party to pass.

Ahead of him Tarzan saw a well-worn road leading down into a dense forest in which huge, live oaks predominated, though interspersed with other varieties of trees, among which he recognized acacias and a variety of plane tree as well as a few cedars.

Shortly after passing through the gate the officer in charge gave the command to halt at a small village of conical huts that was inhabited by Negroes not unlike the Bagegos, but armed with pikes and swords similar to those carried by the legionaries.

Preparations were immediately made to camp in the village, the natives turning over their huts to the soldiers, quite evidently, judging from the expressions on their faces, with poor grace. The legionaries took possession of whatever they wished and ordered their hosts about with all the authority and assurance of conquerors.

At this village a ration of corn and dried fish was issued to the prisoners. They were given no shelter, but were permitted to gather deadwood and build a fire, around which they clustered, still chained neck to neck.

Numerous birds, strange to Tarzan, flitted among the branches of the trees overhead and numerous monkeys chattered and scolded, but monkeys were no novelty to Tarzan of the Apes, who was far more interested in noting the manners and customs of his captors.

Presently an acorn fell upon Tarzan's head, but as acorns might be expected to fall from oak trees he paid no attention to the occurrence until a second and third acorn in rapid succession struck him squarely from above, and then he glanced up to see a little monkey perched upon a low branch just above him.

"So-o, Nkima!" he exclaimed. "How did you get here?"

"I saw them take you from the village of the Gomangani. I followed."

"You came through the gorge, Nkima?"

"Nkima was afraid that the rocks would come together and crush him," said the little monkey, "so he climbed to the top and came over the mountains along the edge. Far, far below he could hear the Tarmangani and the Gomangani walking along the bottom. Away up there the wind blew and little Nkima was cold and the spoor of Sheeta the leopard was everywhere and there were great baboons who chased little Nkima, so that he was glad when he came to the end of the mountain and saw the forest far below. It was a very steep mountain. Even little Nkima was afraid, but he found the way to the bottom."

"Nkima had better run home," said Tarzan. "This forest is full of strange monkeys."

"I am not afraid," said Nkima. "They are little monkeys and they are all afraid of Nkima. They are homely little monkeys. They are not so beautiful as Nkima, but Nkima has seen some of the shes looking at him and admiring him. It is not a bad place for Nkima. What are the strange Tarmangani going to do with Tarzan of the Apes?"

"I do not know, Nkima," said the ape-man.

"Then Nkima will go back and fetch Muviro and the Waziri."

"No," said the ape-man. "Wait until I find the Tarmangani for whom we are searching. Then you may go back with a message for Muviro."

That night Tarzan and the other prisoners slept upon the hard ground in the open and, after it was dark, little Nkima came down and snuggled in his master's arms and there he lay all night, happy to be near the great Tarmangani he loved.

As morning dawned, Ogonyo, who had been captured with the other Bagegos, opened his eyes and looked about him. The camp of the soldiers was just stirring. Ogonyo saw some of the legionaries emerging from the huts that they had commandeered. He saw his fellow prisoners huddled close together for warmth and at a little distance from them lay the white man whom he had so recently guarded in the prison hut in the village of Nyuto, his chief. As his eyes rested upon the white man, he saw the head of a little monkey arise from the encircling arms of the sleeper. He saw it cast a glance in the direction of the legionaries emerging from the huts and then he saw it scamper quickly to a nearby tree and swing quickly into the branches above.

Ogonyo gave a cry of alarm that awakened the prisoners near him.

"What is the matter, Ogonyo?" cried one of them.

"The ghost of my grandfather!" he exclaimed. "I saw him again. He came out of the mouth of the white man who calls himself Tarzan. He has put a curse upon us because we kept the white man prisoner. Now we are prisoners ourselves and soon we shall be killed and eaten." The others nodded their heads solemnly in confirmation.

Food similar to that given to them the night before was given to the prisoners, and after they and the legionaries had eaten, the march was resumed in a southerly direction along the dusty road.

Until noon they plodded through the dust toward the south, passing through other villages similar to that at which they had camped during the night, and then they turned directly east into a road that joined the main road at this point. Shortly afterward Tarzan saw before him, stretching across the road to the right and left as far as he could see through the forest, a lofty rampart surmounted by palisades and battlements. Directly ahead the roadway swung to the left just inside the outer line of the rampart and passed through a gateway that was flanked by lofty towers. At the base of the rampart was a wide moat through which a stream of water moved slowly, the moat being spanned by a bridge where the road crossed it.

There was a brief halt at the gateway while the officer commanding the company conferred with the commander of the gate, and then the legionaries and their prisoners filed through and Tarzan saw stretching before him not a village of native huts, but a city of substantial buildings.

Those near the gate were one-story stucco houses, apparently built around an inner courtyard, as he could see the foliage of trees rising high above the roofs, but at a distance down the vista of a long avenue he saw the outlines of more imposing edifices rising to a greater height.

As they proceeded along the avenue they saw many people upon the streets and in the doorways of the houses—brown and black people, clothed for the most part in tunics and cloaks, though many of the Negroes were almost naked. In the vicinity of the gateway there were a few shops, but as they proceeded along the avenue these gave way to dwellings that continued for a considerable distance until they reached a section that seemed to be devoted to shops of a better grade and to public buildings. Here they began to encounter white men, though the proportion of them to the total population seemed quite small.

The people they passed stopped to look at the legionaries and their prisoners and at intersections little crowds formed and quite a number followed them, but these were mostly small boys.

The ape-man could see that he was attracting a great deal of attention and the people seemed to be commenting and speculating upon him. Some of them called to the legionaries, who answered them good-naturedly, and there was considerable joking and chaffing—probably, Tarzan surmised, at the expense of the unfortunate prisoners.

During the brief passage through the city Tarzan came to the conclusion that the Negro inhabitants were the servants, perhaps slaves; the brown men, the soldiers and shopkeepers, while the whites formed the aristocratic or patrician class.

Well within the city the company turned to the left into another broad avenue and shortly afterward approached a great circular edifice constructed of hewn granite blocks. Arched apertures flanked by graceful columns rose tier upon tier to a height of forty or fifty feet, and above the first story all of these arches were open. Through them Tarzan could see that the enclosure was without a roof and he guessed that this lofty wall enclosed an arena, since it bore a marked resemblance to the Colosseum at Rome.

As they came opposite the building the head of the column turned and entered it beneath a low, wide arch and here they were led through numerous corridors in the first story of the building and down a flight of granite steps into gloomy, subterranean chambers, where, opening from a long corridor, the ends of which were lost in darkness in both directions, were a series of narrow doorways before which swung heavy iron gates. In parties of four or five the prisoners were unchained and ordered into the dungeons that lay behind.

Tarzan found himself with Lukedi and two other Bagegos in a small room constructed entirely of granite blocks. The only openings were the narrow, grated doorway, through which they entered, and a small, grated window in the top of the wall opposite the door, and through this window came a little light and air. The grating was closed upon them, the heavy padlock snapped, and they were left alone to wonder what fate lay in store for them.

8

MALLIUS LEPUS CONDUCTED von Harben from the quarters of the captain of the gate in the south wall of the island city of Castrum Mare and, summoning a soldier, bade him fetch Gabula.

"You shall come with me as my guest, Erich von Harben," announced Mallius Lepus, "and, by Jupiter, unless I am mistaken, Septimus Favonius will thank me for bringing such a find. His dinners lag for want of novelty, for long since has he exhausted all the possibilities of Castrum Mare. He has even had a Negro chief from the Western forest as his guest of honor, and once he invited the aristocracy of Castrum Mare to meet a great ape.

"His friends will be mad to meet a barbarian chief from Germania—you are a chief, are you not?" and as von Harben was about to reply, Mallius Lepus stayed him with a gesture. "Never mind! You shall be introduced as a chief and if I do not know any different I cannot be accused of falsifying."

Von Harben smiled as he realized how alike was human nature the world over and in all periods of time.

"Here is your slave now," said Mallius. "As the guest of Septimus Favonius you will have others to do your bidding, but doubtless you will want to have your own bodyservant as well."

"Yes," said von Harben. "Gabula has been very faithful. I should hate to part with him."

Mallius led the way to a long shedlike building beneath the inner face of the rampart. Here were two litters and a number of strapping bearers. As Mallius appeared eight of these sprang to their stations in front and behind one of the litters and carried it from the shed, lowering it to the ground again before their master.

"And tell me, if you have visited Rome recently, does my litter compare favorably with those now used by the nobles?" demanded Mallius.

"There have been many changes, Mallius Lepus, since the Rome of which your historian, Sanguinarius, wrote. Were I to tell you of even the least of them, I fear that you would not believe me."

"But certainly there could have been no great change in the style of litters," argued Mallius, "and I cannot believe that the patricians have ceased to use them."

"Their litters travel upon wheels now," said von Harben.

"Incredible!" exclaimed Mallius. "It would be torture to bump over the rough pavements and country roads on the great wooden wheels of oxcarts. No, Erich von Harben, I am afraid I cannot believe that story."

"The city pavements are smooth today and the countryside is cut in all directions by wide, level highways over which the litters of the modern citizens of Rome roll at great speed on small wheels with soft tires—nothing like the great wooden wheels of the oxcarts you have in mind, Mallius Lepus."

The officer called a command to his carriers, who broke into a smart run.

"I warrant you, Erich von Harben, that there be no litters in all Rome that move at greater speed than this," he boasted.

"How fast are we traveling now?" asked von Harben.

"Better than eighty-five hundred paces an hour," replied Mallius.

"Fifty thousand paces an hour is nothing unusual for the wheeled litters of today," said von Harben. "We call them automobiles."

"You are going to be a great success," cried Mallius, slapping von Harben upon the shoulder. "May Jupiter strike me dead if the guests of Septimus Favonius do not say that I have made a find indeed. Tell them that there be litter-carriers in Rome today who can run fifty thousand paces in an hour and they will acclaim you the greatest entertainer as well as the greatest liar Castrum Mare has ever seen."

Von Harben laughed good-naturedly. "But you will have to admit, my friend, that I never said that there were litter-bearers who could run fifty thousand paces an hour," he reminded Mallius.

"But did you not assure me that the litters traveled that fast? How then may a litter travel unless it is carried by bearers. Perhaps the litters of today are carried by horses. Where are the horses that can run fifty thousand paces in an hour?"

"The litters are neither carried nor drawn by horses or men, Mallius," said von Harben.

The officer leaned back against the soft cushion of the carriage, roaring with laughter. "They fly then, I presume," he jeered. "By Hercules, you must tell this all over again to Septimus Favonius. I promise you that he will love you."

They were passing along a broad avenue bordered by old trees. There was no pavement and the surface of the street was deep with dust. The houses were built quite up to the street line and where there was space between adjacent houses a high wall closed the aperture, so that each side of the street presented a solid front of masonry broken by arched gateways, heavy doors, and small unglazed windows, heavily barred.

"These are residences?" asked von Harben, indicating the buildings they were passing.

"Yes," said Mallius.

"From the massive doors and heavily barred windows I

should judge that your city is overrun with criminals," commented von Harben.

Mallius shook his head. "On the contrary," he said, "we have few criminals in Castrum Mare. The defenses that you see are against the possible uprising of slaves or invasions by barbarians. Upon several occasions during the life of the city such things have occurred, and so we build to safeguard against disaster in the event that there should be a recurrence of them, but, even so, doors are seldom locked, even at night, for there are no thieves to break in, no criminals to menace the lives of our people. If a man has done wrong to a fellow man he may have reason to expect the dagger of the assassin, but if his conscience be cleared he may live without fear of attack."

"I cannot conceive of a city without criminals," said von Harben. "How do you account for it?"

"That is simple," replied Mallius. "When Honus Hasta revolted and founded the city of Castrum Mare in the 953rd year of Rome, Castra Sanguinarius was overrun with criminals, so that no man dared go abroad at night without an armed bodyguard, nor was anyone safe within his own home, and Honus Hasta, who became the first Emperor of the East, swore that there should be no criminals in Castrum Mare and he made laws so drastic that no thief or murderer lived to propagate his kind. Indeed, the laws of Honus Hasta destroyed not only the criminal, but all the members of his family, so that there was none to transmit to posterity the criminal inclinations of a depraved sire.

"There are many who thought Honus Hasta a cruel tyrant, but time has shown the wisdom of many of his acts and certainly our freedom from criminals may only be ascribed to the fact that the laws of Honus Hasta prevented the breeding of criminals. So seldom now does an individual arise who steals or wantonly murders that it is an event of as great moment as any that can occur, and the entire city takes a holiday to see the culprit and his family destroyed."

Entering an avenue of more pretentious homes, the litter-bearers halted before an ornate gate where Lepus and Erich descended from the litter. In answer to the summons of the former, the gate was opened by a slave and von Harben followed his new friend across a tiled forecourt into an inner garden, where beneath the shade of a tree a stout, elderly man was writing at a low desk. It was with something of a thrill that von Harben noted the ancient Rome inkstand, the reed pen, and the roll of parchment that the man was using as naturally as though they had not been quite extinct for a thousand years.

"Greetings, Uncle!" cried Lepus, and as the older man turned toward them, "I have brought you a guest such as no citizen of Castrum Mare has entertained since the founding of the city. This, my uncle, is Erich von Harben, barbarian chief from far Germania." Then to von Harben, "My revered uncle, Septimus Favonius."

Septimus Favonius arose and greeted von Harben hospitably, yet with such a measure of conscious dignity as to carry the suggestion that a barbarian, even though a chief and a guest, could not be received upon a plane of actual social equality by a citizen of Rome.

Very briefly Lepus recounted the occurrences leading to his meeting with von Harben. Septimus Favonius seconded his nephew's invitation to be their guest, and then, at the suggestion of the older man, Lepus took Erich to his apartments to outfit him with fresh apparel.

An hour later, Erich, shaved and appareled as a young Roman patrician, stepped from the apartment, which had been placed at his disposal, into the adjoining chamber, which was a part of the suite of Mallius Lepus.

"Go on down to the garden," said Lepus, "and when I am dressed I shall join you there."

As von Harben passed through the home of Septimus Favonius on his way to the garden court, he was impressed by the peculiar blending of various cultures in the architecture and decoration of the home.

The walls and columns of the building followed the simplest Grecian lines of architecture, while the rugs, hangings, and mural decorations showed marked evidence of both oriental and savage African influences. The latter he could understand, but the source of the oriental designs in many of the decorations was quite beyond him, since it was obvious that The Lost Tribe had had no intercourse with the outside world, other than with the savage Bagegos, for many centuries.

And when he stepped out into the garden, which was of considerable extent, he saw a further blending of Rome and savage Africa, for while the main part of the building was roofed with handmade tile, several porches were covered with native grass thatch, while a small outbuilding at the far end of the garden was a replica of a Bagego hut except that the walls were left unplastered, so that the structure appeared in the nature of a summerhouse. Septimus Favonius had left the garden and von Harben took advantage of the fact to examine his surroundings more closely. The garden was laid out with winding, graveled walks, bordered by shrubs and flowers, with an occasional tree, some of which gave evidence of great age.

The young man's mind, his eyes, his imagination were so fully occupied with his surroundings that he experienced a sensation almost akin to shock as he followed the turning of the path around a large ornamental shrub and came face-to-face with a young woman.

That she was equally surprised was evidenced by the consternation apparent in her expression as she looked wide-eyed into the eyes of von Harben. For quite an appreciable moment of time they stood looking at one another. Von Harben thought that never in his life had he seen so beautiful a girl. What the girl thought, von Harben did not know. It was she who broke the silence.

"Who are you?" she asked, in a voice little above a whisper, as one might conceivably address an apparition that had arisen suddenly and unexpectedly before him.

"I am a stranger here," replied von Harben, "and I owe you an apology for intruding upon your privacy. I thought that I was alone in the garden."

"Who are you?" repeated the girl. "I have never seen your face before or one like yours."

"And I," said von Harben, "have never seen a girl like you. Perhaps I am dreaming. Perhaps you do not exist at all, for it does not seem credible that in the world of realities such a one as you could exist."

The girl blushed. "You are not of Castrum Mare," she said. "That I can see." Her tone was a trifle cold and slightly haughty.

"I have offended you," said von Harben. "I ask your pardon. I did not mean to be offensive, but coming upon you so unexpectedly quite took my breath away."

"And your manners, too?" asked the girl, but now her eyes were smiling.

"You have forgiven me?" asked von Harben.

"You will have to tell me who you are and why you are here before I can answer that," she replied. "For all I know you might be an enemy or a barbarian."

Von Harben laughed. "Mallius Lepus, who invited me here, insists that I am a barbarian," he said, "but even so I am the guest of Septimus Favonius, his uncle."

The girl shrugged. "I am not surprised," she said. "My father is notorious for the guests he honors."

"You are the daughter of Favonius?" asked von Harben.

"Yes, I am Favonia," replied the girl, "but you have not yet told me about yourself. I command you to do so," she said, imperiously.

"I am Erich von Harben of Germania," said the young man.

"Germania!" exclaimed the girl. "Cæsar wrote of Germania, as did Sanguinarius. It seems very far away."

"It never seemed so far as now," said von Harben; "yet the three thousand miles of distance seem nothing by comparison with the centuries of time that intervene."

The girl puckered her brows. "I do not understand you," she said.

"No," said von Harben, "and I cannot blame you."

"You are a chief, of course?" she asked.

He did not deny the insinuation, for he had been quick to see from the attitude of the three patricians he had met that the social standing of a barbarian in Castrum Mare might be easily open to question, unless his barbarism was somewhat mitigated by a title. Proud as he was of his nationality, von Harben realized that it was a far cry from the European barbarians of Cæsar's day to their cultured descendants of the twentieth century and that it would probably be impossible to convince these people of the changes that have taken place since their history was written; and, also, he was conscious of a very definite desire to appear well in the eyes of this lovely maiden of a bygone age.

"Favonia!" exclaimed von Harben. He scarcely breathed the name.

The girl looked up at him questioningly. "Yes!" she said.

"It is such a lovely name," he said. "I never heard it spoken before."

"You like it?" she asked.

"Very much, indeed."

The girl puckered her brows in thought. She had beautiful penciled brows and a forehead that denoted an intelligence that was belied by neither her eyes, her manner, nor her speech. "I am glad that you like my name, but I do not understand why I should be glad. You say that you are a barbarian, and yet you do not seem like a barbarian. Your appearance and your manner are those of a patrician, though perhaps you are over-bold with a young woman you have never met before, but that I ascribe to the ignorance of the barbarian and so I forgive it."

"Being a barbarian has its compensations," laughed von Harben, "and perhaps I am a barbarian. I may be again forgiven if I say you are quite the most beautiful girl I have ever seen and the only one—I could—" he hesitated.

"You could what?" she demanded.

"Even a barbarian should not dare to say what I was about to say to one whom I have known scarce half a dozen minutes."

"Whoever you may be, you show rare discrimination," came in a sarcastic tone in a man's voice directly behind von Harben.

The girl looked up in surprise and von Harben wheeled about simultaneously, for neither had been aware of the presence of another. Facing him von Harben saw a short, dark, greasy-looking young man in an elaborate tunic, his hand resting upon the hilt of the short sword that hung at his hip. There was a sarcastic sneer upon the face of the newcomer.

"Who is your barbarian friend, Favonia?" he demanded.

"This is Erich von Harben, a guest in the home of Septimus Favonius, my father," replied the girl, haughtily; and to von Harben, "This is Fulvus Fupus, who accepts the hospitality of Septimus Favonius so often that he feels free to criticize another guest."

Fupus flushed. "I apologize," he said, "but one may never know when to honor or when to ridicule one of Septimus Favonius's guests of honor. The last, if I recall correctly, was an ape, and before that there was a barbarian from some outer village—but they are always interesting and I am sure that the barbarian, Erich von Harben, will prove no exception to the rule." The man's tone was sarcastic and obnoxious to a degree, and it was with difficulty that von Harben restrained his mounting temper.

Fortunately, at this moment, Mallius Lepus joined them and von Harben was formally presented to Favonia. Fulvus Fupus thereafter paid little attention to von Harben, but devoted his time assiduously to Favonia. Von Harben knew from their conversation that they were upon friendly and intimate terms and he guessed that Fupus was in love with Favonia, though he could not tell from the girl's attitude whether or not she returned his affection.

There was something else that von Harben was sure of—that he too was in love with Favonia. Upon several occasions in life he had thought that he was in love, but his sensations and reactions upon those other occasions had not been the same in either kind or degree as those which he now experienced. He found himself hating Fulvus Fupus, whom he had known scarce a quarter of an hour and whose greatest offense, aside from looking lovingly at Favonia, had been a certain arrogant sarcasm of speech and manner—certainly no sufficient warrant for a sane man to wish to do murder, and yet Erich von Harben fingered the butt of his Luger, which he had insisted upon wearing in addition to the slim dagger with which Mallius Lepus had armed him.

Later, when Septimus Favonius joined them, he suggested that they all go to the baths and Mallius Lepus whispered to von Harben that his uncle was already itching to exhibit his new find.

"He will take us to the Baths of Cæsar," said Lepus, "which are patronized by the richest patricians only, so have a few good stories ready, but save your best ones, like that you told me about the modern Roman litters, for the dinner that my uncle is sure to give tonight—for he will have the best of Castrum Mare there, possibly even the Emperor himself."

The Baths of Cæsar were housed in an imposing building, of which that portion facing on the avenue was given over to what appeared to be exclusive shops. The main entrance led to a large court where the warmth with which the party was greeted by a number of patrons of the Baths already congregated there attested to the popularity of Favonius, his daughter, and his nephew, while it was evident to von Harben that there was less enthusiasm manifested for Fulvus Fupus.

Servants conducted the bathers to the dressing rooms, the men's and women's being in different quarters of the building.

After his clothes were removed, von Harben's body was anointed with oils in a warm room and then he was led into a hot room and from there with the other men he passed into a large apartment containing a plunge where both the men and women gathered. About the plunge were seats for several hundred people, and in the Baths of Cæsar these were constructed of highly polished granite.

While von Harben enjoyed the prospect of a swim in the clear, cold water of the frigidarium, he was much more interested by the opportunity it afforded him to be with Favonia again. She was swimming slowly around the pool when he entered the room and, making a long, running dive, von Harben slipped easily and gracefully into the water, a few strokes bringing him to her side. A murmur of applause that followed meant nothing to von Harben, for he did not know that diving was an unknown art among the citizens of Castrum Mare.

Fulvus Fupus, who had entered the frigidarium behind von Harben, sneered as he saw the dive and heard the applause. He had never seen it done before, but he could see that the thing was very easy, and realizing the advantages of so graceful an accomplishment, he determined at once to show the assembled patricians, and especially Favonia, that he was equally a master of this athletic art as was the barbarian.

Running, as he had seen von Harben run, toward the edge of the pool, Fulvus Fupus sprang high into the air and came straight down upon his belly with a resounding smack that sent the wind out of him and the water splashing high in all directions.

Gasping for breath, he managed to reach the side of the pool, where he clung while the laughter of the assembled patricians brought the scarlet of mortification to his face. Whereas before he had viewed von Harben with contempt and some slight suspicion, he now viewed him with contempt, suspicion, and hatred. Disgruntled, Fupus clambered from the pool and returned immediately to the dressing room, where he donned his garments.

"Going already, Fupus?" demanded a young patrician who was disrobing in the apodyterium.

"Yes," growled Fupus.

"I hear you came with Septimus Favonius and his new find. What sort may he be?"

"Listen well, Cæcilius Metellus," said Fupus. "This man who calls himself Erich von Harben says that he is a chief from Germania, but I believe otherwise."

"What do you believe?" demanded Metellus, politely, though evidently with no considerable interest.

Fupus came close to the other. "I believe him to be a spy from Castra Sanguinarius," he whispered, "and that he is only pretending that he is a barbarian."

"But they say that he does not speak our language well," said Metellus.

"He speaks it as any man might speak it who wanted to pretend that he did not understand it or that it was new to him," said Fupus.

Metellus shook his head. "Septimus Favonius is no fool," he

said. "I doubt if there is anyone in Castra Sanguinarius, sufficiently clever to fool him to such an extent."

"There is only one man who has any right to judge as to that," snapped Fupus, "and he is going to have the facts before I am an hour older."

"Whom do you mean?" asked Metellus.

"Validus Augustus, Emperor of the East—I am going to him at once."

"Don't be a fool, Fupus," counseled Metellus. "You will only get yourself laughed at or possibly worse. Know you not that Septimus Favonius is high in the favor of the Emperor?"

"Perhaps, but is it not also known that he was friendly with Cassius Hasta, nephew of the Emperor, whom Validus Augustus accused of treason and banished. It would not take much to convince the Emperor that this Erich von Harben is an emissary of Cassius Hasta, who is reputed to be in Castra Sanguinarius."

Cæcilius Metellus laughed. "Go on then and make a fool of yourself, Fupus," he said. "You will probably bring up at the end of a rope."

"The end of a rope will terminate this business," agreed Fupus, "but von Harben will be there, not I."

9

As NIGHT FELL upon the city of Castra Sanguinarius, the gloom of the granite dungeons beneath the city's Colosseum deepened into blackest darkness, which was relieved only by a rectangular patch of starlit sky where barred windows pierced the walls.

Squatting upon the rough stone floor, his back against the wall, Tarzan watched the stars moving in slow procession across the window's opening. A creature of the wild, impatient of restraint, the ape-man suffered the mental anguish of the caged beast—perhaps, because of his human mind, his suffering was greater than would have been that of one of the lower orders, yet he endured with even greater outward stoicism than the beast that paces to and fro seeking escape from the bars that confine it.

As the feet of the beast might have measured the walls of its dungeon, so did the mind of Tarzan, and never for a waking moment was his mind not occupied by thoughts of escape.

Lukedi and the other inmates of the dungeon slept, but Tarzan still sat watching the free stars and envying them, when he became conscious of a sound, ever so slight, coming from the arena, the floor of which was about on a level with the sill of the little window in the top of the dungeon wall. Something was moving, stealthily and cautiously, upon the sand of the arena. Presently, framed in the window, silhouetted against the sky, appeared a familiar figure. Tarzan smiled and whispered a word so low that a human ear could scarce have heard it, and Nkima slipped between the bars and dropped to the floor of the dungeon. An instant later the little monkey snuggled close to Tarzan, its long, muscular arms clasped tightly about the neck of the ape-man.

"Come home with me," pleaded Nkima. "Why do you stay in this cold, dark hole beneath the ground?"

"You have seen the cage in which we sometimes keep Jad-bal-ja, the Golden Lion?" demanded Tarzan.

"Yes," said Nkima.

"Jad-bal-ja cannot get out unless we open the gate," explained Tarzan. "I too am in a cage. I cannot get out until they open the gate."

"I will go and get Muviro and his Gomangani with the sharp sticks," said Nkima. "They will come and let you out."

"No, Nkima," said Tarzan. "If I cannot get out by myself, Muviro could not get here in time to free me, and if he came many of my brave Waziri would be killed, for there are fighting men here in far greater numbers than Muviro could bring." After awhile Tarzan slept, and curled up within his arms slept Nkima, the little monkey, but when Tarzan awoke in the morning Nkima was gone.

Toward the middle of the morning soldiers came and the door of the dungeon was unlocked and opened to admit several of them, including a young white officer, who was accompanied by a slave. The officer addressed Tarzan in the language of the city, but the ape-man shook his head, indicating that he did not understand; then the other turned to the slave with a few words and the latter spoke to Tarzan in the Bagego dialect, asking him if he understood it.

"Yes," replied the ape-man, and through the interpreter the officer questioned Tarzan.

"Who are you and what were you, a white man, doing in the village of the Bagegos?" asked the officer.

"I am Tarzan of the Apes," replied the prisoner. "I was

looking for another white man who is lost somewhere in these mountains, but I slipped upon the cliffside and fell and while I was unconscious the Bagegos took me prisoner, and when your soldiers raided the Bagego village they found me there. Now that you know about me, I presume that I shall be released."

"Why?" demanded the officer. "Are you a citizen of Rome?"

"Of course not," said Tarzan. "What has that to do with it?"

"Because if you are not a citizen of Rome it is quite possible that you are an enemy. How do we know that you are not from Castrum Mare?"

Tarzan shrugged. "I do not know," he said, "how you would know that since I do not even know what Castrum Mare means."

"That is what you would say if you wished to deceive us," said the officer, "and you would also pretend that you could not speak or understand our language, but you will find that it is not going to be easy to deceive us. We are not such fools as the people of Castrum Mare believe us to be."

"Where is this Castrum Mare and what is it?" asked Tarzan.

The officer laughed. "You are very clever," he said.

"I assure you," said the ape-man, "that I am not trying to deceive you. Believe me for a moment and answer one question."

"What is it you wish to ask?"

"Has another white man come into your country within the last few weeks? He is the one for whom I am searching."

"No white man has entered this country," replied the officer, "since Marcus Crispus Sanguinarius led the Third Cohort of the Tenth Legion in victorious conquest of the barbarians who inhabited it eighteen hundred and twenty-three years ago."

"And if a stranger were in your country you would know it?" asked Tarzan.

"If he were in Castra Sanguinarius, yes," replied the officer, "but if he had entered Castrum Mare at the east end of the valley I should not know it; but come, I was not sent here to answer questions, but to fetch you before one who will ask them."

At a word from the officer, the soldiers who accompanied him conducted Tarzan from the dungeon, along the corridor through which he had come the previous day and up into the city. The detachment proceeded for a mile through the city streets to an imposing building, before the entrance to which there was stationed a military guard whose elaborate cuirasses, helmets, and crests suggested that they might be a part of a select military organization.

The metal plates of their cuirasses appeared to Tarzan to be of gold, as did the metal of their helmets, while the hilts and scabbards of their swords were elaborately carved and further ornamented with colored stones ingeniously inlaid in the metal, and to their gorgeous appearance was added the final touch of scarlet cloaks.

The officer who met the party at the gate admitted Tarzan, the interpreter, and the officer who had brought him, but the guard of soldiery was replaced by a detachment of resplendent men-at-arms similar to those who guarded the entrance to the palace.

Tarzan was taken immediately into the building and along a wide corridor, from which opened many chambers, to a large, oblong room flanked by stately columns. At the far end of the apartment a large man sat in a huge, carved chair upon a raised dais.

There were many other people in the room, nearly all of whom were colorfully garbed in bright cloaks over colored tunics and ornate cuirasses of leather or metal, while others wore only simple flowing togas, usually of white. Slaves, messengers, officers were constantly entering or leaving the chamber. The party accompanying Tarzan withdrew between the columns at one side of the room and waited there.

"What is this place?" asked Tarzan of the Bagego interpreter, "and who is the man at the far end of the room?"

"This is the throne room of the Emperor of the West and that is Sublatus Imperator himself."

For some time Tarzan watched the scene before him with interest. He saw people, evidently of all classes, approach the throne and address the Emperor, and though he could not understand their words, he judged that they were addressing pleas to their ruler. There were patricians among the suppliants, brown-skinned shopkeepers, barbarians resplendent in their savage finery, and even slaves.

The Emperor, Sublatus, presented an imposing figure. Over a tunic of white linen, the Emperor wore a cuirass of gold. His sandals were of white with gold buckles, and from his shoulders fell the purple robe of the Cæsars. A fillet of embroidered linen about his brow was the only other insignia of his station.

Directly behind the throne were heavy hangings against which were ranged a file of soldiers bearing poles surmounted by silver eagles and various other devices, and banners, of the meaning and purpose of which Tarzan was ignorant. Upon every column along the side of the wall were hung shields of various shapes over crossed banners and standards similar to those ranged behind the Emperor. Everything pertaining to the embellishment of the room was martial, the mural decorations being crudely painted scenes of war.

Presently a man, who appeared to be an official of the court, approached them and addressed the officer who had brought Tarzan from the Colosseum.

"Are you Maximus Præclarus?" he demanded.

"Yes," replied the officer.

"Present yourself with the prisoner."

As Tarzan advanced toward the throne surrounded by the detachment of the guard, all eyes were turned upon him, for he was a conspicuous figure even in this assemblage of gorgeously appareled courtiers and soldiers, though his only garments were a loincloth and a leopard skin. His suntanned skin, his shock of black hair, and his gray eyes might not alone have marked him especially in such an assemblage, for there were other dark-skinned, black-haired, gray-eyed men among them, but there was only one who towered inches above them all and he was Tarzan. The undulating smoothness of his easy stride suggested even to the mind of the proud and haughty Sublatus the fierce and savage power of the king of beasts, which perhaps accounted for the fact that the Emperor, with raised hand, halted the party a little further from the throne than usual.

As the party halted before the throne, Tarzan did not wait to be questioned, but, turning to the Bagego interpreter, said: "Ask Sublatus why I have been made a prisoner and tell him that I demand that he free me at once."

The man quailed. "Do as I tell you," said Tarzan.

"What is he saying?" asked Sublatus of the interpreter.

"I fear to repeat such words to the Emperor," replied the man.

"I command it," said Sublatus.

"He asked why he has been made a prisoner and demands that he be released at once."

"Ask him who he is," said Sublatus, angrily, "that he dares issue commands to Sublatus Imperator."

"Tell him," said Tarzan, after the Emperor's words had been translated to him, "that I am Tarzan of the Apes, but if that means as little to him as his name means to me, I have other means to convince him that I am as accustomed to issuing orders and being obeyed as is he."

"Take the insolent dog away," replied Sublatus with trembling voice after he had been told what Tarzan's words had been.

The soldiers laid hold of Tarzan, but he shook them off. "Tell him," snapped the ape-man, "that as one white man to another I demand an answer to my question. Tell him that I did not approach his country as an enemy, but as a friend, and that I shall look to him to see that I am accorded the treatment to which I am entitled, and that before I leave this room."

When these words were translated to Sublatus, the purple of his enraged face matched the imperial purple of his cloak.

"Take him away," he shrieked. "Take him away. Call the guard. Throw Maximus Præclarus into chains for permitting a prisoner to thus address Sublatus."

Two soldiers seized Tarzan, one his right arm, the other his left, but he swung them suddenly together before him and with such force did their heads meet that they relaxed their grasps upon him and sank unconscious to the floor, and then it was that the ape-man leaped with the agility of a cat to the dais where sat the Emperor, Sublatus.

So quickly had the act been accomplished and so unexpected was it that there was none prepared to come between Tarzan and the Emperor in time to prevent the terrible indignity that Tarzan proceeded to inflict upon him.

Seizing the Emperor by the shoulder, he lifted him from his throne and wheeled him about and then grasping him by the scruff of the neck and the bottom of his cuirass, he lifted him from the floor just as several pikemen leaped forward to rescue Sublatus. But when they were about to menace Tarzan with their pikes, he used the body of the screaming Sublatus as a shield so that the soldiers dared not to attack for fear of killing their Emperor.

"Tell them," said Tarzan to the Bagego interpreter, "that if any man interferes with me before I have reached the street, I shall wring the Emperor's neck. Tell him to order them back. If he does, I shall set him free when he is out of the building. If he refuses, it will be at his own risk."

When this message was given to Sublatus, he stopped screaming orders to his people to attack the ape-man and instead warned them to permit Tarzan to leave the palace. Carrying the Emperor above his head, Tarzan leaped from the dais and as he did so the courtiers fell back in accordance with the commands of Sublatus, who now ordered them to turn their backs that they might not witness the indignity that was being done their ruler.

Down the long throne room and through the corridors to the outer court Tarzan of the Apes carried Sublatus Imperator above his head and at the command of the ape-man the black interpreter went ahead, but there was no need for him, since Sublatus kept the road clear as he issued commands in a voice that trembled with a combination of rage, fear, and mortification.

At the outer gate the members of the guard begged to be permitted to rescue Sublatus and avenge the insult that had been put upon him, but the Emperor warned them to permit his captor to leave the palace in safety, provided he kept his word and liberated Sublatus when they had reached the avenue beyond the gate.

The scarlet-cloaked guard fell back grumbling, their eyes filled with anger because of the humiliation of their Emperor. Even though they had no love for him, yet he was the personification of the power and dignity of their government, and the scene that they witnessed filled them with mortification as the half-naked barbarian bore their commander-in-chief through the palace gates out into the tree-bordered avenue beyond, while the interpreter marched ahead, scarce knowing whether to be more downcast by terror or elated through pride in this unwonted publicity.

The city of Castra Sanguinarius had been carved from the primeval forest that clothed the west end of the canyon, and with unusual vision the founders of the city had cleared only such spaces as were necessary for avenues, buildings, and similar purposes. Ancient trees overhung the avenue before the palace and in many places their foliage overspread the low housetops, mingling with the foliage of the trees in inner courtyards.

Midway of the broad avenue the ape-man halted and lowered Sublatus to the ground. He turned his eyes in the direction of the gateway through which the soldiers of Sublatus were crowding out into the avenue.

"Tell them," said Tarzan to the interpreter, "to go back into the palace grounds; then and then only shall I release their Emperor," for Tarzan had noted the ready javelins in the hands of many of the guardsmen and guessed that the moment his body ceased to be protected by the near presence of Sublatus it would be the target and the goal of a score of the weapons.

When the interpreter deliver the ape-man's ultimatum to them, the guardsmen hesitated, but Sublatus commanded them to obey, for the barbarian's heavy grip upon his shoulder convinced him that there was no hope that he might escape alive or uninjured unless he and his soldiers acceded to the creature's demand. As the last of the guardsmen passed back into the palace courtyard Tarzan released the Emperor and as Sublatus hastened quickly toward the gate, the guardsmen made a sudden sally into the avenue.

They saw their quarry turn and take a few quick steps, leap high into the air and disappear amidst the foliage of an overhanging oak. A dozen javelins hurtled among the branches of the tree. The soldiers rushed forward, their eyes strained upward, but the quarry had vanished.

Sublatus was close upon their heels. "Quick!" he cried. "After him! A thousand denarii to the man who brings down the barbarian."

"There he goes!" cried one, pointing.

"No," cried another. "I saw him there among the foliage. I saw the branches move," and he pointed in the opposite direction.

And in the meantime the ape-man moved swiftly through the trees along one side of the avenue, dropped to a low roof, crossed it and sprang into a tree that rose from an inner court, pausing there to listen for signs of pursuit. After the manner of a wild beast hunted through his native jungle, he moved as silently as the shadow of a shadow, so that now, although he crouched scarce twenty feet above them, the two people in the courtyard below him were unaware of his presence.

But Tarzan was not unaware of theirs and as he listened to the noise of the growing pursuit, that was spreading now in all directions through the city, he took note of the girl and the man in the garden beneath him. It was apparent that the man was wooing the maid, and Tarzan needed no knowledge of their spoken language to interpret the gestures, the glances, and the facial expressions of passionate pleading upon the part of the man or the cold aloofness of the girl.

Sometimes a tilt of her head presented a partial view of her profile to the ape-man and he guessed that she was very beautiful, but the face of the young man with her reminded him of the face of Pamba the rat.

It was evident that his courtship was not progressing to the liking of the youth and now there were evidences of anger in his tone. The girl rose haughtily and with a cold word turned away, and then the man leaped to his feet from the bench upon which they had been sitting and seized her roughly by the arm. She turned surprised and angry eyes upon him and had half voiced a cry for help when the rat-faced man clapped a hand across her mouth and with his free arm dragged her into his embrace.

Now all this was none of Tarzan's affair. The shes of the city of Castra Sanguinarius meant no more to the savage ape-man than did the shes of the village of Nyuto, chief of the Bagegos. They meant no more to him than did Sabor the lioness and far less than did the shes of the tribe of Akut or of Toyat the king ape—but Tarzan of the Apes was often a creature of impulses; now he realized that he did not like the rat-faced young man, and that he never could like him, while the girl that he was mal-treating seemed to be doubly likable because of her evident aversion to her tormentor.

The man had bent the girl's frail body back upon the bench. His lips were close to hers when there was a sudden jarring of the ground beside him and he turned astonished eyes upon the figure of a half-naked giant. Steel-gray eyes looked into his beady black ones, a heavy hand fell upon the collar of his tunic, and he felt himself lifted from the body of the girl and then hurled roughly aside.

He saw his assailant lift his victim to her feet and his little eyes saw, too, another thing: the stranger was unarmed! Then it was that the sword of Fastus leaped from its scabbard and that Tarzan of the Apes found himself facing naked steel. The girl saw what Fastus would do. She saw that the stranger who protected her was unarmed and she leaped between them, at the same time calling loudly, "Axuch! Sarus! Mpingu! Hither! Quickly!"

Tarzan seized the girl and swung her quickly behind him,

and simultaneously Fastus was upon him. But the Roman had reckoned without his host and the easy conquest over an unarmed man that he had expected seemed suddenly less easy of accomplishment, for when his keen Spanish sword swung down to cleave the body of his foe, that foe was not there.

Never in his life had Fastus witnessed such agility. It was as though the eyes and body of the barbarian moved more rapidly than the sword of Fastus, and always a fraction of an inch ahead.

Three times Fastus swung viciously at the stranger, and three times his blade cut empty air, while the girl, wide-eyed with astonishment, watched the seemingly unequal duel. Her heart filled with admiration for this strange young giant, who, though he was evidently a barbarian, looked more the patrician than Fastus himself. Three times the blade of Fastus cut harmlessly through empty air—and then there was a lightninglike movement on the part of his antagonist. A brown hand shot beneath the guard of the Roman, steel fingers gripped his wrist, and an instant later his sword clattered to the tile walk of the courtyard. At the same moment two white men and a Negro hurried breathlessly into the garden and ran quickly forward— two with daggers in their hands and one, the black, with a sword.

They saw Tarzan standing between Fastus and the girl. They saw the man in the grip of a stranger. They saw the sword clatter to the ground, and naturally they reached the one conclusion that seemed possible—Fastus was being worsted in an attempt to protect the girl against a stranger.

Tarzan saw them coming toward him and realized that three to one are heavy odds. He was upon the point of using Fastus as a shield against his new enemies when the girl stepped before the three and motioned them to stop. Again the tantalizing tongue that he could almost understand and yet not quite, as the girl explained the circumstances to the newcomers while Tarzan still stood holding Fastus by the wrist.

Presently the girl turned to Tarzan and addressed him, but

he only shook his head to indicate that he could not understand her; then, as his eyes fell upon the Negro, a possible means of communicating with these people occurred to him, for the Negro resembled closely the Bagegos of the outer world.

"Are you a Bagego?" asked Tarzan in the language of that tribe.

The man looked surprised. "Yes," he said, "I am, but who are you?"

"And you speak the language of these people?" asked Tarzan, indicating the young woman and Fastus and ignoring the man's query.

"Of course," said the Negro. "I have been a prisoner among them for many years, but there are many Bagegos among my fellow prisoners and we have not forgotten the language of our mothers."

"Good," said Tarzan. "Through you this young woman may speak to me."

"She wants to know who you are, and where you come from, and what you were doing in her garden, and how you got here, and how you happened to protect her from Fastus, and—"

Tarzan held up his hand. "One at a time," he cried. "Tell her I am Tarzan of the Apes, a stranger from a far country, and I came here in friendship seeking one of my own people who is lost."

Now came an interruption in the form of loud pounding and hallooing beyond the outer doorway of the building.

"See what that may be, Axuch," directed the girl, and as the one so addressed, and evidently a slave, humbly turned to do her bidding, she once more addressed Tarzan through the interpreter.

"You have won the gratitude of Dilecta," she said, "and you shall be rewarded by her father."

At this moment Axuch returned followed by a young officer. As the eyes of the newcomer fell upon Tarzan they went wide and he started back, his hand going to the hilt of his sword, and simultaneously Tarzan recognized him as Maximus Præclarus, the young patrician officer who had conducted him from the Colosseum to the palace.

"Lay off your sword, Maximus Præclarus," said the young girl, "for this man is no enemy."

"And you are sure of that, Dilecta?" demanded Præclarus. "What do you know of him?"

"I know that he came in time to save me from this swine who would have harmed me," said the girl haughtily, casting a withering glance at Fastus.

"I do not understand," said Præclarus. "This is a barbarian prisoner of war who calls himself Tarzan and whom I took this morning from the Colosseum to the palace at the command of the Emperor, that Sublatus might look upon the strange creature, whom some thought to be a spy from Castrum Mare."

"If he is a prisoner, what is he doing here, then?" demanded the girl. "And why are you here?"

"This fellow attacked the Emperor himself and then escaped from the palace. The entire city is being searched and I, being in charge of a detachment of soldiers assigned to this district, came immediately hither, fearing the very thing that has happened and that this wild man might find you and do you harm."

"It was the patrician, Fastus, son of Imperial Cæsar, who would have harmed me," said the girl. "It was the wild man who saved me from him."

Maximum Præclarus looked quickly at Fastus, the son of Sublatus, and then at Tarzan. The young officer appeared to be resting upon the horns of a dilemma.

"There is your man," said Fastus, with a sneer. "Back to the dungeons with him."

"Maximus Præclarus does not take orders from Fastus," said the young man, "and he knows his duty without consulting him."

"You will arrest this man who has protected me, Præclarus?" demanded Dilecta.

"What else may I do?" asked Præclarus. "It is my duty."

"Then do it," sneered Fastus.

Præclarus went white. "It is with difficulty that I can keep my hands off you, Fastus," he said. "If you were the son of Jupiter himself, it would not take much more to get yourself choked. If you know what is well for you, you will go before I lose control of my temper."

"Mpingu," said Dilecta, "show Fastus to the avenue."

Fastus flushed. "My father, the Emperor, shall hear of this," he snarled; "and do not forget, Dilecta, your father stands none too well in the estimation of Sublatus Imperator."

"Get gone," cried Dilecta, "before I order my slave to throw you into the avenue."

With a sneer and a swagger Fastus quit the garden, and when he had gone Dilecta turned to Maximus Præclarus.

"What shall we do?" she cried. "I must protect this noble stranger who saved me from Fastus, and at the same time you must do your duty and return him to Sublatus."

"I have a plan," said Maximus Præclarus, "but I cannot carry it out unless I can talk with the stranger."

"Mpingu can understand and interpret for him," said the girl.

"Can you trust Mpingu implicitly?" asked Præclarus.

"Absolutely," said Dilecta.

"Then send away the others," said Præclarus, indicating Axuch and Sarus; and when Mpingu returned from escorting Fastus to the street he found Maximus Præclarus, Dilecta, and Tarzan alone in the garden.

Præclarus motioned Mpingu to advance. "Tell the stranger that I have been sent to arrest him," he said to Mpingu, "but tell him also that because of the service he has rendered Dilecta I wish to protect him, if he will follow my instructions."

"What are they?" asked Tarzan when the question had been put to him. "What do you wish me to do?"

"I wish you to come with me," said Præclarus, "to come with me as though you are my prisoner. I shall take you in the direction of the Colosseum and when I am opposite my own home I shall give you a signal so that you will understand that the house is mine. Immediately afterward I will make it possible for you to escape into the trees as you did when you quit the palace with Sublatus. Go, then, immediately to my house and remain there until I return. Dilecta will send Mpingu there now to warn my servants that you are coming. At my command they will protect you with their lives. Do you understand?"

"I understand," replied the ape-man, when the plan had been explained to him by Mpingu.

"Later," said Præclarus, "we may be able to find a way to get you out of Castra Sanguinarius and across the mountains."

10

THE CARES OF state rested lightly upon the shoulders of Validus Augustus, Emperor of the East, for though his title was imposing his domain was small and his subjects few. The island city of Castrum Mare boasted a population of only a trifle more than twenty-two thousand people, of which some three thousand were whites and nineteen thousand of mixed blood, while outside the city, in the villages of the lake dwellers and along the eastern shore of Mare Orientis, dwelt the balance of his subjects, comprising some twenty-six thousand Negroes.

Today, reports and audiences disposed of, the Emperor had withdrawn to the palace garden to spend an hour in conversation with a few of his intimates, while his musicians, concealed within a vine-covered bower, entertained him. While he was thus occupied a chamberlain approached and announced that the patrician Fulvus Fupus begged an audience of the Emperor.

"Fulvus knows that the audience hour is past," snapped the Emperor. "Bid him come on the morrow."

"He insists, most glorious Cæsar," said the chamberlain, "that his business is of the utmost importance and that it is only because he felt that the safety of the Emperor is at stake that he came at this hour."

"Bring him here then," commanded Validus, and, as the chamberlain turned away, "Am I never to have a moment's relaxation without some fool like Fulvus Fupus breaking in upon me with some silly story?" he grumbled to one of his companions.

When Fulvus approached the Emperor a moment later, he was received with a cold and haughty stare.

"I have come, most glorious Cæsar," said Fulvus, "to fulfill the duty of a citizen of Rome, whose first concern should be the safety of his Emperor."

"What are you talking about?" snapped Validus. "Quick, out with it!"

"There is a stranger in Castrum Mare who claims to be a barbarian from Germania, but I believe him to be a spy from Castrum Sanguinarius where, it is said, Cassius Hasta is an honored guest of Sublatus, in that city."

"What do you know about Cassius Hasta and what has he to do with it?" demanded Validus.

"It is said—it is rumored," stammered Fulvus Fupus, "that—"

"I have heard too many rumors already about Cassius Hasta," exclaimed Validus. "Can I not dispatch my nephew upon a mission without every fool in Castrum Mare lying awake nights to conjure motives, which may later be ascribed to me?"

"It is only what I heard," said Fulvus, flushed and uncomfortable. "I do not know anything about it. I did not say that I knew."

"Well, what did you hear?" demanded Validus. "Come, out with it."

"The talk is common in the Baths that you sent Cassius Hasta away because he was plotting treason and that he went at once to Sublatus, who received him in a friendly fashion and that together they are planning an attack upon Castrum Mare."

Validus scowled. "Baseless rumor," he said; "but what about this prisoner? What has he to do with it and why have I not been advised of his presence?"

"That I do not know," said Fulvus Fupus. "That is why I felt it doubly my duty to inform you, since the man who is harboring the stranger is a most powerful patrician and one who might well be ambitious."

"Who is he?" asked the Emperor.

"Septimus Favonius," replied Fupus.

"Septimus Favonius!" exclaimed Validus. "Impossible."

"Not so impossible," said Fupus, boldly, "if glorious Cæsar will but recall the friendship that ever existed between Cassius Hasta and Mallius Lepus, the nephew of Septimus Favonius. The home of Septimus Favonius was the other home of Cassius Hasta. To whom, then, sooner might he turn for aid than to this powerful friend whose ambitions are well known outside the palace, even though they may not as yet have come to the ears of Validus Augustus?"

Nervously the Emperor arose and paced to and fro, the eyes of the others watching him narrowly; those of Fulvus Fupus narrowed with malign anticipation.

Presently Validus halted and turned toward one of his courtiers. "May Hercules strike me dead," he cried, "if there be not some truth in what Fulvus Fupus suggests!" and to Fupus, "What is this stranger like?"

"He is a man of white skin, yet of slightly different complexion and appearance than the usual patrician. He feigns to speak our language with a certain practiced stiltedness that is intended to suggest lack of familiarity. This, I think, is merely a part of the ruse to deceive."

"How did he come into Castrum Mare and none of my officers report the matter to me?" asked Validus.

"That you may learn from Mallius Lepus," said Fulvus Fupus, "for Mallius Lepus was in command of the Porta Decumana when some of the barbarians of the lake villages brought him there, presumably a prisoner, yet Cæsar knows how easy it would have been to bribe these creatures to play such a part."

"You explain it so well, Fulvus Fupus," said the Emperor, "that one might even suspect you to have been the instigator of the plot, or at least to have given much thought to similar schemes."

"Cæsar's ever brilliant wit never deserts him," said Fupus, forcing a smile, though his face paled.

"We shall see," snapped Validus, and turning to one of his officers, "Order the arrest of Septimus Favonius, and Mallius Lepus and this stranger at once."

As he ceased speaking a chamberlain entered the garden and approached the Emperor. "Septimus Favonius requests an audience," he announced. "Mallius Lepus, his nephew, and a stranger are with him."

"Fetch them," said Validus, and to the officer who was about to depart to arrest them, "Wait here. We shall see what Septimus Favonius has to say."

A moment later the three entered and approached the Emperor. Favonius and Lepus saluted Validus and then the former presented von Harben as a barbarian chief from Germania.

"We have already heard of this barbarian chief," said Validus, with a sneer. Favonius and Lepus glanced at Fupus. "Why was I not immediately notified of the capture of this prisoner?" This time the Emperor directed his remarks to Mallius Lepus.

"There has been little delay, Cæsar," replied the young officer. "It was necessary that he be bathed and properly clothed before he was brought here."

"It was not necessary that he be brought here," said Validus. "There are dungeons in Castrum Mare for prisoners from Castra Sanguinarius."

"He is not from Castra Sanguinarius," said Septimus Favonius.

"Where are you from and what are you doing in my country?" demanded Validus, turning upon von Harben.

"I am from a country that your historians knew as Germania," replied Erich.

"And I suppose you learned to speak our language in Germania," sneered Validus.

"Yes," replied von Harben, "I did."

"And you have never been to Castra Sanguinarius?"

"Never."

"I presume you have been to Rome," laughed Validus.

"Yes, many times," replied von Harben.

"And who is Emperor there now?"

"There is no Roman Emperor," said von Harben.

"No Roman Emperor!" exclaimed Validus. "If you are not a spy from Castra Sanguinarius, you are a lunatic. Perhaps you are both, for no one but a lunatic would expect me to believe such a story. No Roman Emperor, indeed!"

"There is no Roman Emperor," said von Harben, "because there is no Roman Empire. Mallius Lepus tells me that your country has had no intercourse with the outside world for more than eighteen hundred years. Much can happen in that time—much has happened. Rome fell, over a thousand years ago. No nation speaks its language today, which is understood by priests and scholars only. The barbarians of Germania, of Gallia, and of Britannia have built empires and civilizations of tremendous power, and Rome is only a city in Italia."

Mallius Lepus was beaming delightedly. "I told you," he whispered to Favonius, "that you would love him. By Jupiter, I wish he would tell Validus the story of the litters that travel fifty thousand paces an hour!"

There was that in the tone and manner of von Harben that compelled confidence and belief, so that even the suspicious Validus gave credence to the seemingly wild tales of the stranger and presently found himself asking questions of the barbarian.

Finally the Emperor turned to Fulvus Fupus. "Upon what proof did you accuse this man of being a spy from Castra Sanguinarius?" he demanded.

"Where else may he be from?" asked Fulvus Fupus. "We know he is not from Castrum Mare, so he must be from Castra Sanguinarius."

"You have no evidence then to substantiate your accusations?"

Fupus hesitated.

"Get out," ordered Validus, angrily. "I shall attend to you later."

Overcome by mortification, Fupus left the garden, but the malevolent glances that he shot at Favonius, Lepus, and Erich boded them no good. Validus looked long and searchingly at von Harben for several minutes after Fupus quit the garden as though attempting to read the soul of the stranger standing before him.

"So there is no Emperor at Rome," he mused, half aloud. "When Sanguinarius led his cohort out of Ægyptus, Nerva was Emperor. That was upon the sixth day before the calends of February in the 848th year of the city in the second year of Nerva's reign. Since that day no word of Rome has reached the descendants of Sanguinarius and his cohort."

Von Harben figured rapidly, searching his memory for the historical dates and data of ancient history that were as fresh in his mind as those of his own day. "The sixth day before the calends of February," he repeated; "that would be the twenty-seventh day of January in the 848th year of the city—why, January twenty-seventh, A.D. 98, is the date of Nerva's death," he said.

"Ah, if Sanguinarius had but known," said Validus, "but Ægyptus is a long way from Rome and Sanguinarius was far to the south up the Nilus before word could have reached his post by ancient Thebæ that his enemy was dead. And who became Emperor after Nerva? Do you know that?"

"Trajan," replied von Harben.

"Why do you, a barbarian, know so much concerning the history of Rome?" asked the Emperor.

"I am a student of such things," replied von Harben. "It has been my ambition to become an authority on the subject."

"Could you write down these happenings since the death of Nerva?"

"I could put down all that I could recall, or all that I have read," said von Harben, "but it would take a long time."

"You shall do it," said Validus, "and you shall have the time."

"But I had not planned remaining on in your country," dissented von Harben.

"You shall remain," said Validus. "You shall also write a history of the reign of Validus Augustus, Emperor of the East."

"But—" interjected von Harben.

"Enough!" snapped Validus. "I am Cæsar. It is a command."

Von Harben shrugged and smiled. Rome and the Cæsars, he realized, had never seemed other than musty parchment and weather-worn inscriptions cut in crumbling stone, until now.

Here, indeed, was a real Cæsar. What matter it that his empire was naught but a few square miles of marsh, an island and swampy shoreland in the bottom of an unknown canyon, or that his subjects numbered less than fifty thousand souls— the first Augustus himself was no more a Cæsar than was his namesake, Validus.

"Come," said Validus. "I shall take you to the library myself, for that will be the scene of your labors."

In the library, which was a vaultlike room at the end of a long corridor, Validus displayed with pride several hundred parchment rolls neatly arranged upon shelves.

"Here," said Validus, selecting one of the rolls, "is the story of Sanguinarius and the history of our country up to the founding of Castrum Mare. Take it with you and read it at your leisure, for while you shall remain with Septimus Favonius, whom with Mallius Lepus I shall hold responsible for you, every day you shall come to the palace and I shall dictate to you the history of my reign. Go, now, with Septimus Favonius and at this hour tomorrow attend again upon Cæsar."

When they were outside the palace of Validus Augustus, von Harben turned to Mallius Lepus. "It is a question whether I am prisoner or guest," he said, with a rueful smile.

"Perhaps you are both," said Mallius Lepus, "but that you are even partially a guest is fortunate for you. Validus Augustus is vain, arrogant, and cruel. He is also suspicious, for he knows that he is not popular, and Fulvus Fupus had evidently almost succeeded in bringing your doom upon you and ruin to Favonius and myself before we arrived. What strange whim altered the mind of Cæsar I do not know, but it is fortunate for you that it was altered; fortunate, too, for Septimus Favonius and Mallius Lepus."

"But it will take years to write the history of Rome," said von Harben.

"And if you refuse to write it you will be dead many more years than it would take to accomplish the task," retorted Mallius Lepus, with a grin.

"Castrum Mare is not an unpleasant place in which to live," said Septimus Favonius.

"Perhaps you are right," said von Harben, as the face of the daughter of Favonius presented itself to his mind.

Returned to the home of the host, the instinct of the archæologist and the scholar urged von Harben to an early perusal of the ancient papyrus roll that Cæsar had loaned him, so that no sooner was he in the apartments that had been set aside for him than he stretched himself upon a long sofa and untied the cords that confined the roll.

As it unrolled before his eyes he saw a manuscript in ancient Latin, marred by changes and erasures, yellowed by age. It was quite unlike anything that had previously fallen into his hands during his scholarly investigations into the history and literature of ancient Rome. For whereas such other original ancient manuscripts as he had had the good fortune to examine had been the work of clerks or scholars, a moment's glance at this marked it as the laborious effort of a soldier unskilled in literary pursuits.

The manuscript bristled with the rough idiom of far-flung

camps of veteran legionaries, with the slang of Rome and Egypt of nearly two thousand years before, and there were references to people and places that appeared in no histories or geographies known to modern man—little places and little people that were without fame in their own time and whose very memory had long since been erased from the consciousness of man, but yet in this crude manuscript they lived again for Erich von Harben—the quæstor who had saved the life of Sanguinarius in an Egyptian town that never was on any map, and there was Marcus Crispus Sanguinarius himself who had been of sufficient importance to win the enmity of Nerva in the year 90 A.D. while the latter was consul—Marcus Crispus Sanguinarius, the founder of an empire, whose name appears nowhere in the annals of ancient Rome.

With mounting interest von Harben read the complaints of Sanguinarius and his anger because the enmity of Nerva had caused him to be relegated to the hot sands of this distant post below the ancient city of Thebæ in far Ægyptus.

Writing in the third person, Sanguinarius had said:

"Sanguinarius, a præfect of the Third Cohort of the Tenth Legion, stationed below Thebæ in Ægyptus in the 846th year of the city, immediately after Nerva assumed the purple, was accused of having plotted against the Emperor.

"About the fifth day before the calends of February in the 848th year of the city a messenger came to Sanguinarius from Nerva commanding the præfect to return to Rome and place himself under arrest, but this Sanguinarius had no mind to do, and as no other in his camp knew the nature of the message he had received from Nerva, Sanguinarius struck the messenger down with his dagger and caused the word to be spread among his men that the man had been an assassin sent from Rome and that Sanguinarius had slain him in self-defense.

"He also told his lieutenants and centurions that Nerva was sending a large force to destroy the cohort and he prevailed upon them to follow up the Nilus in search of a new country where they might establish themselves far from the malignant power of a jealous Cæsar, and upon the following day the long march commenced.

"It so happened that shortly before this a fleet of one hundred and twenty vessels landed at Myos-hormos, a port of Ægyptus on the Sinus Arabius. This merchant fleet annually brought rich merchandise from the island of Taprobana—silk, the value of which was equal to its weight in gold, pearls, diamonds, and a variety of aromatics and other merchandise, which was transferred to the backs of camels and brought inland from Myos-hormos to the Nilus and down that river to Alexandria, whence it was shipped to Rome.

"With this caravan were hundreds of slaves from India and far Cathay and even light-skinned people captured in the distant northwest by Mongol raiders. The majority of these were young girls destined for the auction block at Rome. And it so chanced that Sanguinarius met this caravan, heavy with riches and women, and captured it. During the ensuing five years the cohort settled several times in what they hoped would prove a permanent camp, but it was not until the 853rd year of Rome that, by accident, they discovered the hidden canyon where now stands Castra Sanguinarius."

"You find it interesting?" inquired a voice from the doorway, and looking up von Harben saw Mallius Lepus standing on the threshold.

"Very," said Erich.

Lepus shrugged his shoulders. "We suspect that it would have been more interesting had the old assassin written the truth," said Lepus. "As a matter of fact, very little is known concerning his reign, which lasted for twenty years. He was assassinated in the year 20 Anno Sanguinarii, which corresponds to the 873rd year of Rome. The old buck named the city after himself, decreed a calendar of his own, and had his head stamped on gold coins, many of which are still in existence. Even today we use his calendar quite as much as that of our Roman ancestors, but in Castrum Mare we have tried to forget the example of Sanguinarius as much as possible."

"What is this other city that I have heard mentioned so

often and that is called Castra Sanguinarius?" asked von Harben.

"It is the original city founded by Sanguinarius," replied Lepus. "For a hundred years after the founding of the city conditions grew more and more intolerable until no man's life or property was safe, unless he was willing to reduce himself almost to the status of a slave and continually fawn upon the Emperor. It was then that Honus Hasta revolted and led a few hundred families to this island at the eastern end of the valley, founding the city and the empire of Castrum Mare. Here, for over seventeen hundred years, the descendants of these families have lived in comparative peace and security, but in an almost constant state of war with Castra Sanguinarius.

"From mutual necessity the two cities carry on a commerce that is often interrupted by raids and wars. The suspicion and hatred that the inhabitants of each city feel for the inhabitants of the other is fostered always by our Emperors, each of whom fears that friendly communication between the two cities would result in the overthrow of one of them."

"And now Castrum Mare is happy and contented under Cæsar?" asked Erich.

"That is a question that it might now be safe to answer honestly," said Lepus, with a shrug.

"If I am going to the palace every day to write the history of Rome for Validus Augustus and receive from him the story of his reign," said von Harben, "it might be well if I knew something of the man, otherwise there is a chance for me to get into serious trouble, which might conceivably react upon you and Septimus Favonius, whom Cæsar has made responsible for me. If you care to forewarn me, I promise you that I shall repeat nothing that you may tell me."

Lepus, leaning lightly against the wall by the doorway, played idly with the hilt of his dagger as he took thought before replying. Presently he looked up, straight into von Harben's eyes.

"I shall trust you," he said; "first, because there is that in you which inspires confidence, and, second, because it cannot profit you to harm either Septimus Favonius or myself. Castrum Mare is not happy with its Cæsar. He is arrogant and cruel—not like the Cæsars to which Castrum Mare has been accustomed.

"The last Emperor was a kindly man, but at the time of his death his brother, Validus Augustus, was chosen to succeed him because Cæsar's son was, at that time, but a year old.

"This son of the former Emperor, a nephew of Validus Augustus, is called Cassius Hasta. And because of his popularity he has aroused the jealousy and hatred of Augustus, who recently sent him away upon a dangerous mission to the west end of the valley. There are many who consider it virtual banishment, but Validus Augustus insists that this is not the fact. No one knows what Cassius Hasta's orders were. He went secretly by night and was accompanied by only a few slaves.

"It is believed that he has been ordered to enter Castra Sanguinarius as a spy, and if such is the case his mission amounts practically to a sentence of death. If this were known for a fact, the people would rise against Validus Augustus, for Cassius Hasta was the most popular man in Castrum Mare.

"But enough. I shall not bore you with the sorrows of Castrum Mare. Take your reading down into the garden where in the shade of the trees, it is cooler than here and I shall join you presently."

As von Harben lay stretched upon the sward beneath the shade of a tree in the cool garden of Septimus Favonius, his mind was not upon the history of Sanguinarius, nor upon the political woes of Castrum Mare so much as they were upon plans for escape.

As a scholar, an explorer, and an archæologist he would delight in remaining here for such a time as might be necessary for him to make an exploration of the valley and study the government and customs of its inhabitants, but to remain cooped up in the vaultlike library of the Emperor of the East writing the history of ancient Rome in Latin with a reed pen on papyrus rolls in no way appealed to him.

The rustle of fresh linen and the soft fall of sandaled feet upon the graveled garden walk interrupted his trend of thought and as he looked up into the face of Favonia, daughter of Septimus Favonius, the history of ancient Rome together with half-formulated plans for escape were dissipated from his mind by the girl's sweet smile, as is a morning mist by the rising sun.

11

As MAXIMUS PRÆCLARUS led Tarzan of the Apes from the home of Dion Splendidus in the city of Castra Sanguinarius, the soldiers, gathered by the doorway, voiced their satisfaction in oaths and exclamations. They liked the young patrician who commanded them and they were proud that he should have captured the wild barbarian single-handed.

A command from Præclarus brought silence and at a word from him they formed around the prisoner, and the march toward the Colosseum was begun. They had proceeded but a short distance when Præclarus halted the detachment and went himself to the doorway of a house fronting on the avenue through which they were crossing. He halted before the door, stood in thought for a moment, and then turned back toward his detachment as though he had changed his mind about entering, and Tarzan knew that the young officer was indicating to him the home in which he lived and in which the ape-man might find sanctuary later.

Several hundred yards farther along the street, after they had resumed the march, Præclarus halted his detachment beneath the shade of great trees opposite a drinking fountain, which was built into the outside of a garden wall close beside an unusually large tree, which, overspreading the avenue upon one side and the wall on the other, intermingled its branches with those of other trees growing inside the garden beyond.

Præclarus crossed the avenue and drank at the fountain and returning inquired by means of signs if Tarzan would drink. The ape-man nodded in assent and Præclarus gave orders that he be permitted to cross to the fountain.

Slowly Tarzan walked to the other side of the avenue. He stooped and drank from the fountain. Beside him was the bole of a great tree; above him was a leafy foliage that would conceal him from the sight and protect him from the missiles of the soldiers. Turning from the fountain, a quick step took him behind the tree. One of the soldiers shouted a warning to Præclarus, and the whole detachment, immediately suspicious, leaped quickly across the avenue, led by the young patrician who commanded them, but when they reached the fountain and the tree their prisoner had vanished.

Shouting their disappointment, they gazed upward into the foliage, but there was no sign there of the barbarian. Several of the more active soldiers scrambled into the branches and then Maximus Præclarus, pointing in the direction opposite to that in which his home lay, shouted: "This way, there he goes!" and started on a run down the avenue, while behind him strung his detachment, their pikes ready in their hands.

Moving silently through the branches of the great trees that overhung the greater part of the city of Castra Sanguinarius, Tarzan paralleled the avenue leading back to the home of Maximus Præclarus, halting at last in a tree that overlooked the inner courtyard or walled garden, which appeared to be a distinguishing feature of the architecture of the city.

Below him he saw a matronly woman of the patrician class, listening to a tall Negro who was addressing her excitedly. Clustered about the woman and eagerly listening to the words of the speaker were a number of slaves, both men and women.

Tarzan recognized the speaker as Mpingu, and, though he could not understand his words, realized that the man was preparing them for his arrival in accordance with the instructions given him in the garden of Dion Splendidus by Maximus Præclarus, and that he was making a good story of it was evidenced by his excited gesticulation and the wide eyes and open mouths of the listening men.

The woman, listening attentively and with quiet dignity of mien, appeared to be slightly amused, but whether at the story itself or at the unrestrained excitement of Mpingu, Tarzan did not know.

She was a regal-looking woman of about fifty, with graying hair and with the poise and manner of that perfect self-assurance which is the hallmark of assured position; that she was a patrician to her fingertips was evident, and yet there was that in her eyes and the little wrinkles at their corners that bespoke a broad humanity and a kindly disposition.

Mpingu had evidently reached the point where his vocabulary could furnish no adequate superlatives wherewith to describe the barbarian who had rescued his mistress from Fastus, and he was acting out in exaggerated pantomime the scene in the garden of his mistress, when Tarzan dropped lightly to the sward beside him. The effect upon the Negroes of this unexpected appearance verged upon the ludicrous, but the white woman was unmoved to any outward sign of surprise.

"Is this the barbarian?" she asked the Mpingu.

"It is he," replied the black.

"Tell him that I am Festivitas, the mother of Maximus Præclarus," the woman directed Mpingu, "and that I welcome him here in the name of my son."

Through Mpingu, Tarzan acknowledged the greetings of

Festivitas and thanked her for her hospitality, after which she instructed one of her slaves to conduct the stranger to the apartments that were placed at his disposal.

It was late afternoon before Maximus Præclarus returned to his home, going immediately to Tarzan's apartments. With him was the same man who had acted as interpreter in the morning.

"I am to remain here with you," said the man to Tarzan, "as your interpreter and servant."

"I venture to say," said Præclarus through the interpreter, "that this is the only spot in Castra Sanguinarius that they have not searched for you and there are three centuries combing the forests outside the city, though by this time Sublatus is convinced that you have escaped. We shall keep you here in hiding for a few days when, I think, I can find the means to get you out of the city after dark."

The ape-man smiled. "I can leave whenever I choose," he said, "either by day or by night, but I do not choose to leave until I have satisfied myself that the man for whom I am searching is not here. But, first, let me thank you for your kindness to me, the reason for which I cannot understand."

"That is easily explained," said Præclarus. "The young woman whom you saved from attack this morning is Dilecta, the daughter of Dion Splendidus. She and I are to be married. That, I think, will explain my gratitude."

"I understand," said Tarzan, "and I am glad that I was fortunate enough to come upon them at the time that I did."

"Should you be captured again, it will not prove so fortunate for you," said Præclarus, "for the man from whom you saved Dilecta is Fastus, the son of Sublatus, and now the Emperor will have two indignities to avenge; but if you remain here you will be safe, for our slaves are loyal and there is little likelihood that you will be discovered."

"If I remain here," said Tarzan, "and it should be discovered that you had befriended me, would not the anger of the Emperor fall upon you?"

Maximus Præclarus shrugged. "I am daily expecting that,"

he said, "not because of you, but because the son of the Emperor wishes to marry Dilecta. Sublatus needs no further excuse to destroy me. I should be no worse off were he to learn that I have befriended you than I now am."

"Then, perhaps, I may be of service to you if I remain," said Tarzan.

"I do not see how you can do anything but remain," said Præclarus. "Every man, woman, and child in Castra Sanguinarius will be on the lookout for you, for Sublatus has offered a huge reward for your capture, and besides the inhabitants of the city there are thousands of barbarians outside the walls who will lay aside every other interest to run you down."

"Twice today you have seen how easily I can escape from the soldiers of Sublatus," said Tarzan, smiling. "Just as easily can I leave the city and elude the barbarians in the outer villages."

"Then why do you remain?" demanded Præclarus.

"I came here searching for the son of a friend," replied Tarzan. "Many weeks ago the young man started out with an expedition to explore the Wiramwazi Mountains in which your country is located. His people deserted him upon the outer slopes, and I am convinced that he is somewhere within the range and very possibly in this canyon. If he is here and alive, he will unquestionably come sooner or later to your city where, from the experience that I have gained, I am sure that he will receive anything but friendly treatment from your Emperor. This is the reason that I wish to remain somewhere in the vicinity, and now that you have told me that you are in danger, I may as well remain in your home where it is possible I may have an opportunity to reciprocate your kindness to me."

"If the son of your friend is in this end of the valley, he will be captured and brought to Castra Sanguinarius," said Maximus Præclarus, "and when that occurs I shall know of it, since I am detailed to duty at the Colosseum—a mark of the disfavor of Sublatus, since this is the most distasteful duty to which an officer can be assigned."

"Is it possible that this man for whom I am searching might be in some other part of the valley?" asked Tarzan.

"No," replied Præclarus. "There is only one entrance to the valley, that through which you were brought, and while there is another city at the eastern end, he could not reach it without passing through the forest surrounding Castra Sanguinarius, in which event he would have been captured by the barbarians and turned over to Sublatus."

"Then I shall remain here," said Tarzan, "for a time."

"You shall be a welcome guest," replied Præclarus.

For three weeks Tarzan remained in the home of Maximus Præclarus. Festivitas conceived a great liking for the bronzed barbarian, and soon tiring of carrying on conversation with him through an interpreter, she set about teaching him her own language, with the result that it was not long before Tarzan could carry on a conversation in Latin; nor did he lack opportunity to practice his new accomplishment, since Festivitas never tired of hearing stories of the outer world and of the manners and customs of modern civilization.

And while Tarzan of the Apes waited in Castra Sanguinarius for word that von Harben had been seen in the valley, the man he sought was living the life of a young patrician attached to the court of the Emperor of the East, and though much of his time was pleasantly employed in the palace library, yet he chafed at the knowledge that he was virtually a prisoner and was often formulating plans for escape—plans that were sometimes forgotten when he sat beneath the spell of the daughter of Septimus Favonius.

And often in the library he discovered only unadulterated pleasure in his work, and thoughts of escape were driven from his mind by discoveries of such gems as original Latin translations of Homer and to hitherto unknown manuscripts of Vergil, Cicero, and Cæsar—manuscripts that dated from the days of the young republic and on down the centuries to include one of the early satires of Juvenal.

Thus the days passed, while far off in another world a frightened little monkey scampered through the upper terraces of a distant forest.

12

A PENCHANT FOR boasting is not the prerogative of any time, or race, or individual, but is more or less common to all. So it is not strange that Mpingu, filled with the importance of the secret that he alone shared with his mistress and the household of Maximus Præclarus, should have occasionally dropped a word here and there that might impress his listeners with his importance.

Mpingu meant no harm. He was loyal to the house of Dion Splendidus and he would not willingly have brought harm to his master or his master's friend, but so it is often with people who talk too much, and Mpingu certainly had done that. The result was that upon a certain day, as he was bartering in the marketplace for provisions for the kitchen of Dion Splendidus, he felt a heavy hand laid upon his shoulder and turning, he was astonished to find himself looking into the face of a centurion of the palace guard, behind whom stood a file of legionaries.

"You are Mpingu, the slave of Dion Splendidus?" demanded the centurion.

"I am," replied the man.

"Come with us," commanded the centurion.

Mpingu drew back, afraid, as all men feared the soldiers of Cæsar. "What do you want of me?" he demanded. "I have done nothing."

"Come, barbarian," ordered the soldier. "I was not sent to confer with you, but to get you!" And he jerked Mpingu roughly toward him and pushed him back among the soldiers.

A crowd had gathered, as crowds gathered always when a man is arrested, but the centurion ignored the crowd as though it did not exist, and the people fell aside as the soldiers marched away with Mpingu. No one questioned or interfered, for who would dare question an officer of Cæsar? Who would interfere in behalf of a slave?

Mpingu thought that he would be taken to the dungeons beneath the Colosseum, which was the common jail in which all prisoners were confined; but presently he realized that his captors were not leading him in that direction, and when finally it dawned upon him that the palace was their goal he was filled with terror.

Never before had Mpingu stepped foot within the precincts of the palace grounds, and when the imperial gate closed behind him he was in a mental state bordering upon collapse. He had heard stories of the cruelty of Sublatus, of the terrible vengeance wreaked upon his enemies, and he had visions that paralyzed his mind so that he was in a state of semi-consciousness when he was finally led into an inner chamber where a high dignitary of the court confronted him.

"This," said the centurion, who had brought him, "is Mpingu, the slave of Dion Splendidus, whom I was commanded to fetch to you."

"Good!" said the official. "You and your detachment may remain while I question him." Then he turned upon Mpingu. "Do you know the penalties one incurs for aiding the enemies of Cæsar?" he demanded.

Mpingu's lower jaw moved convulsively as though he would reply, but he was unable to control his voice.

"They die," growled the officer, menacingly. "They die terrible deaths that they will remember through all eternity."

"I have done nothing," cried Mpingu, suddenly regaining control of his vocal cords.

"Do not lie to me, barbarian," snapped the official. "You aided in the escape of the prisoner who called himself Tarzan and even now you are hiding him from your Emperor."

"I did not help him escape. I am not hiding him," wailed Mpingu.

"You lie. You know where he is. You boasted of it to other slaves. Tell me where he is."

"I do not know," said Mpingu.

"If your tongue were cut out, you could not tell us where he is," said the Roman. "If red-hot irons were thrust into your eyes, you could not see to lead us to his hiding-place; but if we find him without your help, and we surely shall find him, we shall need neither your tongue nor your eyes. Do you understand?"

"I do not know where he is," repeated Mpingu.

The Roman turned away and struck a single blow upon a gong, after which he stood in silence until a slave entered the room in response to the summons. "Fetch tongs," the Roman instructed the slave, "and a charcoal brazier with burning-irons. Be quick."

After the slave had left, silence fell again upon the apartment. The official was giving Mpingu an opportunity to think, and Mpingu so occupied the time in thinking that it seemed to him that the slave had scarcely left the apartment before he returned again with tongs and a lighted burner, from the glowing heart of which protruded the handle of a burning-iron.

"Have your soldiers throw him to the floor and hold him," said the official to the centurion.

It was evident to Mpingu that the end had come; the officer was not even going to give him another opportunity to speak.

"Wait!" he shrieked.

"Well," said the official, "you are regaining your memory?"

"I am only a slave," wailed Mpingu. "I must do what my masters command."

"And what did they command?" inquired the Roman.

"I was only an interpreter," said Mpingu. "The white barbarian spoke the language of the Bagegos, who are my people. Through me they talked to him and he talked to them."

"And what was said?" demanded the inquisitor.

Mpingu hesitated, dropping his eyes to the floor.

"Come, quickly!" snapped the other.

"I have forgotten," said Mpingu.

The official nodded to the centurion. The soldiers seized Mpingu and threw him roughly to the floor, four of them holding him there, one seated upon each limb.

"The tongs!" directed the official, and the slave handed the instrument to the centurion.

"Wait!" screamed Mpingu. "I will tell you."

"Let him up," said the official; and to Mpingu: "This is your last chance. If you go down again, your tongue comes out and your eyes, too."

"I will talk," said Mpingu. "I did but interpret, that is all. I had nothing to do with helping him to escape or hiding him."

"If you tell us the truth, you will not be punished," said the Roman. "Where is the white barbarian?"

"He is hiding in the home of Maximus Præclarus," said Mpingu.

"What has your master to do with this?" commanded the Romans.

"Dion Splendidus has nothing to do with it," replied Mpingu. "Maximus Præclarus planned it."

"That is all," said the official to the centurion. "Take him away and keep him under guard until you receive further orders. Be sure that he talks to no one."

A few minutes later the official who had interrogated Mpingu entered the apartment of Sublatus while the Emperor was in conversation with his son Fastus.

"I have located the white barbarian, Sublatus," announced the official.

"Good!" said the Emperor. "Where is he?"

"In the home of Maximus Præclarus."

"I might have suspected as much," said Fastus.

"Who else is implicated?" asked Sublatus.

"He was caught in the courtyard of Dion Splendidus," said

Fastus, "and the Emperor has heard, as we all have, that Dion Splendidus has long had eyes upon the imperial purple of the Cæsars."

"The slave says that only Maximus Præclarus is responsible for the escape of the barbarian," said the official.

"He was one of Dion Splendidus's slaves, was he not?" demanded Fastus.

"Yes."

"Then it is not strange that he would protect his master," said Fastus.

"Arrest them all," commanded Sublatus.

"You mean Dion Splendidus, Maximus Præclarus, and the barbarian Tarzan?" asked the official.

"I mean those three and the entire household of Dion Splendidus and Maximus Præclarus," replied Sublatus.

"Wait, Cæsar," suggested Fastus; "twice already has the barbarian escaped from the legionaries. If he receives the slightest inkling of this, he will escape again. I have a plan. Listen!"

An hour later a messenger arrived at the home of Dion Splendidus carrying an invitation to the senator and his wife to be the guests of a high court functionary that evening at a banquet. Another messenger went to the home of Maximus Præclarus with a letter urging the young officer to attend an entertainment being given that same evening by a rich young patrician.

As both invitations had emanated from families high in favor with the Emperor, they were, in fact, almost equivalent to commands, even to as influential a senator as Dion Splendidus, and so there was no question either in the minds of the hosts or in the minds of the guests but that they would be accepted.

Night had fallen upon Castra Sanguinarius. Dion Splendidus and his wife were alighting from their litter before the home of their host and Maximus Præclarus was already drinking with his fellow guests in the banquet hall of one of Castra Sanguinarius's wealthiest citizens. Fastus was there, too, and Maximus Præclarus was surprised and not a little puzzled at the friendly attitude of the prince.

"I always suspect something when Fastus smiles at me," he said to an intimate.

In the home of Dion Splendidus, Dilecta sat among her female slaves, while one of them told her stories of the wild African village from which she had come.

Tarzan and Festivitas sat in the home of Máximus Præclarus, the Roman matron listening attentively to the stories of savage Africa and civilized Europe that she was constantly urging her strange guest to tell her. Faintly they heard a knock at the outer gate and, presently, a slave came to the apartment where they sat to tell them that Mpingu, the slave of Dion Splendidus, had come with a message for Tarzan.

"Bring him hither," said Festivitas, and, shortly, Mpingu was ushered into the room.

If Tarzan or Festivitas had known Mpingu better, they would have realized that he was under great nervous strain; but they did not know him well, and so they saw nothing out of the way in his manner or bearing.

"I have been sent to fetch you to the home of Dion Splendidus," said Mpingu to Tarzan.

"That is strange," said Festivitas.

"Your noble son stopped at the home of Dion Splendidus on his way to the banquet this evening and as he left I was summoned and told to come hither and fetch the stranger to my master's house," explained Mpingu. "That is all I know about the matter."

"Maximus Præclarus gave you those instructions himself?" asked Festivitas.

"Yes," replied Mpingu.

"I do not know what his reason can be," said Festivitas to Tarzan, "but there must be some very good reason, or he would not run the risk of your being caught."

"It is very dark out," said Mpingu. "No one will see him."

"There is no danger," said Tarzan to Festivitas. "Maximus Præclarus would not have sent for me unless it were necessary. Come, Mpingu!" And he arose, bidding Festivitas good-bye.

Tarzan and Mpingu had proceeded but a short distance

down the avenue when the black motioned the ape-man to the side of the street, where a small gate was let into a solid wall.

"We are here," said Mpingu.

"This is not the home of Dion Splendidus," said Tarzan, immediately suspicious.

Mpingu was surprised that this stranger should so well remember the location of a house that he had visited but once, and that more than three weeks since, but he did not know the training that had been the ape-man's through the long years of moving through the trackless jungle that had trained his every sense and faculty to the finest point of orientation.

"It is not the main gate," replied Mpingu, quickly, "but Maximus Præclarus did not think it safe that you be seen entering the main gate of the home of Dion Splendidus in the event that, by any chance, you were observed. This way leads into a lane that might connect with any one of several homes, and once in it there is little or no chance of apprehension."

"I see," said Tarzan. "Lead the way."

Mpingu opened the gate and motioned Tarzan in ahead of him, and as the ape-man passed through into the blackness beyond there fell upon him what seemed to be a score of men and he was borne down in the same instant that he realized that he had been betrayed. So rapidly did his assailants work that it was a matter of seconds only before the ape-man found shackles upon his wrists, the one thing that he feared and hated most.

WHILE ERICH VON Harben wooed Favonia beneath a summer moon in the garden of Septimus Favonius in the island city of Castrum Mare, a detachment of the brown legionaries of Sublatus Imperator dragged Tarzan of the Apes and Mpingu, the slave of Dion Splendidus, to the dungeons beneath the Colosseum of Castra Sanguinarius—and far to the south a little monkey shivered from cold and terror in the topmost branches of a jungle giant, while Sheeta the panther crept softly through the black shadows far below.

In the banquet hall of his host, Maximus Præclarus reclined upon a sofa far down the board from Fastus, the guest of honor. The prince, his tongue loosed by frequent drafts of native wine, seemed in unusually good spirits, radiating self-satisfaction. Several times he had brought the subject of conversation around to the strange white barbarian, who had insulted his sire and twice escaped from the soldiers of Sublatus.

"He would never have escaped from me that day," he boasted, throwing a sneer in the direction of Maximus Præclarus, "nor from any other officer who is loyal to Cæsar."

"You had him, Fastus, in the garden of Dion Splendidus," retorted Præclarus. "Why did you not hold him?"

Fastus flushed. "I shall hold him this time," he blurted.

"This time?" queried Præclarus. "He has been captured again?" There was nothing in either the voice or expression of the young patrician of more than polite interest, though the words of Fastus had come with all the unexpected suddenness of lightning out of a clear sky.

"I mean," explained Fastus, in some confusion, "that if he is again captured I, personally, shall see that he does not escape," but his words did not allay the apprehensions of Præclarus.

All through the long dinner Præclarus was cognizant of a sensation of foreboding. There was a menace in the air that was apparent in the veiled hostility of his host and several others who were cronies of Fastus.

As early as was seemly he made his excuses and departed. Armed slaves accompanied his litter through the dark avenues of Castra Sanguinarius, where robbery and murder slunk among the shadows hand in hand with the criminal element that had been permitted to propagate itself without restraint; and when at last he came to the doorway at his home and had alighted from his litter he paused and a frown of perplexity clouded his face as he saw that the door stood partially ajar, though there was no slave there to receive him.

The house seemed unusually quiet and lifeless. The night light, which ordinarily a slave kept burning in the forecourt when a member of the household was away, was absent. For an instant Præclarus hesitated upon the threshold and then, throwing his cloak back from his shoulders to free his arms, he pushed the door open and stepped within.

In the banquet hall of a high court functionary the guests yawned behind their hands from boredom, but none dared leave while Cæsar remained, for the Emperor was a guest there that evening. It was late when an officer brought a message to Sublatus—a message that the Emperor read with a satisfaction he made no effort to conceal.

"I have received an important message," said Sublatus to his host, "upon a matter that interests the noble Senator Dion Splendidus and his wife. It is my wish that you withdraw with the other guests, leaving us three here alone."

When they had gone he turned to Dion Splendidus. "It has

long been rumored, Splendidus," he remarked, "that you aspire to the purple."

"A false rumor, Sublatus, as you should well know," replied the senator.

"I have reason to believe otherwise," said Sublatus, shortly. "There cannot be two Cæsars, Splendidus, and you well know the penalty for treason."

"If the Emperor has determined, for personal reasons or for any reason whatever, to destroy me, argument will avail me nothing," said Splendidus, haughtily.

"But I have other plans," said Sublatus, "—plans that might be overturned should I cause your death."

"Yes?" inquired Splendidus, politely.

"Yes," assented Sublatus. "My son wishes to marry your daughter, Dilecta, and it is also my wish, for thus would the two most powerful families of Castra Sanguinarius be united and the future of the empire assured."

"But our daughter, Dilecta, is betrothed to another," said Splendidus.

"To Maximus Præclarus?" inquired Sublatus.

"Yes," replied the senator.

"Then let me tell you that she shall never wed Maximus Præclarus," said the Emperor.

"Why?" inquired Splendidus.

"Because Maximus Præclarus is about to die."

"I do not understand," said Splendidus.

"Perhaps when I tell you that the white barbarian, Tarzan, has been captured, you will understand why Præclarus is about to die," said Sublatus, with a sneer.

Dion Splendidus shook his head negatively. "I regret," he said, "that I do not follow Cæsar."

"I think you do, Splendidus," said the Emperor, "but that is neither here nor there, since it is Cæsar's will that there be no breath of suspicion upon the sire of the next Empress of Castra Sanguinarius. So permit me to explain what I am sure that you already know. After the white barbarian escaped from my soldiers he was found by Maximus Præclarus in your garden. My son, Fastus, witnessed the capture. One of your own slaves acted as interpreter between the barbarian and Maximus, who arranged that the barbarian should escape and take refuge in the home of Maximus. Tonight he was found there and captured, and Maximus Præclarus has been placed under arrest. They are both in the dungeons beneath the Colosseum. It is improbable that these things should have transpired entirely without your knowledge, but I shall let it pass if you give your word that Dilecta shall marry Fastus."

"During the entire history of Castra Sanguinarius," said Dion Splendidus, "it has been our boast that our daughters have been free to choose their own husbands—not even a Cæsar might command a free woman to marry against her will."

"That is true," replied Sublatus, "and for that very reason I do not command—I am only advising."

"I cannot answer for my daughter," said Splendidus. "Let the son of Cæsar do his own wooing as becomes the men of Castra Sanguinarius."

Sublatus arose. "I am only advising," but his tone belied his words. "The noble senator and his wife may retire to their home and give thought to what Cæsar has said. In the course of a few days Fastus will come for his answer."

By the light of the torch that illuminated the interior of the dungeon into which he was thrust by his captors, Tarzan saw a white man and several Negroes chained to the walls. Among the blacks was Lukedi, but when he recognized Tarzan he evinced only the faintest sign of interest, so greatly had his confinement weighed upon his mind and altered him.

The ape-man was chained next to the only other white in the dungeon, and he could not help but notice the keen interest that this prisoner took in him from the moment that he entered until the soldiers withdrew, taking the torch with them, leaving the dungeon in darkness.

As had been his custom while he was in the home of Maximus Præclarus, Tarzan had worn only his loincloth and leopard skin, with a toga and sandals out of courtesy for Festivitas when he appeared in her presence. This evening, when he started out with Mpingu, he had worn the toga as a disguise, but in the scuffle that preceded his capture it had been torn from him, with the result that his appearance was sufficient to arouse the curiosity of his fellow prisoners, and as soon as the guards were out of hearing the man spoke to him.

"Can it be," he asked, "that you are the white barbarian whose fame has penetrated even to the gloom and silence of the dungeon?"

"I am Tarzan of the Apes," replied the ape-man.

"And you carried Sublatus out of his palace above your head and mocked at his soldiers!" exclaimed the other. "By the ashes of my imperial father, Sublatus will see that you die the death."

Tarzan made no reply.

"They say you run through the trees like a monkey," said the other. "How then did you permit yourself to be recaptured?"

"It was done by treachery," replied Tarzan, "and the quickness with which they locked the shackles upon me. Without these," and he shook the manacles upon his wrists, "they could not hold me. But who are you and what did you do to get yourself in the dungeons of Cæsar?"

"I am in the dungeon of no Cæsar," replied the other. "This creature who sits upon the throne of Castra Sanguinarius is no Cæsar."

"Who then is Cæsar?" inquired Tarzan.

"Only the Emperors of the East are entitled to be called Cæsar," replied the other.

"I take it that you are not of Castra Sanguinarius then," suggested the ape-man.

"No," replied the other, "I am from Castrum Mare."

"And why are you a prisoner?" asked Tarzan.

"Because I am from Castrum Mare," replied the other.

"Is that a crime in Castra Sanguinarius?" asked the ape-man.

"We are always enemies," replied the other. "We trade occasionally under a flag of truce, for we have things that they want and they have things that we must have, but there is much raiding and often there are wars, and then whichever side is victorious takes the things by force that otherwise they would be compelled to pay for."

"In this small valley what is there that one of you may have that the other one has not already?" asked the ape-man.

"We of Castrum Mare have the iron mines," replied the other, "and we have the papyrus swamps and the lake, which give us many things that the people of Castra Sanguinarius can obtain only from us. We sell them iron and paper, ink, snails, fish, and jewels, and many manufactured articles. In their end of the valley they mine gold, and as they control the only entrance to the country from the outside world, we are forced to obtain our slaves through them as well as new breeding-stock for our herds.

"As the Sanguinarians are naturally thieves and raiders and are too lazy to work and too ignorant to teach their slaves how to produce things, they depend entirely upon their gold mine and their raiding and trading with the outer world, while we, who have developed many skilled artisans, have been in a position for many generations that permitted us to obtain much more gold and many more slaves than we need in return for our manufactured articles. Today we are much richer than the Sanguinarians. We live better. We are more cultured. We are happier and the Sanguinarians are jealous and their hatred of us has increased."

"Knowing these things," asked Tarzan, "how is it that you came to the country of your enemies and permitted yourself to be captured?"

"I was delivered over treacherously into the hands of Sublatus by my uncle, Validus Augustus, Emperor of the East," replied the other. "My name is Cassius Hasta, and my father was Emperor before Validus. Validus is afraid that I may wish to seize the purple, and for this reason he plotted to get rid of me without assuming any responsibility for the act; so he conceived the idea of sending me upon a military mission, after bribing one of the servants who accompanied me to deliver me into the hands of Sublatus."

"What will Sublatus do with you?" asked Tarzan.

"The same thing that he will do with you," replied Cassius

Hasta. "We shall be exhibited in the triumph of Sublatus, which he holds annually, and then in the arena we shall amuse them until we are slain."

"And when does this take place?" asked Tarzan.

"It will not be long now," replied Cassius Hasta. "Already they have collected so many prisoners to exhibit in the triumph and to take part in the combats in the arena that they are forced to confine Negroes and whites in the same dungeons, a thing they do not ordinarily do."

"Are these Negroes held here for this purpose?" asked the ape-man.

"Yes," replied the other.

Tarzan turned in the direction of Lukedi, whom he could not see in the darkness. "Lukedi!" he called.

"What is it?" asked the black, listlessly.

"You are well?" asked Tarzan.

"I am going to die," reported Lukedi. "They will feed me to lions or burn me upon a cross or make me fight with other warriors, so that it will be all the same for Lukedi. It was a sad day when Nyuto, the chief, captured Tarzan."

"Are all these men from your village?" asked Tarzan.

"No," replied Lukedi. "Most of them are from the villages outside the walls of Castra Sanguinarius."

"Yesterday they called us their own people," spoke up a man, who understood the language of the Bagego, "and tomorrow they make us kill one another to entertain Cæsar."

"You must be very few in numbers or very poor in spirit," said Tarzan, "that you submit to such treatment."

"We number nearly twice as many as the people in the city," said the man, "and we are brave warriors."

"Then you are fools," said Tarzan.

"We shall not be fools forever. Already there are many who would rise against Sublatus and the whites of Castra Sanguinarius."

"The Negroes of the city as well as those of the outer villages hate Cæsar," said Mpingu, who had been brought to the dungeon with Tarzan.

The statements of the men furnished food for thought to

Tarzan. He knew that in the city there must be hundreds and perhaps thousands of African slaves and many thousands of others in the outer villages. If a leader should arise among them, the tyranny of Cæsar might be brought to an abrupt end. He spoke of the matter to Cassius Hasta, but the patrician assured him that no such leader would ever arise.

"We have dominated them for so many centuries," he explained, "that fear of us is an inherited instinct. Our slaves will never rise against their masters."

"But if they did?" asked Tarzan.

"Unless they had a white leader they could not succeed," replied Hasta.

"And why not a white leader then?" asked Tarzan.

"That is unthinkable," replied Hasta.

Their conversation was interrupted by the arrival of a detachment of soldiers, and as they halted before the entrance to the dungeon and threw open the gate Tarzan saw, in the light of their torches, that they were bringing another prisoner. As they dragged the man in, he recognized Maximus Præclarus. He saw that Præclarus recognized him, but as the Roman did not address him, Tarzan kept silent, too. The soldiers chained Præclarus to the wall, and after they had left and the dungeon was in darkness again, the young officer spoke.

"I see now why I am here," said Præclarus, "but even when they set upon me and arrested me in the vestibule of my home, I had guessed as much, after piecing together the insinuations of Fastus at the banquet this evening."

"I have been fearful that by befriending me you would bring disaster upon yourself," said Tarzan.

"Do not reproach yourself," said Præclarus. "Fastus or Sublatus would have found another excuse. I have been doomed from the moment that the attention of Fastus fixed itself upon Dilecta. To attain his end it was necessary that I be destroyed. That is all, my friend, but yet I wonder who it could have been that betrayed me."

"It was I," said a voice out of the darkness.

"Who is that that speaks?" demanded Præclarus.

"It is Mpingu," said Tarzan. "He was arrested with me when

we were on the way to the home of Dion Splendidus to meet you."

"To meet me!" exclaimed Præclarus.

"I lied," said Mpingu, "but they made me."

"Who made you?" demanded Præclarus.

"The officers of Cæsar and Cæsar's son," replied Mpingu. "They dragged me to the palace of the Emperor and held me down upon my back and brought tongs to tear out my tongue and hot irons to burn out my eyes. Oh, master, what else could I do? I am only a poor slave and I was afraid and Cæsar is very terrible."

"I understand," said Præclarus. "I do not blame you, Mpingu."

"They promised to give me my liberty," said the slave, "but instead they have chained me in this dungeon. Doubtless I shall die in the arena, but that I do not fear. It was the tongs and the red-hot irons that made me a coward. Nothing else could have forced me to betray the friend of my master."

There was little comfort upon the cold, hard stones of the dungeon floor, but Tarzan, inured to hardship from birth, slept soundly until the coming of the jailer with food awakened him several hours after sunrise. Water and coarse bread were doled out to the inmates of the dungeon by slaves in charge of a surly half-caste in the uniform of a legionary.

As he ate, Tarzan surveyed his fellow prisoners. There was Cassius Hasta of Castrum Mare, son of a Cæsar, and Maximus Præclarus, a patrician of Castra Sanguinarius and captain of Legionaries. These, with himself, were the only whites. There was Lukedi, the Bagego who had befriended him in the village of Nyuto, and Mpingu, the slave of Dion Splendidus, who had betrayed him, and now, in the light from the little barred window, he recognized also another Bagego—Ogonyo, who still cast fearful eyes upon Tarzan as one might upon any person who was on familiar terms with the ghost of one's grandfather.

In addition to these three, there were five strapping warriors from the outer villages of Castra Sanguinarius, picked men chosen because of their superb physiques for the gladiatorial contests that would form so important a part of the games that would shortly take place in the arena for the glorification of Cæsar and the edification of the masses. The small room was so crowded that there was barely space upon the floor for the eleven to stretch their bodies, yet there was one vacant ring in the stone wall, indicating that the full capacity of the dungeon had not been reached.

Two days and nights dragged slowly by. The inmates of the cell amused themselves as best they could, though the Negroes were too downcast to take a lively interest in anything other than their own sad forebodings.

Tarzan talked much with these and especially with the five warriors from the outer villages. From long experience with them he knew the minds and the hearts of these men, and it was not difficult for him to win their confidence and, presently, he was able to instil within them something of his own courageous self reliance, which could never accept or admit absolute defeat.

He talked with Præclarus about Castra Sanguinarius and with Cassius Hasta about Castrum Mare. He learned all that they could tell him about the forthcoming triumph and games; about the military methods of their people, their laws and their customs until he, who all his life had been accounted taciturn, might easily have been indicated for loquacity by his fellow prisoners, yet, though they might not realize it, he asked them nothing without a well-defined purpose.

Upon the third day of his incarceration another prisoner was brought to the crowded cell in which Tarzan was chained. He was a young white man in the tunic and cuirass of an officer. He was received in silence by the other prisoners, as seemed to be the custom among them, but after he had been fastened to the remaining ring and the soldiers who had brought him had departed, Cassius Hasta greeted him with suppressed excitement.

"Cæcilius Metellus!" he exclaimed.

The other turned in the direction of Hasta's voice, his eyes not yet accustomed to the gloom of the dungeon.

"Hasta!" he exclaimed. "I would know that voice were I to hear it rising from the blackest depths of Tartarus."

"What ill fortune brought you here?" demanded Hasta.

"It is no ill fortune that unites me with my best friend," replied Metellus.

"But tell me how it happened," insisted Cassius Hasta.

"Many things have happened since you left Castrum Mare," replied Metellus. "Fulvus Fupus has wormed his way into the favor of the Emperor to such an extent that all of your former friends are under suspicion and in actual danger. Mallius Lepus is in prison. Septimus Favonius is out of favor with the Emperor and would be in prison himself were it not that Fupus is in love with Favonia, his daughter. But the most outrageous news that I have to communicate to you is that Validus Augustus has adopted Fulvus Fupus and has named him as his successor to the imperial purple."

"Fupus a Cæsar!" cried Hasta, in derision. "And sweet Favonia? It cannot be that she favors Fulvus Fupus?"

"No," replied Metellus, "and that fact lies at the bottom of all the trouble. She loves another, and Fupus, in his desire to possess her, has utilized the Emperor's jealousy of you to destroy every obstacle that stands in his way."

"And whom does Favonia love?" asked Cassius Hasta. "It cannot be Mallius Lepus, her cousin?"

"No," replied Metellus, "it is a stranger. One whom you have never known."

"How can that be?" demanded Cassius Hasta. "Do I not know every patrician in Castrum Mare?"

"He is not of Castrum Mare."

"Not a Sanguinarian?" demanded Cassius Hasta.

"No, he is a barbarian chieftain from Germania."

"What nonsense is this?" demanded Hasta.

"I speak the truth," replied Metellus. "He came shortly after you departed from Castrum Mare, and being a scholar well versed in the history of ancient and modern Rome he won the favor of Validus Augustus, but he brought ruin upon himself and upon Mallius Lepus and upon Septimus Favonius by winning the love of Favonia and with it the jealous hatred of Fulvus Fupus."

"What is his name?" asked Cassius Hasta.

"He calls himself Erich von Harben," replied Metellus.

"Erich von Harben," repeated Tarzan. "I know him. Where is he now? Is he safe?"

Cæcilius Metellus turned his eyes in the direction of the ape-man. "How do you know Erich von Harben, Sanguinarian?" he demanded. "Perhaps then the story that Fulvus Fupus told Validus Augustus is true—that this Erich von Harben is in reality a spy from Castra Sanguinarius."

"No," said Maximus Præclarus. "Do not excite yourself. This Erich von Harben has never been in Castra Sanguinarius, and my friend here is not himself a Sanguinarian. He is a white barbarian from the outer world, and if his story be true, and I have no reason to doubt it, he came here in search of this Erich von Harben."

"You may believe this story, Metellus," said Cassius Hasta. "These both are honorable men and since we have been in prison together we have become good friends. What they tell you is the truth."

"Tell me something of von Harben," insisted Tarzan. "Where is he now and is he in danger from the machinations of this Fulvus Fupus?"

"He is in prison with Mallius Lepus in Castrum Mare," replied Metellus, "and if he survives the games, which he will not, Fupus will find some other means to destroy him."

"When are the games held?" asked Tarzan.

"They start upon the ides of August," replied Cassius Hasta.

"And it is now about the nones of August," said Tarzan.

"Tomorrow," corrected Præclarus.

"We shall know it then," said Cassius Hasta, "for that is the date set for the triumph of Sublatus."

"I am told that the games last about a week," said Tarzan. "How far is it to Castrum Mare?"

"Perhaps an eight hours' march for fresh troops," said

Cæcilius Metellus; "but why do you ask? Are you planning on making a trip to Castrum Mare?"

Tarzan noted the other's smile and the ironic tone of his voice. "I am going to Castrum Mare," he said.

"Perhaps you will take us with you," laughed Metellus.

"Are you a friend of von Harben?" asked Tarzan.

"I am a friend of his friends and an enemy of his enemies, but I do not know him well enough to say that he is my friend."

"But you have no love for Validus Augustus, the Emperor?" asked Tarzan.

"No," replied the other.

"And I take it that Cassius Hasta has no reason to love his uncle, either?" continued Tarzan.

"You are right," said Hasta.

"Perhaps I shall take you both, then," said Tarzan.

The two men laughed.

"We shall be ready to go with you when you are ready to take us," said Cassius Hasta.

"You may count me in on the party, too," said Maximus Præclarus, "if Cassius Hasta will remain my friend in Castrum Mare."

"That I promise, Maximus Præclarus," said Cassius Hasta.

"When do we leave?" demanded Metellus, shaking his chain.

"I can leave the moment that these shackles are struck from me," said the ape-man, "and that they must do when they turn me into the arena to fight."

"There will be many legionaries to see that you do not escape, you may rest assured of that," Cassius Hasta reminded him.

"Maximus Præclarus will tell you that I have twice escaped from the legionaries of Sublatus," said Tarzan.

"That he has," declared Præclarus. "Surrounded by the Emperor's guard, he escaped from the very throne room of Sublatus and he carried Cæsar above his head through the length of the palace and out into the avenue beyond."

"But if I am to take you with me, it will be more difficult," said the ape-man, "and I would take you because it would please me to frustrate the plans of Sublatus and also because two of you, at least, could be helpful to me in finding Erich von Harben in the city of Castrum Mare."

"You interest me," said Cassius Hasta. "You almost make me believe that you can accomplish this mad scheme."

14

A GREAT SUN, rising into a cloudless sky, ushered in the nones of August. It looked down upon the fresh-raked sands of the deserted arena; upon the crowds that lined the Via Principalis that bisected Castra Sanguinarius.

Brown artisans and tradesmen in their smart tunics jostled one another for places of vantage along the shady avenue. Among them moved barbarians from the outer villages, sporting their finest feathers and most valued ornaments and skins, and mingling with the others were the slaves of the city, all eagerly waiting for the pageant that would inaugurate the triumph of Sublatus.

Upon the low rooftops of their homes the patricians reclined upon rugs at every point where the avenue might be seen between or beneath the branches of the trees. All Castra Sanguinarius was there, technically to honor Cæsar, but actually merely to be entertained.

The air buzzed with talk and laughter; hawkers of sweetmeats and trinkets elbowed through the crowd crying their wares; legionaries posted at intervals the full distance from the palace to the Colosseum kept the center of the avenue clear.

Since the evening of the preceding day the throng had been gathering. During the cold night they had huddled with close-drawn cloaks. There had been talk and laughter and brawls and near-riots, and many would-be spectators had been hauled off to the dungeons where their exuberance might be permitted to cool against cold stone.

As the morning dragged on the crowd became restless. At first, as some patrician who was to have a part in the pageant passed in his ornate litter he would be viewed in respectful and interested silence, or if he were well known and favorably thought of by the multitude he might be greeted with cheers; but with the passing of time and the increasing heat of the day each occasional litter that passed elicited deep-throated groans or raucous catcalls as the patience and the temper of the mob became thinner.

But presently from afar, in the direction of the palace, sounded the martial notes of trumpets. The people forgot their fatigue and their discomfort as the shrill notes galvanized them into joyous expectancy.

Slowly along the avenue came the pageant, led by a score of trumpeters, behind whom marched a maniple of the imperial guard. Waving crests surmounted their burnished helmets, the metal of two hundred cuirasses, pikes, and shields shot back the sunlight that filtered through the trees beneath which they marched. They made a proud showing as they strode haughtily between the lines of admiring eyes, led by their patrician officers in gold and embossed leather and embroidered linen.

As the legionaries passed, a great shout of applause arose. A roar of human voices that started at the palace rolled slowly along the Via Principalis toward the Colosseum as Cæsar himself, resplendent in purple and gold, rode alone in a chariot drawn by lions led on golden leashes by huge blacks.

Cæsar may have expected for himself the plaudits of the populace, but there was a question as to whether these were elicited as much by the presence of the Emperor as by the sight of the captives chained to Cæsar's chariot, for Cæsar was an old story to the people of Castra Sanguinarius, while the prisoners were a novelty and, furthermore, something that promised rare sport in the arena.

Never before in the memory of the citizens of Castra Sanguinarius had an Emperor exhibited such noteworthy captives in his triumph. There was Nyuto, the chief of the Bagegos. There was Cæcilius Metellus, a centurion of the legions of the Emperor; but perhaps he who aroused their greatest enthusiasm because of the mad stories that had been narrated of his feats of strength and agility was the great white barbarian, with a shock of black hair and his well-worn leopard skin.

The collar of gold and the golden chain that held him in leash to the chariot of Cæsar, curiously enough, imparted to his appearance no suggestion of fear or humiliation. He walked proudly with head erect—a lion tethered to lions—and there was that in the easy sinuosity of his stride that accentuated his likeness to the jungle beasts that drew the chariot of Cæsar along the broad Via Principalis of Castra Sanguinarius.

As the pageant moved its length slowly to the Colosseum the crowd found other things to hold their interest. There were the Bagego captives chained neck to neck and stalwart gladiators resplendent in new armor. White men and brown men were numbered among these and many warriors from the outer villages.

To the number of two hundred they marched—captives, condemned criminals, and professional gladiators—but before them and behind them, and on either side marched veteran legionaries whose presence spoke in no uncertain terms of the respect in which Cæsar held the potential power of these bitter, savage fighting-men.

There were floats depicting historic events in the history of Castra Sanguinarius and ancient Rome. There were litters bearing the high officers of the court and the senators of the city, while bringing up the rear were the captured flocks and herds of the Bagegos.

That Sublatus failed to exhibit Maximus Præclarus in his triumph evidenced the popularity of this noble young Roman, but Dilecta, watching the procession from the roof of her father's house, was filled with anxiety when she noted the absence of her lover, for she knew that sometimes men who entered the dungeons of Cæsar were never heard of more—but there was none who could tell her whether Maximus Præclarus lived or not, and so with her mother she made her way to the Colosseum to witness the opening of the games. Her heart was heavy lest she should see Maximus Præclarus entered there, and his blood upon the white sand, yet, also, she feared that she might not see him and thus be faced by the almost definite assurance that he had been secretly done to death by the agents of Fastus.

A great multitude had gathered in the Colosseum to witness the entry of Cæsar and the pageant of his triumph, and the majority of these remained in their seats for the opening of the games, which commenced early in the afternoon. It was not until then that the sections reserved for the patricians began to fill.

The loge reserved for Dion Splendidus, the senator, was close to that of Cæsar. It afforded an excellent view of the arena and with cushions and rugs was so furnished as to afford the maximum comfort to those who occupied it.

Never had a Cæsar essayed so pretentious a fête; entertainment of the rarest description was vouchsafed each lucky spectator, yet never before in her life had Dilecta loathed and dreaded any occurrence as she now loathed and dreaded the games that were about to open.

Always heretofore her interest in the contestants had been impersonal. Professional gladiators were not of the class to come within the ken or acquaintance of the daughter of a patrician. The warriors and slaves were to her of no greater importance than the beasts against which they sometimes contended, while the condemned criminals, many of whom expiated their sins within the arena, aroused within her heart only the remotest suggestion of sympathy. She was a sweet and lovely girl, whose sensibilities would doubtless have been shocked by the brutality of the prize-ring or a varsity football game, but she could look upon the bloody cruelties of a Roman arena without a qualm, because by custom and heredity they had become a part of the national life of her people.

But today she trembled. She saw the games as a personal menace to her own happiness and the life of one she loved, yet by no outward sign did she divulge her perturbation. Calm, serene, and entirely beautiful, Dilecta, the daughter of Dion Splendidus, awaited the signal for the opening of the games that was marked by the arrival of Cæsar.

Sublatus came, and after he had taken his seat there emerged from one of the barred gates at the far end of the arena the head of a procession, again led by trumpeters, who were followed by those who were to take part in the games during the week. It consisted for the most part of the same captives who had been exhibited in the pageant, to which were added a number of wild beasts, some of which were led or dragged along by slaves, while others, more powerful and ferocious, were drawn in wheeled cages. These consisted principally of lions and leopards, but there were also a couple of bull buffaloes and several cages in which were confined huge manlike apes.

The participants were formed in a solid phalanx facing Sublatus, where they were addressed by the Emperor, freedom and reward being promised the victors; and then, sullen and lowering, they were herded back to their dungeons and cages.

Dilecta's eyes scanned the faces of the contestants as they stood in solid rank before the loge of Cæsar, but nowhere among them could she discover Maximus Præclarus. Breathless and tense, with fearful apprehension, she leaned forward in her seat across the top of the arena wall as a man entered the loge from behind and sat upon the bench beside her.

"He is not there," said the man.

The girl turned quickly toward the speaker. "Fastus!" she exclaimed. "How do you know that he is not there?"

"It is by my order," replied the prince.

"He is dead," cried Dilecta. "You have had him killed."

"No," denied Fastus, "he is safe in his cell."

"What is to become of him?" asked the girl.

"His fate lies in your hands," replied Fastus. "Give him up and promise to become the wife of Fastus and I will see that he is not forced to appear in the arena."

"He would not have it so," said the girl.

Fastus shrugged. "As you will," he said, "but remember that his life is in your hands."

"With sword, or dagger, or pike he has no equal," said the girl, proudly. "If he were entered in the contest, he would be victorious."

"Cæsar has been known to pit unarmed men against lions," Fastus reminded her, tauntingly. "Of what avail then is prowess with any weapon?"

"That would be murder," said Dilecta.

"A harsh term to apply to an act of Cæsar," returned Fastus, menacingly.

"I speak my mind," said the girl; "Cæsar or no Cæsar. It would be a cowardly and contemptible act, but I doubt not that either Cæsar or his son is capable of even worse." Her voice trembled with scathing contempt.

With a crooked smile upon his lips, Fastus arose. "It is not a matter to be determined without thought," he said, "and your answer concerns not Maximus Præclarus alone, nor you, nor me."

"What do you mean?" she asked.

"There are Dion Splendidus and your mother, and Festivitas, the mother of Præclarus!" And with this warning he turned and left the loge.

The games progressed amid the din of trumpets, the crash of arms, the growling of beasts, and the murmuring of the great audience that sometimes rose to wild acclaim or deep-throated, menacing disapproval. Beneath fluttering banners and waving scarfs the cruel, terrible thousand-eyed thing that is a crowd looked down upon the blood and suffering of its fellow men, munching sweetmeats while a victim died and cracking coarse jokes as slaves dragged the body from the arena and raked clean sand over crimsoned spots.

Sublatus had worked long and carefully with the præfect in charge of the games that the resultant program might afford the greatest possible entertainment for Cæsar and the populace, thus winning for the Emperor a certain popularity that his own personality did not command.

Always the most popular events were those in which men of

the patrician class participated, and so he counted much upon Cassius Hasta and Cæcilius Metellus, but of even greater value for his purpose was the giant white barbarian, who already had captured the imagination of the people because of his exploits.

Wishing to utilize Tarzan in as many events as possible, Sublatus knew that it would be necessary to reserve the more dangerous ones for the latter part of the week, and so upon the first afternoon of the games Tarzan found himself thrust into the arena, unarmed, in company with a burly murderer, whom the master of the games had clothed in loincloth and leopard skin similar to Tarzan.

A guard escorted them across the arena and halted them in the sand below the Emperor, where the master of the games announced that these two would fight with bare hands in any way that they saw fit and that he who remained alive or alone in the arena at the end of the combat would be considered victorious.

"The gate to the dungeons will be left open," he said, "and if either contestant gets enough he may quit the arena, but who-ever does so forfeits the contest to the other."

The crowd booed. It was not to see such tame exhibitions as this that they had come to the Colosseum. They wanted blood. They wanted thrills, but they waited, for perhaps this contest might afford comedy—that they enjoyed, too. If one greatly outclassed the other, it would be amusing to see the weaker seek escape. They cheered Tarzan and they cheered the low-browed murderer. They shouted insults at the noble patrician who was master of the games, for they knew the safety and irresponsibility of numbers.

As the word was given the contestants to engage one another Tarzan turned to face the low-browed, hulking brute against whom he had been pitted and he saw that someone had been at pains to select a worthy antagonist for him. The man was somewhat shorter than Tarzan, but great, hard muscles bulged beneath his brown hide, bulking so thick across his back and shoulders as almost to suggest deformity. His long arms hung almost to his knees, and his thick, gnarled legs sug-gested a man of bronze upon a pedestal of granite. The fellow circled Tarzan, looking for an opening. He scowled ferociously as though to frighten his adversary.

"There is the gate, barbarian," he cried in a low voice, pointing to the far end of the arena. "Escape while you are yet alive."

The crowd roared in approbation. It enjoyed glorious sallies such as these. "I shall tear you limb from limb," shouted the murderer, and again the crowd applauded.

"I am here," said Tarzan, calmly.

"Flee!" screamed the murderer, and lowering his head he charged like an angry bull.

The ape-man sprang into the air and came down upon his antagonist, and what happened happened so quickly that no one there, other than Tarzan, knew how it had been accomplished; only he knew that he clamped a reverse headlock upon the murderer.

What the crowd saw was the hulking figure hurtling to a hard fall. They saw him lying half-stunned upon the sand, while the giant barbarian stood with folded arms looking down upon him.

The fickle crowd rose from its benches, shrieking with delight. *Habet! Habet!* they cried, and thousands of closed fists were outstretched with the thumbs pointing downward, but Tarzan only stood there waiting, as the murderer, shaking his head to clear his brain, crawled slowly to his feet.

The fellow looked about him half-bewildered and then his eyes found Tarzan and with a growl of rage he charged again. Again the terrible hold was clamped upon him, and again he was hurled heavily to the floor of the arena.

The crowd screamed with delight. Every thumb in the Colosseum was pointed downward. They wanted Tarzan to kill his adversary. The ape-man looked up into Cæsar's loge, where sat the master of the games with Sublatus.

"Is not this enough?" he demanded, pointing at the prostrate figure of the stunned gladiator.

The præfect waved a hand in an all-including gesture which took in the audience. "They demand his death," he said. "While he remains alive in the arena, you are not the victor."

"Does Cæsar require that I kill this defenseless man?" demanded Tarzan, looking straight into the face of Sublatus.

"You have heard the noble præfect," replied the Emperor, haughtily.

"Good," said Tarzan. "The rules of the contest shall be fulfilled." He stooped and seized the unconscious form of his antagonist and raised it above his head. "Thus I carried your Emperor from his throne room to the avenue!" he shouted to the audience.

Screams of delight measured the appreciation of the populace, while Cæsar went white and red in anger and mortifications. He half rose from his seat, but what he contemplated was never fulfilled, for at that instant Tarzan swung the body of the murderer downward and back like a huge pendulum and then upward with a mighty surge, hurling it over the arena wall, full into the loge of Sublatus, where it struck Cæsar, knocking him to the floor.

"I am alive and alone in the arena," shouted Tarzan, turning to the people, "and by the terms of the contest I am victor," and not even Cæsar dared question the decision that was voiced by the shrieking, screaming, applauding multitude.

15

BLOODY DAYS FOLLOWED restless nights in comfortless cells, where lice and rats joined forces to banish rest. When the games began there had been twelve inmates in the cell occupied by Tarzan, but now three empty rings dangled against the stone wall, and each day they wondered whose turn was next.

The others did not reproach Tarzan because of his failure to free them, since they had never taken his optimism seriously. They could not conceive of contestants escaping from the arena during the games. It simply was not done and that was all that there was to it. It never had been done, and it never would be.

"We know you meant well," said Præclarus, "but we knew better than you."

"The conditions have not been right, as yet," said Tarzan, "but if what I have been told of the games is true, the time will come."

"What time could be propitious," asked Hasta, "while more than half of Cæsar's legionaries packed the Colosseum?"

"There should be a time," Tarzan reminded him, "when all the victorious contestants are in the arena together. Then we shall rush Cæsar's loge and drag him into the arena. With Sublatus as a hostage we may demand a hearing and get it. I venture to say that they will give us our liberty in return for Cæsar."

341

"But how can we enter Cæsar's loge?" demanded Metellus.

"In an instant we may form steps with living men stooping, while others step upon their backs as soldiers scale a wall. Perhaps some of us will be killed, but enough will succeed to seize Cæsar and drag him to the sands."

"I wish you luck," said Præclarus, "and, by Jupiter, I believe that you will succeed. I only wish that I might be with you."

"You will not accompany us?" demanded Tarzan.

"How can I? I shall be locked in this cell. Is it not evident that they do not intend to enter me in the contests? They are reserving for me some other fate. The jailer has told me that my name appears in no event."

"But we must find a way to take you with us," said Tarzan.

"There is no way," said Præclarus, shaking his head, sadly.

"Wait," said Tarzan. "You commanded the Colosseum guards, did you not?"

"Yes," replied Præclarus.

"And you had the keys to the cells?" asked the ape-man.

"Yes," replied Præclarus, "and to the manacles as well."

"Where are they?" asked Tarzan. "But no, that will not do. They must have taken them from you when they arrested you."

"No, they did not," said Præclarus. "As a matter of fact, I did not have them with me when I dressed for the banquet that night. I left them in my room."

"But perhaps they sent for them?"

"Yes, they sent for them, but they did not find them. The jailer asked me about them the day after I was arrested, but I told him that the soldiers took them from me. I told him that because I had hidden them in a secret place where I keep many valuables. I knew that if I had told them where they were they would take not only the keys, but my valuables as well."

"Good!" exclaimed the ape-man. "With the keys our problem is solved."

"But how are you going to get them?" demanded Præclarus, with a rueful smile.

"I do not know," said Tarzan. "All I know is that we must have the keys."

"We know, too, that we should have our liberty," said Hasta, "but knowing it does not make us free."

Their conversation was interrupted by the approach of soldiers along the corridor. Presently a detachment of the palace guard halted outside their cell. The jailer unlocked the door and a man entered with two torch-bearers behind him. It was Fastus.

He looked around the cell. "Where is Præclarus?" he demanded, and then, "Ah, there you are!"

Præclarus did not reply.

"Stand up, slave!" ordered Fastus, arrogantly. "Stand up, all of you. How dare you sit in the presence of a Cæsar!" he exclaimed.

"Swine is a better title for such as you," taunted Præclarus.

"Drag them up! Beat them with your pikes!" cried Fastus to the soldiers outside the doorway.

The command of the Colosseum guard, who stood just behind Fastus, blocked the doorway. "Stand back," he said to the legionaries. "No one gives orders here except Cæsar and myself, and you are not Cæsar yet, Fastus."

"I shall be one day," snapped the prince, "and it will be a sad day for you."

"It will be a sad day for all Castra Sanguinarius," replied the officer. "You said that you wished to speak to Præclarus? Say what you have to say and be gone. Not even Cæsar's son may interfere with my charges."

Fastus trembled with anger, but he knew that he was powerless. The commander of the guard spoke with the authority of the Emperor, whom he represented. He turned upon Præclarus.

"I came to invite my good friend, Maximus Præclarus, to my wedding," he announced, with a sneer. He waited, but Præclarus made no reply. "You do not seem duly impressed, Præclarus," continued the prince. "You do not ask who is to be the happy bride. Do you not wish to know who will be the next Empress in Castra Sanguinarius, even though you may not live to see her upon the throne beside Cæsar?"

The heart of Maximus Præclarus stood still, for now he knew why Fastus had come to the dungeon-cell, but he gave no sign of what was passing within his breast, but remained seated in silence upon the hard floor, his back against the cold wall.

"You do not ask me whom I am to wed, nor when," continued Fastus, "but I shall tell you. You should be interested. Dilecta, the daughter of Dion Splendidus, will have none of a traitor and a felon. She aspires to share the purple with a Cæsar. In the evening following the last day of the games Dilecta and Fastus are to be married in the throne room of the palace."

Gloating, Fastus waited to know the result of his announcement, but if he had looked to surprise Maximus Præclarus into an exhibition of chagrin he failed, for the young patrician ignored him so completely that Fastus might not have been in the cell at all for all the attention that the other paid to him.

Maximus Præclarus turned and spoke casually to Metellus and the quiet affront aroused the mounting anger of Fastus to such an extent that he lost what little control he had of himself. Stepping quickly forward, he stooped and slapped Præclarus in the face and then spat upon him, but in doing so he had come too close to Tarzan and the ape-man reached out and seized him by the ankle, dragging him to the floor.

Fastus screamed a command to his soldiers. He sought to draw his dagger or his sword, but Tarzan took them from him and hurled the prince into the arms of the legionaries, who had rushed past the commander of the Colosseum guard and entered the cell.

"Get out now, Fastus," said the latter. "You have caused enough trouble here already."

"I shall get you for this," hissed the prince, "all of you," and he swept the inmates of the cell with an angry, menacing glance.

Long after they had gone, Cassius Hasta continued to chuckle. "Cæsar!" he exclaimed. "Swine!"

As the prisoners discussed the discomfiture of Fastus and sought to prophesy what might come of it, they saw a wavering light reflected from afar in the corridor before their cell.

"We are to have more guests," said Metellus.

"Perhaps Fastus is returning to spit on Tarzan," suggested Cassius Hasta, and they all laughed.

The light was advancing along the corridor, but it was not accompanied by the tramp of soldiers' feet.

"Whoever comes comes silently and alone," said Maximus Præclarus.

"Then it is not Fastus," said Hasta.

"But it might be an assassin sent by him," suggested Præclarus.

"We shall be ready for him," said Tarzan.

A moment later there appeared beyond the grating of the cell door the commander of the Colosseum guards, who had accompanied Fastus and who had stood between the prince and the prisoner.

"Appius Applosus!" exclaimed Maximus Præclarus. "He is no assassin, my friends."

"I am not the assassin of your body, Præclarus," said Applosus, "but I am indeed the assassin of your happiness."

"What do you mean, my friend?" demanded Præclarus.

"In his anger Fastus told me more than he told you."

"He told you what?" asked Præclarus.

"He told me that Dilecta had consented to become his wife only in the hope of saving her father and mother and you, Præclarus, and your mother, Festivitas."

"To call him swine is to insult the swine," said Præclarus. "Take word to her, Applosus, that I would rather die than to see her wed to Fastus."

"She knows that, my friend," said the officer, "but she thinks also of her father and her mother and yours."

Præclarus's chin dropped upon his chest. "I had forgotten that," he moaned. "Oh, there must be some way to stop it."

"He is the son of Cæsar," Applosus reminded him, "and the time is short."

"I know it! I know it!" cried Præclarus, "but it is too hideous. It cannot be."

"This officer is your friend, Præclarus?" asked Tarzan, indicating Appius Applosus.

"Yes," said Præclarus.

"You would trust him fully?" demanded the ape-man.

"With my life and my honor," said Præclarus.

"Tell him where your keys are and let him fetch them," said the ape-man.

Præclarus brightened instantly. "I had not thought of that," he cried, "but no, his life would be in jeopardy."

"It already is," said Applosus. "Fastus will never forget or forgive what I said tonight. You, Præclarus, know that I am already doomed. What keys do you want? Where are they? I will fetch them."

"Perhaps not when you know what they are," said Præclarus.

"I can guess," replied Appius Applosus.

"You have been in my apartment often, Applosus?"

The other nodded affirmatively.

"You recall the shelves near the window where my books lie?"

"Yes."

"The back of the third shelf slides to one side and behind it, in the wall, you will find the keys."

"Good, Præclarus. You shall have them," said the officer.

The others watched the diminishing light as Appius Applosus departed along the corridor beneath the Colosseum.

The last day of the games had come. The bloodthirsty populace had gathered once more as eager and enthusiastic as though they were about to experience a new and unfamiliar thrill, their appetites swept as clean of the memories of the past week as were the fresh sands of the arena of the brown stains of yesterday.

For the last time the inmates of the cell were taken to enclosures nearer to the entrance to the arena. They had fared better, perhaps, than others, for of the twelve rings only four were empty.

Maximus Præclarus alone was left behind. "Good-bye," he said. "Those of you who survive the day shall be free. We shall not see one another again. Good luck to you and may the gods give strength and skill to your arms—that is all that I can ask of them, for not even the gods could give you more courage than you already possess."

"Applosus has failed us," said Hasta.

Tarzan looked troubled. "If only you were coming out with us, Præclarus, we should not then need the keys."

From within the enclosure, where they were confined, Tarzan and his companions could hear the sounds of combat and the groans and hoots and applause of the audience, but they could not see the floor of the arena.

It was a very large room with heavily barred windows and a door. Sometimes two men, sometimes four, sometimes six would go out together, but only one, or two, or three returned. The effect upon the nerves of those who remained uncalled was maddening. For some the suspense became almost unendurable. Two attempted suicide and others tried to pick quarrels with their fellow prisoners, but there were many guards within the room and the prisoners were unarmed, their weapons being issued to them only after they had quit the enclosure and were about to enter the arena.

The afternoon was drawing to a close. Metellus had fought with a gladiator, both in full armor. Hasta and Tarzan had heard the excited cries of the populace. They had heard cheer after cheer, which indicated that each man was putting up a skillful and courageous fight. There was an instant of silence and then the loud cries of *"Habet! Habet!"*

"It is over," whispered Cassius Hasta.

Tarzan made no reply. He had grown to like these men, for he had found them brave and simple and loyal and he, too, was inwardly moved by the suspense that must be endured until one or the other returned to the enclosure; but he gave no outward sign of his perturbation, and while Cassius Hasta paced nervously to and fro Tarzan of the Apes stood silently, with folded arms, watching the door. After awhile it opened and Cæcilius Metellus crossed the threshold.

Cassius Hasta uttered a cry of relief and sprang forward to embrace his friend.

Again the door swung open and a minor official entered. "Come," he cried, "all of you. It is the last event."

Outside the enclosure each man was given a sword, dagger, pike, shield, and a hempen net, and one by one, as they were thus equipped, they were sent into the arena. All the survivors of the week of combat were there—one hundred of them.

They were divided into two equal parties, and red ribbons were fastened to the shoulders of one party and white ribbons to the shoulders of the other.

Tarzan was among the reds, as were Hasta, Metellus, Lukedi, Mpingu, and Ogonyo.

"What are we supposed to do?" asked Tarzan of Hasta.

"The reds will fight against the whites until all the reds are killed or all the whites."

"They should see blood enough to suit them now," said Tarzan.

"They can never get enough of it," replied Metellus.

The two parties marched to the opposite end of the arena and received their instructions from the præfect in charge of the games, and then they were formed, the reds upon one side of the arena, the whites upon the other. Trumpets sounded and the armed men advanced toward one another.

Tarzan smiled to himself as he considered the weapons with which he was supposed to defend himself. The pike he was sure of, for the Waziri are great spearmen and Tarzan excelled even among them, and with the dagger he felt at home, so long had the hunting knife of his father been his only weapon of protection—but the Spanish sword, he felt, would probably prove more of a liability than an asset, while the net in his hands could be nothing more than a sorry joke. He would like to have thrown his shield aside, for he did not like shields, considering them, as a rule, useless encumbrances, but he had used them before when the Waziri had fought other native tribes, and knowing that they were constructed as a defense against the very weapons that his opponents were using he retained his and advanced with the others toward the white line. He had determined that their only hope lay in accounting for as many of their adversaries in the first clash of arms as was possible, and this word he had passed down the line with the further admonition that the instant that a man had disposed of an antagonist he turn immediately to help the red nearest him, or the one most sorely beset.

As the two lines drew closer, each man selected the opponent opposite him and Tarzan found that he faced a warrior from the outer villages. They came closer. Some of the men, more eager or nervous than the others, were in advance; some, more fearful, lagged behind. Tarzan's opponent came upon him. Already pikes were flying through the air. Tarzan and the warrior hurled their missiles at the same instant, and back of the ape-man's throw was all the skill and all the muscle and all the weight that he could command. Tarzan struck upward with his shield and his opponent's pike struck it a glancing blow, but with such force that the spear haft was shattered, while Tarzan's weapon passed through the shield of his opponent and pierced the fellow's heart.

There were two others down—one killed and one wounded—and the Colosseum was a babble of voices and a bedlam of noise. Tarzan sprang quickly to aid one of his fellows, but another white, who had killed his red opponent, ran to interfere. Tarzan's net annoyed him, so he threw it at a white who was pressing one of the reds and took on his fresh opponent, who had drawn his sword. His adversary was a professional gladiator, a man trained in the use of all his weapons, and Tarzan soon realized that only through great strength and agility might he expect to hold his own with this opponent.

The fellow did not rush. He came in slowly and carefully, feeling out Tarzan. He was cautious because he was an old hand at the business and was imbued with but a single hope—to live. He cared as little for the hoots and jibes of the people as he did for their applause, and he hated Cæsar. He soon discovered that Tarzan was adopting defensive tactics only, but whether this was for the purpose of feeling out his opponent or whether it was part of a plan that would lead up to a sudden and swift surprise, the gladiator could not guess, nor did he care particularly, for he knew that he was master of his weapon and many a corpse had been burned that in life had thought to surprise him.

Judging Tarzan's skill with the sword by his skill with the shield, the gladiator thought that he was pitted against a highly skilled adversary, and he waited patiently for Tarzan to open up his offense and reveal his style. But Tarzan had no style that could be compared with that of the gladiator. What he was awaiting was a lucky chance—the only thing that he felt could assure him victory over this wary and highly skilled swordsman—but the gladiator gave him no openings and he was hoping that one of his companions would be free to come to his assistance, when, suddenly and without warning, a net dropped over his shoulders from behind.

16

CASSIUS HASTA SPLIT the helmet of a burly thief who opposed him, and as he turned to look for a new opponent he saw a white cast a net over Tarzan's head and shoulders from the rear, while the ape-man was engaged with a professional gladiator. Cassius was nearer the gladiator than Tarzan's other opponent and with a cry he hurled himself upon him. Tarzan saw what Cassius Hasta had done and wheeled to face the white who had attacked him from the rear.

The gladiator found Cassius Hasta a very different opponent from Tarzan. Perhaps he was not as skillful with his shield. Perhaps he was not as powerful, but never in all his experience had the gladiator met such a swordsman.

The crowd had been watching Tarzan from the beginning of the event because his great height and his nakedness and his leopard skin marked him from all others. They noted that the first cast of his pike had split the shield of his opponent and dropped him dead and they watched his encounter with the gladiator, which did not please them at all. It was far too slow and they hooted and voiced catcalls. When the white cast the net over him they howled with delight, for they did not know from one day to the next, or from one minute to the next, what their own minds would be the next day or the next minute. They were cruel and stupid, but they were no different from the crowds of any place or any time.

As Tarzan, entangled in the net, turned to face the new

menace, the white leaped toward him to finish him with a dagger and Tarzan caught the net with the fingers of both his hands and tore it asunder as though it had been made of paper, but the fellow was upon him in the same instant. The dagger hand struck as Tarzan seized the dagger wrist. Blood ran from beneath the leopard skin from a wound over Tarzan's heart, so close had he been to death, but his hand stopped the other just in time and now steel fingers closed upon that wrist until the man cried out with pain as he felt his bones crushed together. The ape-man drew his antagonist toward him and seized him by the throat and shook him as a terrier shakes a rat, while the air trembled to the delighted screams of the mob.

An instant later Tarzan cast the lifeless form aside, picked up his sword and shield that he had been forced to abandon, and sought for new foes. Thus the battle waged around the arena, each side seeking to gain the advantage in numbers so that they might set upon the remnant of their opponents and destroy them. Cassius Hasta had disposed of the gladiator that he had drawn away from Tarzan and was now engaged with another swordsman when a second fell upon him. Two to one are heavy odds, but Cassius Hasta tried to hold the second off until another red could come to his assistance.

This, however, did not conform with the ideas of the whites who were engaging him, and they fell upon him with redoubled fury to prevent the very thing that he hoped for. He saw an opening and quick as lightning his sword leaped into it, severing the jugular vein of one of his antagonists, but his guard was down for the instant and a glancing blow struck his helmet and, though it did not pierce it, it sent him stumbling to the sand, half-stunned.

"*Habet! Habet!*" cried the people, for Cassius Hasta had fallen close to one side of the arena where a great number of people could see him. Standing over him, his antagonist raised his forefinger to the audience and every thumb went down.

With a smile the white raised his sword to drive it through Hasta's throat, but as he paused an instant, facing the crowd, in a little play to the galleries for effect, Tarzan leaped across the soft sand, casting aside his sword and shield, reverting to the primitive, to the beast, to save his friend.

It was like the charge of a lion. The crowd saw and was frozen into silence. They saw him spring in his stride several yards before he reached the opposing gladiator and, like a jungle beast, fall upon the shoulders and back of his prey.

Down the two went across the body of Hasta, but instantly the ape-man was upon his feet and in his hands was his antagonist. He shook him as he had shaken the other—shook him into unconsciousness, choking him as he shook, shook him to death, and cast his body from him.

The crowd went wild. They stood upon their benches and shrieked and waved scarfs and helmets and threw many flowers and sweetmeats into the arena. Tarzan stooped and lifted Cassius Hasta to his feet as he saw that he was not killed and consciousness was returning.

Scanning the arena quickly, he saw that fifteen reds survived and but ten whites. This was a battle for survival. There were no rules and no ethics. It was your life or mine and Tarzan gathered the surplus five and set upon the strongest white, who now, surrounded by six swordsmen, went down to death in an instant.

At Tarzan's command the six divided and each three charged another white with the result that by following these tactics the event was brought to a sudden and bloody close with fifteen reds surviving and the last white slain.

The crowd was crying Tarzan's name above all others, but Sublatus was enraged. The affront that had been put upon him by this wild barbarian had not been avenged as he had hoped, but instead Tarzan had achieved a personal popularity far greater than his own. That it was ephemeral and subject to the changes of the fickle public mind did not lessen the indignation and chagrin of the Emperor. His mind could entertain but one thought toward Tarzan. The creature must be destroyed. He turned to the præfect in charge of the games and whispered a command.

The crowd was loudly demanding that the laurel wreaths be

accorded the victors and that they be given their freedom, but instead they were herded back to their enclosure, all but Tarzan.

Perhaps, suggested some members of the audience, Sublatus is going to honor him particularly, and this rumor ran quickly through the crowd, as rumors will, until it became a conviction.

Slaves came and dragged away the corpses of the slain and picked up the discarded weapons and scattered new sand and raked it, while Tarzan stood where he had been told to stand, beneath the loge of Cæsar.

He stood with folded arms, grimly waiting for what he knew not, and then a low groan rose from the crowded stands—a groan that grew in volume to loud cries of anger above which Tarzan caught words that sounded like "Tyrant!" "Coward!" "Traitor!" and "Down with Sublatus!" He looked around and saw them pointing to the opposite end of the arena and, facing in that direction, he saw the thing that had aroused their wrath, for instead of a laurel wreath and freedom there stood eying him a great, black-maned lion, gaunt with hunger.

Toward the anger of the populace Sublatus exhibited, outwardly, an arrogant and indifferent mien. Contemptuously he permitted his gaze to circle the stands, but he whispered orders that sent three centuries of legionaries among the audience in time to overawe a few agitators who would have led them against the imperial loge.

But now the lion was advancing, and the cruel and selfish audience forgot its momentary anger against injustice in the expected thrill of another bloody encounter. Some, who, a moment before, had been loudly acclaiming Tarzan now cheered the lion, though if the lion were vanquished they would again cheer Tarzan. That, however, they did not anticipate, but believed that they had taken sides with the assured winner, since Tarzan was armed only with a dagger, not having recovered his other weapons after he had thrown them aside.

Naked, but for loincloth and leopard skin, Tarzan presented a magnificent picture of physical perfection, and the people of

Castra Sanguinarius gave him their admiration, while they placed their denarii and their talents upon the lion.

They had seen other men that week face other lions bravely and hopelessly and they saw the same courageous bearing in the giant barbarian, but the hopelessness they took for granted the ape-man did not feel. With head flattened, half-crouching, the lion moved slowly toward its prey, the tip of its tail twitching in nervous anticipation, its gaunt sides greedy to be filled. Tarzan waited.

Had he been the lion himself, he scarcely could have better known what was passing in that savage brain. He knew to the instant when the final charge would start. He knew the speed of that swift and deadly rush. He knew when and how the lion would rear upon its hind legs to seize him with great talons and mighty, yellow fangs.

He saw the muscles tense. He saw the twitching tail quiet for an instant. His folded arms dropped to his side. The dagger remained in its sheath at his hip. He waited, crouching almost imperceptibly, his weight upon the balls of his feet, and then the lion charged.

Knowing how accurately the beast had timed its final rush, measuring the distance to the fraction of a stride, even as a hunter approaches a jump, the ape-man knew that the surest way in which to gain the first advantage was to disconcert the charging beast by doing that which he would least expect.

Numa the lion knows that his quarry usually does one of two things—he either stands paralyzed with terror or he turns and flees. So seldom does he charge to meet Numa that the lion never takes this possibility into consideration and it was, therefore, this very thing that Tarzan did.

As the lion charged, the ape-man leaped to meet him, and the crowd sat breathless and silent. Even Sublatus leaned forward with parted lips, forgetful, for a moment, that he was Cæsar.

Numa tried to check himself and rear to meet this presumptuous man-thing, but he slipped a little in the sand and the great paw that struck at Tarzan was ill-timed and missed, for the ape-man had dodged to one side and beneath it, and in the fraction of a second that it took Numa to recover himself he found that their positions had been reversed and that the prey that he would have leaped upon had turned swiftly and leaped upon him.

Full upon the back of the lion sprang Tarzan of the Apes. A giant forearm encircled the maned throat; steel-thewed legs crossed beneath the gaunt, slim belly and locked themselves there. Numa reared and pawed and turned to bite the savage beast upon his back, but the viselike arm about his throat pressed tighter, holding him so that his fangs could not reach their goal. He leaped into the air and when he alighted on the sand shook himself to dislodge the growling man-beast clinging to him.

Holding his position with his legs and one arm, Tarzan, with his free hand, sought the hilt of his dagger. Numa, feeling the life being choked from him, became frantic. He reared upon his hind legs and threw himself upon the ground, rolling upon his antagonist, and now the crowd found its voice again and shouted hoarse delight. Never in the history of the arena had such a contest as this been witnessed. The barbarian was offering such a defense as they had not thought possible and they cheered him, though they knew that eventually the lion would win. Then Tarzan found his dagger and drove the thin blade into Numa's side, just back of his left elbow. Again and again the knife struck home, but each blow seemed only to increase the savage efforts of the lunging beast to shake the man from his back and tear him to pieces.

Blood was mixed with the foam on Numa's jowls as he stood panting upon trembling legs after a last futile effort to dislodge the ape-man. He swayed dizzily. The knife struck deep again. A great stream of blood gushed from the mouth and nostrils of the dying beast. He lurched forward and fell lifeless upon the crimsoned sand.

Tarzan of the Apes leaped to his feet. The savage personal combat, the blood, the contact with the mighty body of the carnivore had stripped from him the last vestige of the thin veneer of civilization. It was no English Lord who stood there with one foot upon his kill and through narrowed lids glared about him at the roaring populace. It was no man, but a wild beast, that raised its head and voiced the savage victory cry of the bull ape, a cry that stilled the multitude and froze its blood. But, in an instant, the spell that had seized him passed. His expression changed. The shadow of a smile crossed his face as he stooped and, wiping the blood from his dagger upon Numa's mane, returned the weapon to its sheath.

Cæsar's jealousy had turned to terror as he realized the meaning of the tremendous ovation the giant barbarian was receiving from the people of Castra Sanguinarius. He well knew, though he tried to conceal the fact, that he held no place in popular favor and that Fastus, his son, was equally hated and despised.

This barbarian was a friend of Maximus Præclarus, whom he had wronged, and Maximus Præclarus, whose popularity with the troops was second to none, was loved by Dilecta, the daughter of Dion Splendidus, who might easily aspire to the purple with the support of such a popular idol as Tarzan must become if he were given his freedom in accordance with the customs and rules governing the contests. While Tarzan waited in the arena and the people cheered themselves hoarse, more legionaries filed into the stands until the wall bristled with glittering pikes.

Cæsar whispered in consultation with the præfect of the games. Trumpets blared and the præfect arose and raised his open palm for silence. Gradually the din subsided and the people waited, listening, expecting the honors that were customarily bestowed upon the outstanding hero of the games. The præfect cleared his throat.

"This barbarian has furnished such extraordinary entertainment that Cæsar, as a special favor to his loyal subjects, has decided to add one more event to the games in which the barbarian may again demonstrate his supremacy. This event will"—but what further the præfect said was drowned in a murmur of surprise, disapproval, and anger, for the people had sensed by this time the vicious and unfair trick that Sublatus was about to play upon their favorite.

They cared nothing for fair play, for though the individual may prate of it at home it has no place in mob psychology, but the mob knew what it wanted. It wanted to idolize a popular hero. It did not care to see him fight again that day and it wanted to thwart Sublatus, whom it hated. Menacing were the cries and threats directed toward Cæsar, and only the glittering pikes kept the mob at bay.

In the arena the slaves were working rapidly; fallen Numa had been dragged away, the sands swept, and as the last slave disappeared, leaving Tarzan again alone within the enclosure, those menacing gates at the far end swung open once more.

17

As Tarzan looked toward the far end of the arena he saw six bull apes being herded through the gateway. They had heard the victory cry roll thunderously from the arena a few minutes before and they came now from their cages filled with excitement and ferocity. Already had they long been surly and irritable from confinement and from the teasing and baiting to which they had been subjected by the cruel Sanguinarians. Before them they saw a man-thing—a hated Tarmangani. He represented the creatures that had captured them and teased them and hurt them.

"I am Gayat," growled one of the bull apes. "I kill."

"I am Zutho," bellowed another. "I kill."

"Kill the Tarmangani," barked Go-yad, as the six lumbered forward—sometimes erect upon their hind feet, sometimes swinging with gnarled knuckles to the ground.

The crowd hooted and groaned. "Down with Cæsar!" "Death to Sublatus!" rose distinctly above the tumult. To a man they were upon their feet, but the glittering pikes held them in awe as one or two, with more courage than brains, sought to reach the loge of Cæsar, but ended upon the pikes of the legionaries instead. Their bodies, lying in the aisles, served as a warning to the others.

Sublatus turned and whispered to a guest in the imperial loge. "This should be a lesson to all who would dare affront Cæsar," he said.

"Quite right," replied the other. "Glorious Cæsar is, indeed, all powerful," but the fellow's lips were blue from terror as he saw how great and menacing was the crowd and how slim and few looked the glittering pikes that stood between it and the imperial loge.

As the apes approached, Zutho was in the lead. "I am Zutho," he cried. "I kill."

"Look well, Zutho, before you kill your friend," replied the ape-man. "I am Tarzan of the Apes."

Zutho stopped, bewildered. The others crowded about him.

"The Tarmangani spoke in the language of the great apes," said Zutho.

"I know him" said Go-yad. "He was king of the tribe when I was a young ape."

"It is, indeed, Whiteskin," said Gayat.

"Yes," said Tarzan, "I am Whiteskin. We are all prisoners here together. These Tarmangani are my enemies and yours. They wish us to fight, but we shall not."

"No," said Zutho, "We shall not fight against Tarzan."

"Good," said the ape-man, as they gathered close around

him, sniffing that their noses might validate the testimony of their eyes.

"What has happened?" growled Sublatus. "Why do they not attack him?"

"He has cast a spell upon them," replied Cæsar's guest.

The people looked on wonderingly. They heard the beasts and the man growling at one another. How could they guess that they were speaking together in their common language? They saw Tarzan turn and walk toward Cæsar's loge, his bronzed skin brushing against the black coats of the savage beasts lumbering at his side. The ape-man and the apes halted below imperial Cæsar. Tarzan's eyes ran quickly around the arena. The wall was lined with legionaries so not even Tarzan might pass these unscathed. He looked up at Sublatus.

"Your plan has failed, Cæsar. These that you thought would tear me to pieces are my own people. They will not harm me. If there are any others that you would turn against me let them come now, but be quick, for my patience is growing short and if I should say the word these apes will follow me into the imperial loge and tear you to shreds."

And that is exactly what Tarzan would have done had he not known that while he doubtless could have killed Sublatus his end would come quickly beneath the pikes of the legionaries. He was not sufficiently well versed in the ways of mobs to know that in their present mood the people would have swarmed to protect him and that the legionaries, with few exceptions, would have joined forces with them against the hated tyrant.

What Tarzan wanted particularly was to effect the escape of Cassius Hasta and Cæcilius Metellus simultaneously with his own, so that he might have the advantage of their assistance in his search for Erich von Harben in the Empire of the East; therefore, when the præfect ordered him back to his dungeon he went, taking the apes with him to their cages.

As the arena gates closed behind him he heard again, above the roaring of the populace, the insistent demand: "Down with Sublatus!"

As the jailer opened the cell door, Tarzan saw that its only occupant was Maximus Præclarus.

"Welcome, Tarzan!" cried the Roman. "I had not thought to see you again. How is it that you are neither dead nor free?"

"It is the justice of Cæsar," replied Tarzan, with a smile, "but at least our friends are free, for I see they are not here."

"Do not deceive yourself, barbarian," said the jailer. "Your friends are chained safely in another cell."

But they won their freedom," exclaimed Tarzan.

"And so did you," returned the jailer, with a grin; "but are you free?"

"It is an outrage," cried Præclarus. "It cannot be done."

The jailer shrugged. "But it is already done," he said.

"And why?" demanded Præclarus.

"Think you that a poor soldier has the confidence of Cæsar?" asked the jailer; "but I have heard the reason rumored. Sedition is in the air. Cæsar fears you and all your friends because the people favor you and you favor Dion Splendidus."

"I see," said Præclarus, "and so we are to remain here indefinitely."

"I should scarcely say indefinitely," grinned the jailer, as he closed the door and locked it, leaving them alone.

"I did not like the look in his eye nor the tone of his voice," said Præclarus, after the fellow was out of hearing. "The gods are unkind, but how can I expect else from them when even my best friend fails me?"

"You mean Appius Applosus?" asked Tarzan.

"None other," replied Præclarus. "If he had fetched the keys, we might yet escape."

"Perhaps we shall in any event," said Tarzan. "I should never give up hope until I were dead—and I have never been dead."

"You do not know either the power or perfidy of Cæsar," replied the Roman.

"Nor does Cæsar know Tarzan of the Apes."

Darkness had but just enveloped the city, blotting out even the dim light of their dungeon cell, when the two men perceived wavering light beams lessening the darkness of the corridor without. The light increased and they knew that someone was approaching, lighting his way with a flaring torch.

Visitors to the dungeon beneath the Colosseum were few in the daytime. Guards and jailers passed occasionally and twice each day slaves came with food, but at night the silent approach of a single torch might more surely augur ill than well. Præclarus and Tarzan dropped the desultory conversation with which they had been whiling away the time and waited in silence for whoever might be coming.

Perhaps the nighttime visitor was not for them, but the egotism of misfortune naturally suggested that he was and that his intentions might be more sinister than friendly. But they had not long to wait and their suspicions precluded any possibility of surprise when a man halted before the barred gateway to their cell. As the visitor fitted the key to the lock Præclarus recognized him through the bars.

"Appius Applosus!" he cried. "You have come!'

"Ps-st!" cautioned Applosus, and quickly opening the gate he stepped within and closed it silently behind him. With a quick glance he surveyed the cell and then extinguished his torch against the stone wall. "It is fortunate that you are alone," he said, speaking in whispers, as he dropped to the floor close to the two men.

"You are trembling," said Præclarus. "What has happened?"

"It is not what has happened but what is about to happen that alarms me," replied Applosus. "You have probably wondered why I had not brought the keys. You have doubtless thought me faithless, but the fact is that up to this instant it has been impossible, although I have stood ready before to risk my life in the attempt, even as I am now doing."

"But why should it be so difficult for the commander of the Colosseum guard to visit the dungeon?"

"I am no longer the commander of the guards," replied Applosus. "Something must have aroused Cæsar's suspicions, for I was removed in the hour that I last left you. Whether someone overheard and reported our plan or whether it was merely my known friendship for you that aroused his misgivings, I may only surmise, but the fact remains that I have been kept on duty constantly at the Porta Prætoria since I was transferred there from the Colosseum. I have not even been permitted to return to my home, the reason given being that Cæsar expects an uprising of the barbarians of the outer villages, which, as we all know, is utterly ridiculous.

"I risked everything to leave my post only an hour ago and that because of a word of gossip that was passed to me by a young officer, who came to relieve another at the gate."

"What said he?" demanded Præclarus.

"He said that an officer of the palace guard had told him that he had been ordered to come to your cell tonight and assassinate both you and this white barbarian. I hastened to Festivitas and together we found the keys that I promised to bring you, but even as I slunk through the shadows of the city's streets, endeavoring to reach the Colosseum unobserved or unrecognized, I feared that I might be too late, for Cæsar's orders are that you are to be dispatched at once. Here are the keys, Præclarus. If I may do more, command me."

"No, my friend," replied Præclarus, "you have already risked more than enough. Go at once. Return to your post lest Cæsar learn and destroy you."

"Farewell then and good luck," said Applosus. "If you would leave the city, remember that Appius Applosus commands the Porta Prætoria."

"I shall not forget, my friend," replied Præclarus, "but I shall not impose further risks upon your friendship."

Appius Applosus turned to leave the cell, but he stopped suddenly at the gate. "It is too late," he whispered. "Look!"

The faint gleams of distant torchlight were cutting the gloom of the corridor.

"They come!" whispered Præclarus. "Make haste!" but instead Appius Applosus stepped quickly to one side of the doorway, out of sight of the corridor beyond, and drew his Spanish sword.

Rapidly the torch swung down the corridor. The scraping of sandals on stone could be distinctly heard, and the ape-man knew that whoever came was alone. A man wrapped in a long dark cloak halted before the barred door and, holding his torch above his head, peered within.

"Maximus Præclarus!" he whispered. "Are you within?"

"Yes," replied Præclarus.

"Good!" exclaimed the other. "I was not sure that this was the right cell."

"What is your errand?" demanded Præclarus.

"I come from Cæsar," said the other. "He sends a note."

"A sharp one?" inquired Præclarus.

"Sharp and pointed," laughed the officer.

"We are expecting you."

"You knew?" demanded the other.

"We guessed, for we know Cæsar."

"Then make your peace with your gods," said the officer, drawing his sword and pushing the door open, "for you are about to die."

There was a cold smile upon his lips as he stepped across the threshold, for Cæsar knew his men and had chosen well the proper type for this deed—a creature without conscience whose envy and jealousy Præclarus had aroused, and the smile was still upon his lips as the sword of Appius Applosus crashed through his helmet to his brain. As the man lunged forward dead, the torch fell from his left hand and was extinguished upon the floor.

"Now go," whispered Præclarus to Applosus, "and maybe the gratitude of those you have saved prove a guard against disaster."

"It could not have turned out better," whispered Applosus. "You have the keys; you have his weapons, and now you have ample time to make your escape before the truth is learned. Good-bye, again. Good-bye, and may the gods protect you."

As Applosus moved cautiously along the dark corridor, Maximus Præclarus fitted keys to their manacles and both men stood erect, freed at last from their hated chains. No need to formulate plans—they had talked and talked of nothing else for weeks, changing them only to meet altered conditions. Now their first concern was to find Hasta and Metellus and the others upon whose loyalty they could depend and to gather around them as many of the other prisoners as might be willing to follow them in the daring adventure they contemplated.

Through the darkness of the corridor they crept from cell to cell and in the few that still held prisoners they found none unwilling to pledge his loyalty to any cause or to any leader that might offer freedom. Lukedi, Mpingu, and Ogonyo were among those they liberated. They had almost given up hope of finding the others when they came upon Metellus and Hasta in a cell close to the entrance to the arena. With them were a number of professional gladiators, who should have been liberated with the other victors at the end of the games, but who were being kept because of some whim of Cæsar that they could not understand and that only inflamed them to anger against the Emperor.

To a man they pledged themselves to follow wherever Tarzan might lead.

"Few of us will come through alive," said the ape-man, when they had all gathered in the large room that was reserved for the contestants before they were ushered into the arena, "but those who do will have been avenged upon Cæsar for the wrongs that he has done them."

"The others will be welcomed by the gods as heroes worthy of every favor," added Præclarus.

"We do not care whether your cause be right or wrong, or whether we live or die," said a gladiator, "so long as there is good fighting."

"There will be good fighting. I can promise you that," said Tarzan, "and plenty of it."

"Then lead on," said the gladiator.

"But first I must liberate the rest of my friends," said the ape-man.

"We have emptied every cell," said Præclarus. "There are no more."

"Oh, yes, my friend," said Tarzan. "There are still others— the great apes."

18

IN THE DUNGEONS of Validus Augustus in Castrum Mare, Erich von Harben and Mallius Lepus awaited the triumph of Validus Augustus and the opening of the games upon the morrow.

"We have nothing to expect but death," said Lepus, gloomily. "Our friends are in disfavor, or in prison, or in exile. The jealousy of Validus Augustus against his nephew, Cassius Hasta, has been invoked against us by Fulvus Fupus to serve his own aims."

"And the fault is mine," said von Harben.

"Do not reproach yourself," replied his friend. "That Favonia gave you her love cannot be held against you. It is only the jealous and scheming mind of Fupus that is to blame."

"My love has brought sorrow to Favonia and disaster to her friends," said von Harben, "and here am I, chained to a stone wall, unable to strike a blow in her defense or theirs."

"Ah, if Cassius Hasta were but here!" exclaimed Lepus. "There is a man. With Fupus adopted by Cæsar, the whole city would arise against Validus Augustus if Cassius Hasta were but here to lead us."

And as they conversed sadly and hopelessly in the dungeons of Castrum Mare, noble guests gathered in the throne room of Sublatus in the city of Castra Sanguinarius, at the opposite end of the valley. There were senators in rich robes and high officers of the court and of the army, resplendent in jewels and embroidered linen, who, with their wives and their daughters, formed a gorgeous, and glittering company in the pillared chamber, for Fastus, the son of Cæsar, was to wed the daughter of Dion Splendidus that evening.

In the avenue, beyond the palace gates, a great crowd had assembled—a multitude of people pushing and surging to and fro, but pressing ever upon the gates up to the very pikes of the legionaries. It was a noisy crowd—noisy with a deep-throated roar of anger.

"Down with the tyrant!" "Death to Sublatus!" "Death to Fastus!" was the burden of their hymn of hate.

The menacing notes filled the palace, reaching to the throne-room, but the haughty patricians pretended not to hear the voice of the cattle. Why should they fear? Had not Sublatus distributed donations to all the troops that very day? Would not the pikes of the legionaries protect the source of their gratuity? It would serve the ungrateful populace right if Sublatus set the legions upon them, for had he not given them such a pageant and such a week of games as Castra Sanguinarius never had known before?

For the rabble without, their contempt knew no bounds now that they were within the palace of the Emperor, but they did not speak among themselves of the fact that most of them had entered by a back gate after the crowd had upset the litter of a noble senator and spilled its passengers into the dust of the avenue.

With pleasure they anticipated the banquet that would follow the marriage ceremony, and while they laughed and chattered over the gossip of the week, the bride sat stark and cold in an upper chamber of the palace surrounded by her female slaves and comforted by her mother.

"It shall not be," she said. "I shall never be the wife of Fastus," and in the folds of her flowing robe she clutched the hilt of a slim dagger.

In the corridor beneath the Colosseum, Tarzan marshaled his forces. He summoned Lukedi and a chief of one of the outer villages, who had been a fellow prisoner with him and with whom he had fought shoulder to shoulder in the games.

"Go to the Porta Prætoria," he said, "and ask Appius Applosus to pass you through the city wall as a favor to Maximus Præclarus. Go then among the villages and gather warriors. Tell them that if they would be avenged upon Cæsar and free to live their own lives in their own way, they must rise now and join the citizens who are ready to revolt and destroy the tyrant. Hasten, there is no time to be lost. Gather them quickly and lead them into the city by the Porta Prætoria, straight to the palace of Cæsar."

Warning their followers to silence, Tarzan and Maximus Præclarus led them in the direction of the barracks of the Colosseum guard, where were quartered the men of Præclarus's own cohort.

It was a motley throng of near-naked warriors from the outer villages, slaves from the city, and brown half-castes, among whom were murderers, thieves, and professional gladiators. Præclarus and Hasta and Metellus and Tarzan led them, and swarming close to Tarzan were Gayat, Zutho, and Go-yad and their three fellow apes.

Ogonyo was certain now that Tarzan was a demon, for who else might command the hairy men of the woods? Doubtless in each of these fierce bodies presided the ghost of some great Bagego chief. If little Nkima had been the ghost of his grandfather, then these must be the ghosts of very great men, indeed. Ogonyo did not press too closely to these savage allies, nor as a matter of fact did any of the others—not even the most ferocious of the gladiators.

At the barracks Maximus Præclarus knew to whom to speak and what to say, for mutiny had long been rife in the ranks of the legionaries. Only their affection for some of their officers, among whom was Præclarus, had kept them thus long in leash, and now they welcomed the opportunity to follow the young patrician to the very gates of Cæsar's palace.

Following a plan that had been decided upon, Præclarus dispatched a detachment under an officer to the Porta Prætoria with orders to take it by force, if they could not persuade Appius Applosus to join them, and throw it open to the warriors from the outer villages when they should arrive.

Along the broad Via Principalis, overhung by giant trees that formed a tunnel of darkness in the night, Tarzan of the Apes led his followers toward the palace in the wake of a few torchbearers, who lighted the way.

As they approached their goal, someone upon the outskirts of the crowd, pressing the palace guard, was attracted by the light of their torches and quickly the word was passed that Cæsar had sent for reinforcements—that more troops were coming. The temper of the crowd, already inflamed, was not improved as this news spread quickly through its ranks. A few, following a self-appointed leader, moved forward menacingly to meet the newcomers.

"Who comes?" shouted one.

"It is I, Tarzan of the Apes," replied the ape-man.

The shout that went up in response to this declaration proved that the fickle populace had not, as yet, turned against him.

Within the palace the cries of the people brought a scowl to the face of Cæsar and a sneer to many a patrician lip, but their reaction might have been far different had they known the cause of the elation of the mob.

"Why are you here?" cried voices. "What are you going to do?"

"We have come to rescue Dilecta from the arms of Fastus and to drag the tyrant from the throne of Castra Sanguinarius."

Roars of approval greeted the announcement. "Death to the tyrant!" "Down with the palace guards!" "Kill them!" "Kill them!" rose from a thousand lips.

The crowd pushed forward. The officer of the guard, seeing the reinforcements, among which were many legionaries, ordered his men to fall back within the palace grounds and close and bar the gate, nor did they succeed in accomplishing this an instant too soon, for as the bolts were shot the crowd hurled itself upon the stout barriers of iron and oak.

A pale-faced messenger hastened to the throne room and to Cæsar's side.

"The people have risen," he whispered, hoarsely, "and many soldiers and gladiators and slaves have joined them. They are throwing themselves against the gates, which cannot hold for long."

Cæsar arose and paced nervously to and fro, and presently he paused and summoned officers.

"Dispatch messengers to every gate and every barracks," he ordered. "Summon the troops to the last man that may be spared from the gates. Order them to fall upon the rabble and kill. Let them kill until no citizen remains alive in the streets of Castra Sanguinarius. Take no prisoners."

As word finds its way through a crowd, as though by some strange telepathic means, so the knowledge soon became common that Sublatus had ordered every legionary in the city to the palace with instructions to destroy the revolutionaries to the last man.

The people, encouraged by the presence of the legionaries led by Præclarus, had renewed their assaults upon the gates, and though many were piked through its bars, their bodies were dragged away by their friends and others took their places, so that the gates sagged and bent beneath their numbers; yet they held and Tarzan saw that they might hold for long—or at least long enough to permit the arrival of the reinforcements that, if they remained loyal to Cæsar, might overcome this undisciplined mob with ease.

Gathering around him some of those he knew best, Tarzan explained a new plan that was greeted with exclamations of approval, and summoning the apes he moved down the dark avenue, followed by Maximus Præclarus, Cassius Hasta, Cæcilius Metellus, Mpingu, and a half dozen of Castra Sanguinarius's most famous gladiators.

The wedding of Fastus and Dilecta was to take place upon the steps of Cæsar's throne. The high priest of the temple stood facing the audience, and just below him, and at one side, Fastus waited, while slowly up the center of the long chamber came the bride, followed by the vestal virgins, who tended the temple's sacred fires.

Dilecta was pale, but she did not falter as she moved slowly forward to her doom. There were many who whispered that she looked the Empress already, so noble was her mien, so stately her carriage. They could not see the slim dagger clutched in her right hand beneath the flowing bridal robes. Up the aisle she moved, but she did not halt before the priest as Fastus had done—and as she should have done—but passed him and mounting the first few steps toward the throne she halted, facing Sublatus.

"The people of Castra Sanguinarius have been taught through all the ages that they may look to Cæsar for protection," she said. "Cæsar not only makes the law—he is the law. He is either the personification of justice or he is a tyrant. Which, Sublatus, are you?"

Cæsar flushed. "What mad whim is this, child?" he demanded. "Who has set you to speak such words to Cæsar?"

"I have not been prompted," replied the girl, wearily. "It is my last hope and though I knew beforehand that it was futile, I felt that I must not cast it aside as useless before putting it to the test."

"Come! Come!" snapped Cæsar. "Enough of this foolishness. Take your place before the priest and repeat your marriage vows."

"You cannot refuse me," cried the girl, stubbornly. "I appeal to Cæsar, which is my right as a citizen of Rome, the mother city that we have never seen, but whose right to citizenship has been handed down to us from our ancient sires. Unless the spark of freedom is to be denied us, you cannot refuse me that right, Sublatus."

The Emperor paled and then flushed with anger. "Come to me tomorrow," he said. "You shall have whatever you wish."

"If you do not hear me now, there will be no tomorrow," she said. "I demand my rights now."

"Well," demanded Cæsar, coldly, "what favor do you seek?"

"I seek no favor," replied Dilecta. "I seek the right to know if the thing for which I am paying this awful price has been done, as it was promised."

"What do you mean?" demanded Sublatus. "What proof do you wish?"

"I wish to see Maximus Præclarus here alive and free,"

replied the girl, "before I pledge my troth to Fastus. That, as you well know, was the price of my promise to wed him."

Cæsar arose angrily. "That cannot be," he said.

"Oh, yes, it can be," cried a voice from the balcony at the side of the chamber, "for Maximus Præclarus stands just behind me."

19

EVERY EYE TURNED in the direction of the balcony from which came the voice of the speaker. A gasp of astonishment arose from the crowded room.

"The barbarian!" "Maximus Præclarus!" cried a score of voices.

"The guard! The guard!" screamed Cæsar, as Tarzan leaped from the balcony to one of the tall pillars that supported the roof and slid quickly to the floor, while behind him came six hairy apes.

A dozen swords flashed from their scabbards as Tarzan and the six leaped toward the throne. Women screamed and fainted. Cæsar shrank back upon his golden seat, momentarily paralyzed by terror.

A noble with bared blade leaped in front of Tarzan to bar his way, but Go-yad sprang full upon him. Yellow fangs bit once into his neck and, as the great ape arose and standing on the body of his kill roared forth his victory cry, the other nobles shrank back. Fastus, with a scream, turned and fled, and Tarzan leaped to Dilecta's side. As the apes ascended the steps to the dais, Cæsar, jabbering with terror, scuttled from his seat and hid, half-fainting, behind the great throne that was the symbol of his majesty and his power.

But it was not long before the nobles and officers and soldiers in the apartment regained the presence of mind that the sudden advent of this horrid horde had scattered to the four winds, and now, seeing only the wild barbarian and six unarmed beasts threatening them, they pushed forward. Just then a small door beneath the balcony from which Tarzan had descended to the floor of the throne room was pushed open, giving entrance to Maximus Præclarus, Cassius Hasta, Cæcilius Metellus, Mpingu, and the others who had accompanied Tarzan over the palace wall beneath the shadows of the great trees into which the ape-man and the apes had assisted their less agile fellows.

As Cæsar's defenders sprang forward they were met by some of the best swords in Castra Sanguinarius, as in the forefront of the fighting were the very gladiators whose exploits they had cheered during the week. Tarzan passed Dilecta to Mpingu, for he and Præclarus must lend a hand in the fighting.

Slowly, Dilecta's defenders fell back before the greater number of nobles, soldiers, and guardsmen who were summoned from other parts of the palace. Back toward the little door they fell, while shoulder to shoulder with the gladiators and with Maximus Præclarus and Hasta and Metellus, Tarzan fought and the great apes spread consternation among all because of their disposition to attack friend as well as foe.

And out upon the Via Principalis the crowd surged and the great gates gave to a shrieking mob that poured into the palace grounds, overwhelming the guards, trampling them—trampling their own dead and their own living.

But the veteran legionaries who composed the palace guard made a new stand at the entrance to the palace. Once more they checked the undisciplined rabble, which had by now grown to such proportions that the revolting troops, who had joined them, were lost in their midst. The guard had dragged an onager to the palace steps and were discharging stones into the midst of the crowd, which continued to rush forward to fall upon the pikes of the palace defenders.

In the distance trumpets sounded from the direction of the Porta Decumana, and from the Porta Principalis Dextra came the sound of advancing troops. At first those upon the outskirts of the mob, who had heard these sounds, did not interpret them correctly. They cheered and shouted. These cowards that hang always upon the fringe of every crowd, letting others take the risks and do the fighting for them, thought that more troops had revolted and that the reinforcements were for them. But their joy was short-lived, for the first century that swung into the Via Principalis from the Porta Decumana fell upon them with pike and sword until those who were not slain escaped, screaming, in all directions.

Century after century came at the double. They cleared the Via Principalis and fell upon the mob within the palace court until the revolt dissolved into screaming individuals fleeing through the darkness of the palace grounds, seeking any shelter that they might find, while terrible legionaries pursued them with flaming torches and bloody swords.

Back into the little room from which they had come fell Tarzan and his followers. The doorway was small and it was not difficult for a few men to hold it, but when they would have retreated through the window they had entered and gone back into the palace grounds to seek escape across the walls in the shadows of the old trees, they saw the grounds swarming with legionaries and realized that the back of the revolt had been broken.

The anteroom in which they had taken refuge would barely accommodate them all, but it offered probably the best refuge they could have found in all the palace of Sublatus, for there were but two openings in it—the single small doorway leading into the throne room and an even smaller window letting into the palace gardens. The walls were all stone and proof against any weapons at the disposal of the legionaries; yet if the uprising had failed and the legionaries had not joined the people, as they had expected, of what value this temporary sanctuary? The instant that hunger and thirst assailed them this same room would become their prison cell and torture chamber—and perhaps for many of them a vestibule to the grave.

"Ah, Dilecta," cried Præclarus, in the first moment that he could seize to go to her side, "I have found you only to lose you again. My rashness, perhaps, has brought you death."

"Your coming saved me from death," replied the girl, drawing the dagger from her gown and exhibiting it to Præclarus. "I chose this as husband rather than Fastus," she said, "so if I die now I have lived longer than I should have, had you not come; and at least I die happy, for we shall die together."

"This is no time to be speaking of dying," said Tarzan. "Did you think a few hours ago that you would ever be together again? Well, here you are. Perhaps in a few more hours everything will be changed and you will be laughing at the fears you are now entertaining."

Some of the gladiators, who were standing near and had overheard Tarzan's words, shook their heads.

"Any of us who gets out of this room alive," said one, "will be burned at the stake, or fed to lions, or pulled apart by wild buffalo. We are through, but it has been a good fight, and I for one thank this great barbarian for this glorious end."

Tarzan shrugged and turned away. "I am not dead yet," he said, "and not until I am dead is it time to think of it—and then it will be too late."

Maximus Præclarus laughed. "Perhaps you are right," he said. "What do you suggest? If we stay here, we shall be slain, so you must have some plan for getting us out."

"If we can discern no hope of advantage through our own efforts," replied Tarzan, "we must look elsewhere and await such favors of fortune as may come from without, either through the intervention of our friends beyond the palace grounds or from the carelessness of the enemy himself. I admit that just at present our case appears desperate, but even so I am not without hope; at least we may be cheered by the realization that whatever turn events may take it must be for the better, since nothing could be worse."

"I do not agree with you," said Metellus, pointing through the window. "See, they are setting up a small ballista in the garden. Presently our condition will be much worse than it is now."

"The walls appear substantial," returned the ape-man. "Do you think they can batter them down, Præclarus?"

"I doubt it," replied the Roman, "but every missile that comes through the window must take its toll, as we are so crowded here that all of us cannot get out of range."

The legionaries that had been summoned to the throne room had been held at the small doorway by a handful of gladiators and the defenders had been able to close and bar the stout oaken door. For a time there had been silence in the throne room and no attempt was made to gain entrance to the room upon that side; while upon the garden side two or three attempts to rush the window had been thwarted, and now the legionaries held off while the small ballista was being dragged into place and trained upon the palace wall.

Dilecta having been placed in an angle of the room where she would be safest, Tarzan and his lieutenants watched the operations of the legionaries in the garden.

"They do not seem to be aiming directly at the window," remarked Cassius Hasta.

"No," said Præclarus. "I rather think they intend making a breach in the wall through which a sufficient number of them can enter to overpower us."

"If we could rush the ballista and take it," mused Tarzan, "we could make it rather hot for them. Let us hold ourselves in readiness for that, if their missiles make it too hot for us in here. We shall have some advantage if we anticipate their assault by a sortie of our own."

A dull thud upon the door at the opposite end of the room brought the startled attention of the defenders to that quarter. The oak door sagged and the stone walls trembled to the impact.

Cassius Hasta smiled wryly. "They have brought a ram," he said.

And now a heavy projectile shook the outer wall and a piece of plaster crumbled to the floor upon the inside—the ballista had come into action. Once again the heavy battering ram shivered the groaning timbers of the door and the inmates of the room could hear the legionaries chanting the hymn of the ram to the cadence of which they swung it back and heaved it forward.

The troops in the garden went about their duty with quiet, military efficiency. Each time a stone from the ballista struck the wall there was a shout, but there was nothing spontaneous in the demonstration, which seemed as perfunctory as the mechanical operation of the ancient war-engine that delivered its missiles with almost clocklike regularity.

The greatest damage that the ballista appeared to be doing was to the plaster on the inside of the wall, but the battering ram was slowly but surely shattering the door at the opposite side of the room.

"Look," said Metellus, "they are altering the line of the ballista. They have discovered that they can effect nothing against the wall."

"They are aiming at the window," said Præclarus.

"Those of you who are in line with the window lie down upon the floor," commanded Tarzan. "Quickly! the hammer is falling upon the trigger."

The next missile struck one side of the window, carrying away a piece of the stone, and this time the result was followed by an enthusiastic shout from the legionaries in the garden.

"That's what they should have done in the beginning," commented Hasta. "If they get the walls started at the edge of the window, they can make a breach more quickly there than elsewhere."

"That is evidently what they are planning on doing," said Metellus, as a second missile struck in the same place and a large fragment of the wall crumbled.

"Look to the door," shouted Tarzan, as the weakened timbers sagged to the impact of the ram.

A dozen swordsmen stood ready and waiting to receive the legionaries, whose rush they expected the instant that the door fell. At one side of the room the six apes crouched, growling, and kept in leash only by the repeated assurances of Tarzan that the man-things in the room with them were the friends of the ape-man.

As the door crashed, there was a momentary silence, as each side waited to see what the other would do, and in the lull that ensued there came through the air a roaring sound ominous and threatening, and then the shouts of the legionaries in the throne room and the legionaries in the garden drowned all other sounds.

The gap around the window had been enlarged. The missiles of the ballista had crumbled the wall from the ceiling to the floor, and as though in accordance with a prearranged plan the legionaries assaulted simultaneously, one group rushing the doorway from the throne room, the other the breach in the opposite wall.

Tarzan turned toward the apes and pointing in the direction of the breached wall, shouted: "Stop them, Zutho! Kill, Go-yad! Kill!"

The men near him looked at him in surprise and perhaps they shuddered a little as they heard the growling voice of a beast issue from the throat of the giant barbarian, but instantly they realized he was speaking to his hairy fellows, as they saw the apes spring forward with bared fangs and, growling hideously, throw themselves upon the first legionaries to reach the window. Two apes went down, pierced by Roman pikes, but before the beastly rage of the others Cæsar's soldiers gave back.

"After them," cried Tarzan to Præclarus. "Follow them into the garden. Capture the ballista and turn it upon the legionaries. We will hold the throne room door until you have seized the ballista, then we shall fall back upon you."

After the battling apes rushed the three patricians, Maximus Præclarus, Cassius Hasta, and Cæcilius Metellus, leading gladiators, thieves, murderers, and slaves into the garden, profiting by the temporary advantage the apes had gained for them.

Side by side with the remaining gladiators Tarzan fought to hold the legionaries back from the little doorway until the balance of his party had won safely to the garden and seized the ballista. Glancing back he saw Mpingu leading Dilecta from the room in the rear of the escaped prisoners. Then he turned again to the defense of the doorway, which his little party held stubbornly until Tarzan saw the ballista in the hands of his own men, and, giving step-by-step across the room, he and they backed through the breach in the wall.

At a shout of command from Præclarus, they leaped to one side. The hammer fell upon the trigger of the ballista, which Præclarus had lined upon the window, and a heavy rock drove full into the faces of the legionaries.

For a moment the fates had been kind to Tarzan and his fellows, but it soon became apparent that they were little if any better off here than in the room they had just quitted, for in the garden they were ringed by legionaries. Pikes were flying through the air, and though the ballista and their own good swords were keeping the enemy at a respectful distance, there was none among them who believed that they could for long withstand the superior numbers and the better equipment of their adversaries.

There came a pause in the fighting, which must necessarily be the case in hand-to-hand encounters, and as though by tacit agreement each side rested. The three whites watched the enemy closely. "They are preparing for a concerted attack with pikes," said Præclarus.

"That will write finis to our earthly endeavors," remarked Cassius Hasta.

"May the gods receive us with rejoicing," said Cæcilius Metellus.

"I think the gods prefer them to us," said Tarzan.

"Why?" demanded Cassius Hasta.

"Because they have taken so many more of them to heaven this night," replied the ape-man, pointing at the corpses lying about the garden, and Cassius Hasta smiled, appreciatively.

"They will charge in another moment," said Maximus Præclarus, and turning to Dilecta he took her in his arms and kissed her. "Good-bye, dear heart," he said. "How fleeting is happiness! How futile the hopes of mortal man!"

"Not good-bye, Præclarus," replied the girl, "for where you go I shall go," and she showed him the slim dagger in her hand.

"No," cried the man. "Promise me that you will not do that."

"And why not? Is not death sweeter than Fastus?"

"Perhaps you are right," he said, sadly.

"They come," cried Cassius Hasta.

"Ready!" shouted Tarzan. "Give them all we have. Death is better than the dungeons of the Colosseum."

20

FROM THE FAR end of the garden, above the din of breaking battle, rose a savage cry—a new note that attracted the startled attention of the contestants upon both sides. Tarzan's head snapped to attention. His nostrils sniffed the air. Recognition, hope, surprise, incredulity surged through his consciousness as he stood there with flashing eyes looking out over the heads of his adversaries.

In increasing volume the savage roar rolled into the garden of Cæsar. The legionaries turned to face the vanguard of an army led by a horde of warriors, glistening giants from whose proud heads floated white feather warbonnets and from whose throats issued the savage war cry that had filled the heart of Tarzan—the Waziri had come.

At their head Tarzan saw Muviro and with him was Lukedi, but what the ape-man did not see, and what none of those in the garden of Cæsar saw until later, was the horde of warriors from the outer villages of Castra Sanguinarius that, following the Waziri into the city, were already overrunning the palace seeking the vengeance that had so long been denied them.

As the last of the legionaries in the garden threw down their arms and begged Tarzan's protection, Muviro ran to the ape-man and, kneeling at his feet, kissed his hand, and at the same instant a little monkey dropped from an overhanging tree onto Tarzan's shoulder.

"The gods of our ancestors have been good to the Waziri," said Muviro, "otherwise we should have been too late."

"I was puzzled as to how you found me," said Tarzan, "until I saw Nkima."

"Yes, it was Nkima," said Muviro. "He came back to the country of the Waziri, to the land of Tarzan, and led us here. Many times we would have turned back thinking that he was mad, but he urged us on and we followed him, and now the big Bwana can come back with us to the home of his own people."

"No," said Tarzan, shaking his head, "I cannot come yet. The son of my good friend is still in this valley, but you are just in time to help me rescue him, nor is there any time to lose."

Legionaries, throwing down their arms, were running from the palace, from which came the shrieks and groans of the dying and the savage hoots and cries of the avenging horde. Præclarus stepped to Tarzan's side.

"The barbarians of the outer villages are attacking the city, murdering all who fall into their hands," he cried. "We must gather what men we can and make a stand against them. Will these warriors, who have just come, fight with us against them?"

"They will fight as I direct," replied Tarzan, "but I think it will not be necessary to make war upon the barbarians. Lukedi, where are the white officers who command the barbarians?"

"Once they neared the palace," replied Lukedi, "the warriors became so excited that they broke away from their white leaders and followed their own chieftain."

"Go and fetch their greatest chief," directed Tarzan.

During the half hour that followed, Tarzan and his lieutenants were busy reorganizing their forces into which were incorporated the legionaries who had surrendered to them, in caring for the wounded, and planning for the future. From the palace came the hoarse cries of the looting soldiers, and Tarzan had about abandoned hope that Lukedi would be able to persuade a chief to come to him when Lukedi returned, accompanied by two warriors from the outer villages, whose bearing and ornaments proclaimed them chieftains.

"You are the man called Tarzan?" demanded one of the chiefs.

The ape-man nodded. "I am," he said.

"We have been looking for you. This Bagego said that you have promised that no more shall our people be taken into slavery and no longer shall our warriors be condemned to the arena. How can you, who are yourself a barbarian, guarantee this to us?"

"If I cannot guarantee it, you have the power to enforce it yourself," replied the ape-man, "and I with my Waziri will aid you, but now you must gather your warriors. Let no one be killed from now on who does not oppose you. Gather your warriors and take them into the avenue before the palace and then come with your subchiefs to the throne room of Cæsar. There we shall demand and receive justice, not for the moment but for all time. Go!"

Eventually the looting horde was quieted by their chiefs and withdrawn to the Via Principalis. Waziri warriors manned the shattered gate of Cæsar's place and lined the corridor to the throne room and the aisle to the foot of the throne. They formed a half circle about the throne itself, and upon the throne of Cæsar sat Tarzan of the Apes with Præclarus and Dilecta and Cassius Hasta and Cæcilius Metellus and Muviro about him, while little Nkima sat upon his shoulder and complained bitterly, for Nkima, as usual, was frightened and cold and hungry.

"Send legionaries to fetch Sublatus and Fastus," Tarzan

directed Præclarus, "for this business must be attended to quickly, as within the hour I march on Castrum Mare."

Flushed with excitement, the legionaries that had been sent to fetch Sublatus and Fastus rushed into the throne room. "Sublatus is dead!" they cried. "Fastus is dead! The barbarians have slain them. The chambers and corridors above are filled with the bodies of senators, nobles, and officers of the legion."

"Are none left alive?" demanded Præclarus, paling.

"Yes," replied one of the legionaries, "there were many barricaded in another apartment who withstood the onslaught of the warriors. We explained to them that they are now safe and they are coming to the throne room," and up the aisle marched the remnants of the wedding guests, the sweat and blood upon the men evidencing the dire straits from which they had been delivered, the women still nervous and hysterical. Leading them came Dion Splendidus, and at sight of him Dilecta gave a cry of relief and pleasure and ran down the steps of the throne and along the aisle to meet him.

Tarzan's face lighted with relief when he saw the old senator, for his weeks in the home of Festivitas and his long incarceration with Maximus Præclarus in the dungeons of the Colosseum had familiarized him with the politics of Castra Sanguinarius, and now the presence of Dion Splendidus was all that he needed to complete the plans that the tyranny and cruelty of Sublatus had forced upon him.

He rose from the throne and raised his hand for silence. The hum of voices ceased. "Cæsar is dead, but upon someone of you must fall the mantle of Cæsar."

"Long live Tarzan! Long live the new Cæsar!" cried one of the gladiators, and instantly every Sanguinarian in the room took up the cry.

The ape-man smiled and shook his head. "No," he said, "not I, but there is one here to whom I offer the imperial diadem upon the condition that he fulfill the promises I have made to the barbarians of the other villages.

"Dion Splendidus, will you accept the imperial purple with the understanding that the men of the outer villages shall be forever free; that no longer shall their girls or their boys be pressed into slavery, or their warriors forced to do battle in the arena?" Dion Splendidus bowed his head in assent—and thus did Tarzan refuse the diadem and create a Cæsar.

21

THE YEARLY TRIUMPH of Validus Augustus, Emperor of the East, had been a poor thing by comparison with that of Sublatus of Castra Sanguinarius, though dignity and interest was lent the occasion by the presence of the much-advertised barbarian chieftain, who strode in chains behind Cæsars chariot.

The vain show of imperial power pleased Validus Augustus, deceiving perhaps the more ignorant of his subjects, and would have given Erich von Harben cause for laughter had he not realized the seriousness of his position.

No captive chained to the chariot of the greatest Cæsar that ever lived had faced a more hopeless situation than he. What though he knew that a regiment of marines or a squadron of Uhlans might have reduced this entire empire to vassalage? What though he knew that the mayor of many a modern city could have commanded a fighting force far greater and much more effective than this little Cæsar? The knowledge was only tantalizing, for the fact remained that Validus Augustus was supreme here and there was neither regiment of marines nor squadron of Uhlans to question his behavior toward the subject of a great republic that could have swallowed his entire empire without being conscious of any discomfort. The triumph was over. Von Harben had been returned to the cell that he occupied with Mallius Lepus.

"You are back early," said Lepus. "How did the triumph of Validus impress you?"

"It was not much of a show, if I may judge by the amount of enthusiasm displayed by the people."

"The triumphs of Validus are always poor things," said Lepus. "He would rather put ten talents in his belly or on his back than spend one denarius to amuse the people."

"And the games," asked von Harben, "will they be as poor?"

"They do not amount to much," said Lepus. "We have few criminals here and as we have to purchase all our slaves, they are too valuable to waste in this way. Many of the contests are between wild beasts, an occasional thief or murderer may be pitted against a gladiator, but for the most part Validus depends upon professional gladiators and political prisoners—enemies or supposed enemies of Cæsar. More often they are like you and I—victims of the lying and jealous intrigues of favorites. There are about twenty such in the dungeons now, and they will furnish the most interesting entertainment of the games."

"And if we are victorious, we are freed?" asked von Harben.

"We shall not be victorious," said Mallius Lepus. "Fulvus Fupus has seen to that, you may rest assured."

"It is terrible," muttered von Harben.

"You are afraid to die?" asked Mallius Lepus.

"It is not that," said von Harben. "I am thinking of Favonia."

"And well you may," said Mallius Lepus. "My sweet cousin would be happier dead than married to Fulvus Fupus."

"I feel so helpless," said von Harben. "Not a friend, not even my faithful body servant, Gabula."

"Oh, that reminds me," exclaimed Lepus. "They were here looking for him this morning."

"Looking for him? Is he not confined in the dungeon?"

"He was, but he was detailed with other prisoners to prepare the arena last night, and during the darkness of early morning he is supposed to have escaped—but be that as it may, they were looking for him."

"Good!" exclaimed von Harben. "I shall feel better just knowing that he is at large, though there is nothing that he can do for me. Where could he have gone?"

"Castrum Mare is ill guarded along its waterfront, but the lake itself and the crocodiles form a barrier as efficacious as many legionaries. Gabula may have scaled the wall, but the chances are that he is hiding within the city, protected by other slaves or, possibly, by Septimus Favonius himself."

"I wish I might feel that the poor, faithful fellow had been able to escape the country and return to his own people," said von Harben.

Mallius Lepus shook his head. "That is impossible," he said. "Though you came down over the cliff, he could not return that way, and even if he could find the pass to the outer world, he would fall into the hands of the soldiers of Castra Sanguinarius or the barbarians of their outer villages. No, there is no chance that Gabula will escape."

The time passed quickly, all too quickly, between the hour that Erich von Harben was returned to his cell, following his exhibition in the triumph of Validus Augustus, and the coming of the Colosseum guards to drive them into the arena.

The Colosseum was packed. The loges of the patricians were filled. The haughty Cæsar of the East sat upon an ornate throne, shaded by a canopy of purple linen. Septimus Favonius sat with bowed head in his loge and with him was his wife and Favonia. The girl sat with staring eyes fixed upon the gateway from which the contestants were emerging. She saw her cousin, Mallius Lepus, emerge and with him Erich von Harben, and she shuddered and closed her eyes for a moment.

When she opened them again the column was forming and the contestants were marched across the white sands to receive the commands of Cæsar. With Mallius Lepus and von Harben marched the twenty political prisoners, all of whom were of the patrician class. Then came the professional gladiators—coarse, brutal men, whose business it was to kill or be killed. Leading these, with a bold swagger, was one who had been champion gladiator of Castrum Mare for five years. If the people had an idol, it was he. They roared their approval of him. "Claudius Taurus! Claudius Taurus!" rose above a babel of voices. A few mean thieves, some frightened slaves, and a half dozen lions completed the victims that were to make a Roman holiday.

Erich von Harben had often been fascinated by the stories of the games of ancient Rome. Often had he pictured the Colosseum packed with its thousands and the contestants upon the white sand of the arena, but now he realized that they had been but pictures—but the photographs of his imagination. The people in those dreams had been but picture people—automatons, who move only when we look at them. When there had been action on the sand the audience had been a silent etching, and when the audience had roared and turned its thumbs down the actors had been mute and motionless.

How different, this! He saw the constant motion in the packed stands, the mosaic of a thousand daubs of color that became kaleidoscopic with every move of the multitude. He heard the hum of voices and sensed the offensive odor of many human bodies. He saw the hawkers and vendors passing along the aisles shouting their wares. He saw the legionaries stationed everywhere. He saw the rich in their canopied loges and the poor in the hot sun of the cheap seats.

Sweat was trickling down the back of the neck of the patrician marching just in front of him. He glanced at Claudius Taurus. He saw that his tunic was faded and that his hairy legs were dirty. He had always thought of gladiators as clean-limbed and resplendent. Claudius Taurus shocked him.

As they formed in solid rank before the loge of Cæsar, von Harben smelled the men pressing close behind him. The air was hot and oppressive. The whole thing was disgusting. There was no grandeur to it, no dignity. He wondered if it had been like this in Rome.

And then he looked up into the loge of Cæsar. He saw the man in gorgeous robes, sitting upon his carved throne. He saw naked slaves swaying long-handled fans of feathers above the head of Cæsar. He saw large men in gorgeous tunics and cuirasses of shining gold. He saw the wealth and pomp and circumstance of power, and something told him that after all ancient Rome had probably been much as this was—that its populace had smelled and that its gladiators had had hairy legs with dirt on them and that its patricians had sweated behind the ears.

Perhaps Validus Augustus was as great a Cæsar as any of them, for did he not rule half of his known world? Few of them had done more than this.

His eyes wandered along the row of loges. The præfect of the games was speaking and von Harben heard his voice, but the words did not reach his brain, for his eyes had suddenly met those of a girl.

He saw the anguish and hopeless horror in her face and he tried to smile as he looked at her, a smile of encouragement and hope, but she only saw the beginning of the smile, for the tears came and the image of the man she loved was only a dull blur like the pain in her heart.

A movement in the stands behind the loges attracted von Harben's eyes and he puckered his brows, straining his faculties to assure himself that he must be mistaken, but he was not. What he had seen was Gabula—he was moving toward the imperial loge, where he disappeared behind the hangings that formed the background of Cæsar's throne.

Then the præfect ordered them from the arena and as von Harben moved across the sand he tried to find some explanation of Gabula's presence there—what errand had brought him to so dangerous a place?

The contestants had traversed but half the width of the arena returning to their cells when a sudden scream, ringing out behind them, caused them all to turn. Von Harben saw that the disturbance came from the imperial loge, but the scene that met his startled gaze seemed too preposterous to have greater substance than a dream. Perhaps it was all a dream. Perhaps there was no Castrum Mare. Perhaps there was no Validus Augustus. Perhaps there was no—ah, but that could not be true, there was a Favonia and this preposterous thing then that he was looking at was true too. He saw a man holding Cæsar by the throat and driving a dagger into his heart with the other, and the man was Gabula.

It all happened so quickly and was over so quickly that scarcely had Cæsar's shriek rung through the Colosseum than he lay dead at the foot of his carved throne, and Gabula, the assassin, in a single leap had cleared the arena wall and was running across the sand toward von Harben.

"I have avenged you, Bwana!" cried Gabula. "No matter what they do to you, you are avenged."

A great groan arose from the audience and then a cheer as someone shouted: "Cæsar is dead!"

A hope flashed to the breast of von Harben. He turned and grabbed Mallius Lepus by the arm. "Cæsar is dead," he whispered. "Now is our chance."

"What do you mean?" demanded Mallius Lepus.

"In the confusion we can escape. We can hide in the city and at night we can take Favonia with us and go away."

"Where?" asked Mallius Lepus.

"God! I do not know," exclaimed von Harben, "but anywhere would be better than here, for Fulvus Fupus is Cæsar and if we do not save Favonia tonight, it will be too late."

"You are right," said Mallius Lepus.

"Pass the word to the others," said von Harben. "The more there are who try to escape the better chance there will be for some of us to succeed."

The legionaries and their officers as well as the vast multitude could attend only upon what was happening in the loge of Cæsar. So few of them had seen what really occurred there that as yet there had been no pursuit of Gabula.

Mallius Lepus turned to the other prisoners. "The gods have been good to us," he cried. "Cæsar is dead and in the confusion we can escape. Come!"

As Mallius Lepus started on a run toward the gateway that led to the cells beneath the Colosseum, the shouting prisoners fell in behind him. Only those of the professional gladiators who were freemen held aloof, but they made no effort to stop them.

"Good luck!" shouted Claudius Taurus, as von Harben passed him. "Now if someone would kill Fulvus Fupus we might have a Cæsar who is a Cæsar."

The sudden rush of the escaping prisoners so confused and upset the few guards beneath the Colosseum that they were easily overpowered and a moment later the prisoners found themselves in the streets of Castrum Mare.

"Where now?" cried one.

"We must scatter," said Mallius Lepus. "Each man for himself."

"We shall stick together, Mallius Lepus," said von Harben.

"To the end," replied the Roman.

"And here is Gabula," said von Harben, as the Negro joined them. "He shall come with us."

"We cannot desert the brave Gabula," said Mallius Lepus, "but the first thing for us to do is to find a hiding-place."

"There is a low wall across the avenue," said von Harben, "and there are trees beyond it."

"Come, then," said Mallius Lepus. "It is as good for now as any other place."

The three men hurried across the avenue and scaled the low wall, finding themselves in a garden so overgrown with weeds and underbrush that they at once assumed that it was deserted. Creeping through the weeds and forcing their way through the underbrush, they came to the rear of a house. A broken door, hanging by one hinge, windows from which the wooden blinds had fallen, an accumulation of rubbish upon the threshold marked the dilapidated structure as a deserted house.

"Perhaps this is just the place for us to hide until night," said von Harben.

"Its proximity to the Colosseum is its greatest advantage," said Mallius Lepus, "for they will be sure to believe that we have rushed as far from our dungeon as we could. Let us go in and investigate. We must be sure that the place is uninhabited."

The rear room, which had been the kitchen, had a crumbling brick oven in one corner, a bench, and a dilapidated table.

Crossing the kitchen, they entered an apartment beyond and saw that these two rooms constituted all that there was to the house. The front room was large and as the blinds at the windows facing the avenue had not fallen, it was dark within it. In one corner they saw a ladder reaching to a trapdoor in the ceiling, which evidently led to the roof of the building, and two or three feet below the ceiling and running entirely across the end of the room where the ladder arose was a false ceiling, which formed a tiny loft just below the roof-beams, a place utilized by former tenants as a storage room. A more careful examination of the room revealed nothing more than a pile of filthy rags against one wall, the remains perhaps of some homeless beggar's bed.

"It could not have been better," said Mallius Lepus, "if this had been built for us. Why, we have three exits if we are hard pressed—one into the back garden, one into the avenue in front, and the third to the roof."

"We can remain in safety, then," said von Harben, "until after dark, when it should be easy to make our way unseen through the dark streets to the home of Septimus Favonius."

22

EAST ALONG THE Via Mare from Castra Sanguinarius marched five thousand men. The white plumes of the Waziri nodded at the back of Tarzan. Stalwart legionaries followed

Maximus Præclarus, while the warriors of the outer villages brought up the rear.

Sweating slaves dragged catapults, ballistæ, testudones, huge battering rams, and other ancient engines of war. There were scaling ladders and wall hooks and devices for throwing fire balls into the defenses of an enemy. The heavy engines had delayed the march and Tarzan had chafed at the delay, but he had to listen to Maximus Præclarus and Cassius Hasta and Cæcilius Metellus, all of whom had assured him that the fort, which defended the only road to Castrum Mare, could not be taken by assault without the aid of these mechanical engines of war.

Along the hot and dusty Via Mare the Waziri swung, chanting the war-songs of their people. The hardened legionaries, their heavy helmets dangling against their breasts from cords that passed about their necks, their packs on forked sticks across their shoulders, their great oblong shields hanging in their leather covers at their backs, cursed and grumbled as become veterans, while the warriors from the outer villages laughed and sang and chattered as might a party of picnickers.

As they approached the fort with its moat and embankment and palisade and towers, slaves were bearing the body of Validus Augustus to his palace within the city, and Fulvus Fupus, surrounded by fawning sycophants, was proclaiming himself Cæsar, though he trembled inwardly in contemplation of what fate might lie before him—for though he was a fool he knew that he was not popular and that many a noble patrician with a strong following had a better right to the imperial purple than he.

Throughout the city of Castrum Mare legionaries searched for the escaped prisoners and especially for the slave who had struck down Validus Augustus, though they were handicapped by the fact that no one had recognized Gabula, for there were few in the city and certainly none in the entourage of Cæsar who was familiar with the face of the black from distant Urambi.

A few of the thieves and five or six gladiators, who were

condemned felons and not freemen, had clung together in the break for freedom and presently they found themselves in hiding in a low part of the city, in a den where wine could be procured and where there were other forms of entertainment for people of their class.

"What sort of a Cæsar will this Fulvus Fupus make?" asked one.

"He will be worse than Validus Augustus," said another. "I have seen him in the Baths where I once worked. He is vain and dull and ignorant; even the patricians hate him."

"They say he is going to marry the daughter of Septimus Favonius."

"I saw her in the Colosseum today," said another. "I know her well by sight, for she used to come to the shop of my father and make purchases before I was sent to the dungeons."

"Have you ever been to the house of Septimus Favonius?" asked another.

"Yes, I have," said the youth. "Twice I took goods there for her inspection, going through the forecourt and into the inner garden. I know the place well."

"If one like her should happen to fall into the hands of a few poor convicts they might win their freedom and a great ransom," suggested a low-browed fellow with evil, cunning eyes.

"And be drawn asunder by wild oxen for their pains."

"We must die anyway if we are caught."

"It is a good plan."

They drank again for several minutes in silence, evidencing that the plan was milling in their minds.

"The new Cæsar should pay an enormous ransom for his bride."

The youth rose eagerly to his feet. "I will lead you to the home of Septimus Favonius and guarantee that they will open the gate for me and let me in, as I know what to say. All I need is a bundle and I can tell the slave that it contains goods that my father wishes Favonia to inspect."

"You are not such a fool as you look."

"No, and I shall have a large share of the ransom for my part in it," said the youth.

"If there is any ransom, we shall share and share alike."

Night was falling as Tarzan's army halted before the defenses of Castrum Mare. Cassius Hasta, to whom the reduction of the fort had been entrusted, disposed his forces and supervised the placing of his various engines of war.

Within the city Erich von Harben and Mallius Lepus discussed the details of their plans. It was the judgment of Lepus to wait until after midnight before making any move to leave their hiding-place.

"The streets will be deserted then," said Mallius Lepus, "except for an occasional patrol upon the principal avenue, and these may be easily eluded, since the torches that they carry proclaim their approach long before there is any danger of their apprehending us. I have the key to the gate of my uncle's garden, which insures that we may enter the grounds silently and unobserved."

"Perhaps you are right," said von Harben, "but I dread the long wait and the thought of further inaction seems unbearable."

"Have patience, my friend," said Mallius Lepus. "Fulvus Fupus will be too busy with his new Cæsarship to give heed to aught else for some time, and Favonia will be safe from him, certainly for the next few hours at least."

And as they discussed the matter, a youth knocked upon the door of the home of Septimus Favonius. Beneath the shadow of the trees along the wall darker shadows crouched. A slave bearing a lamp came to the door in answer to the knocking and, speaking through a small grille, asked who was without and the nature of his business.

"I am the son of Tabernarius," said the youth. "I have brought fabrics from the shop of my father that the daughter of Septimus Favonius may inspect them."

The slave hesitated.

"You must remember me," said the youth. "I have been here

often," and the slave held the light a little bit higher and peered through the grille.

"Yes," he said, "your face is familiar. I will go and ask my mistress if she wishes to see you. Wait here."

"These fabrics are valuable," said the youth, holding up a bundle, which he carried under his arm. "Let me stand just within the vestibule lest thieves set upon me and rob me."

"Very well," said the slave, and opening the gate he permitted the youth to enter. "Remain here until I return."

As the slave disappeared into the interior of the house, the son of Tabernarius turned quickly and withdrew the bolt that secured the door. Opening it quickly, he leaned out to voice a low signal.

Instantly the denser shadows beneath the shadowy trees moved and were resolved into the figures of men. Scurrying like vermin, they hurried through the doorway and into the home of Septimus Favonius, and into the anteroom off the vestibule the son of Tabernarius hustled them. Then he closed both doors and waited.

Presently the slave returned. "The daughter of Septimus Favonius recalls having ordered no goods from Tabernarius," he said, "nor does she feel in any mood to inspect fabrics this night. Return them to your father and tell him that when the daughter of Septimus Favonius wishes to purchase she will come herself to his shop."

Now this was not what the son of Tabernarius desired and he racked his crafty brain for another plan, though to the slave he appeared but a stupid youth, staring at the floor in too much embarrassment even to take his departure.

"Come," said the slave, approaching the door and laying hold of the bolt, "you must be going."

"Wait," whispered the youth, "I have a message for Favonia. I did not wish anyone to know it and for that reason I spoke of bringing fabrics as an excuse."

"Where is the message and from whom?" demanded the slave, suspiciously.

"It is for her ears only. Tell her this and she will know from whom it is."

The slave hesitated.

"Fetch her here," said the youth. "It will be better that no other member of the household sees me."

The slave shook his head. "I will tell her," he said, for he knew that Mallius Lepus and Erich von Harben had escaped from the Colosseum and he guessed that the message might be from one of these. As he hastened back to his mistress the son of Tabernarius smiled, for though he knew not enough of Favonia to know from whom she might reasonably expect a secret message, yet he knew there were few young women who might not, at least hopefully, expect a clandestine communication. He had not long to wait before the slave returned and with him came Favonia. Her excitement was evident as she hastened eagerly forward toward the youth.

"Tell me," she cried, "you have brought word from him."

The son of Tabernarius raised a forefinger to his lip to caution her to silence. "No one must know that I am here," he whispered, "and no ears but yours may hear my message. Send your slave away."

"You may go," said Favonia to the slave. "I will let the young man out when he goes," and the slave, glad to be dismissed, content to be relieved of responsibility, moved silently away into the shadows of a corridor and thence into that uncharted limbo into which pass slaves and other lesser people when one has done with them.

"Tell me," cried the girl, "what word do you bring? Where is he?"

"He is here," whispered the youth, pointing to the anteroom.

"Here?" exclaimed Favonia, incredulously.

"Yes, here," said the youth. "Come," and he led her to the door and as she approached it he seized her suddenly and, clapping a hand over her mouth, dragged her into the dark anteroom beyond.

Rough hands seized her quickly and she was gagged and bound. She heard them converse in low whispers.

"We will separate here," said one. "Two of us will take her to the place we have selected. One of you will have to leave the note for Fulvus Fupus so the palace guards will find it. The rest of you scatter and go by different routes to the deserted house across from the Colosseum. Do you know the place?"

"I know it well. Many is the night that I have slept there."

"Very well," said the first speaker, who seemed to be the leader, "Now be off. We have no time to waste."

"Wait," said the son of Tabernarius, "the division of the ransom has not yet been decided. Without me you could have done nothing. I should have at least half."

"Shut up or you will be lucky if you get anything," growled the leader.

"A knife between his ribs would do him good," muttered another.

"You will not give me what I asked?" demanded the youth.

"Shut up," said the leader. "Come along now, men," and carrying Favonia, whom they wrapped in a soiled and ragged cloak, they left the home of Septimus Favonius unobserved; and as two men carried a heavy bundle through the dark shadows beneath the shadowy trees the son of Tabernarius started away in the opposite direction. . . .

A youth in soiled and ragged tunic and rough sandals approached the gates of Cæsar's palace. A legionary challenged him, holding him at a distance with the point of his pike.

"What do you loitering by the palace of Cæsar by night?" demanded the legionary.

"I have a message for Cæsar," replied the youth.

The legionary guffawed. "Will you come in or shall I send Cæsar out to you?" he demanded, ironically.

"You may take the message to him yourself, soldier," replied the other, "and if you know what is good for you, you will not delay."

The seriousness of the youth's voice finally compelled the attention of the legionary. "Well," he demanded, "out with it. What message have you for Cæsar?"

"Hasten to him and tell him that the daughter of Septimus Favonius has been abducted and that if he hastens he will find her in the deserted house that stands upon the corner opposite the chariot entrance to the Colosseum."

"Who are you?" demanded the legionary.

"Never mind," said the youth. "Tomorrow I shall come for my reward," and he turned and sped away before the legionary could detain him.

"At this rate midnight will never come," said von Harben.

Mallius Lepus laid a hand upon the shoulder of his friend. "You are impatient, but remember that it will be safer for Favonia, as well as for us, if we wait until after midnight, for the streets now must be full of searchers. All afternoon we have heard soldiers passing. It is a miracle that they have not searched this place."

"Ps-st!" cautioned von Harben. "What was that?"

"It sounded like the creaking of the gate in front of the house," said Mallius Lepus.

"They are coming," said von Harben.

The three men seized the swords with which they had armed themselves, after they had rushed the Colosseum guard, and following a plan they had already decided upon in the event that searchers approached their hiding-place, they scaled the ladder and crept out upon the roof. Leaving the trapdoor pushed slightly to one side, they listened to the sounds that were now coming from below, ready to take instant action should there be any indication that the searchers might mount the ladder to the roof.

Von Harben heard voices coming from below. "Well, we made it," said one, "and no one saw us. Here come the others now," and von Harben heard the gate creak again on its rusty hinges; then the door of the house opened and he heard several people enter.

"This is a good night's work," said one.

"Is she alive? I cannot hear her breathe."

"Take the gag from her mouth."

"And let her scream for help?"

"We can keep her quiet. She is worth nothing to us dead."

"All right, take it out."

"Listen, you, we will take the gag out of your mouth, but if you scream it will be the worse for you."

"I shall not scream," said a woman's voice in familiar tones that set von Harben's heart to palpitating, though he knew that it was nothing more than his imagination that suggested the seeming familiarity.

"We shall not hurt you," said a man's voice, "if you keep quiet and Cæsar sends the ransom."

"And if he does not send it?" asked the girl.

"Then, perhaps, your father, Septimus Favonius, will pay the price we ask."

"Heavens!" muttered von Harben. "Did you hear that, Lepus?"

"I heard," replied the Roman.

"Then come," whispered von Harben. "Come, Gabula, Favonia is below."

Casting discretion to the wind, von Harben tore the trap from the opening in the roof and dropped into the darkness below, followed by Mallius Lepus and Gabula.

"Favonia!" he cried. "It is I. Where are you?"

"Here," cried the girl.

Rushing blindly in the direction of her voice, von Harben encountered one of the abductors. The fellow grappled with him, while, terrified by fear that the legionaries were upon them, the others bolted from the building. As they went they left the door open and the light of a full moon dissipated the darkness of the interior, revealing von Harben struggling with a burly fellow who had seized the other's throat and was now trying to draw his dagger from it sheath.

Instantly Mallius Lepus and Gabula were upon him, and a quick thrust of the former's sword put a definite period to the earthly rascality of the criminal. Free from his antagonist, von Harben leaped to his feet and ran to Favonia, where she lay upon a pile of dirty rags against the wall. Quickly he cut her bonds and soon they had her story.

"If you are no worse for the fright," said Mallius Lepus, "we may thank these scoundrels for simplifying our task, for here we are ready to try for our escape a full three hours earlier than we had hoped."

"Let us lose no time, then," said von Harben. "I shall not breathe freely until I am across the wall."

"I believe we have little to fear now," said Mallius Lepus. "The wall is poorly guarded. There are many places where we can scale it, and I know a dozen places where we can find boats that are used by the fishermen of the city. What lies beyond is upon the knees of the gods."

Gabula, who had been standing in the doorway, closed the door quickly and crossed to von Harben. "Lights are coming down the avenue, Bwana," he said. "I think many men are coming. Perhaps they are soldiers."

The four listened intently until they made out distinctly the measured tread of marching men.

"Some more searchers," said Mallius Lepus. "When they have passed on their way, it will be safe to depart."

The light from the torches of the legionaries approached until it shone through the cracks in the wooden blinds, but it did not pass on as they had expected. Mallius Lepus put an eye to an opening in one of the blinds.

"They have halted in front of the house," he said. "A part of them are turning the corner, but the rest are remaining."

They stood in silence for what seemed a long time, though it was only a few minutes, and then they heard sounds coming from the garden behind the house and the light of torches was visible through the open kitchen door.

"We are surrounded," said Lepus. "They are coming in the front way. They are going to search the house."

"What shall we do?" cried Favonia.

"The roof is our only hope," whispered von Harben, but even as he spoke the sound of sandaled feet was heard upon the roof and the light of torches shone through the open trap.

"We are lost," said Mallius Lepus. "We cannot defeat an entire century of legionaries."

"We can fight them, though," said von Harben.

"And risk Favonia's life uselessly?" said Lepus.

"You are right," said von Harben, sadly, and then, "Wait, I have a plan. Come, Favonia, quickly. Lie down here upon the floor and I will cover you with these rags. There is no reason why we should all be taken. Mallius Lepus, Gabula, and I may not escape, but they will never guess that you are here, and when they are gone you can easily make your way to the guardhouse in the Colosseum, where the officer in charge will see that you are given protection and an escort to your home."

"Let them take me," said the girl. "If you are to be captured, let me be captured also."

"It will do no good," said von Harben. "They will only separate us, and if you are found here with us it may bring suspicion upon Septimus Favonius."

Without further argument she threw herself upon the floor, resigned in the face of von Harben's argument, and he covered her over with the rags that had been a beggar's bed.

23

BY THE TIME that Cassius Hasta had disposed his forces and placed his engines of war before the defenses of Castrum Mare, he discovered that it was too dark to open his assault that day, but he could carry out another plan that he had and so he advanced toward the gate, accompanied by Tarzan, Metellus, and Præclarus and preceded by torchbearers and a legionary bearing a flag of truce.

Within the fort great excitement had reigned from the moment that the advancing troops had been sighted. Word had been sent to Fulvus Fupus and reinforcements had been hurried to the fort. It was assumed by all that Sublatus had inaugurated a new raid upon a larger scale than usual, but they were ready to meet it, nor did they anticipate defeat. As the officer commanding the defenders saw the party approaching with a flag of truce, he demanded from a tower gate the nature of their mission.

"I have two demands to make upon Validus Augustus," said Cassius Hasta. "One is that he free Mallius Lepus and Erich von Harben and the other is that he permit me to return to Castrum Mare and enjoy the privileges of my station."

"Who are you?" demanded the officer.

"I am Cassius Hasta. You should know me well."

"The gods are good!" cried the officer.

"Long live Cassius Hasta! Down with Fulvus Fupus!" cried a hoarse chorus of rough voices.

Someone threw open the gates, and the officer, an old friend of Cassius Hasta, rushed out and embraced him.

"What is the meaning of all this?" demanded Cassius Hasta. "What has happened?"

"Validus Augustus is dead. He was assassinated at the games today and Fulvus Fupus has assumed the title of Cæsar. You are indeed come in time. All Castrum Mare will welcome you."

Along the Via Mare from the castle to the lakeshore and across the pontoon bridge to the island marched the army of the new Emperor of the East, while the news spread through the city and crowds gathered and shrieked their welcome to Cassius Hasta.

In a deserted house across the avenue from the Colosseum four fugitives awaited the coming of the legionaries of Fulvus Fupus. It was evident that the soldiers intended to take no chances. They entirely surrounded the building and they seemed to be in no hurry to enter.

Von Harben had had ample time to cover Favonia with the rags, so that she was entirely concealed before the legionaries entered simultaneously from the garden, the avenue, and the roof, torchbearers lighting their way.

"It is useless to resist," said Mallius Lepus to the officer who accompanied the men in from the avenue. "We will return to the dungeons peaceably."

"Not so fast," said the officer. "Where is the girl?"

"What girl?" demanded Mallius Lepus.

"The daughter of Septimus Favonius, of course."

"How should we know?" demanded von Harben.

"You abducted her and brought her here," replied the officer. "Search the room," he commanded, and a moment later a legionary uncovered Favonia and raised her to her feet.

The officer laughed as he ordered the three men disarmed.

"Wait," said von Harben. "What are you going to do with the daughter of Septimus Favonius? Will you see that she has a safe escort to her father's house?"

"I am taking my orders from Cæsar," replied the officer.

"What has Cæsar to do with this?" demanded von Harben.

"He has ordered us to bring Favonia to the palace and to slay her abductors upon the spot."

"Then Cæsar shall pay for us all with legionaries," cried von Harben, and with his sword he fell upon the officer in the doorway, while Gabula and Mallius Lepus, spurred by a similar determination to sell their lives as dearly as possible, rushed those who were descending the ladder and entering the kitchen door. Taken by surprise and momentarily disconcerted by the sudden and unexpected assault, the legionaries fell back. The officer, who managed to elude von Harben's thrust, escaped from the building and summoned a number of the legionaries who were armed with pikes.

"There are three men in that room," he said, "and a woman. Kill the men, but be sure that the woman is not harmed."

In the avenue the officer saw people running, heard them shouting. He saw them stop as they were questioned by some of his legionaries, whom he had left in the avenue. He had not given the final order for his pikemen to enter the building because his curiosity had momentarily distracted his attention. As he turned now, however, to order them in, his attention was again distracted by a tumult of voices that rose in great cheers and rolled up the avenue from the direction of the bridge that connects the city with the Via Mare and the fort. As he turned to look, he saw the flare of many torches and now he heard the blare of trumpets and the thud of marching feet.

What had happened? He had known, as had everyone in Castrum Mare, that the forces of Sublatus were camped before the fort, but he knew that there had been no battle and so this could not be the army of Sublatus entering Castrum Mare, but it was equally strange if the defenders of Castrum Mare should be marching away from the fort while it was menaced by an enemy army. He could not understand these things, nor could he understand why the people were cheering.

As he stood there watching the approach of the marching column, the shouts of the people took on form and he heard the name of Cassius Hasta distinctly.

"What has happened?" he demanded, shouting to the men in the street.

"Cassius Hasta has returned at the head of a big army, and Fulvus Fupus has already fled and is in hiding."

The shouted question and the equally loud reply were heard by all within the room.

"We are saved," cried Mallius Lepus, "for Cassius Hasta will harm no friend of Septimus Favonius. Aside now, you fools, if you know when you are well off," and he advanced toward the doorway.

"Back, men," cried the officer. "Back to the avenue. Let no hand be raised against Mallius Lepus or these other friends of Cassius Hasta, Emperor of the East."

"I guess this fellow knows which side his bread is buttered on," commented von Harben, with a grin.

Together Favonia, von Harben, Lepus, and Gabula stepped from the deserted building into the avenue. Approaching them they saw the head of a column of marching men; flaming torches lighted the scene until it was almost as bright as day.

"There is Cassius Hasta," exclaimed Mallius Lepus. "It is indeed he, but who are those with him?"

"They must be Sanguinarians," said Favonia. "But look, one of them is garbed like a barbarian, and see the strange warriors with their white plumes that are marching behind them."

"I have never seen the like in all my life," exclaimed Mallius Lepus.

"Neither have I," said von Harben, "but I am sure that I recognize them, for their fame is great and they answer the description that I have heard a thousand times."

"Who are they?" asked Favonia.

"The white giant is Tarzan of the Apes, and the warriors are his Waziri fighting men."

At sight of the legionaries standing before the house, Cassius Hasta halted the column.

"Where is the centurion in command of these troops?" he demanded.

"It is I, glorious Cæsar," replied the officer, who had come to arrest the abductors of Favonia.

"Does it happen that you are one of the detachments sent out by Fulvus Fupus to search for Mallius Lepus and the barbarian, von Harben?"

"We are here, Cæsar," cried Mallius Lepus, while Favonia, von Harben, and Gabula followed behind him.

"May the gods be praised!" exclaimed Cassius Hasta, as he embraced his old friend. "But where is the barbarian chieftain from Germania, whose fame has reached even to Castra Sanguinarius?"

"This is he," said Mallius Lepus. "This is Erich von Harben."

Tarzan stepped nearer. "You are Erich von Harben?" he asked in English.

"And you are Tarzan of the Apes, I know," returned von Harben, in the same language.

"You look every inch a Roman," said Tarzan with a smile.

"I feel every inch a barbarian, however," grinned von Harben.

"Roman or barbarian, your father will be glad when I bring you back to him."

"You came here in search of me, Tarzan of the Apes?" demanded von Harben.

"And I seemed to have arrived just in time," said the ape-man.

"How can I ever thank you?" exclaimed von Harben.

"Do not thank me, my friend," said the ape-man. "Thank little Nkima!"

TARZAN:
THE CLASSICS
Two jungle adventures for the price of one!
Published by Del Rey® Books.